MW01613467

RIBBON OF LOVE

by

Donna R. Causey

DEDICATED

To my husband Wayne and two sons Mike and Brian
Thank you for all your love and support

ACKNOWLEDGEMENTS

Henry and Mary (Wilson) Pattenden's story is the result of my imagination based on actual court records and historical events that took place in England and the Eastern Shore of Virginia. Much of the history of the Eastern Shore has been preserved in the book *"Ye Kingdom of Accawmacke"* by Jennings Cropper Wise, a book I consulted frequently when writing this novel, as well as many other historical books of England and early Accomack, Virginia.

The seed for this novel was planted when I attended a family reunion with my mother Ellorine Cottingham Morgan. The reunion took place at Wesley Chapel, a small historic Church in Bibb County, Alabama. Wesley Chapel, originally named Cottingham Chapel, was one of the first churches in the Bibb County area.

At the reunion, I was spell-bound as I listened to the many family stories related by my cousin and family historian, Hal Cottingham. His enthusiasm for family history and genealogy was contagious. For many years, Hal was known as the "go to" person in Bibb County for genealogy information on local families. With the help of his wife, Edna Earle, he accumulated a considerable amount of historical and genealogical data on local Bibb County, Alabama families.

I visited Hal shortly after the reunion and he graciously allowed me to make copies of the Cottingham records he and his wife had compiled. I returned home with a box full of documents, letters, court records, and etc. on many generations of Cottinghams. As I studied this treasure trove of letters and stories, I developed an overwhelming desire to tell the stories of my ancestors.

As I continued writing, I researched historical events and made trips to England and the Eastern Shore of Virginia. I'll never forget the special moment when I stood on the land where my first direct ancestor, Mary (Willson) Pattenden, resided on Plantation Creek. It was truly an unforgettable feeling and created a desire within me to understand her world and the impetus that led her to America. *Ribbon of Love* was born when I decided to share her story with others.

Along with my mother, Ellorine Cottingham Morgan, who encouraged me to write this novel, I would also like to give special thanks to my good friends, Jackie Shugart, Elizabeth King and Gail Farris who cheered me on, helped edit and provided suggestions for improvement. Most of all I would like to thank my immediate family, my husband Wayne, and my two sons Mike and Brian for supporting me in this journey through our families past.

Last but not least, I am grateful to all my ancestors who recorded and documented records of their lives. This novel would not exist without these initial records.

Donna R. Causey

TO THE READER

The events and characters in this novel have been derived from 17th century England and American history as well as court records from the Eastern Shore, Virginia. While, the Eastern Shore of Virginia is an actual place and the people named in this novel, family connections, and historic events are basically true; this novel is entirely a work of fiction and a product of my imagination.

Sometimes it's difficult to separate actual history from fiction in historical fiction novels so I've have included an Appendix at the end to clarify some of the questions the reader may have.

Though I diligently researched, I was unable to discover the author of the poem at the beginning of this novel but it so closely relates to Mary's life that I had to include it in *Ribbon of Love*.

Ribbon of Love is the first in the Series, *Tapestry of Love,* about my ancestors. I am currently working on the next in the Series, *Faith and Courage.*

My life is but a weaving
Between my Lord and me...
I may not choose the colors;
He knows what they should be;
For He can view the pattern
Upon the upper side,
While I can see it only
on this, the under side.
Sometimes He weaveth sorrow,
Which seemth strange to me;
But I will trust His judgment
And work on faithfully.
"Tis He who fills the shuttle;
He knows just what is best;
So I shall weave in earnest
And leave with Him the rest.
Not till the loom is silent
And the shuttles cease to fly,
Shall God unroll the canvas
And explain the reason why
The dark threads are as needful,
In the weaver's skillful hand,
As the treads of gold and silver
In the pattern He has planned.

Unknown

CHAPTER ONE

June 30, 1637, London, England

The air was stifling hot and the streets crowded when Henry Pattenden arrived in London's market square. Tension and excitement filled the air as everyone jockeyed for the best position to witness the event. Henry managed to find a fairly empty space with an unobstructed view in the shade of a building.

He glanced around at the people. Few seemed intent on trading but were instead congregated in small clusters conversing intensely. Children and dogs dashed about, stirring clouds of dust and nearly toppled adults with their play as they darted among them. Henry's attention was drawn to loud shouts in the street.

"Ye pushed first," a boy shouted defiantly. He stood with fists curled ready for a fight and angrily stared down at a crying child.

The child on the ground had a scraped knee and blood was flowing from his split lip.

"Me didna...Ye did," the injured boy cried.

Two women, both dressed in plain garb were conversing quietly but stopped their conversation when the boys' shouts rang out. They glanced in the direction of the two boys and frowned. Then, as if on cue, both turned and walked rapidly toward the boys. The crowd parted to allow the women's passage.

The older woman yanked the standing child by his ear before the altercation escalated.

"Owwww, Mum! Ye'll pull me ear off," hollered the boy.

"And ye'll deserve it!" she retorted. "Liz, how's ye youngun?"

"Not much harm done....just a scratch on his knee but this cut lip is bleeding some...she replied. She dabbed at the small child's lip with a handkerchief. "Best we go home and clean it up...guess that's the end of excitement for ye today young man."

At her words, the child stopped wailing and gave two loud sniffs. "Nay, Mum....it's, it's okay now,.....see the bleeding's stopped!" he stammered, as he pushed her hand away from his face and

1

swiped his own hand across his mouth, smearing blood on his cheek.

"Stopped, eh...that was quick." She gave the other woman a wink. "Well...mayhaps ye can stay a while longer....if ye promise not to run or fight." She looked up at the other woman and smiled, "Sarah, have ye ever seen anyone heal so fast?"

Before the other woman could answer, the child sprang up, and attempted to run off but his mother quickly caught his arm.

"Wait Jules...ye need to be cleaned up a little more first."

With a firm hold on his arm she led him toward the water trough on the side street where Pattenden was leaning against a post. He gave her a brief nod but avoided eye contact and immediately averted his gaze toward the other woman who remained in the street.

The old woman stood with her hands on her hips as she frowned at her son. The boy turned away but before he could leave, she reached out, caught his chin in a tight grasp....lowered her face to his level, and scowled deeply into his eyes. Her harsh words rose above the street noise as she growled. "Jeremiah...stay out of fights today of all days...there's enough mischief happening as is."

"Aw Mum," the boy whined as he tried to wrestle loose. In the next instant, he broke free and headed toward some larger boys congregated in a small group playing marbles. As he ran, he shouted back to his mother, "Jules started it!"

His mother watched him flee. "That's what ye always say.....always someone else's fault," she muttered under her breath, "Ye'll be the death of me yet."

Henry continued watching the woman as she shaded her eyes with one hand then shifted her gaze toward the center of the New Palace Yard. His eyes followed her gaze.

The old woman gave a huge sigh and squinted at the gaunt, stark, wooden scaffold in the New Palace Yard. The pillory was placed squarely in the middle. A post in the center of the skeleton of torture was fitted with three stocks radiating out like spokes in a wheel. Each stock had holes so the heads and hands of three men could be confined in a standing position.

Henry's attention returned to the woman as she grumbled, "There's enough trouble today...that's for sure!"

She rubbed her dusty hands on her plain dark gray dress, gave a slight shiver, even though it was miserably hot, and pulled her ragged shawl around her tighter. She ambled in the general direction her friend had taken toward a group of common women lining the street. The old woman lifted her skirt as she walked, in an attempt to avoid the dung and muck from the many horses and cattle on the street.

Henry studied the group of women she joined. All were similarly dressed in dull colors of faded brown or gray. Aprons covered their bodices and their hair was completely hidden by a small lace fringed rochet. Young children pulled at the long skirts of some of the women while others gently rocked small infants, cradled in their arms as they chatted.

The men, standing with the group of women, wore plain jerkins with short leather breeches and appeared to be in an intense debate. Some of the men held grim expressions on their faces and often cast furtive glances around as if anticipating danger.

An argument broke out between two men near the center of the street, diverting Henry's attention, but it was soon broken up by other men near them. Henry's gaze returned to the scaffold.

Among the crowd near the platform, small clusters of colorfully dressed people appeared as bright flowers in a barren field. The men were clad in fashionably starched collars and high topped gloves with colorful jerkins and were more vocal in their conversation...often pointing and laughing loudly from time to time. Henry was dressed in similar fashion but restrained from joining them.

The women in this group were elegantly adorned in starched collars and colorful dresses, tight fitting bodices with ruffles around their waist above a full skirt covering many petticoats.

Henry stretched and removed his coat as the sun beat down and the morning wore on. He continued to quietly observe the ever increasing throng and patiently waited by a post.

Gradually, what had been quiet murmuring, changed to grumbling. Soon, loud shouts penetrated the drone of conversation as some of the men became more agitated in their conversation.

An obviously inebriated, man, near Henry, shouted above

the murmuring crowd, "Me thinks it's about time something was done about them. They've been allowed free rein in their writing too long, whilst we take the brunt of the suffering."

'Ayes, and Nays' filled the air as the people agreed or disagreed with the man.

Buoyed by the response from the crowd, the now animated drunk jumped on a crate and continued his tirade. "Me say let's hang 'um' all, they be just trouble makers anyway."

Before he could continue, a couple of men with strong muscular arms grabbed the drunk by the shirt collar and threw him to the ground. "Go home ye old drunk," the man exclaimed. "Ye don't know what ye're talking about."

Henry laughed silently to himself as the penitent man crawled off to the side and disappeared in the crowd. A bench in front of a shop was empty and Henry was tired of standing in one place all morning so he walked over to the bench and sat down. He continued to watch families drift in from the outlying countryside.

The mass of people now swelled and overflowed into the dusty side streets. The overwhelming smell of fish, poultry, overripe produce, and other food mixed with the stink of dung and waste permeated the air and sickened his senses. Many of the people pressed toward the center of the Palace Yard in their attempt to acquire a good view of the scaffold. Whole families seemed intent on watching the spectacle.

After a time, Henry stood up and walked toward the scaffold. He moved to the edge of the crowd, closer to the street and smiled at a blond-haired girl, about four years of age. She held her father's hand as he maneuvered among the people. In her other hand, she held a doll, trailing it behind her in the dirt.

The loud tramp of many horses was heard on the street and the crowd jostled one another to get out of the way. In the chaos, someone stepped on the child's doll and it was ripped from her hands. It lay near the middle of the street directly in the path of the oncoming horses.

Panicked at the loss of her doll, the child screamed, "Wait, Papa!" and released her grip from his hand. She ran toward the street in order to retrieve it but at the same instant, soldiers on horseback appeared.

Henry watched in horror as they bore down on the spot

4

where the child stood with her doll. She froze when she saw the horses pounding the ground toward her and began screaming, "Papa! Papa!"

Her father was at the back of the crowd vainly searching for his screaming child while Henry was near the street witnessing a potential tragedy unfold before his eyes. He reacted instantly, rushed toward the street, reached out, grabbed the child by her dusty blue pinafore and pulled her to safety seconds before she would have been crushed by the horses' hooves.

Her grateful father quickly joined them, collected the little girl in his arms and shook Henry's hand as he said, "Thank ye....Thank ye... friend!" The little girl whimpered as she clasped her father's neck tightly.

"Aye, ye would have done the same...glad to help," Henry replied as he patted the crying child gently on her back. Then he glanced behind the man at some foot soldiers walking among the people. Henry turned away quickly and tried to become invisible within the crowd.

After the horse soldiers passed, a hush fell over the assemblage as a heavily guarded cart appeared. Only the loud creak of cart wheels penetrated the quiet. Then....all at once, en masse, the people lining the street, pushed toward the cart, blocking its movement. Soldiers promptly responded by surrounding the cart with swords drawn. They forced men, women and children to separate as the driver threaded the cart through a narrow path toward the New Palace Yard.

"They got ye now!" shouted someone from the crowd. "Now ye'll see how it feels," he continued. His jeer was isolated from the silent shock of onlookers, only pockets of quiet mumbling could be heard.

The rolling prison passed three boys with a pile of stones collected for the occasion. One boy shouted "Heretic" and threw a stone at a man in the cart, hitting him on his cheek. The prisoner hit by the rock was William Prynne, a barrister of Lincoln's Inn. He was startled for a moment but continued to stare straight ahead. Other rocks, vegetables and debris began to fly at the men chained to the wagon's sides and all three men lowered their heads as they tried to dodge the pelting from children.

Henry grimaced when a rock hit Dr. John Bastwick's

forehead and blood flowed from the deep gash. Dr. Bastwick had been educated at the esteemed Emmanuel College and taught Henry everything he knew about medicine. He hated to see him treated so badly.

Next to Dr. Bastwick, stood Rev. Henry Burton, the Puritan divine who greatly encouraged Dr. Bastwick's in his writing.

All three men had been taken to the STAR CHAMBER by Bishop Laud and found guilty of sedition. The STAR CHAMBER created a sensation in England when they ordered a highly unusual punishment for the three men. They were ordered to be pilloried and their ears cut off before the public. Such savage punishment was not typically given to such distinguished gentlemen.

Fights broke out among the mob around the cart, as adults attempted to halt the rock throwers and Henry was happy to see that the usual barrage of mockery and abuse of the prisoners was wanting. Even in their humiliation the three men commanded respect among the majority of onlookers.

The cart reached the scaffold and the soldiers began extricating the men from the chains connected to the cart. All of a sudden, the crowd parted abruptly as some young maidens pushed near the front and threw herbs and flowers in the path the prisoners would take to the platform. Just as quickly as they appeared, the girls disappeared in the multitude before the guards could stop them. Some of the soldiers attempted to kick the flowers aside and cover the herbs with dust with little success.

Pyrnne was released from his chains first and started his ascent to the platform. A child threw a rock at Pyrnne but it missed and ricocheted off the post hitting the executioner instead.

"Good shot!" someone shouted and several people laughed. Some of the soldiers on the ground mingled among the mob searching for the perpetrator but to no avail.

This interlude allowed Bastwick's wife, who had been standing near the prisoners, to quickly grasp her husband's face and kiss the ears he was about to lose.

Henry's heart went out to her as she was roughly pushed aside by a guard. Briefly forgetting his fear of being recognized, Henry joined in the shouts of anger that rang out among the congregation over her treatment.

Bastwick looked toward his wife and said, "Don't be

frightened."

"Farewell, my dearest, be of comfort, I am not dismayed," she replied.

The guard pushed Dr. Bastwick forward toward the scaffold and the crowd shouted their disapproval. The guards completely surrounded Rev. Burton as he made his way to the scaffold and no further disruption occurred.

Prisoners were normally allowed to speak before their sentences were executed and Pyrnne spoke first. At the sound of his voice, silence fell over the assemblage as they strained to hear. First, he repeated a great part of the Court's Proceedings that had taken the cause for confession. Then he cited two Statues against libeling the Queen in the time of Queen Mary and Queen Elizabeth.

"In these instances," he proclaimed, "the offender being lawfully convicted by verdict, his own confession, or by the oaths of two sufficient witnesses, witnesses brought face to face at his Trial, should have both his ears cut off, unless he paid 100£ within one month, and should suffer three months for payment, and suffer six months, imprisonment."

"I challenge ye, Look at the times of Queen Mary and Queen Elizabeth, and the times now of King Charles and how far more dangerous it is now to write against a Bishop or two, than against a King or Queen."

Shouts of acclamation rang out from the populace.

He continued, "The most there was during the Queen Mary and Queen Elizabeth's time were but six months imprisonment in ordinary Prisons...And the Delinquent might redeem his ears for 200£, and had two months time for payment but no fine...while here today we are fined 5000£ a piece, to be perpetually imprisoned in the remotest Castles, where no friends permitted and to lose our ears without redemption."

More cheers bellowed from the rabble. Soon the New Palace Yard was thundering with hurrahs of approbation.

Encouraged, Pyrnne pressed on, "Then there was no stigmatization; here we must be branded on both Cheeks...then a legal Conviction was requisite, here all to be taken pro confesso without verdict, confession, or so much as one witness! If the people knew what times they had been cast and what changes of laws, religions, and ceremonies had been made by one man, they

7

would look upon them. If they look upon them, the people might see that no degree or profession was exempt from the prelates' malice...for here is a divine for the soul, a physician for the body, and a lawyer for the estates...and the next to be censured in STAR CHAMBER is likely to be a bishop! If all the Martyrs that suffered in Queen Mary's days are called fanatical heretics, factious fellows, traitors and rebels, condemned by the Holy Church, what can we look for?"

The mass of people became more and more vocal in their affirmation and the executioner began to sense trouble so he ordered Pyrnne bound and placed in the stocks and the guards quickly followed his orders. The executioner raised the top board to bind Pyrnne's head. He scowled as he noted a problem. Pyrnne had previously been punished by the STAR CHAMBER and both of his ears were cut off at the time. Though an obvious attempt had been made to sew the ears back on... clearly only stumps of his ears remained.

Someone shouted, "Me hope Archbishop Laud won't be too disappointed since Pyrnne has no ears to cut off." Laughter rang out.

Once Pyrnne was encased in the stocks, the executioner moved to secure Bastwick without allowing him to speak so Pyrnne continued his discourse.

"Silence!" barked, the executioner. "Nail his ears to the stocks!"

The guards quickly obeyed and tears filled Pyrnne's eyes but he did not flinch or shout out as they completed the gruesome task.

Next, Rev. Burton was brought to the platform and roughly bound by the guards.

A few people were congregated next to the scaffold near Rev. Burton. A man asked, "Is the pillory not uneasy for ye neck and shoulders?"

Rev. Burton replied, "How can Christ yoke be uneasy? He bears the heavier end and I bear the lighter; and if mine were too heavy, he would bear that too."

The crowd cheered.

After all three men were encased in the stocks securely, the executioner stood in the center of the platform and read aloud:

"The following named men are hereby convicted of the crime of sedition by the Court of High Commission: William Prynne, barrister, Dr. John Bastwick and Rev. Henry Burton. They are condemned to stand not less than two hours in the pillory, amputation of both ears and to pay severally a fine of 5000£ to the king and to be imprisoned for life."

After reading the order, a guard nailed the charge to the center post of the pillory.

The executioner returned to Pyrnne and paused briefly to decide what to do about his ears.

Prynne calmly said, "Come friend....on with it...I fear not for Christ sustains me."

Clearly angered by his comment, the executioner swung his sword at the right stump of his ear. Blood spurted on the executioner and formed rivulets on the platform. Pyrnne appeared dazed for a moment but remained steady. Then the executioner cut the left stump so close that he took away a piece of Pyrnne's cheek. Blood stained the platform under Pyrnne and poured onto the ground below. A few men hissed and threw rotten vegetables and rocks at the executioner but halted when the soldiers rushed into the crowd with swords drawn.

Henry retreated to the back of the crowd.

Disgusted, the executioner moved on to cut off Bastwick's ears. With a sharp swing, he sliced the right ear off and in another swing, hacked at the left ear. A massive amount of blood flowed onto the scaffold and a groan swelled up from the people. A piece of Bastwick's left ear hung against his cheek.

Dazed briefly, Bastwick regained his composure and shouted in anguish, "If I had a thousand lives, I would give them up for the cause."

Some confusion occurred near the steps and Henry peered above their heads as he tried to see. In an instant, Bastwick's wife darted past the guards, climbed onto the platform and rushed toward her husband. She then quickly gathered his ears in a handkerchief before the executioner shoved her to the floor, almost pushing her off the scaffold.

Henry joined in the roar bellowed from the mob at her cruel treatment.

A guard grabbed her arm roughly but she shoved him away

and proudly stood. With a hand stained from her husband's bloody ears, she pushed away a lock of her curly brown hair from her eyes, turned and walked slowly and deliberately toward the ladder amid shouts of approval from the crowd. When she reached the edge of the platform tears flowed from her eyes, clouding her vision. She wiped them away with her blood-stained hand. Her tears mingled with her husband's blood and stained her cheeks bright red. She slowly descended each rung and fell to the ground crying. A group of ladies quickly gathered around to console her.

The executioner was clearly frustrated at this point. He drew his sword high above his head and with one swift down stroke sliced off Rev. Burton's right ear so close that his temporal artery was opened. Blood gushed out in a strong spurt, splattering the executioners' chest. With another stroke, he cut off his other ear. Blood flowed to the platform forming a pool of red beneath the divine's head and drips of blood penetrated the platform, staining the ground below.

For a moment Rev. Burton appeared faint, but he regained his strength and exclaimed, "Christ is a good Master, and worth suffering for! If the world would but know his goodness and had tasted his sweetness; all would come and be his servants!"

Shouts of acclamation bellowed from the assemblage.

Next a hot iron with the letters S. L. engraved on them for the crime of sedition was brought to the scaffold and Pyrnne taunted the executioner, "Come friend, come, burn me! cut me! I have learned to fear the fire of hell, and not what man can do unto me, Come; scar me! Scar me!"

"Nay, ye need worry not...ye shall have what's due," laughed the executioner. Then he looked at the iron and exclaimed, "The iron has grown cold, fire it again, this scoundrel wants fire!"

The iron was reheated and returned red-hot to the executioner. He grabbed the iron and quickly pressed the glowing implement of torture against Prynne's right cheek...and left it there for an excruciating long time...the stench of cooking flesh filled the air and some ladies in the crowd covered their noses with handkerchiefs in an attempt to block the suffocating odor.

"The punishment was to brand him, not cook 'em!" shouted a burly man near the pillory.

The executioner, now visibly excited by the crowd's reaction smiled menacingly and began to twist and press the instrument of torment harder against Prynne's cheek as he waited for the iron to cool.

Tears of anguish flowed from Prynne's eyes but he did not cry out. Finally, the executioner withdrew the iron. Pyrnne exclaimed, "The more I am beaten down, the more I am lifted up."

Disgusted, the executioner barked to a waiting soldier, "The fire doth grow cold... heat it again." The iron was reheated and returned to the executioner's waiting hand. "Let's see how ye like this one," he barked, with a smirk on his face. Again, the red-hot iron was pressed on Pyrnne's left cheek where the skin had been ripped away.

Tears flowed from Pyrnne's eyes but he continued to stare straight ahead. Ironically, the iron, slowed the blood that had been flowing from his cheek.

The iron was reheated and the executioner pressed it against Bastwick's cheek. A whimper was heard in the crowd and a soldier on the platform pointed to Bastwick's wife's pale face. The executioner turned toward her, nodded at the soldier and smiled. He ordered the iron fired and this time, as he thrust the iron against Bastwick's other cheek, it made a sizzling noise like bacon frying on a skillet. A collective groan came from the assemblage. Henry turned his back to the scaffold. His face was ashen.

The executioner laughed and exclaimed, "Where is ye Christ now?"

Bastick's wife began to wail loudly.

Bastwick closed his eyes for a minute, then opened them and said, "Sweet wife, be of good cheer! Christ sustains me."

The executioner angrily threw the iron at the soldier waiting to reheat it. When it was returned red-hot, he quickly pressed it against the left cheek of Rev. Burton. Obviously wanting to be through with his task, the executioner branded the right cheek without reheating the iron.

The divine shouted, "Christ is a Good Master, I gladly suffer for thee!"

His duty completed, the executioner, frustrated by his victims' responses, climbed down the ladder from the platform and hurriedly left the Yard by horseback.

The spectacle was over so the people began to disperse.

Three soldiers remained to guard the scaffold. A small pocket of plainly dressed individuals remained in close proximity and offered encouraging words to the men. Bastwick's wife stood next to the scaffold, quietly weeping.

Henry stood off in the distance and tried to decide what to do. He feared he might be arrested if he neared the scaffold. Archbishop Laud was already suspicious of him. He looked at Bastwick's wife and thought of his own wife, then retreated to a bench in front of a shop where he could view the scene unnoticed.

A few moments later, a horse was heard galloping swiftly toward the scaffold. The executioner had returned. He angrily dismounted and with a scowl on his face, mounted the platform in four steps. He drew his sword and hacked off the remainder of Bastwick's ear. A massive amount of blood flowed on the platform. The executioner spat on the blood and piece of ear, clamored down the ladder, mounted his horse and rode promptly away.

Astonished by the executioner's reappearance, Henry whispered to a man standing near him, "What do ye think provoked that?"

"Ahhh, I heard that Archbishop Laud had spies in the crowd and he wasn't happy with the executioner's service so Laud ordered him to return and complete the job on Bastwick's ear. Laud's never happy with anything these days. Join me in a pint of ale. I'm tired of watching this farce."

Henry looked back at Bastwick's wife weeping at the base of the scaffold then turned and said, "Nay, I think I'll wait here a while."

"Suit yeself," the man said and left.

Two boys, equipped with a stash of rocks, rotten vegetables and manure, began pelting the men. Bastwick, Pyrnne and Burton's heads were tightly bound in the stocks and they could not move their heads to advert the items thrown.

"Good-un John!" yelled on of the boys to the other when a tomato splattered above Burton's right eye.

The other boy laughed as he grabbed a huge rock... "Watch, this-un! I'll tear the top of his head off."

A gigantic, red-haired man with strong muscular arms, and a long red beard angrily stomped over to the boys and grabbed each by one arm. "Ye boys get out of here now or I'll break both of ye're arms!" he bellowed.

"But we won't get our coins!" cried one boy.

"What coins?" the man asked contemptuously.

"The coins from that man."

Henry looked in the direction the boy pointed at a distant cleric on a street corner, who was quickly retreating from the scene.

"Well, ye don't deserve coins from the likes of him, especially harming good men as these. Now, leave before ye lose the use of ye're arms."

The boys reluctantly walked away...muttering to themselves.

The day wore on and the hot sun bore down on the three men on the platform. Henry stood on a side corner but remained in the shadows. Mrs. Bastwick stood near the scaffold, offering encouragement to her husband whenever the guards were distracted. Occasionally, a wandering child threw a stone or rotten vegetable at the men but he was quickly admonished by adults nearby. Throughout the ordeal, the three men defended their faith to all who would listen.

In the early afternoon, another rumor circulated among the people. Henry overheard a conversation between two bystanders.

"Did ye hear that Archbishop Laud tis disturbed by their talk?" one man said as he pointed to the three men on the scaffold.

"Well, how's he plan to stop it. Cut out their tongues?"

"I wouldn't be surprised but he made a motion to the Lords who are now sitting in the STAR CHAMBER to gag Pyrnne or have some censure on them."

As the rumor spread, people began to congregate around the men again, anticipating more excitement but Henry remained on the side street silently willing the end of the punishment. Later, word came that Laud's motion to the Lords did not succeed. Murmurings and rumors continued circulating among the people throughout the day.

Around dusk, Henry watched as the men were finally removed from their ordeal.

As Bastwick descended the platform, he drew from his ear a blood soaked sponge, raised it to the remaining stragglers around the scaffold and said "Blessed be my God who hath counted me worthy and enabled me to suffer for his sake; and as now I have lost some of my blood, so I am ready to spill every drop in the veins for this cause for which I now have suffered, which is for maintaining the truth of God, and the honor of my King against popish usurpation. Let God be glorified and the King live forever."

His words, stirred those assembled around the scaffold and they cheered their approval. Soon others joined the group.. Sensing possible trouble, a soldier guarding Bastwick, grabbed Bastwick's arm and pushed him down the ladder, causing him to tumble to the ground. The soldiers on the ground instantly pulled Bastwick to the waiting cart and chained him to the side. One stuffed a cloth in Bastwick's mouth, preventing him from speaking.

Prynne and Burton were released from the scaffold but both men appeared faint so offered no remarks. They were led down to the waiting cart and chained to the sides. The cart slowly left the New Palace Yard. The remaining assemblage observed with sadness the gruesome faces and mangled ears of the men.

Henry watched patiently, a silent witness to the grizzly scene. He remained until the cart was no longer visible. Then he walked slowly away deep in thought.

CHAPTER TWO

March 1, 1638 Gravesend, England

Dr. Henry Pattenden was pacing again. He was painfully thin and Mary, his wife, often chided him that he would never gain weight because he was always pacing. She was probably right but it was his way of releasing tension. Presently, he stopped and shouted up the stairs.

"Are ye ready, Mary? The coach will be here soon. We must be at the station by 8:00 or ye will miss it."

In their bedroom upstairs, Mary was uneasy. She never liked being away from her husband and this was at an especially difficult time for them both. She hated to increase his stress but so many decisions had been forced on her lately and right now, her mind had gone blank and she was in a quandary. Crates and trunks filled the small rented room, making it hard to move or even see what was in each.

"What am I forgetting?"

Thoughts flooded her mind making it hard to focus on the task at hand. She tried to concentrate but then the anxiety she had been experiencing daily overwhelmed her again. Fear of an unknown country with unknown people brought icy chills to Mary's small body. A piercing thought plunged into her heart with the realization that on this trip, she might be saying the final goodbyes to her world...and worst of all....saying goodbye to her family. How could she ever cope without her loving family around her? She thought of her mother and her warmth and constant devotion. Then her father and his strong defense of his family that always made Mary feel safe. Even her siblings and their loyalty would be terrible to leave behind.

But she must start a new life, depending on and trusting just one man. A man she had only known a short time. Could she really put her faith in their love for one another? Especially since she now carried a secret....even from him.

15

"Henry... I mustn't keep him waiting any longer," she said aloud, as her thoughts returned to the present. "Well, whatever I forgot, it will just have to stay forgotten....Henry," she shouted down the staircase. "The trunk tis ready."

Henry climbed the stairs and stood at the door of the bedroom for a minute and looked lovingly at his wife. Her long dark hair was tucked under her white rochet but a few tendrils escaped, framing her face with curls like a halo. Her big gray eyes never failed to enchant him and even though they were in a hurry, he couldn't resist. He quietly walked over to her and bent down to steal a quick kiss. As his lips touched hers, Mary reached up to touch his face. His kind, loving concern for her shone back in his eyes and she knew the answer. Forcing the fearful anxiety back into a far corner compartment, Mary exclaimed, "Oh Henry, just think we'll soon start our exciting adventure. Oh, I do love ye dear husband."

"And I love ye," he replied, "but we must be on our way. The coach will not wait." After one last glance around the room, Mary followed her husband down the steps.

Three days later, Dr. Henry Pattenden stood on the edge of the quay stroking his chin as he stared into the vast emptiness of water ahead. He was gripped by another one of his melancholy moods...the moods were occurring with more frequency and were difficult to overcome when Mary was not around. She was aware of the overwhelming despair her husband suffered and on these occasions, her cheerful disposition often enabled the young bride to tease his dark moods away but she was visiting her family now and he couldn't shake his frame of mind. Henry missed her positive disposition. She always found something optimistic about any situation and he needed her happy reassurance now as he struggled with self-doubt.

Am I being foolish? Is this some wild idea that will only bring pain to Mary as well?

Though she tried to maintain an enthusiastice attitude as the departure time drew near, Henry was cognizant of Mary's growing despondency. He knew what it felt like to lose a family and hated to put her through the same pain. Henry recalled the day he first met Mary, a beautiful child with big gray eyes and a bubbling personality but when he returned to claim her as his bride, he was amazed at what an attractive young lady she had become. The scene unfolded in his mind as if it was yesterday. He laughed to himself as he recalled his bold entrance into her life.

There was Mary, smiling at him shyly as she stood behind her father in a gray linen shift that matched the gray in her large eyes. Her long dark hair, draped around her porcelain face was tied with a simple gray ribbon. Henry had come to claim his bride.

"Young man, her father exclaimed, ye are correct....Mary was promised to ye by an agreement ye father and I made some eighteen odd years ago...our first born were to be wed...but she is not yet fifteen and knows ye not."

"A promise is a promise, Sir," Henry added. "And I am in need of a wife today. I have a trade and plan to start my life."

"Henry, I intend to keep my promise to ye dear departed father. Lord knows, he was my closest and dearest friend, but understand me position. Mary's me first-born. I must be sure that she is happy with ye.... besides, she still needs more time to learn to become a good wife for ye. Why ye two have never met and ye haven't even had a proper courtship. She is young yet. Stay a while with us so that the two of ye may know each other better before marrying. I am sure ye'll not regret the wait."

"Aye, ye give me cause to ponder, Sir. I have land in the New World and hoped to set sail in a month but as ye say, I do need a properly trained wife. How long do ye think it will be before she is ready?"

"Who knows?" Mary's father laughed. "But ye'll know when the time is right if ye spend more time with her before ye marry."

"Well Sir, I guess ye leave me no choice but to wait but I will not be staying here. I have a place of me own and if it will be with ye're approval, I plan to court Mary."

Henry laughed to himself, as he recalled their subsequent courtship. He was awkward talking with Mary and she was very shy. Her father had been correct though. It was worth the wait and when they were finally married, on September 12th, her sixteenth birthday, Henry realized just how deeply he had fallen in love with

17

Mary.

His thoughts returned to their engagement in the spring of 1637. Mary's brother, George, as was the custom, presented Mary with a beautiful horseshoe he made for them. Mary's clan tartan ribbon, Scottish thistle and satin ribbon roses were engraved on it She wore the horseshoe on her wrist all summer for good luck but the horseshoe was quite heavy and Henry chuckled aloud as he recalled a comment Mary made toward the end of summer.

"Henry, we should have the most luck in the world if the weight of this horseshoe means anything! Me thinks George, added extra weight for spite. It would be just like him to do so.... but since we'll need every bit of good luck in this new country of yours, it's worth the pain."

Mary decided on the date of their wedding, as she stated, "Ye will never forget me birthday and anniversary this way and as it's said that when ye marry in September's shine, your living will be rich and fine."

Three weeks before the date of their marriage, the wedding banns announced their upcoming nuptials in the church each Sunday while she and Henry stayed away as required because Mary said.... "Of course we don't want bad luck to follow."

The day of Henry and Mary's wedding dawned bright and beautiful. Henry remembered the vision of Mary walking down the aisle in the church in her long white linen shift, carrying her favorite yellow mums.

"She was truly a beautiful bride," Henry whispered to himself as he continued to reminiscence about their wedding.

The priest took the ring from a pillow and touched the thumb, the first finger, and then the second finger of Mary's hand as he declared, "In the name of the Father, the Son, and the Holy Ghost." He placed the ring on Mary's third finger and said "Amen."

The priest repeated the same with Henry's ring. Then came the magical moment when Henry and Mary first kissed as man and wife.

As they left the church, all their friends and family showered Mary's head with wheat. Henry chuckled to himself as he recalled the expression on Mary's face when she forgot to duck and wheat flew in her eye, blinding her. She laughed as Henry managed to catch her before she fell down the church steps.

Oh, how I miss your laughter. I can't wait to see you again, sweet Mary!

Even at the age of sixteen, Mary was mature beyond her years...especially after a particularly bad day when death seemed to be everywhere and he knew he was helpless to prevent it.

Mary is indispensable to me now. But, am I being selfish by dragging her to the Colonies with me? Mayhaps, I should go first and send for her when I am settled.

Henry abandoned the idea as soon as it came to mind.

I can not imagine life without her. Why would I want to even try but is this adventure fair to her?

The quay was a busy place but Henry was oblivious to the noise surrounding him until his reverie was broken by a loud, "Well, Halloa!"

Henry glanced down the quay and saw the robust, rosy-cheeked figure of William Berriman, dressed in a red jerkin and leather breeches, advancing toward him.

"Never thought I'd see the like's of ye here so early this morning." William said. "Not with a pretty bride at home."

"I thought I'd come down and check on the repairs," Henry responded, then continued. "Mary is visiting her family....What brings ye here?"

Henry liked Berriman. Though he hadn't known him but a few days, Berriman had already proved to be a valuable friend by allowing Henry to store some of his medical supplies in the space he was allotted on the Elizabeth.

"Just checking on repairs, same as ye." replied Berriman as he joined Henry. "It's hard to wait...spending me profits on the high rent in town. Have ye heard the sail date yet? I hope it will be soon. I need to be on me way now. I've bought ten more indentures to take to Virginia and need to sell them before planting time."

"Why do you sell indentured servants? Don't they help ye with planting?"

"I couldn't manage without them....tried to a few years ago...went bust...but I have all I need....now, I just want their headrights. There's always people wanting to go to the Colonies these days and I aim to transport any of them that want to go...of course in exchange for their headrights."

"Exchange for their headrights?"

"Aye, headrights, ye know that every person traveling to Virginia receives a headright of 50 acres and by paying for their transport, in exchange for that headright, I gain a tidy sum of acres with little cost to me...they also are indentured to me for seven years...I can use them to plant and harvest my land or sell them to other needy planters at a handsome profit...either way, I can't lose." Berriman laughed...."Great system and perfectly legal."

"Sounds like it. Maybe, I'll look into purchasing some indentures. I know we could use the help,"

"Ye say ye bride's with her family. She hasn't backed out of traveling to the Colonies, has she?"

"On the contrary, she's anxious to leave but I wanted her to have time to say good-bye to her family without me around. She's trying to talk her parents into following us to the Colonies. She really hates to leave them here with all this turmoil in England."

"I know tis trying to leave family but it's for the best. Tis not safe here in England for ye both...especially with ye're connection with Bastwick and that atrocity Laud perpetrated on him. Who knows what Laud will do next? Have ye heard where Bastwick was sent?"

"Sicily, I believe, but I didn't want to ask too many questions. Laud's already suspicious enough of my connection with Bastwick and has made several queries about me. That's why I feel compelled to leave England as soon as possible."

"Ye be doing the right thing. With me living in Virginia, and traipsing back and forth between here and there, I haven't kept up with things here in England. I thought William Laud was a Protestant. What got him so riled against Bastwick?"

"The whole thing started right after Laud, succeeded to the archbishopric of Canterbury on the death of the Abbot. Bastwick printed two treatises in the Netherlands and Laud thought they were targeted at him so he had Bastwick fined, excommunicated and prohibited from practicing medicine. His books were burned and he was imprisoned."

"But writing treatises is hardly enough to have him pilloried, him being a gentleman as well."

"I guess everyone was fooled by Laud. He seems to hold opinions closely aligned with the Pope and is King Charles right-hand in putting down religious liberties. Laud's action only intensified Bastwick's beliefs and he responded with two more books, one written in English, in which he charged that bishops were the enemies of God and 'the tail of the beast!'."

"Tail of the beast....strong language. Is that when Laud retaliated with the STAR CHAMBER?"

"Aye, he took Bastwick and two other Puritan activists, William Prynne and Rev. Henry Burton to the STAR CHAMBER where they were prosecuted at the same time. They were censured and condemned to pay a fine of 5000 pounds each. After that the men were set in the New Palace Yard, and suffered the torture of having their ears cut off. In addition, these good men were branded and banished to imprisonment for life in remote parts of the kingdom without access to pen or paper."

"The punishment is unbelievable, particularly since all were honest gentlemen. At least you will be out of Laud's grasp in Virginia."

"True, there is little left for me to do here, though in a way I feel I am betraying Dr. Bastwick. He's an honorable man. Without him, I would not be a surgeon today. After my father died, he took me in and taught me everything I know. When he closed his medical practice, I went to the Colonies for a brief time and was not involved with him much after that, but there's no telling what Laud might do next. Did ye hear that he very nearly caused a riot at St. Giles in Scotland?"

"Nay, I hadn't heard....What happened?" asked Berriman.

"I heard that the Dean of Edinburgh was clad in canonicals and began reading from the new Liturgy for worship. Well, the people started shouting and a young girl...I believe her name was Janet Geddes.... actually threw a stool at the Dean of Edinburgh."

"Brave lass, this Janet Geddes. What did the Dean do then?"

"He panicked and actually ran from the room....the Bishop of Edinburgh tried to continue the service but the people called him 'A Pope and Antichrist!' They both barely managed to escape and only with the help of their magistrates. Since then, I heard that the Privy Council of Scotland sent a representative to King Charles to state the feelings of the Scots but the King has declared all who opposed the new Liturgy as traitors."

"Someone told me that King Charles was raising an army but I didna know what for. Do ye think he will go against

Scotland?"

"Who knows what he'll do next? I just hope Mary's family doesn't get involved in it all. I really hate to leave them here."

"Ye are doing the right thing by going to the colonies. Imagine what would happen once Laud discovered ye're connection with Bastwick. Think of ye pretty young wife. Would ye want her to go through such torment?"

Henry grimaced as he was reminded of the scene at the pillory when Bastwick's weeping wife retrieved his hacked off ears and held them close to her breast as she walked away with tears streaming down her cheeks. He knew that scene would be etched in his mind forever.

The thought of putting Mary through such a horrible ordeal was something I could never face. It will be safer for Mary in the Colonies.

"How does ye young bride feel about traveling to Virginia?"

"She's anxious to go but still worried. Mary fears for her parents' safety but she knows our move is for the best. I wish her parents would agree to go as well but they're determined to stay in England. I know life will be difficult for her in Virginia. My brief visit there assured me of that."

"Aye, that is true....but it is far away from Laud and all his ordinances...and that is worth more than anything here. So ye have been to Virginia already, when were ye there?"

"As I said, I studied under Dr. Bastwick but after he stopped treating the sick and began writing, I left him for a time and was hired as the surgeon on a trip to Virginia. I stayed about a year in Jamestown and acquired about 200 acres. I returned to England about a year ago to wed Mary just in time to witness Bastwick being pilloried."

"Ye said ye have 200 acres. Where do ye plan to settle?"

"At first, I thought about Jamestown but Mary has an uncle in Accawmacke and he's encouraged us to settle there. We plan to stay with him for a while after we reach Virginia."

"Accawmacke, ye say, why that's where I have my plantation. What's Mary's uncle's name?"

"Henry Willson, do ye know him?"

"Ye wife's uncle is Henry Willson? Why of course I know Henry! He married me Mum in England after me father died. Then

22

he left for Virginia with his bother John and sent for us after things were a little more settled. I remember I was around nineteen at the time of arrival in Virginia and having been educated in England, I was shocked by the primitiveness of Virginia but quickly learned to love her. He and me Mum live near me place on Old Plantation Creek. I believe he's one of the oldest planters in Accawmacke. I heard he arrived around twenty years ago."

"That must be him. He settled in Virginia quite a while back."

Berriman continued, "My sister-in-law Elizabeth is there too, she married Henry Carsley, Jr., me 'brother' from Mum's first marriage. He talked me into coming to the colonies and my land is next to their plantation. I've been helping her some after me brother died a couple of years ago. They have two daughters Agnis, and Francis. Me brother Henry Carsley, Jr. and Henry Willson were always arguing over who arrived in Virginia first. A better man can not be found.   Henry helped set up the salt mines on Smith Island when Accawmacke was first settled."

"The salt mines, is there salt in Accawmacke?"

Berriman laughed, "Of course, there's salt...a whole ocean full....If they had not set up the salt works to secure salt by evaporation from the ocean, Virginia may never have been settled.... there was no other way to preserve meat. Men can't survive long when they only have fresh meat. The salt works were first set up by Sir Thomas Dale around 1614 but Henry Willson's group really made the Salt Works profitable."

"I see, but evaporation seems to be a very hard way to make salt."

"True, it was, until old man Mile Pirket was sent to Virginia to manage the works. Somehow he and a few other men, including Henry Willson managed to make a profit. Henry went to Accawmacke to help with the salt works, fell in love with the Eastern Shore and stayed. Say, since ye have relatives in Accawmacke, ye ought to settle there. Ye could do worse."

"Well that would be good for Mary. It would be nice to be near a relative, even one she doesn't know well."

"We didna get bothered by Jamestown much since tis a way's across the bay which would be good for ye since ye want to stay out of Laud's reach. The further from that man's hooks the better, I say. Jamestown receives orders from England that we in Accawmacke often ignore. Though I won't deceive you, there are tough times ahead but in Accawmacke a man can build a good life if he is willing to work."

"I'm not afraid of work but I just hope it won't be too hard on Mary. She's heard many stories about the savages in Virginia and I'm afraid they've terrified her. Is it true that the Indians are friendly in Accawmacke? Her uncle wrote us that they've never had trouble with them."

"Aye, in my part of the woods around Old Plantation Creek the Accawmacke are friendly, though I wouldn't turn me back on them. But there has never been anything like the savagery perpetrated on the people in Jamestown. Why they say, before that massacre on the western shore in 1622, Devedeavon, the Laughing King of the Accawmacke warned of the uprising. His warning saved Jamestown from total devastation since everyone was prepared with guns and ammunition. We owe a lot to the Laughing King. The land, however, is worth any tribulation. The soil is so fertile and the weather so mild that I've produced two crops each year I've been there and no stones to break a plough. The forests are filled with wildlife and there's all manner of fish or shellfish just for the taking. The salt works at Old Plantation creek supply salt to most of Virginia. I'd say it's a regular paradise and I can't wait to get back."

"Well, ye certainly make Accawmacke sound appealing."

"Say, why don't ye and Mary come stay with me and Sarah a spell when we reach Virginia and see for yeself."

"That's a very kind offer. Of course, we plan to stay with Mary's uncle first but I'm sure Mary will enjoy visiting with ye wife. I understand there aren't too many women in Virginia."

"Aye, that's true. Sarah will enjoy visiting with ye missus. She gets a mite lonely sometimes for womanly company."

A loud racket down the quay startled Henry and Berriman. They looked in the direction of the sound and saw soldiers racing toward them. Henry was briefly alarmed as they drew nearer but gave a sigh of relief as they ran past them and went further down the quay.

Henry and Berriman watched as a man untying a skiff glanced up and saw the soldiers heading in his direction. His fearful eyes darted around for some chance of escape, seeing none, he jumped into the water. Two soldiers dived in after him, and they struggled with the man briefly before finally subduing him. Then the soldiers heaved him out of the water and onto the pier. His hands were quickly bound behind him and two soldiers hauled him down the wharf, one soldier on each arm. As they neared Henry and William, the man could be heard repeating the words, "I can do all things through Christ, who strengtheneth me," over and over again.

William looked at Henry and said, "I'd say the Elizabeth won't be leaving any too soon for either of us."

CHAPTER THREE

March, 1638, Cranbrook, England

Mary opened her eyes to the graying dawn of morning and for a brief instant she felt a sense of panic in the strange room but as she became more alert, thoughts of last night's late arrival came to her, and she smiled. Silent beams of light began to penetrate the cracks in the roof and walls and creep over the sleeping figures like fingers, first lightly touching, then, softly caressing each one until they were all bathed in the glorious glow. How welcome was the sunlight after the unrelenting rain that plagued her final days of packing and planning.

Thoughts of moving so far away from family, friends and everything she knew filled Mary's every waking moment as she sorted and packed the necessary items needed for their new home. It had been hard deciding what to take with them, especially since so little was known about their destination and they were limited to such a small space on the ship.

Henry was a lot of help in the decisions since he had been to the Colonies and knew some of the needs. He often wrote lists for her of items they would need on any hard surface available. She laughed to herself as she thought of some of the strange places she found his lists....from the fireplace mantle to the wooden flour bin, Henry's writing was everywhere. She teased him about the many scribbles but secretly, enjoyed seeing his handwriting in unexpected places. When she discovered a list in a strange place, she couldn't help but laugh and it eased the increasing tension she felt from their impending journey.

But how can I manage without my loom?

A loom had been such an integral part of Mary's life but it was just too large and Henry insisted that it must be left behind. He reassured her they could build one anew in the Colonies. It was hard to believe that most people built their own furniture and many other items.

What do people use until they had the time to build their furniture?

As she eliminated more and more items she thought she could not do without, Mary's spirits over the great adventure dampened right along with the streets of London so Henry suggested this trip to see her family and he took care of the remaining details for their journey. The visit seemed to have helped since she awoke in better spirits this morning.

As she looked at her brothers and sisters, Mary's thoughts returned to her family and the fact that this might be the last time she would see them. She glanced at her still sleeping sister, Anne, who was snuggled under the coverlet next to her and a deep feeling of sadness suddenly overwhelmed her. Tears trickled down her cheeks as images of the happy days she and her sister spent flowed through her mind. Life, though hard, was simple compared to the problems she encountered now.

I wonder if things would have been so hard if our family had remained in Steeton in the two-room cottage great-grandfather built. He had to start life all over again too, just like me, and everything turned out okay.

Realizing her mother would probably be up now preparing breakfast, Mary started to arise to assist her but as she threw back the coverlet, the movement caused her sister, Anne, to stir.

I'll just wait a little longer because I'll probably just wake everyone getting up.

It was still very chilly in the early morning and she pulled the coverlet back and snuggled a little closer to Anne. She let her mind wander as she recalled other early mornings with her family and realized how much she missed the quiet talks she and her mother often had as they prepared breakfast while her brothers and sisters slept. She needed time to talk with her now without her brothers and sisters around.

Mary had known for about a month that she was carrying their first-born child but she was hesitant of telling Henry. He had so many things to take care of as he prepared for their voyage, she didn't want to add an additional burden of an expectant wife so Mary kept the impending birth a secret.

I wonder how Henry will feel about me having a bairn. I know he wants children but this is not exactly the right time.

Knowing Henry, he would probably make me stay in England if he knew... and that is the last thing I want to do. I couldn't tolerate living in England without him. After all, we'll be in the Colonies long before our bairn is born and I never felt better in my life. I just need to know what to expect that's all. Still I've heard illness is often rampant on the voyages to the Colonies. If I fell ill, Henry would need to know then. Perhaps I ought to tell him sooner...but only after we're safely on the ship. Maybe Mum can help me decide what to do.

Mary snuggled deeper in the covers as the sunlight filled the room and continued to reflect on her life.

Had it just been only one year since marriage to Henry? So much has happened since then that it seemed much longer.

Mary grimaced as she recalled the inane fits of giggles she and her sisters often had as they planned and dreamed about their futures. All those plans were in vain because unbeknownst to her; Mary's father had already determined the course of her life long before she'd ever been born.

Mary's father and Henry's father were close friends during the War and after returning home, the two men ensured their continued alliance by arranging marriage contracts between their first-born sons and daughters.

Henry's father had been the parson of Nettlestead and Mary learned of the marriage contract on her tenth birthday but she had not been concerned since marriage still seemed so far in the future. Tragedy struck when Henry's father, two brothers and a sister died of the "Black Death" in 1624 and left Henry as the sole support of his mother and two sisters at the young age of twelve.

She thought the marriage contract might not be fulfilled after Henry's father's death but she was wrong. She smiled as she recalled that fateful day on her fifteenth birthday when he appeared at their door.

Luckily, Henry's persistence and hard work paid off and Dr. Bastwick had taken an interest in him, and given him a position in his apothecary business. Later, after his mother's remarriage, he was apprenticed to Dr. Bastwick to study physick but when Bastwick began writing, Henry seemed to have disappeared for a few years until that fateful day when the tall, dark haired Henry, with his brooding brown eyes unexpectedly appeared on her doorstep.

She remembered standing behind her father as he answered the door and when Henry emphatically stated,

"Ye made a promise with me father and I've come to claim me wife."

And when she heard her father say, "I intend to keep me promise," she became terrified. Henry was a complete stranger to her and quite a bit older and she was completely awestruck by him. She remembered being thankful that her father convinced Henry to wait awhile to marry until they courted.

What a courtship! Neither one of us knew what to say to each other.

At first, he seemed to be quite pompous but as the year passed, she soon realized how very wrong her first impression had been. She discovered that Henry was really a very caring person with an insatiable thirst for knowledge and what she had mistaken for arrogance was instead a strong drive to improve his lot in life.

When Henry started talking, he couldn't stop. The floodgates were open.

Henry told her about his anguish over his father's death and how he then forced to become the bread-winner for the family at an early age and how Dr. Bastwick took an interest in him and gave him a future.

Henry would never have made it after his father died without all that ambition and that same ambition was leading them to The Colonies. No, I wouldn't change a thing even though my life has been turned upside down.

Mary heard a rustling sound below and knew her mother was stirring the fire to warm the small cottage so she eased out of the covers very carefully trying not to disturb her sister and quietly climbed down the ladder from the loft. Her mother was kneading dough for bread on the table by the fire. Mary glanced in the parlour at her parent's bed and she gave a sigh of relief. She loved her father but she really wanted to talk to her mother first about the expected birth and she was glad he left early today.

"Tis nice to have ye here Mary. I hope ye slept well," her mother said without looking up from her kneading. "I was afraid the wee ones would talk ye to death last night. I hope they didn't wear ye out."

"I slept very well...we didn't talk too long because I was tired but we'll have more time today."

Her mother's gray hair was tied in a knot in back but small wisps fell down around her face occasionally, falling in eyes as her knarled hands kneaded the bread dough.

How old Mum has become since I've been away.

The thought of never seeing her again beset Mary and she had to look away to avoid the tears that filled her eyes. This homecoming was going to be a lot harder than she anticipated. She needed to get her mind on something else or she'd never make it through this visit without constantly crying.

"Can I help ye with the meal?" Mary said as she walked over to the fire in order to stir the gruel in the huge iron pot hanging over the fire.

Her mother smiled at her then and said, "Seems like old times. We had many a fine morning working together, didna we?"

"Yes Mum. I miss them and I'll miss them even more after I've gone. Do ye realize that I may never see ye again?" Her eyes misted as she said the words and Mary admonished herself for expressing the thoughts that kept racing in her mind.

"I know," her mother said. "I've been thinking the same thing but we shouldn't let those thoughts ruin ye visit."

"If ye would come to the colonies with us, we could see each other every day. It is becoming so difficult to have meetings here now and I hear that in the colonies it is much safer to meet. The land is very bountiful there so Papa wouldn't have to work as hard and there is no worry about the plague," Mary rapidly exclaimed.

"Now Mary, we've been over this before. Ye father and me are getting too old to start over again and it would be too hard for the wee ones. We'll just manage here like we said. God will take care of us. Besides the numbers of our faith are increasing and King Charles will not be able ignore us much longer. Things should get better here too. I've heard talk about changes coming soon. But all this chatter about the colonies just makes us sad. Let's talk about something else."

"Where's Papa? I had hoped to visit with him too."

"Oh, he said he'd be back early this evening. He left in the wee hours this morning so he could leave work early and have a nice long visit with ye."

Mary's father was a weaver, a trade the family had been in since their days in Steeton. With the loom from their cottage in Steeton, they were able to reestablish themselves again in the small village of Rochester and her great-grandfather, George Willson had been Alderman of Rochester until his death in 1629. He always hated collecting money from the poor of Rochester and many times money from the Willson household took the place of the fee of some poor family in Rochester.

The Willson family still seemed to be doing quite well though. Her father had added a kitchen and buttery since her last visit, though Mary's brothers and sisters said that mother complained constantly about her father's gardening tools in the buttery. Recently, Mary's father had purchased additional land and Grandfather Willson and her brothers were farming the new land to add to their income.

Maybe they'll be okay. At least they aren't living in London with the continual threat of the "Black Death" as well.

Still she couldn't help but worry about her parents. Life was becoming difficult in England. Many nights their meetings had been rudely interrupted by soldiers. Her father always managed to make peace with them but the interruptions had been more frequent the last couple of years.

"When's the bairn due?" her mother abruptly asked.

"What! How did ye know?"

"Oh, when ye have been around as many births as I have, ye have a way of knowing these things. Ye still haven't answered me. When is it due?"

"Somewhere around October I believe but we should be in the colonies by then. That's what I wanted to talk to ye about. I wish ye were going to be with me when the time comes. I know Henry will be with me but I'm a little anxious about having a wee one just now."

"Oh, ye'll be fine. All the women in me family have an easy time of the 'lying in.'...I wish I could be with ye too, being me first grandchild. What does Henry think about having a wee one?"

"I haven't told him yet and don't ye tell him either. I don't want him to know until we are on our way."

"Why, may I ask? Does he not want bairns?"

"On nay, I mean, I'm sure he wants a bairn but I'm afraid he

32

will make me stay in England until after it's born if he knew. He worries about me so much but I couldn't stand to stay in England without him."

"Well, I don't know, I still think ye need to tell him but I suppose ye are right. He will probably make ye stay here. Men worry too much about women having bairns but it's just as normal as cats having kittens. Still there's no telling how bad the conditions will be in the Colonies. I suppose there's little hope of convincing ye to stay here with us until after the wee one is born," she said with questioning eyes directed at Mary.

They both looked up when they heard the clamor of Anne climbing down the ladder from the sleeping loft.

"Just remember to try and rest as much as ye can, we'll talk more later," whispered her Mother.

"I thought ye had gone again. Why didna ye wake me?" Anne exclaimed. "I was afraid ye left without saying good'bye."

"Now ye know I'd never do that. Come," Mary said as she picked up the water pail hanging on the wall. I'm sure mum will need some water soon and we'll talk on the way to the village well before the wee ones get up and I want to see Cranbrook one last time in the early morning."

Cranbrook, once the center of the woollen industry, attracted many Flemish weavers, fullers and dyers from Flanders who settled there years ago due to the water power, timber and labor available and Mary's father moved his family from Rochester to Cranbrook for the same reasons.

Since Queen Elizabeth had prohibited the exportation of cloth for dyeing and finishing, the industry was now on the decline but unnumbered flocks of sheep still grazed the gentle hills surrounding Cranbrook as Mary and her sister walked along the brook which had swelled from the recent rains.

"Have ye a beau yet, Anne?" Mary queried.

"Nay, no one special. I'm sure Papa will have something to say about it anyway like he did with ye."

"I hope ye will be as lucky in his choice as I have been."

33

"It doesn't sound so lucky to me, with him dragging ye off to some strange country. I don't want to ever leave Cranbrook much less England."

"Life doesn't always turn out as ye plan Anne but ye just have to learn to accept what comes ye way."

"Do ye know where ye will live in the Colonies?"

"We'll stay with Uncle Henry at first. We really haven't had much time to plan much past our trip. It has all been in such a hurry. Ye know Bishop Laud has been asking many questions about Henry since Dr. Bastwick ordeal with the STAR CHAMBER. I just hope Henry is not implicated before we leave. We have been living in fear these past few months, waiting for a knock on the door. At least, in the Colonies we will be far away from Bishop Laud. I hope ye will all be safe here in Cranbrook."

"Aye, I feel sure we will. Papa and Mum are careful about keeping the meetings secret and our friends here in Cranbrook would not give us away."

As they passed the free grammar school, a small dog darted out in front of them chasing a speckled chicken and spattered the two young girls with mud.

"Oh me, now we'll really need that water," exclaimed Mary, as she attempted to wipe away some of the mud on her dress. "We'd better get that water soon so we can clean up before breakfast."

CHAPTER FOUR

March 10, 1638 Cranbrook, England

As dusk approached, a nightingale perched in a nearby tree began its soaring crescendo of music. The bird's sweet song filled the air. Mary, her grandfather, brothers and sisters gathered by the glowing fire complacently enjoying the warmth while their mother rocked baby Sarah to sleep. They were all anxiously waiting for Papa's return home.

"I wonder if there will be nightingales in the colonies," said Mary. "I'll certainly miss them if they aren't."

"Aye, their music has a way of making the evenings special," agreed her grandfather. "Me Papa used to say they were calling us to our home in the days when we were wandering across the country after leaving Steeton."

"Tell us again about Steeton Grandpapa," Mary declared.

"Aye, ye have heard it many times but it's a tale worth repeating. Steeton was a grand place. We had a fine timber-framed home and with me Papa's extra earnings from weaving, we added a hall and a fine parlour. Everything was wonderful until Sir Guy threw us off the land."

Mary's grandfather's voice filled with bitterness as he recalled that day. "Ye know it was the sheep that ruined us and the sheep again that saved us. We were lucky that the loom was secured before our house was torn down or we never would have been able to make a new start."

"How did the sheep ruin ye?" Anne queried.

"Our landlord, Sir Guy Fairfax needed more land for his sheep and since they offered higher profits than the taking of rents, he cast his greedy eyes upon the village community land and raised the rents. Me papa still was able to hang on for a while until that terrible day when him drove us off the land. We nearly starved that first year wandering around the country looking for a place to make a new start."

Mary's Grandpapa became very quiet as he looked into the fire with misted eyes and said, "Me mum died that first year one cold night in April."

"Wouldn't any of our relatives take ye in?" Mary asked.

"They wanted to but because so many others were traveling the countryside without a home, townspeople were afraid we were a threat because we'd work for practically anything to keep from starving. A law was made which forbade more than one family to occupy a house so our friends and relatives couldn't take us in without breaking that law. We even had a song about our plight. I used to sing it to ye when ye were a wee thing.

Commons to close and kepe
Poor folk for bred to cry and wepe;
Towns pulled down to pasture shepe;
This is the new gyse.

"I remember that song, but never understood it until now," Mary said sadly.

"Ye know if it wasn't for the 'Black Death', we'd probably still be looking for a home. When we reached Rochester so many people died and many houses were vacant. With the loom we saved, me papa started weaving.   It's strange that something as terrible as the Black Death would be a life saver for us."

"Weren't ye afraid of living in a house where someone died from the 'Black Death?" queried Mary's brother Robert.

"Aye, we were, but at least it was a home. We would probably all have died if we'd remained vagabonds much longer."

Mary's brother, George exclaimed, "Papa says the 'Black Death' is judgment by God for England's evil ways and until the King repents of his evil ways the 'Black Death' will not leave."

"Henry doesn't go along with that belief," Mary said softly. "He feels that it's caused by crowded living conditions since it occurred mainly in London. Ye know it's not in the colonies and he hopes to find out why. Maybe he'll find the cure there."

"Aye, I hope he will," Mary's grandfather added.

The door flew open with a strong gust of wind and Papa tromped in bringing a rush of cold air into the toasty room.

"Aye, ye all look mighty warm and happy," he said. Edward Willson was a tall, thin man with wavy, dark hair and deep-set piercing gray eyes. Everyone said Mary had her father's eyes though she more nearly resembled her mother, Margaret.

"Here ye have all been sitting happily chatting by the fire while I've been out fighting this dastardly wind and working me fingers to the bone." he exclaimed with a mischievous smile.

"Papa, Papa, what's in the package?" shouted six year old Elizabeth.

"Why, what package? I don't know what package ye're talking about," he replied, as he quickly hid a packet he was carrying under his coat.

Elizabeth ran to him and started tugging at his coat. "The package under ye coat, Papa...under ye coat."

With a flourish he pulled the package out and said, "Ye mean this package."

"Yes, papa, yes, what's in the package?"

"Hush, Elizabeth," admonished her mother, "Ye will wake Sarah with all that clamoring and I'm sure ye papa is tired after his long day."

"Why, if a little girl gives her papa a big hug and is very quiet while I eat, maybe I'll let her know what's in the package," he replied as he gave her a wink. He laid the package on the table and swept Elizabeth up in his arms and gave her a big bear hug but she never took her eyes off the package. "And, how is my beautiful married daughter this fine evening?" he said as he glanced over the shoulder of the exuberant Elizabeth. "Mary, the sight of ye here is as welcome as the roses in May."

"I'm fine papa...it's good to be home...though it won't be for long..." Mary said, blinking back her tears.

"Aye, but we must relish this visit while ye are here...and not be lamenting over the days ahead."

"Henry was hoping that I could talk ye into following us this summer."

"Now, Mary, ye know that's not going to happen. Ye mum and I are far too old to attempt such a long journey and start over again in a new country especially with the wee ones."

"But, I'm so worried about ye staying here."

"Aye, it's a worrisome time in England these days but I'm sure God will take care of us. But right now, I'd like to enjoy some of ye mum's fine cooking."

"I was wondering if ye had forgotten about eating," Mary's

mother exclaimed as she placed a warm bowl of stew and a half a loaf of fresh bread on the table. "I'm afraid the wee ones didn't leave much for ye. They were ravenous tonight."

"I'm sorry I'm late getting home but it was for a good cause. I had something special to complete tonight," and he gave his wife a wink.

"Sorry, papa, I guess we were a little greedy tonight," Robert said, as he sat down beside his father. "But grandpa worked us pretty hard today."

"Humph," grandpa snorted, "Ye young people today don't know what hard work is...why when I was ye age..."

Elizabeth interrupted with a plaintive plea, "Papa, ye need to eat, so we can open the package."

"Ye are right, Elizabeth, but mind ye manners; Grandpa was talking."

"Oh, I was through anyway," said grandpa. "Have ye any news from London?"

"Aye, I hear that King Charles has declared the Scots National Covenant treason and the Covenanters as rebels. He's raising an army to put them down."

"But surely, he must realize that the Covenant was not against him, but only against the use of the Prayer book and other Popery relics," Margaret exclaimed.

"The only thing King Charles is worried about is his power," retorted Mary's grandfather.

"Aye, he thinks his power over Scotland is threatened by the Covenant and he is determined to dissolve it even if by force...but that's enough talk about our King. I want to enjoy this visit with Mary...it will be short enough. How long can ye stay?"

"Henry thinks we'll be sailing within the next couple of weeks. I'm anxious to be on our way...the waiting has become intolerable...but again, I don't know if I'm really ready to go. We'll be so far away."

"I wish ye didna have to leave as well...but it is really not safe in England for the two of ye. I know God must have a special plan for ye both in the Colonies. Have ye heard from me brother, Henry? I sent a packet to him months ago and told him to contact ye."

"Aye, we received a reply and plan to stay with him when we

reach Virginia for a while. He left such a long time ago and I never really knew him. Why did he leave England?"

"Henry Willson always had an adventuresome spirit and when he heard about the opportunities available in the Colonies, he just felt compelled to go there, I guess. He talked me brother, John, into going with him and they settled there years ago. John died not too long ago but I understand Henry has done quite well...though I don't hear from him much. Just the same, I'm glad he's over there so there will be some family for ye. I'm sure he'll be a lot of help."

Elizabeth silently watched her father finish his last morsel of food and could contain herself no longer. "Papa, I've been very good...now can we see what's in the package?"

"Well, Elizabeth, I don't know," he teased. "Maybe, we ought to wait until tomorrow to open it. It is late and tis time ye went to bed."

"Oh Papa, please, please, open it now. I'll never sleep a wink thinking about it."

"Aye, well, I guess we'd better open it so ye can get some rest," he chortled as he began untying the string holding the wrapping.

Then he looked at Mary seriously and said, "Mary, I know ye don't have a lot of room on the ship to stow belongings so ye Mum and I had a hard time deciding what to give ye. We finally decided ye could always use some extra cloth for dresses and such, so this is some fine broadcloth from our family's own loom. But, ye Mum said that a young lady shouldn't always have to be so practical so we have something special as well and I just finished tonight. It took a little longer than I thought so that's why I was late. I wanted it to be perfect."

As her father lifted the broadcloth, a delicate, intricately designed silk ribbon was revealed underneath. "Ye Mum suggested the ribbon Mary, but we all created the design. It is a reminder of home and the love that remains here for ye. Christ has given us this love and has made our family beautiful and strong just like this ribbon. Remember it as a ribbon of love that ties and forever binds us to ye no matter how far the distance. We will always love and be praying for ye even though distance keeps us apart."

He lifted the ribbon up and held it closer so Mary could see the design.

"Notice, there are nine strands of color in the ribbon," he continued. "Each color represents a member of our family. The strands are very fragile alone and they follow different paths just as each member of our family will follow a different path in their life but when the strands are woven and tied together a strong bond is created resulting in a beautiful design. "

"When ye reach the Colonies and begin life there, ye will be creating a totally new direction for our family's design. As ye follow this new path, always remember the love that ties ye to us...a family that has been here for generations, long before Grandpa's time. The path our ancestor's chose in life created a design for our family today. Most of all, ye must remember to keep God's love in the design, for His love is what makes our family strong and beautiful. It is the tie that binds our love to each other. With His love in ye life, our family's design will remain beautiful and strong and our hearts will be forever bound just like the strands in this ribbon."

This was too much for Mary and tears freely flowed down her cheeks as she said between sobs, "Oh Papa, I'll treasure this ribbon forever."

"It's not only from me, Mary, it's from ye whole family," he said. "We created the design together....don't forget to thank them as well."

"Oh yes, thank ye, thank ye all!" she exclaimed. "I'll treasure and keep this ribbon with me always and feel ye presence in me life as long as it is with me...and most of all, Papa," she said with all the strength in her voice she could muster..."I won't forget the love within it."

"What color am I?" chirped Elizabeth.

They all laughed as Papa pulled her into his lap. "Oh, ye are yellow because ye remind me of sunshine," he said with a smile.

"Now, isn't it time ye started thinking about sleep. The sun has to arise very early tomorrow morning."

As Mary climbed down the ladder on the morning of her

departure, her mother looked up from where she was stirring the gruel. "Aye, Mary, I'm glad ye arose before the wee ones. I was afraid ye be too tired from the party last night."

"I am a little tired but I don't want to waste a second of time sleeping when I could be visiting with my family instead. It will be a long time before I see ye all again."

"Aye, I understand. I hope ye have room for a few more items to take with ye. I have something I want to give ye and didn't want questions from the wee ones."

"Mum, ye have already been too generous. Unless, it's telling me that ye will soon join me in my journey to the colonies, I can't think of anything else I'd need."

"Maybe, not quite yet, Mary, but ye will need it soon," her mother replied mysteriously, as she led Mary to the Parlour. Margaret pulled open the lower drawer of the big chest in the Parlour and began to take out some delicately embroidered items. "I want ye to have my childbed linen, Mary. Ye will need it soon enough for ye lying in and I know it will be hard to come by in the Colonies."

"Oh Mum, I hate to take it. Ye are still young and I may have another brother and sister yet."

"Nay, I doubt that Mary but if I do, I will be better able to get more here in England than ye will in the Colonies. My Mum gave me this linen Mary and because ye are me eldest daughter, it should go to ye. I didna know when we'll see each other again and I wanted to make sure ye had it for ye're 'lying in'"

Mary fingered the beautiful linen, and tears welled up in her eyes again. "Oh, Mum, will I ever stop crying. I haven't even left and all I can think about is how much I'll miss ye."

Margaret drew her to her breast and Mary could control herself no longer and sobbed on her shoulder.

After a time Margaret softly replied, "Mary, I feel the same but it's for the best. I so want to see my first grandchild.....maybe, ye and Henry will be able to return to England if things become a little safer here."

"I hope so," Mary replied. "That hope keeps me going. I can't bear the thought of never seeing ye again."

"Well now, we both should stop this crying," Margaret said and she stood and tried to compose herself. "We need to cook the victuals or we'll have some hungry wee ones grumbling soon. "Let's see if we can only think of pleasant things today so our last memories will be good ones."

"Ye're right., I didna want to remember a gloomy last day with my family. Just give me a minute and I'll try to stop the tears as I pack this linen away," Mary replied in a choked voice.

Margaret went back to her duties in the kitchen and Mary stood up and gave a long last look around her parent's room, trying to imprint the vision of it deeply within her memory. Seeing her swollen eyes in the looking glass, she splashed water on her face and pinched her pale cheeks. She brushed back her disheveled hair, tying it in a bun with the ribbon her family had given her then covered her head with her rochet. She picked up the delicate linen and walked into the kitchen. Her mother was again stirring the gruel at the fire with her back to Mary.

Oh Mum, how I wish ye would come with us. I feel so alone. How will I ever manage without me family? I love Henry so much but it is so hard to leave ye.

She bit her lip, forcing back the tears and carefully packed the precious linen in her bags.

CHAPTER FIVE

April 25, 1638 Atlantic Ocean

With the break in the weather, Mary climbed up from the ladies' cabin to walk on the main deck in the hope that a little fresh air would ease the nausea that plagued her since leaving England. She leaned against the railing breathing in the fresh salty air and tried to ignore the stench emanating from the ship. Oh, to smell clean air again but that should be a while. The captain said it would take approximately two months to arrive in Virginia.

Mary recalled her last days in England when she and Henry waited at the Inn at Gravesend for the ship to sail. When they were notified that the ship was ready, 115 passengers went on a barge to the ship with their belongings. The *Elizabeth* was a little under 200 feet long with three masts. After the custom-house officer came on board to peruse their packets and get fees, they finally set sail around sunset and soon caught up with the other ships in the fleet.

The *Elizabeth* had been sailing for twenty days now and during that time, the crowded ship was battered by squall after squall. The forty-six ships in the original fleet sailing from Gravesend had been separated in one of the storms and the Elizabeth was sailing with only two others in the rough sea.

Mary reeled as another wave of nausea rippled through her body just as Henry happened to climb up from the hold.

"Mary, I thought ye would still be resting. Ye are not well. Why didn't ye call for me? I'm worried about ye're sickness." He touched her forehead and gave a sigh of relief when he found no fever.

"I thought the fresh air might do me some good and since the rain has stopped, it seemed a good opportunity."

"Ye are probably right. Fresh air and sun is what everyone needs, the foul air in the hold has become unbearable. Ye must take better care though and not work so hard, I noticed ye helping

Sarah Brown with her wee ones last night. Don't do too much work until ye are feeling better."

"I know, but with four children sick, she's having a very difficult time tending to them all. I just felt someone needed to lend a hand."

"Aye, she does have an arduous task taking care of so many sick ones but do rest more. I wish I knew what made them so ill. It seems to be more than just the usual sea-sickness but I may be just worrying about nothing."

Mary shivered as a strong north-westerly breeze blew across the deck. "I hope we're not in for some more rough weather. I think we've had enough to last a life time."

Henry put his arm around Mary's shoulders as he gently guided her toward the cabin assigned to the women and children. "I'll look in on ye after a while. Try to get some rest."

"It might be a little difficult just now. Everything is still wet from these continual storms and we need to dry some of the bedding before the rain starts again. I need to go back and see what I can manage to dry out though and I'm sure Sarah needs help...but what about ye, Henry? Ye have not slept in two nights. Ye can not continue to go without sleep or ye'll be ill as well."

"Aye, the life of a ship surgeon," laughed Henry. "I'll stop soon. I just need to look in on Berriman's indenture servant John Trehearne. He was quite ill before last night's ordeal and I'm a worried about him."

Captain Potts came out of the round house and seeing Henry, crossed over to speak with him as Mary climbed down the ladder to the ladies cabin. "How many sick have we, Henry?"

"About thirty-five so far...most due to rough sea.... Ten of them I'm not exactly sure what ails them...I'm afraid it might be ship's fever. If we could ever have calmer waters, I'll be able to discern their ailments better."

"I'm afraid that won't be happening today. Our latitude places us in an area of turbulent waters and my officer's on watch saw a spout early this morning to the east. We'll probably be in for more of the same. At least with this good trade-wind, we made about fifty or sixty more leagues since yesterday. At this rate we should reach the Azores in a few days if we have no more set-backs."

"At least that's some good news. Do ye think there is much chance of boiling the kettle before we face another storm? We'll all be sick soon if we don't eat something besides the cheese and water we've had the last couple of days."

"Maybe, if we hurry....but some of the passengers look like they could care less about food. Not too many have their sea legs on this trip, I'd say."

"Ye're right about that, I just hope that's all it is," replied Henry.

"I agree. We don't need to be battling ship's fever as well as the weather."

As if in answer, a strong gust of wind blew Henry's hat off his head, tumbled across the wooden deck and finally into the raging waters. The startled men looked off into the waters after it and Henry said, "I hope that's not an omen of things to come."

Lightening strikes flickered across the distant horizon before the women finished clearing the remains of the first cooked meal in days. The main deck seemed to be littered with colorful fall leaves with all the drying clothing lying around and a few children, still sick from fever lay on damp bedding watching the dark clouds form overhead. As the drops of rain began to hit the deck, the women scrambled to gather the children, bedding, and clothing.

Sarah was near panic as she rushed to round up her four sick children before they were drenched.

"Jane," she shouted to her oldest, "Are ye able to carry Susan?"

"Yes, Mum, I'll try," the sick child replied.

Mary rushed to Sarah's side and said. "Jane, ye grab Joseph's hand and ye both climb down the ladder. I'll carry Susan."

"Oh, thank ye, Mary. Praise be to God that ye are with us on this ship."

Mary smiled, "No need for thanks. Ye take care of the children. I'll come back for the bedding."

At the ladder, near panic was taking place, it was taking too long for each person to climb down the ladder to the hold. The children were being pushed aside.

Henry forced his way to the ladder and shouted, "Move aside.... let me stand on the ladder and we can hand the children down...sick ones first......that will be faster!"

45

Surprisingly, the mob responded and let Henry take command of the situation. Children were lifted, hand over hand to each other and quickly transported to the waiting hands in the hold but not without screams from the frightened children.

"MUM, MUM!" wailed a particularly strong toddler. It took some strength to hold him as he wrestled with the hands transporting him to the hold.

After releasing the docile Susan to waiting hands, Mary rushed back to retrieve the bedding as heavy raindrops began to penetrate her clothing.

"Well, so much for trying to dry everything out!" shouted Mary above the storm to a fellow passenger.

"Aye, seems something or someone is against us on this trip!" the passenger responded.

Once the full force of the rain came, all the women and children were safely in the cabin and loud curses could be heard from the seamen above as the cold rain pelted the hands topside.

Around noon, the fierce storm hit. It quickly turned into a ferocious gale with mountainous waves battering the ship.

Henry joined Captain Potts, who had stepped out briefly from the round house to check on the crew.

"Do ye think we'll make it through this one okay?" Henry shouted with worry in his voice.

"Aye, we'll survive. I've been through worse. Tis damage to this old brig that I'm worried about," replied the captain as calmly as he could under the conditions.

"There will be more sickness too, I'm afraid. We need some dry days soon," Henry retorted with frustration.

A huge wave suddenly loomed ahead....and Captain Potts shouted, "Lower the main yard men!"

The crew complied, cursing all the while and the main yard was down just before the wave hit the ship. Henry grabbed a rope attached to the side of the round house as the crushing wave enveloped the deck with water just in time to avoid being swept overboard.

After the wave dissipated, Captain Potts exclaimed, "Henry, we don't need to lose our only ship surgeon. Return to the hold and we'll take care of the deck."

"Aye, Captain. I'll check on the passengers."

46

Before Henry left the deck, a loud crack was heard and the startled men stared in amazement as the fore-mast fell over and crashed broadside along the ship.

The hands were quickly roused to action as Captain Potts barked, "Move men, free the fore-mast before she pulls the main-mast down!" The hands with axes in hand ran to break it free from the ship before further damage ensued.

Henry, seeing the chaos, realized he was in the way and darted down the ladder to the hold.

The whole trim and rigging of the ship depended on the stays and tackle fixed to the fore-mast and it was no easy job breaking it free.

As the men worked feverishly, a piercing howl rang out from a seaman on the half deck and all eyes followed his pointed finger to the gigantic wave looming over the forecastle of the ship where most of the men were working. Before they could react, the wave crashed down over the forecastle sweeping two hands with it into the raging sea.

"Save them, men!" yelled Captain Potts.

A seaman on the main deck threw a rope to the helpless men in the water, but at the same moment, another enormous wave slammed against the side of the ship forcing everyone to grab hold of anything available to avoid being swallowed up by the angry sea as well. As the hands regained their footing, they peered into the thrashing water.

"Captain, they're gone!" screamed an anguished hand.

The foremast was gone and only the shrouds that remained were loose and useless. The rigging of the fore-mast was pulling hard on the main-topmast. It was evident to all topside that the main-topmast would soon follow if something wasn't done quickly.

Captain Potts bellowed above the roar of the storm, "Cut the rigging before we all perish with them!"

"How, do we do that Captain?" bawled a deck hand in anguish.

"I can do it Captain!" a hand yelled and before anyone could stop him, a brave hand with ax in hand climbed up to cut the rigging holding the main-topmast.

"Ye can do it Johnny!" yelled a fellow hand.

All watched intently, as the young lad hacked at the

rigging....each blow caused a line to snap, endangering him even more. When the last line was cut, the lad began his long scamper down.

Suddenly, another huge wave appeared on the horizon.

"Hurry, man!" Captain Potts exclaimed.

"Come on, Johnny!" an anguish hand yelled. "He'll never make it," shouted another.

Just as he reached the half-way point the wave hit, and engulfed the ship in a deadly crush of water. After the wave abated, all the men looked up. The rigging was gone but Johnny was no longer on the mast.

A loud "Thud" broke the men's thoughts and forced them into action. The fore-mast lay broadside against the Elizabeth and became a battering ram pounding the side of the ship with each wave.

"We're all going to die!" echoed from below deck amid the frenzied screams and cries from terrified women and children between decks. Sounds of chaos below deck filled the air as the hands scrambled to free the foremast before it broke through the ship.

"Quickly, men" We need to free that fore-mast now!" bellowed Captain Potts. "But, by God be careful, we don't want to lose another man!"

All the hands, with axes in hand, scrambled to cut the lines attaching the fore-mast. Lines snapped free with loud 'POPS" The next swell swung the fore-mast away from the ship.

"Careful men!" yelled the Captain. "She's coming back."

The men watched cautiously as they continued to hack away at the lines. On the returning swing, a deafening 'CRAAACK" pierced the air as it hit the windward side of the ship between decks. A huge gaping whole was left below the main deck as it swung away. For a brief moment all that could be heard was the loud pops of the snapping lines and a tremendous SHUSHING sound as the sea water poured into the hold below deck while the stunned passengers took in the horror before them.

"Awwwwhhh" pierced the air as the ear-splitting scream from a small child broke through the consciousness of the people below deck.

Then additional screams pelted the air from below: "God

Save Us!" "We're doomed!" "Help Us!" "Mummy, Mummy!"

The crew continued to work frantically on-deck and finally, the last line was cut so the Captain barked at the men, "Good work men! Now get down there, fix that leak immediately, before she takes on too much water!"

The crew hastened down below deck to an astonishing scene of orderly confusion. Several passengers, carpenters by trade, were frantically trying to seal the gap with any board they could find while all the remaining women and children were using every conceivable vessel to bale water out of the cabin. They were in a line and passing the water hand over hand, up a ladder and out of the hold.

"Here, here, we'll take over now!" said a deck-hand as he jostled a man out of the way.

"Nay, let us help!" said the man. "We need to do something!"

With the aid of the hands, the gap was soon sealed with only a little water seeping around the edges and the hold was no longer in danger of being flooded.

The passengers spent a fitful night of prayers and terror as the storm continued to rage but no further damage occurred.

Toward morning, the storm subsided and a thick fog settled over the water like an immense veil obscuring the horizon as the crippled ship bobbed in the swirling waters. Henry was on deck with Berriman as they watched the bowsprit, devoid of her rigging, toss up and down at the mercy of the waves. The other two remaining ships traveling with them were no longer visible.

"I hope the gale didn't frighten Mrs. Pattenden too much," said Berriman.

"I don't think anyone could help but be frightened after that storm. I hope it's the last one we see. In ye trips back and forth to England, have ye ever seen one that bad?"

"Aye, I've seen many a storm, but that was one of the worse. "We should be reaching calmer waters once we reach the Azores. We'll have some fruit from the islands as well. The peaches there are a treat to behold."

"I just hope we make it soon. The Captain said we're

starting to run low on water....that is if ye count that brackish stuff in the barrels water. How is ye man Trehearne today?"

"Not well, not well at all. He's much worse after last night. His fever just doesn't seem to break and he was talking quite out of his head all night. I really hate to see it. I've grown to like Trehearne. After his indenture, I'd thought about offering him a share of my land. He's a real hard worker. Do ye think it's ship's fever?"

"I'm afraid so. I'm expecting many more to fall ill soon. I just hope we reach the Azores soon."

"Aye, I'm with ye on that but as crippled as this ship is now, we need a lot of luck."

CHAPTER SIX

April 28, 1638, Atlantic Ocean

On the twenty-third day at sea, the sun broke through the clouds and the wind dissipated, but it did little to lift the spirits of the passengers. One of Mrs. Brown's children passed away during the night and a solemn group stood on the main deck holding a brief funeral before sending the small body into the depths of the ocean.

Mary leaned against her husband in stoic silence as they both watched James Brown stiffly hold the arms of his distraught wife as the parson spoke.

"Oh Lord, as we stand here bereaved at the loss of little Anna, we know not the reason thou hast chosen her to be with ye but we trust and accept ye wisdom. We pray ye console her family and all that mourn her passing. Be with us Lord as we continue our journey to this unknown country. Guide our way and help us stay true to thy cause."

Everyone then sang...The Twenty-Third Psalm. Afterwards, four hands walked over to the small body of little Anna. Before they reached her, Sarah Brown broke free of her husband and lay over the wrapped prostrate body of her child preventing them from picking the child up and cried out "Nay, not the water. She's afraid of the water."

Her husband with the parsons help gently lifted his wife all the while quietly saying, "It's okay Sarah, she's with God now. This is only the shell of her body. Anna's safe with God."

With his words, she finally relented and allowed the seamen to lift the small body and gently slide it over the leeward side of the ship into the waiting waters. As the small form disappeared from view, Sarah, overcome with grief, fell to the deck and cried out, "Why, oh why Lord. She's such a wee child." The passengers wordlessly walked by her and gave her a hug or a gentle pat as she continued to cry inconsolably.

After a few minutes, the small clusters of people gathered on the deck began climbing down the ladder to the cabins between decks to boil the kettle for the morning meal. Mary remained with her husband on deck and he held her close as they looked off into the distant horizon.

"I just wish we'd reach land soon or we may be having many more deaths in the next few days," said Henry.

"How many are sick now?" Mary queried.

"About fifty at last count...I hope ye won't be one of them. I'm concerned about ye health."

"I suspect this sickness is normal for someone in my condition."

"What do ye mean?"

"Why, ye being a surgeon, I thought ye would have guessed by now," Mary said, looking up at him, quizzically. "We'll be having a wee one once we reach Virginia, though it doesn't look like it is quite the right time now after witnessing Sarah's misery."

"Oh Mary...a child, Henry whispered in her ear and gave her a tight affectionate squeeze as he tried not to disturb the still distraught Sarah crying softly on her husband's shoulder. Suddenly his body became rigid and he exclaimed, "How long have ye known? Ye should never have attempted this journey in ye condition."

"About two months but that's exactly why I didn't tell ye until now. I ye might make me stay in England and I couldn't endure having our first child without ye near."

"I admit, I'd have a bad time of it without ye, but still there's no telling what difficulties we'll be facing in Virginia. It would have been much safer for ye to stay in England with ye're family until after the birth."

"Aye, maybe so, but it's too late now. I'm sure I'll be fine, though I'll be glad when we reach land."

"Please be very careful. I wish ye hadn't helped Sarah so much with her children. I'm afraid the illness might affect ye too. In fact, ye feel a little warm now," he said as he caressed her cheek. "I want ye to rest the remainder of the day....no helping others for a while."

"Aye, aye doctor, I admit, I'm feeling a little tired and Mum did say I should rest as much as possible."

"Ye're Mum knew before we left? I'm surprised she didn't make ye stay with her in Cranbrook."

"She tried but realized I wouldn't stay and besides, she trusts God to take care of us. We had a good talk on my last visit and she told me that all the women in our family have an easy time with their lying in."

"I hope she's right because ye'll need all the strength one can muster once we reach Virginia. I'm afraid it won't be an easy life for us. I just hope the task will not be insurmountable."

"We really didn't have much choice. There was no future left for us in England. At least in the Colonies we can build a new life free from the worries we faced there."

"Still we may be facing even bigger problems in the Colonies. I wish these doubts that plague me would wane but I still have the feeling that I'm creating more burdens instead of making a better life for us."

"Life will always be perfect as long as I have ye with me so never worry about that."

James Brown approached Henry and said, "Doctor, would ye come and look at my oldest daughter, Elizabeth? I'm afraid she might join little Anna if her fever doesn't break soon. Sarah says that she hasn't eaten anything for three days now. I don't think Sarah could bear it if she died too...I should never have made this trip. It was difficult at home but at least we still had all our children."

"I'll go right now to see her. We need to get Sarah to rest too or she'll be sick as well," Henry replied. As the two men walked over to Sarah, Henry not looking back, shouted over his shoulder above the roar of the waves, "Mary, remember, I'm ordering ye to get some rest."

"Aye, I will," she said. "I just want to get a little more air, before going down to the cabin. Go along, I'll be fine."

The salty air filled Mary's senses and she reflected on how far away she was from her family now. She instinctively reached up as the wind tore at her white rochet covering the soft dark locks of hair, bound tightly with the ribbon her family gave her before she left.

Oh, I miss ye all so much already. How will I ever make it without ye but I must be brave for Henry.

After, a few more minutes, she slowly walked to the ladder and descended below deck to help with the preparations of the morning meal.

Later that day, Mary became violently ill. Several more passengers and crew became ill as well and Henry moved all the sick to the large cabin for the women and children so they might be more easily cared for but he rarely left Mary's side as she thrashed about and talked out of her head from the fever and he was up most nights wiping her brow with moist cloths.

Henry ordered the cabin to be continually washed down and the sick were draped with "devil's dung" in the hope that it would stop the spread of the sickness. Henry was glad he had a great deal of the plant with him though it made the ship reek even more, it would surely ward off further vapors from the dilapidated ship.

He used aconite for fever and continually ministered to the sick, taking little rest for himself. He only resorted to bleeding with the sickest patients when all hope of other cures was lost.

Henry's ideas were a little different from the other surgeons regarding bleeding. He accepted the declaration of William Harvey, the King's surgeon, that the same blood passed continuously throughout the body instead of the prevalent belief that blood was made in the liver then sent to the heart to mix with 'vital spirits' from the air.

He reasoned that if the same blood passed continuously throughout the body then it might weaken the patient even more by blood letting by diminishing the amount of blood needed by the body. His persistence paid off as gradually the number of sick diminished.

The stink of the ship was still overwhelming and he was constantly treating people for scurvy, mouth-rot and other mouth sores due to the highly salted state of the food and filthy water and he often had to scrape the lice from their bodies.

Once when he was dealing with this dreadful task on an elderly man, the man exclaimed, "Oh, If only I were back home, even lying in my pigsty! Ah, dear God, if I only had once again a piece of good bread or a fresh drop of water"....then the man fell into a deep depression from which no one could arouse him. The man's continual groans and lamentations went on day and night, depressing everyone around him until he died five days later.

Luckily he did not have to resort to bleeding Mary since she began to improve immediately. Her fever finally broke on the thirtieth day at sea. She was moved to the main deck away from the stench on the first sunny day so that she might gain some strength from the sunshine and Henry kept some clean water hidden for her so she could avoid drinking the black, dirty water, filled with worms. Henry encouraged her to drink ale frequently to quench her thirst.

Elizabeth Brown, now fully recovered, was on the main deck along with Sarah's other two children one day and they entertained Mary with their antics.

As the children played in the sunshine, a forehand, perched high on the rigging of the main top-mast gave a shout, 'LAND HO!' and passengers below deck bustled up the ladder to see. The *Elizabeth* had been at sea for five long weeks and their spirits could not be contained now that land was visible in the distance. Shouts of glee and prayers of thanks filled the air as the throng of passengers, some half-dead revived and crawled up from the hold to gaze at land from afar.

"Thanks be to God!" rang out over and over again and a few people began to dance on the main deck. By afternoon, as if to intentionally persecute them, the wind died down, leaving the crippled ship sitting silently on the water.

The wait became almost unbearable for the distraught passengers. To be so close to land, yet so far was torturous and a good deal of bickering broke out among them. Food supplies were now being rationed as well and the ship needed to be restocked or they would soon be in danger of starvation. The numerous rats which plagued the ship were sometimes snared and eaten to provide additional sustenance to the larger families. The ship sat in the sun for seven more days then late on the fortieth-seventh day at sea, a slight whisper of breeze began late in the evening and the ship began to bob on the gentle waves and slowly advanced toward land.

CHAPTER SEVEN

May 20, 1638, Island of Fyall

The island of Fyall in the western islands was paradise to the bedraggled passengers and crew of the Elizabeth. There was an abundance of fish and fowl as well as fresh peaches from the trees on the island and excellent wines. The ailing passengers were able to recuperate while the ship was repaired and other passengers took short excursions to the island to restock their personal store of food. It seemed that providence had smiled on them at last.

Captain Potts was standing on the main deck watching his hands bring water back to the ship on the long boat when the exhausted Henry, climbing up the ladder to the deck, lost his footing, grabbed his chest and fell back into the hold. Hearing the clamor, Captain Potts and other passengers ran to see what happened.

Henry was lying at the bottom of the ladder between decks, gasping for breath and clutching his chest.

Berriman, kneeled beside Henry and asked, "Henry, what is it? What do ye need?"

Between gasps, Henry whispered, "Get Mary, she'll know what to do."

"Someone, find his wife, and bring her to my cabin at once!" the Captain ordered. "And, ye two," he said, looking at two hands standing near, "Move him to my cabin, but be easy with him!"

Mary was immediately at his side and held his hand as he was carried to the cabin. "Oh, Henry, what is it? What do ye want me to do?"

"It's my heart, Mary," Henry weakly gasped, "And ye must be brave. I need ye to prepare medicine from the foxglove leaves in our supplies."

Mary summoned all her courage and tried to say with a voice belying her fear, "I know ye'll be all right, just tell me what I need to do." She listened attentively as he guided her in the preparation of the medication between gasps of breath and soon it was ready to be administered.

Though still weak from her bout of fever, she wouldn't leave Henry's side and though she took little nourishment herself, she made sure that Henry had fresh water and food whenever he was awake. After about a week of her tender administrations, Henry regained some of his strength and was finally able to stand for short periods of time.

Captain Potts looked in on Henry frequently, and delayed sailing while Henry was recuperating. Many passengers, now rested, objected to the delay but Captain Potts would not be budged.

"This ship won't leave, until I'm ready," he said wryly at the most recent complainer. And with a piercing look, retorted, "Aren't ye the strange one to complain? Weren't ye sick with fever a few weeks back? If it weren't for Henry, ye would probably be fish food by now."

At that, the admonished passenger stole away without further comment.

On June 6th, the Captain, after consulting with Henry, decided that he was strong enough to travel and gave the command to set sail. The newly repaired Elizabeth, freshly stocked with black pigs and peaches, was again on its way to Virginia. For once, the weather remained fair and a good trade wind carried the ship fifty or sixty leagues in twenty-four hours. Luckily, since Henry was in no condition to treat the sick, illness on ship seemed to have abated with the change in diet and fresh water.

Henry was gaining strength everyday and Mary finally felt safe enough to leave his side. One morning she ventured to the main deck for a breath of fresh air and in the turbulent water spied a number of strange, large fish and asked one of the seamen what they were.

"Porpoises, miss....bad omen....means we'll have bad weather soon."

"Oh, I hope not,' she replied, "I don't think we could stand anymore. But, I wish Henry could see these strange fish though!" she exclaimed and ran back to the ladder to report her sighting to him.

"Henry, I wish ye could go up to the main deck! There are porpoises everywhere, why there are so many ye could walk on the water stepping on them like stones."

William Berriman was leaning on a post nearby smoking his pipe and overheard Mary. He responded, "Porpoises ye say...why Henry, I think it is time we get ye on the main deck for a while. Ye must see these porpoises. Besides, it will do ye good to get away from this stench. Wait here and I'll get me man Trehearne to help."

In a few minutes, he was back with Trehearne and the two hoisted Henry between them. Mary grabbed a blanket and climbed the ladder. Trehearne climbed halfway up the ladder and reached back to support Henry as he gingerly climbed the ladder while William supported him below. The sun was shining and Henry gave a deep sigh as he reached the top of the deck.

"This was a great idea, Mary," Henry said. This fresh air makes me feel better already. Now let's see those porpoises!"

The two men supported Henry as he walked over to join Mary on the leeward side of the ship and they all gazed in amazement at the porpoises frolicking in the water.

"I don't think I've ever seen quite so many at one time," said Berriman.

"I hope that seaman wasn't right," Mary said.

"What do ye mean, Mary?" asked Henry.

"He said that the porpoises are a bad omen and mean we'll have bad weather. I don't think fish so happy could be a bad omen."

"I'm afraid they may be right, Mary. These seamen are often quite accurate in predicting signs," said Berriman. "But maybe it will hold off for a while. Captain Potts told me this morning that we are nearing Cape Hatteras and that means maybe only another week or two before we're in Virginia."

"None too soon for me," retorted Henry. "I'm ready to get off this ship."

"Where will we land, Mr. Berriman?" asked John.

"Point Comfort, if all goes well. The sea tends to have a

mind of its own and has blown many a ship off course."

"Well, anywhere that we land, I'll just be happy to be on land," Mary said. "Henry needs to get off this ship so he can get well."

"I'll be fine soon, Mary, with the care ye have given me....why I should be well before we land."

"I hope so," replied Mary. Looking up at Berriman, Mary queried, "What should we expect when we get to Virginia, Mr. Berriman?"

"Aye, call me Will, Mary....after all, we're to be neighbors," he replied with a wink. Then he gave a long sigh. "I won't fool ye Mary, life in Virginia is nothing like London. Why in Accawmacke we don't even have a town yet.... just a good many houses along the shore. We've really have no need for a town."

"No town!" Mary exclaimed. "How do ye get supplies?"

"What we don't grow, catch or kill comes from Jamestown or the ships from England but most people only grow tobacco. The sea is our road and most supplies come from England. Tobacco is like gold in Virginia; we don't waste our time and land growing much else. "

"But doesn't it take a long time to get supplies that way, depending on ships from England?" Mary asked.

"Aye, it does take a while. But a man can become quite wealthy while waiting," Berriman laughed.

"What about the Indians, Mr. uhh...Will?

"If ye settle in Accawmacke, ye needn't worry about them. The Laughing King is our friend and has never attacked anyone in Accawmacke."

"The Laughing King....that's a strange name. Who is he?"

"He's the chief of the Accawmacke Indians who live on the island with us. He is a very likable fellow. The Indians are a curious lot but I'm sure ye will grow accustomed to them."

Trying to allay Mary's fears, Henry added, "Remember that massacre in Jamestown we heard about a few years back? Will told me that The Laughing King warned the settlers about the uprising in time for them to defend themselves. A lot of lives were saved because of his warning."

"Aye, the Laughing King is a real friend," Berriman remarked.

Trehearne, had been listening intently to this conversation, and asked, "Will I be helping with this tobacco growing, Mr. Berriman? I don't know anything about growing tobacco. I've always been a ship caulker."

"Aye and that ye will remain. Eventually, I want to have ships of my own sailing to England with my tobacco so I'm in need of ye talents. But one day maybe ye may own a tobacco plantation of ye own," said Berriman as he winked at Henry. "Many a man has started just like ye."

"Sounds like Virginia's the right place for me," said Trehearne. "I just wish this old ship would get us there soon."

"Aye, me too, Trehearne, me too!" Henry exclaimed.

CHAPTER EIGHT

June 18, 1638, Point Comfort, Virginia

Later that month, the Elizabeth reached Point Comfort Virginia and the passengers gave thanks to God for their safe passage while they waited for the Commander to come aboard. None of the passengers or crew were allowed to disembark until the Commander of the fort obtained a true list of all persons with their names, birthplaces and occupations.

Finally, Commander Andrews arrived before dusk and after being satisfied that he had the necessary information from Captain Potts, he then administered the Oath of Supremacy and Allegiance to the King to all on board as the sun was setting over the horizon.

"I don't think we'll ever get off this tub," grumbled Berriman to Henry. "Now its nightfall, we'll have to spend another night on ship."

"Well, at least we know tomorrow we can disembark," said Henry. He stood against the railing for balance, trying not to reveal how weak he still felt. Mary was by his side, ready to assist him if he needed her support, sensing the strain the long wait had placed on him.

"Humph," Commander Andrews cleared his throat as he tried to get everyone's attention. "I would like to welcome ye all to Virginia by regulation of the General Assembly of Virginia, I must collect six pence tax for each passenger before ye will be allowed to disembark."

"What's this?" shouted Captain Potts. "There's never been any tax before now. What are ye talking about man?"

"That's true, the tax is new but still it is required," Commander Andrews declared while he glared menacingly at Captain Potts. He added, "No one will be allowed off this ship until their tax is paid."

At this statement, the astonished passengers protested bitterly, shaking their fists at the Commander, but he held his ground and shouted above the melee.

"I'll return tomorrow to collect the tax and guards will be posted so anyone planning to leave this ship without payment during the night will be shot on sight," then he left the ship quickly before the passengers became more belligerent.

"That tax is not right. They can't hold us prisoners here," exclaimed an old man behind Henry and Mary. "I didna have a pence left. All I had in the world was spent in England taking care of me family waiting for the Elizabeth to sail."

"The same for me," said another passenger. "How will we ever get off this ship? I have six wee ones plus me wife. That comes to forty-eight pence. Where does he think we'll obtain that much tax while remaining on this ship?"

Listening to their complaints, William Berriman declared, "Maybe, I can be of service. If ye want to sell one of ye headrights to me, I'll pay the tax for ye entire family."

"Aye, that seems fair," exclaimed the man with six children, "I'll do it. One less headright, won't hurt me none."

Trading for tax in exchange for headrights continued among the passengers the rest of the evening and by morning most of the passengers sold enough headrights to secure their share of the required tax and the more wealthy planters were greatly benefited by the additional headrights.

Mary spent the evening completing her packing and urged Henry to rest. She knew the next day would be demanding for him. Since his illness, Henry was able to rest quite a bit since space on the main deck was confined and there was little else to do. But now she knew that once they were on land he would not be so willing to take care of himself. He hated appearing weak and would push himself beyond his endurance.

Morning dawned with a slight mist and the Commander, true to his word, returned to the ship to collect the tax due. The mist turned to a deluge by mid-morning before most of the passengers disembarked. The only passengers remaining on ship were men whom the Captain planned to sale as indentured servants to regain the cost of their transportation.

Before leaving England, Henry had dismissed their servants as a precaution to avoid any possible link to their whereabouts in Virginia; but not having servants to carry their supplies presented them with a dilemma on their arrival, especially now that he was still so weak. To solve their problem, he bought two of the indentured servants from the Captain to assist them and the men began loading the Pattenden's supplies on one of the wagons Berriman kindly procured for them.

Mary watched Henry as he tried to walk upright to the wagon, each breath seemed to be an extreme exertion for him but he avoided any assistance.

She looked around at the dwellings surrounding the dock and gave a sigh.

I hope he regains his strength soon. I don't know what I would do without him in this strange country. Maybe, things will look better once we reach the town. After all, some quays in England don't look much better than this.

The road or trail to Elizabeth City was filled with ruts and slushy mud from the recent rain which made the ride even more treacherous than normal. As they jostled along, Berriman could be heard whistling in the wagon ahead. He seemed to have gained renewed energy from their arrival in Virginia despite the rain.

Henry looked at Mary and smiled. "Not quite as warm a welcome as I would have wished for ye Mary.....but things should improve once we are settled in at ye Uncle's house."

"Are we headed for Accawmacke now?" she asked.

"Nay, it's on the other side of the bay. We'll have to take a boat to reach it and won't leave until tomorrow at the earliest. We'll be staying with ye Cousin Rev. John Willson near the Elizabeth River tonight so at least ye will be with some family," Henry said smiling sheepishly.

"Rev. John Willson.....I didn't even know I had a cousin in Elizabeth City."

"Ye Uncle Henry mentioned he had a nephew in Elizabeth City in his last letter. I made arrangements to stay with him before we left and wanted to keep it a surprise. I knew it would take a little while to find a boat headed toward Accawmacke and I didn't want ye to have to stay with strangers."

"Oh, Henry, what a nice surprise!....I already miss my family so much and it will be nice to be around a relative once again even if I don't know anything about him."

"From what I understand, he has been the minister at the Elizabeth River Parish for just a few years but I know little else."

"No matter, he's still family....what a great surprise!"

Happy with the news, Mary speculated what her cousin would be like. It took her mind off Henry's health for a while and helped to pass the time as the oxen trudged slowly along the well-worn path ahead seemingly oblivious to their surroundings.

But Mary was not oblivious; she was overwhelmed by the huge trees lining the trail. Unspoiled forests covered the land as far as the eye could see.

No wonder so much wood had been transported to England from Virginia. Yet it still seems the forests have been untouched.

Many trees were new to Mary but the more familiar trees were thicker and taller than at home and the colors in the forest with dogwood, honeysuckle and wild rose was a sight to behold. Occasionally, a deer was spied frolicking in the woods and numerous birds filled the air with song. White herons, red-headed woodpeckers, cardinals and blackbirds were brighter than the English species.

Since it was nearing dusk, she listened for the nightingale but instead her ears were filled with the music of thousands of frogs and insects. She became aware of something stinging her arms and looked down at the numerous bites she had already incurred from flying insects on her arm. Swarms would periodically become so thick in front of her face that her vision was blocked and just breathing was difficult without inhaling some of the insects.

Surely, everything must grow well here. We should be able to succeed in this paradise.

Many times she saw what appeared to be a clearing in the woods but realized that it was just some dead tree with rings about shoulder height around the tree but around the base of the tree some young plants were growing.

What strange disease could be killing those trees yet still allow those plants to grow around it.

As the group moved further away from the bustling quay and Fort Monroe, Mary sensed someone staring at her. She glanced to the side into the woods surrounding them and was startled by some children with the strangest color skin she had ever seen staring at them. Behind them stood a young maiden, clad only in apron made of some type hide. She had dark black hair pulled back sharply and piled on her head. The young maiden had a child strapped to her back on some kind of board. Mary blushed as she stared in awe at them. The children were chattering and laughing in some unknown tongue while pointing at the wagons.

Mary became even more uneasy when she saw another tall, scantily clad male, standing stoically beside the path ahead. She squeezed Henry's arm for comfort.

"Don't worry Mary, they're just curious," he said in a soothing tone. "The Indians around this area trade with us and they're just checking out the latest arrivals from England. Stay calm, we're not far from Elizabeth City now."

Henry eased her anxiety, somewhat, but Mary's mind still raced with the horror tales reported in England about the Indians savagery and she pressed closer to him. This first glimpse of the dreaded Indians unnerved her and she would be thankful when they reached her cousin's house.

After a time, the wooded trail came to an end and they ferried the wagons across a small river. As they neared the other side, a clearing revealed a cluster of small, rough clapboard houses outside a Fort at the mouth of the river. Stumps of fresh, felled trees permeated the landscape and the air was filled with smoke from the numerous, burning fires smoldering in the misty rain. Berriman's wagon halted after crossing the river and he climbed down from his wagon and walked back to the Pattenden's wagon.

"I guess this is where I leave ye good folk," he said. "I'll be going on to Jamestown to take care of some business there but the offer about staying with us in Accawmacke still holds. As soon as I take care of business in Jamestown, I'm heading for Accawmacke on me boat and if ye would like to accompany me, I can stop by here on my way down the James."

"I would appreciate that Will," said Henry. "We'd have to find transportation to Accawmacke anyway and I'm anxious to see this veritable paradise ye have been talking about. We'll just wait here until ye return from Jamestown."

"Aye, then I'll see ye in a few days. Have a nice visit with ye cousin, Mary."

"Thanks for ye help Will," Mary responded. "I don't know how I would have managed without ye and Trehearne when Henry became ill."

"She's right about that," added Henry. "I probably wouldn't be alive today without ye help."

"That's what neighbors are for," he replied, tipping his hat at his walked back to his wagon. Berriman continued on the trail while Henry and Mary with their two indentured servants, Chris and James, guided the loaded wagon toward the village.

CHAPTER NINE

June 19, 1638 Elizabeth River Parish, Virginia

It didn't take long to find Mary's cousin, Rev. John Willson, since he was the only minister in the Elizabeth River Parish and they were welcomed with open arms. Henry was immediately sent to bed in spite of his protests by Rev. Willson's wife, Hannah, while her husband directed the unloading of the wagon.

"We certainly can't afford to have a surgeon ailing here with as much sickness as we have," fussed Hannah as she flurried around the small house preparing for her guests.

Mary mixed the potion from the foxglove leaves for Henry to take, before helping him settle in the Parlour; then she went to the hall of the house where she found Hannah setting pewter plates on the table and two small children playing with a puppy. One of the children was a small girl around two years of age, with flaxen hair and delicate features. Her smile and laughter lit up the room. The other child, a tall, thin boy with pale skin, was around age seven. He was quieter and appeared to be a little more serious in nature, though their high spirits exuberance over the puppy's antics was quite noisy in the hall.

"Is he all settled in?" asked Hannah.

"Yes, thank ye for insisting that Henry rest. I don't think he would have without ye persuasion."

"Bridget and John come here and meet our cousin." The two children dutifully came over to their mother and Mary was struck by Bridget's deep blue eyes.

"Bridget and John, those are two pretty names for two beautiful children." said Mary, "How old are ye?"

John spoke up and pointed at his sister, "She's three and I'm five but she didna talk much."

"She doesn't get much chance to around here," chuckled Hannah. 'With five wee ones, there's not much chance of getting a word in edgewise. Now, ye two take that poor puppy outside. I'm sure Mr. Pattenden would like to have some quiet time and doesn't need to hear all that barking. Oh, and tell James to fetch a ham from the smokehouse and take it to Molly in the kitchen. I'm sure our visitors are starved after their long journey. Then ye two help Little Eliza pick some berries, but be careful of snakes. They're sure to be out this time of year"

Hannah was a tall, chubby woman with a drawn look. She couldn't have been more than thirty but looked much older. In England, a minister would always have maids and servants to help with the household but it appeared to Mary that none were available to Hannah.

After watching her for a few minutes, Mary asked, "Is there something I can do to help? I'd hate for our visit to inconvenience ye."

"Why, ye are no inconvenience child," Hannah replied. "We love having ye as company. Don't mind me. There's always something to do around here and I guess I don't know when to stop, but let's sit a spell and have a cup of tea. Ye must be exhausted from that long trip."

"Tea would be nice. I admit I'm a little tired."

"Well that settles it. Ye sit there at the table and I'll go put the kettle on the fire...I might be able to scrounge us up a couple of biscuits if the wee ones haven't eaten them all. I need to tell Molly about dinner anyway."

"Where is Molly? I thought we were the only ones here," Mary queried.

"Oh, she's in the outdoor kitchen, we built a kitchen outdoors for summer use because of the heat and the danger of fire. There would be little chance of putting a fire out in this remote country. I'll just be a moment."

And with that she scurried out the house heading for the outdoor kitchen leaving Mary alone in the big hall.

Mary sat down at the table where the family appeared to eat their meals and gave a sigh as she looked around the room. The hall though small, contained quite a bit of furniture and seemed to be the gathering room for the family. Several tables and chairs, a cupboard, chest of drawers, a looking glass, trunks and a bed that must have served as a couch were all neatly arranged in the room. It was so different from her home in England. Though she tried to hold them back, a few tears began to trickle down Mary's cheeks.

Oh, Mum and. Papa, I miss ye so. Will I ever get over this homesickness?

Hearing Hannah return, Mary wiped the tears from her cheeks and glanced in the looking glass across the room as she tried to compose herself.

Hannah came in, breathing hard, and said cheerily, "I declare, I believe that kitchen moves further away every day but at least it keeps the heat away from the house. I hope the tea hasn't cooled too much. There's nothing worse than a cool cup of tea." She pulled two pewter mugs from the cupboard, poured the tea in the mugs and sat down. "Aye, it feels good to get off me feet for a while. Now tell me the news of England and our family there."

At the mention of England, Mary could contain herself no longer and began crying anew.

"Why child, what's wrong? Have I said something to upset ye? I've always had a big mouth!" she admonished herself as she reached over to give Mary's hand a pat.

"Oh no, I'm just a little tired and I guess homesick," Mary said between sobs. "I'm sorry; I just couldn't hold the tears back."

"Aye, I understand, I felt the same way when we first came to the colonies and I can't say my homesickness has completely gone now but then I look at my husband, my five children and this good land, and I know I wouldn't trade any one of them for another day in England. It's a different life for sure but I know in time ye would learn to love Virginia just I have."

"I hope ye are right," Mary sputtered as she tried to smile. "Now this is a fine way to meet a cousin for the first time," she said, as she composed herself a little. "I don't know where the tears came from...I just can't seem to stop them."

"Ye have had a rough time of it. Didna I hear ye husband say that ye ship was in a bad storm and with ye husband taking ill like that.....I'd say ye had plenty to cry about."

"I admit, I didn't expect such a difficult trip...but thanks be to God we got through it okay and now I just need him to recover

71

from his illness."

"We'll all pray for him to regain his strength soon. We certainly need ye husband's skills here in Virginia. I understand ye plan to settle in Accawmacke across the bay."

"Yes, that's our plans for now. We'll be staying with Uncle Henry until we find the land my husband wants to patent."

"Accawmacke is a beautiful place...just not too populated yet but the Indians are all friendly so that is not a worry about them...they are just strange."

"I saw a few on our way in...some children, a maiden with a child and a man. The man seemed quite menacing."

"They were probably some of the Kecoughtan's....they're a friendly tribe and often trade at the post here. It's Opecancanough's warriors ye have to watch out for but they don't usually bother us much around here though and the Eastern Shore Indians are even friendlier, though all Indians take some getting use to. John's dad settled in Accawmacke about fifteen years ago and has never had any trouble with them. We would have stayed in Accawmacke but it's kind of isolated and John was concerned about the wee ones education. He was sent to England for his education but when pirating of ships to England increased, he didn't want to risk sending our boys over. Then he heard that when Mr. Syms died and left land for a school in Elizabeth City so we decided to move here about a year ago."

"A school? ...has it started yet?" Mary asked incredulously.

"Nay, but it shouldn't be much longer. The church had to be built first but it's almost completed now. It's on Mr. Seawelle's Pointe by the garrison. They'll start on the school next. I know I'll be glad when the parsonage is complete. This house gets a mite small at times....but I'm chattering away. I'm dying to hear news from home."

Mary was unsure how to answer Hannah's questions without revealing the troubles Henry had with Bishop Laud. After all Rev. Willson was an Episcopal minister and even though he was her cousin, she was not sure he would understand the present situation in England since he had not been there for a while so she just told her about the Willson family in England leaving the rest for Henry to relate when he felt better.

They had not talked long before three of Hannah's children

returned with a pail full of blackberries and covered in mud. "Look, at ye wee ones. Go clean up some before ye come in here traipsing all that mud. Where has the time gone? I'd better check on our food or we'll not be eating anything tonight."

CHAPTER TEN

June 25, 1638 Elizabeth Parish, Virginia

In the brief time William Berriman was in Jamestown, Henry's health improved considerably. Even though the hospitality of Rev. Willson's family was without exception, Henry became restless, so when Berriman finally returned one morning, five days later, he found Henry anxiously pacing on the porch of the Willson's home.

"Halloa., looks like ye are feeling better," greeted Berriman.

"Aye, the Willson's have been most hospitable and Virginia seems to have been just what the doctor ordered," Henry replied. "However, I'm looking forward to seeing Accawmacke and getting settled in one place. When do ye want to leave?"

"Well, if ye are ready, we can head out now. I'd like to get home soon too before the weather turns bad. I don't want to be caught in a afternoon storm on the Chesapeake. It can be a bit treacherous at times when the wind comes up."

"I'll check with Mary but I think we could be ready very quickly.....just need to gather a few things."

Hearing the conversation between the two men, Rev. Willson walked out on the porch. "Come on in and I'll have me missus make some tea while Henry's men load the boat. I'd like to hear any news ye may have of Jamestown."

The three men walked into the hall and Hannah overhearing her husband's comment about tea went out back to the kitchen to boil the kettle while Henry went in search of Mary.

"Here, Will, have a seat while we talk, it will probably take a little while to load the boat," said Rev. Willson.

"I hope not," Berriman exclaimed. "I don't want the wind to come up too much." He looked a little uneasy as he sat down.

"I'm sure ye will get away soon enough, But tell me what news ye bring from Jamestown? I haven't heard much from there lately. Work on the new parsonage has kept me pretty busy here.

I'm afraid I haven't been much of a host to our company as well."

"On the contrary," Henry contradicted as he walked back into the room. "Ye have been most gracious...I just regret that this illness has inconvenienced ye wife and lovely family. I certainly had no intention of being such a burden."

Hannah returned with hot tea and overhearing the last comment, retorted. "Why, ye have been no trouble at all and I've really enjoyed visiting with ye wife. It becomes a mite lonesome here sometimes even with all the wee ones. There's not too many women folk around to talk to in Virginia yet and I've enjoyed the company...but here I go chattering away again and interrupted ye conversation," she said as she glanced at her husband. "John always says I could talk a fence post to death."

"Hmmm, that's true, Abby, but I still wouldn't trade ye for the quietest lass alive," then he gave her cheek a playful pinch. "Now, William, what have ye to report from Jamestown?"

"Not a lot, the Indians have been somewhat settled lately and of course there's still the complaints against Governor Harvey but there was one bit of information I enjoyed hearing. I checked into that new tax charged on newly arriving passengers and found out something quite interesting," and he looked at Henry with a smile. "It's probably another good reason for ye to settle on the Eastern Shore. It seems that the tax is only for ships arriving on the Western shore, the Eastern Shore is excluded. We need to make sure and land on the Eastern Shore on our next trip from England Henry, so we can avoid the tax."

"Hold on there, William," Henry said laughing. "I haven't exactly decided to settle in Accawmacke yet."

"Aye, but I know ye will, once ye see it."

"William's right about that. I'd go back now if I didn't have this parish to settle," Rev. Willson agreed.

"I did hear of something strange," William continued. "It seems a slave auction took place in the market square of Jamestown a few weeks ago."

"Slave auction, why that's nothing new," Henry scoffed. "There's a slave auction each time a new ship arrives. I bought two indentured servants to help with the supplies from the captain on our ship. What's so new about this slave auction?"

"Aye, indentures are often sold but this slave auction was

selling some blacks direct from Africa.....for life. It seems that a Dutch ship couldn't get rid of twenty-three blacks in the West Indies and decided to bring them here to sell and if ye think about it, maybe a slave for life is not a bad idea. After all, once an indentured servant is trained well in tobacco farming, then his contracts up and ye have to buy another and train him in his place."

"Slaves for life," exclaimed Henry. "Something about that bothers me."

"I agree, Henry," added Rev. Willson. "I don't like the idea of owning a man for life."

"Did he sell all the slaves?" asked Henry.

"Aye, they were bought quickly." William took another sip of tea and contemplated a moment before continuing. "They've had black slaves in the Indies for years...just never thought they'd make it here....but it may not be a bad idea with the labor needed for tobacco farming. A man could really do well with enough help."

Mary appeared in the doorway and Henry stood up, looking at her quizzically. "Has everything been loaded?" he asked.

She nodded and William stood up as well. "Then I guess it's time to sail." Smiling at Rev. Willson's wife he said. "Mrs. Willson I appreciate the tea and cakes, and ye kind hospitality. If ye ever make it over to the Eastern Shore, I'm sure Sarah would love to have ye visit for a spell."

"Thank ye," Hannah replied. "I'll remember that."

Henry added, "And I can't thank ye enough for ye kindness. I didn't think I could take another step when we reached ye house last week and with all the care I received, I'm back on me feet again."

Mary looked wistfully at Hannah and said, "I appreciate all ye advice as well. Please come to visit us once we get settled."

"Aye, we will if we can...but I'm not sure ye know what ye suggesting....with me brood."

Mary quickly replied. "I'm from a big family and miss them....ye will all be more than welcome at our house."

Henry and Mary's two indentured servants, Chris and James, appeared and reported that all was loaded so they departed to board the small boat. Mary gave a quick glance back at Hannah and John then touched the ribbon under her lace cap for reassurance and continued toward the waiting boat with the men.

CHAPTER ELEVEN

July 1638, Eastern Shore, Virginia

Henry Willson had not slept well. A dull pain in his chest gnawed at him most of the night making it difficult to sleep so he arose early and decided to take an early morning walk to alleviate the nagging ache. The gentle breeze from the Atlantic and Chesapeake sweeping across the island always refreshed him and eased his restless spirit.

He looked out over the flat land and recalled his first image of Accawmacke with its luxuriant fields of Indian corn rustling in the breezes from the sea and the bay, while the pungent smell of pine mingled with the sweet scent of wild flowers filled the air. When he and twenty other men were sent over to boil sea water down to salt and catch fish for the people of the James River, he never thought it would eventually become his home. They had been a little wary at first due to their isolation from Jamestown, but the compelling scene captivated him and when they found the Accawmacke Indians to be friendly, he vowed twenty years ago to settle here permanently whenever the opportunity arose. It was a decision he had never regretted. The fertile soil with years of heavy dense growth yielded easily to cultivation and the mild climate enabled him to produce two crops a year. A few years later, Alice joined him and life became even more fulfilling.

I wonder if our new cousins will be as enthralled by Accawmacke as I have been. We could use another doctor here on this side of the creek and they'd make good neighbors.

Realizing that he had been gone quite a while and Alice would be worried, he headed back toward the house. On his arrival, he found everyone already eating breakfast in the dining room.

"I wondered where ye got off to so early this morning," Alice said with a quizzical look. "Is there a problem?"

Alice was now fifty, a little stout but still a beautiful woman in spite of her years. She had grayish hazel eyes that changed with the color she was wearing and her brown hair was tucked neatly under her rochet. As always, she was neatly dressed, no matter the task at hand and her cheery disposition belied the struggles she faced daily managing the Willson household in such a remote location.

"Nay, I was just taking a walk and enjoying the breeze," he replied. "It won't be long now til harvest time....then we'll have our hands full."

He joined them at the table and immediately, a pewter plate was placed in front of him by Anne, their indentured servant. Anne had been with them almost four years and had only three years left on her indenture. She was like a member of the family and they hated losing her. She had a diminutive statue but could do twice the work of anyone her size and was an excellent cook.

"Well, I 'spect ye are mighty hungry.....leaving without breakfast like that. Anne has cooked us up quite a feast. No one can top her biscuits," said Alice. "Would ye like some more Doctor? Ye need plenty of good food to get ye strength back. I know good food must have been hard to come by on the ship."

"Ye are right about the lack of good food," Pattenden replied. "I believe there would be a lot less deaths on ships if we could somehow solve the food problem." He spread some raspberry preserves on his biscuit and asked "How long have ye been in Accawmacke, Henry?"

"Almost twenty years now, I came over on the Sampson in 1619. Life was difficult back then in Virginia so Alice remained in England for about eight years with the children until I could get things settled here. Finally, I just couldn't stand being without them any longer and persuaded her to come over about twelve years ago and she's regretted it ever since," he said with a twinkle in his eye.

"On hush Henry, ye know that's not true," admonished Alice. "Why, ye know I love 'Ye Kingdom of Accawmacke' just as much as ye do."

"Ye Kingdom of Accawmacke?" Mary said quizzically. "What

a strange name. Why is it called that?"

Henry Willson spread some butter on his biscuit and replied. "Well, we are pretty isolated from Jamestown here....like a Kingdom of our own. One day a remark was made on how Accawmacke is like a Kingdom within itself and the name just stuck. Since then even England refers to us as 'Ye Kingdom of Accawmacke,'" he chuckled. "Kind of a bold name for our small settlement, wouldn't ye say?"

"That reminds me of something I've wanted to ask" said Pattenden. "Where exactly is the main settlement in Accawmacke?"

"Why ye saw it when ye came in. It was that cluster of buildings on King's Creek in Town's Fields. I admit it's not much but the Church and court are held there and Alex Mountney has a store there for some supplies. We really haven't had much need for a town since the plantations are so separated by creeks, and inlets. Ships can just land at the plantations' docks. Most of the food we need is grown here and any other necessities come directly from England on the ships. At times though, it is difficult to attend Church when the wind picks up on the Chesapeake so we recently built one here at Fishing Point. Rev. Cotton had been pushing for a new church for a while....the old one at Secretary's Land was in poor condition."

"We have a nice parsonage now....forty feet long with a chimney at each end," chirped in Alice. "There's also a buttery in it."

"That's good to hear," said Mary. "I understand ye have a doctor in Accawmacke as well."

"Aye, Doc Holloway," replied Alice. "But he's over on King's Creek and we really need a doctor here at Plantation Creek so ye see we were very happy to have ye with us, Dr. Pattenden and want to see that ye get well as soon as possible. Give him a little more ham, Anne, his plate is empty."

"Nay, I'm sure I've had enough, Alice," Pattenden laughed and waved the servant away. "Ye have been most hospitable and I should be on feet again in no time." Turning to Henry Willson, he said, "I'm really anxious to see the land, Henry. I'd like to get a patent on acreage as soon as possible and build a house before winter sets in. Do ye think ye will be able to spare a little time to show me around? I'm sure after living here so many years ye are aware of the best area and any suggestion would be invaluable."

"Aye, it's a good time this week. Harvest will be coming soon but right now, work is a little slower than usual. Do ye want to look some this morning?"

"That would be fine with me," Pattenden replied.

"Just don't wear ye self out," Mary said. "Ye must remember to take care of ye heart."

"I think Mary has become the doctor and me the patient," Henry laughed. "It looks like ye will have two new doctors on Plantation Creek, Alice."

Mary blushed at his comment and looked down at her plate.

Sensing that he had embarrassed her, Pattenden quickly, added. "I wouldn't be here today if Mary hadn't been on ship with me. She was right there when I needed her," and he gave her hand a pat and said softly to her, "Don't worry pet, I'll remember. I just want to settle in our own place as soon as possible." He gave her hand a gentle squeeze ...she smiled and looked up at him with loving eyes.

"Aye, I promise not to get him too tired Mary," Willson said. "We'll be back before dark."

Alice said, "Well, ye will want some victuals for this excursion. I'll have Anne prepare something," she continued as she bustled off to the kitchen to make preparations.

Henry Willson looked off in the distance for a moment, I know of just the spot to show ye on Plantation Creek, near William's. The land is good and one could have a sizeable quay."

"William was most helpful to us during the trip and became quite a good friend. I'd like to see his place if possible."

"He's a good friend to have," Willson replied. "William's done quite well for himself with a large plantation at Fishing Point and he's very well respected in Accawmacke though we don't see him much with his trips back and forth to England to sell tobacco and buy headrights. But if ye want to see his plantation today, we'd better get on our way soon or we'll never return before dark. Let's plan on leaving in an hour."

"That's fine. I'll be ready."

After the men left, Alice and Mary sat in the parlour chatting while mending clothes. The room was small by English standards but pleasant. Windows on one side allowed the ladies to enjoy a cool breeze while they worked. Mary was in her fifth month of pregnancy and the oppressive heat and humidity in Elizabeth City had been intolerable. She was thankful for the gentle wind that prevailed on the Eastern Shore.

"When will ye bairn be born?" asked Alice.

"October, I believe and I'm beginning to get a little nervous with it becoming so close."

"Don't worry child, ye are still young and strong. Ye should do fine. What do ye want a boy or girl?"

"Oh, definitely a boy! I'd love to give Henry a boy."

"Aye, everyone wants a boy but a girl is nice too. There are so few women on the Shore and it would be nice to have a few more to chat with. I've been so lonely at times just to talk to another woman."

"William said the same thing about his wife, Sarah. I hadn't realized there were so few women in Virginia."

"The men are certainly in the majority here and don't really understand women ways. I've learned to do many a thing that I've never have done in England. When I first came, I often worked right along with Henry in the fields, plowing and clearing the land just as my daughter-in-law Elizabeth did with my son Henry Carsley, Jr. He was my son from my first marriage. I think she handled it a mite better than me though...she's younger.

"Henry had a small cabin, if ye could call it that. It took a while accepting the ways of life and the harshness of life here. Men don't put much store in the 'niceties'. My grandchildren, Agnis, and Francis......Elizabeth and Henry's children complained quite a bit to their Pa.......God rest his soul......He died a couple of years ago and poor Elizabeth has had a difficult time raising those girls alone... so far she hasn't thought about remarrying..... Henry and William help her when they can.....anyway...all my husband wanted to do was plow up more land for tobacco.. It took some time to convince him to send for more items from England and build a better house."

"Well, it's certainly pleasant now. I hope we will be able to build one near as nice."

"I 'spect it will take a while. Good carpenters are hard to

83

come by, most are building ships rather than houses but maybe ye husband will have better success than we had at first. There are many more carpenters now."

"What can ye tell me about Sarah? William offered to let us stay with him while we looked for our land and mentioned that she was lonely for company."

"Aye, I 'spect she is. They have never been able to have wee ones of their own though they tried. Two died at birth and one boy around the age of three. Sarah has never been the same since the last one died. I imagine life is mighty lonesome for her with William traveling to England each year but he has built up quite a bit of acreage due to those trips. Ye'd think I'd see her more, being me daughter-in-law, but she sort of keeps to herself managing their big plantation. I guess she's still grieving over the loss of her last child. He was a beautiful boy with long curly locks...me third grandchild."

Mary felt a little apprehensive over her own impending birth due to this frank revelation and her face turned ashen.

Alice looked up and said, "Oh, there I go again...putting me foot in me mouth. I'm sure ye child will be fine, Mary. Ye have to remember, life was a bit more difficult in Accawmacke when Sarah had her children. We didn't have a doctor then and there was the continual effort of preparing the land ready for plowing. She didn't take care of herself, always helping William even though she was carrying a bairn and look at my Elizabeth...she had two girls...though between ye and me....I think her husband really wanted at least one boy...those girls are a handful. Ye are lucky, having a husband that's a surgeon. I'm sure everything will go well when is comes time for ye lying in."

"I hope ye're right. I guess I just wish me Mum was here. She always knew about such things and was a mid-wife to many of the women in our town."

"Aye, well I'm a mid-wife as well, and I've been through many births so I'll be happy to help when the time comes."

"I'm so thankful for that. Did ye have anyone to help ye when ye're sons were born?"

"I was lucky. Most of my children were born in England. I married Henry there after me second husband died. They were a good age when we arrived and a tremendous help to us clearing the land. We were a mite crowded in the one-room cabin though. One son and two daughters can be quite much at times."

"Are all ye children close by Alice?"

"Aye, all but one. They're all married except for Mary and she is staying with me daughter-in-law, Elizabeth right now. After me son, Henry, was killed by savages, she moved in with Elizabeth to help."

"Killed by savages! I thought ye said the Indians were friendly here!" Mary exclaimed.

"That's true, Mary. The ones around here are friendly but a few years ago, a more troublesome tribe occasionally made forays to our area. Me son was part of a party that drove them away and he was killed along with several other men....anyway...Henry left Elizabeth with a large plantation and it's been difficult for her so Mary moved in with her. My other daughter, Jane, returned to England. She married last year."

Alice paused a moment then continued with a choked voice...."I had two other children...boys... born after we arrived in Virginia...but they died young. I was sort of old to be having bairns though and this country can be mighty harsh for raising wee ones. I guess that's why I hope ye have a boy. T'would be nice to have another young boy around. William is me only son now and I don't see much of him since he's constantly traveling back and forth to England. Well that's enough chatter about me. Tell me what's happening in England....I'm dying to hear the news."

"I afraid the news is not good. There's quite a bit of dissension. It appears that England is headed back to Catholicism if Bishop Laud has anything to say about it and he's intent on executing or sending to the gaol all that resist him. I'm sure me family will not consent to the changes and I'm very uneasy about their safety. I tried to encourage them to come with us to Virginia but they refused to even consider the trip."

"They still live near Canterbury, don't they, Mary?"

"Aye, and I'm afraid they're too close to Bishop Laud to go unnoticed."

"It's strange, the Catholics and Protestants are constantly fighting in England but here it's different, we get along fine. Why, the Catholics have even let us meet in their chapel until our new church is built!"

"Really?" Mary said incredulously. "That's hard to believe. There is so much bitterness in England between the two groups. I just hope me family doesn't become enmeshed in the troubles there. Papa can be pretty outspoken at times."

"Well, we'll just have to pray that God will take care of them and one day they'll see their way to come to Virginia." Trying to relieve Mary's anguish, she continued. "After all, they'll have a new grandchild they simply must come to see in Virginia."

"I hope ye are right Alice but I still can't help but worry about them."

CHAPTER TWELVE

July, 1638 Plantation Creek, Eastern Shore, Virginia
The sky was filled with puffy clouds as Henry Willson and Dr. Pattenden sailed in Willson's shallop down Old Plantation Creek toward the Chesapeake. A profusion of various shades of green and gold spilled over the banks from the many oaks and maples lining the banks as a gentle breeze billowed the sail and Pattenden was enraptured by the beauty of the scene. The trees were huge with massive trunks from years of growth.

"It must take quite a while to clear a field for planting with such large trees to cut," he said.

"Aye," replied Willson. "If it hadn't been for a trick the Kecoughtans taught us, we'd have starved that first few years trying to clear a field. Instead of cutting the trees, we just strip the bark in a girdle surrounding the tree. It kills the tree, then all we have to do is plant corn around it because the sun is able to reach the ground and we put a fish on top of each to improve the soil. It never fails and keeps us supplied with corn until the trees finally fall, then we are left with a field to plant once we remove the stumps.

"So that's what we saw when we reached Elizabeth City. Mary thought it was some strange disease killing the trees."

"Slapping a large mosquito on his neck, Willson said, "The only thing I don't enjoy about Accawmacke is these pesky insects. Sometimes I think they could eat a man alive."

"I agree and the frogs and katydids make quite a racket when trying to sleep too but I guess one gets use to their noise."

"Aye, after a while they are like a lullaby singing ye to sleep, especially when ye put in a hard day in the field." Henry guided the shallop around a bend in the creek and said, "I think we'll head out to the bay first and let ye see a little more of the northern part of Accawmacke. We'll stop back by William's afterward on our way back. That way we can visit with him a spell if it's okay with ye."

"That'll be fine. I'd like to see a little more of the bay. We headed straight for Plantation Creek from Elizabeth City. William was anxious to return home."

"I 'spect he was, he's been away a longer time and I'm sure he was worried about Sarah. She's been poorly since their last child died."

"How many children does William have? It's strange but all the time we spent on the ship, he never mentioned any."

"That's because he doesn't have any. All his children died at birth... except for one that died at three years. It's been pretty rough for Sarah."

"I'd imagine so. Have they been married long?"

"About five years now."

As the shallop rounded a bend, a flock of geese startled by the boat, took flight and flew out over the bay.

Seeing them, Willson said, "Won't be long now until they're head further south. I'll miss seeing them."

"There seems to be no want of game."

"Tis true. Many a man has made a good living just hunting and trapping in Accawmacke."

The wind picked up as they headed into the bay and Willson noticed the clouds darkening overhead.

"We'll probably not stay on the bay too long. A storm can come up quickly out here and take over a small shallop like this. I'll just head along the west bank so ye can get an idea of the land over there."

Pattenden gazed off into the direction Henry pointed and was immediately in awe of the immense growth of timber on land as far as the eye could see. "Now, I understand why so much lumber is being shipped back to home. There seems to be no end to the trees," he said.

"Aye, but tobacco is the money crop though it takes a lot of work.....Tends to use up the soil though, so ye have to have a good bit of acreage available to move to when it's worn out but there's no shortage of land either. Some have moved even further north into Maryland."

"I thought Maryland was settled by the Catholics."

"That doesn't matter here. Lord Baltimore encourages anyone to move there....Baptists, Methodists....it doesn't matter to him. He just wants the land settled."

As the shallop sailed along the bank, the waves became choppy and the wind became stronger.

"We'd better head into shore for a bit," Willson said as he eyed at the skies overhead. "Looks like a storm's brewing and it will give ye a chance to have a closer look at the soil."

The shallop drifted toward an inlet and when it scraped bottom, the two men got out and waded in the waves toward land. In a few short minutes, rain began to pelt them so they raced across the clearing toward the cover of the distant trees to wait out the storm.

Pattenden, amazed by the fury of the storm, said, "The weather sure came out fast. From the looks of the clouds at home, I thought we'd have a nice day for sailing."

"That's just the nature of the Chesapeake," replied Henry. "Many a man has been killed sailing on her by ignoring the warnings of a storm."

"Well, at least we didn't come upon a rocky shoreline before it hit!" exclaimed Pattenden. "T'would have made it difficult seeking shelter if we'd had to climb a cliff."

"Aye, ye will never see one along the Chesapeake. Not a stone along the whole shoreline nor many inland." Stooping down to grasp a handful of the now damp soil, Willson continued, "All ye find is this rich, sandy loam, ripe for planting."

"From what ye have shown me so far, it certainly seems fruitful. Tell me more about growing tobacco. Ye said it required a lot of labor and land. What type land should I look for to patent?"

"Tis true, but the profit a man can earn makes it worth the effort," replied Willson. "The best land for growing tobacco is along streams and ye will find many in this area. That way the tobacco can be transported down the streams for shipment."

As the two men talked, they heard rustling in the leaves behind them and immediately grew quiet. A tall, dark man carrying a matchlock walked out of the trees and Willson smiled as he immediately recognized him. The man laughed and said, "It looks like ye two decided to set sail on the wrong day. Ye look like a couple of wet puppies....might as well come join me camp."

"Aye, ye are a welcome site," said Willson. "It appears that t'will be a while before this blows over. What brings ye to this part of Accawmacke? I thought ye place was a little further north on Long Creek."

"Been doing a little hunting ....and noticed the two of ye racing across the ground like a couple of wet deer and I thought I'd discovered a new animal in these parts," the man chuckled.

They approached a hastily made tent of deer hide with a timber set in the center holding the hides. The three men gladly, clamored inside and hovered close together to await the end of the storm....none too soon as heavy raindrops began to pelt the deer hide.

Willson shouted above the hammering rain, "Henry, I want ye to meet one of the oldest settlers in Accawmacke, John Savage. His father, Thomas Savage, was the first to settle here. He came to live with the Alogonquin as a mere boy of thirteen but left the western shore after being shot by an arrow and relocated on the Eastern Shore about twenty years ago. John, this here is Dr. Pattenden, husband of my niece. He's planning to settle among us in Accawmacke."

"Well, I'm certainly considering it," Pattenden added. "But it's nice to make ye acquaintance especially at such an opportune time."

"Ye did look like ye needed a little assistance," John replied.

Turning to Pattenden, Henry continued, "If it hadn't been for his father, Tom, the settlers of Jamestown probably would have died. There was many a time he procured corn from the Accawmackes for Jamestown, saving them from starvation after their crops failed. How's Anne doing, John? I heard ye would be having a wee one soon."

"That's true...hopefully a boy...but who knows? "

"John is a good man to tell ye about tobacco farming, Henry. He has a much larger plantation than mine....around 9,000 acres, isn't it John?"

"Whew," whistled Pattenden. "That's a lot to manage."

"Oh, I don't do a lot of farming. I lease out quite a bit....I'd rather trap and hunt."

"He's just being modest," said Willson. "John's a good planter as well as serving as one of our Burgesses. Share some of ye secrets for that sweet tobacco ye produce John? I promise ye, John, has the sweetest tobacco in the area. "

"Well, I think it depends on the soil. I've produced many a crop on the wrong soil and it wasn't near as sweet. The soil around these parts usually produces a pretty good crop though but Henry introduced ye as a doctor. I'd stick to doctoring if I were ye. Tobacco growing can be pretty fickle like a woman."

"I still plan to practice physick some but thought I'd like to try my hand at tobacco farming as well. From what I've hear, a man can make a pretty fair profit rather quickly."

"Aye, that's true, just takes a lot of work," Henry added.

After a time, the tent grew quiet as the rain dissipated and the men exited the tent.

"Sorry to leave such good company John but I promised Pattenden a tour along the Bay and a trip to William's house. We'd better depart before another storm moves in again or we'll never get back before nightfall."

"Ye are right, that's for sure. Storms come up fast around here. I need to get back to hunting as well or Anne will have me hide."

"Good luck on ye hunting John and give my best to Anne," Henry shouted as he and Pattenden walked toward the shallop rollicking in the gentle waves.

The sun was shining when the men reached the shallop and Willson said," We may have time to sail a little further north along the coast before turning back now that the storm has subsided. Maybe we'll be able to reach William's in time for the noon meal and he'll be able to show us around his plantation."

"That would be great," Pattenden replied. "I'd like to see a large working plantation and see how John Trehearne, his indentured servant was doing. He became quite ill on our trip from England."

"Always the doctor," laughed Willson. "I thought ye wanted to be a tobacco planter."

"I guess I'll always feel the need to take care of the sick. I've spent most of my life doing so....but I would like to try some farming."

"Ye may change ye mind once ye see William's plantation."

"True, but I'd believe I'd like to give it a good try at least."

The sun glistened as sparkles on the waves as the shallop headed further north along the shore. Geese honked so loudly as they flew above, that conversation became difficult. Henry pointed to a tributary where a flock of ducks frolicked in the blue green water. All life seemed to be relishing the sunshine after the earlier storm. Henry expertly, maneuvered the small shallop through the meandering creeks as Pattenden gazed at the flora and fauna inland. After a time, Henry turned the shallop downstream and back to Old Plantation Creek. They moved so swiftly and smoothly through the waters that it seemed the land was moving and the small shallop was standing still.

"William's patent starts about here," Henry said, pointing to the left as they glided down Plantation Creek.

A clapboard house sitting on a rise with several smaller houses surrounding it in the distance appeared in view as Willson glided the shallop into dock on the creek. Corn fields around the house gave way to broken and dead trees and waves and waves of a large leafed woody plant.

"So that's the tobacco Berriman refers to as gold," said Pattenden.

"Aye, it may not look like much but his fields of sot-weed bring him quite a handsome profit." Willson said as he pulled the shallop up to the dock. William's servant could be seen coming down to greet the two men.

"I thought that was ye shallop, Mr. Willson. I know Mr. Berriman will be glad to see ye with all the troubles his having."

"What do ye mean troubles? Has something happened?"

"Aye, Mr. Willson. It's Miss Sarah. She's missing."

"Missing? How long?"

"Since yesterday, she left to visit the graves of her wee ones at the high meadow like she does everyday but apparently never came back. We've been looking for her since last night and she seems to have vanished without a trace."

"Where's William now?"

"He's up at the house ...just got back....he's been looking for her all night."

Willson and Pattenden climbed quickly out of the boat and rushed toward the house while the servant tied the shallop to the dock. They found William frantically pacing on his porch giving orders to his servants.

"William, I just heard about Sarah," exclaimed Henry. Have

ye noticed any savages about lately? Do ye think she might have been captured?'"

William looked up and became aware that someone was asking him a question. As the men approached the porch, he exclaimed in anguish, "Henry...she's gone. Sarah's gone."

Trying to sound calm, Henry asked again more gently. "Have ye noticed any savages about William? If she was captured by the savages, we need to arrange a search before they depart from the area. We'll find her."

"I don't know Henry. I've been away...been away too much," and his voice trailed off as his eyes misted. "Poor Sarah, I brought her nothing but misery."

"That's not true, William. Sarah loved ye and there was no way ye could prevent her disappearance."

Pattenden said, "Why don't I stay with William while ye gather others for a search party, Henry. I don't know much about the area around here, and I'm sure I wouldn't be much help searching but perhaps Henry or some of the servants can provide more information about her activities this past week."

"Good idea! I'll leave right away."

Margaret, William's cook, overheard their conversation and added, "Mayhaps I can help, Mr. Willson,"

"What do ye know, child, speak up?" Henry retorted a little too sharply.

Unruffled by his harshness, Margaret quickly replied "I've seen some savages lurking down by the spring a few days ago. They looked different from the usual ones around here...many tattoos...painted faces...pierced ears and noses and dark black hair shaved in the back."

"Could've been the Assateague, Henry declared. Their land is well north of Chingoteague Island. They've given us trouble before....but they don't usually come this far south....still it wouldn't hurt to check it out. Come with me Trehearne...ye can fill me in on where ye have searched so far."

The two men headed briskly toward the shallop while Pattenden continued questioning Berriman.

"Did ye notice anything unusual before Sarah left yesterday, Will?"

"Nay, she was kind of quiet but she's been that way since

she lost the wee one. Sort of surprised me though....I thought she'd be better by now. This last trip to London took a little longer than the others and I know it's been hard on her, alone here, with just the servants. She really didn't seem too excited when I returned, just kept to herself most of the time. Oh, Sarah! Where are ye?" His voice trailed off as he put his head in his hands.

After a few minutes he looked up and continued, "Ye should have seen her when we first married. She was so cheery and full of life...but of course that was in England before I brought her to Virginia....still she managed and made a fine home for us....but when she lost the first wee one...she never seemed to get better...became kind of frail....with the lost of each child, a little of her seemed to die too."

"We'll find her Will...just keep ye hope up."

Henry Willson and Trehearne quickly docked the shallop and walked briskly to the Church. Rev. Cotton, Hungar's parish minister, hearing the news of Sarah from them, rang the Church bell to call others for the search.

In a short while, a large crowd congregated in front of the Church and Henry reported Sarah's disappearance. When he mentioned Margaret's report of the sighting of unknown Indians in the vicinity, harsh shouts rang out.

"Let's go get them murdering savages!' shouted one man.

"We'll teach them to take our women!" another man added.

"Let's not be too hasty," replied Henry trying to calm the rowdy crowd. "We don't know if she's been captured or not. She may have only fallen or something....right now, all we know is that she's missing. The Assateague's may not have even been involved and the Indians around here might steal a little but they'd never been known to capture any of our women. Besides, Margaret's only been in Accawmacke a short while and she's not all that familiar with the Indians around here."

"I agree," said Thomas Savage. "It's not likely that the Assateague's would take Sarah without a reason."

Captain Scarburgh agreed, "Ye may be right but I still believe we should check out the Assateague's village anyway."

Scarburgh was a well-respected citizen in Accawmacke and he took charge of the assemblage. He continued, "I think we should form two search parties, one to check out the Assateague village and the other to search Berriman's plantation."

"Sounds like a good plan." Rev. Cotton responded.

Captain Scarburgh, quickly divided the men into two groups, placing his son Edmund, a noted Indian hater, in charge of the band headed toward the Assateague village. He included Ambrose Dixon, George Cottingham, Henry Willson and other experienced Indian fighters in the group. The other band was headed by Scarburgh. The men quickly dispersed, all were well armed and filled with determination to find Sarah.

CHAPTER THIRTEEN

July 1638, Plantation Creek, Eastern Shore, Virginia

A piercing scream filled the air shortly after the search party left William Berriman's home. Pattenden, still too weak from his recent illness was unable to participate in the search of the plantation and remained behind with the nervous servants. He was sitting on the wide expansive porch anxiously waiting news from the search parties when the scream startled him. It seemed to have come from somewhere inside the house so he rushed in to ascertain the cause. The scream continued then was followed by loud crying. It appeared to be coming from upstairs. He climbed the steps two or three at a time and looked in the two rooms on the second level but found no one. Then he noticed a door to the attic ajar in one of the rooms and realized the cries were coming from there. He rushed in and was overcome by the revolting sight.

From one of the rafters, hung a limp female body with a rope around her neck, a chair was lying on its side below the body. Margaret was kneeling and screaming uncontrollably in the closed room. Without a word, he rushed forward and frantically sought a pulse from Sarah's small wrist but finding none, he moved to console Margaret.

As he reached out to Margaret, she stood, and collapsed on his chest, sobbing uncontrollably. After a few moments, her tears subsided and she asked, "Why'd she do it, Sir? I knew she was sad but she was still young. She could have more wee ones....Oh, poor Mr. William!"

"One never knows the reason one does such things, Margaret. We just have to accept. Perhaps life was too difficult for her to bear here."

Looking at the frail, young figure hanging so grotesquely from the ceiling, Henry's thoughts immediately turned to Mary.

I hope conditions never become so difficult for Mary as it evidently has for this young woman. What kind of situation have I brought her to if one so young and full promise could take her own life?

Henry quickly banished these thoughts and said, "Margaret, help me get her down. William doesn't need to see her like this."

"Ye're right," she said gravely.

"Hold her feet while I cut the rope," Henry said as he righted the chair and stood on it.

Margaret fell to the floor with Sarah's body. She sat with Sarah's head cradled in her lap and gently caressed Sarah's brow as if she was only sleeping. "Aye, poor lass, at least ye are no longer in ye misery."

"Margaret, do ye think ye can help me carry her down and lay her on the bed?"

"Aye, Doctor Pattenden."

They lifted the small body, and Pattenden was astonished at how light Sarah was. She had a fragile beauty about her with, long dark brown hair and small delicate features. Such a waste!

They placed her on the bed in the room next to the attic. Margaret, now more composed, brushed Sarah's hair away from her face with her hand, crossed her arms across her breast and closed her eyes.

"She looks like she is only sleeping, doesn't she? Margaret said.

"Aye, but one from which she'll never awaken."

At this, Margaret began to cry again. "Oh, poor Mr. William....poor Mr. William."

Henry remembered that men were now out searching for Sarah at the Indian village and around the plantation, so he asked, "Margaret, is their anyone we can send to try to and reach the search parties? We need to stop the searches before anyone else is harmed. From what I heard about what took place at the Church, the band of men headed for the Assateagues are intent on retaliation rather than an actual search."

"Powell's still here, mayhaps he could go after them but I don't think he could reach both groups in one day."

"I'll try to find the search party around the plantation if he could go after the group headed for the Assateagues. Will ye be okay here with her?"

"Aye, Doctor Pattenden, but are ye sure ye are up to

searching for them?"

"They're on foot and haven't been gone long, so they shouldn't be too far away. Besides, William needs to know about his wife as soon as possible and he's with them. Don't worry about me. Just tell Powell to head out as soon as possible. We don't need any more people dying over this incident."

Henry left the house quickly, grabbing his cane and hat on the way and headed in the direction of the search party.

Edmund Scarburgh's group of Indian fighters reached the Assateague by noon before Powell was able to overtake them. As the small band approached the sleepy village, only a few Assateague men could be seen on the grounds. Children were playing, while some of the women could be seen in the fields of corn surrounding the village. Other women were pounding the corn near cooking fires. Small bent sapling framed round houses were covered with woven mats of sea grass. The only men visible were a few older men sitting on mats watching the group approach.

"Look sharp, men, do ye see any fair skinned women about?" asked Scarburgh.

"Nay, not a one, but she could be in one of the houses," replied Ambrose Dixon. "I wonder though, where are the young men?"

"Probably, hunting or fishing. Mayhaps, luck holds with us and we'll not be bothered in our search," Scarburgh said. "Let's split up and have a look around while I have a talk with some of the old men.

An elderly man was sitting on a mat and stood up as Scarburgh approached. Scarburgh talked authoritatively to the man, while the other's in the search party began checking inside each house, roughly pushing aside every woman who protested. After a few minutes of futile searching, they joined Scarburgh who was becoming increasingly red-faced as he talked to the man. He turned to the search party and said, "They don't seem to know about Sarah, but I don't believe them. Did ye notice anything unusual while searching the huts?"

"Nay, I don't believe Sarah's here," replied George Cottingham."

"Well, they must have killed her, and I say we need to kill a couple of their women in return!" Scarburgh exclaimed.

Ambrose said, "Don't ye think we ought to make sure first and wait for the other search parties report?"

"We don't have time to spend wasting on these savages," replied Scarburgh. "They've given us enough trouble in the past anyway, if we kill a couple of their women while we're here, mayhaps they'll think twice about bothering us again."

"I'm with ye Captain, said Norton, they need to be taught a lesson and he grabbed an Indian maiden near him who had been pounding corn."

Suddenly, they heard a commotion as the young Assateagues returned victorious from their hunting trip and were surprised to see the small band of menacing white men in the center of their village, roughly holding an Indian maiden. One of the braves picked up his bow and sent an arrow piercing Norton's leg. He immediately let go of the maiden and cried out in pain.

"Load ye weapons men!" Scarburgh shouted. "We'll show these savages what it means to fight."

Before they could load their weapons, a volley of arrows began to fly from the young braves. Clearly outnumbered, Scarburgh's group retreated and scrambled for their waiting shallop, briefly stopping to fire back at the chasing Assateagues as they ran. The search party managed to kill at least five of the young braves. Norton was trailing the group, unable to move quickly due to the arrow in his leg, so Henry Willson and Ambrose Dixon took hold of his arms and pulled him toward the waiting boat. But before they reached the shallop, Henry Willson abruptly fell forward on the ground. An arrow was protruding from his back. Ambrose shouted for help and George Cottingham and Richard Bayly stopped in their tracks, turned and raced back to pick up Henry's now inert body. The two men carried Henry the remaining distance with Ambrose and Norton trailing close behind.

When the men reached the shallop, they quickly piled in the boat and pushed it off the bank. Cottingham and Bayly placed Henry's body in the center while the other men began to furiously

100

paddle. A welcome breeze puffed out the sail and moved the craft speedily away from the village. A few braves attempted to follow in canoes but after a few minutes abandoned the task and returned to their village.

"We'll be back men," Scarburgh exclaimed. "No stinking savage will get the best of a white man. We were just caught off guard. How's Norton, and Willson?" he asked.

"Willson's dead but Norton will make it if we get him back home soon," George Cottingham grimly replied.

They saw a small boat approaching them and recognized Powell, Berriman's indentured servant, at the helm.

"I wonder what he is doing out here," Dixon said, "Maybe the search party found Sarah."

"Not likely," said Scarburgh wryly, "The way those young bucks were acting, they probably killed her."

CHAPTER FOURTEEN

July 1638, Plantation Creek, Eastern Shore, Virginia

Anne, the Willson's indentured servant, was dipping candles near a fire outside when the Ambrose Dixon, George Cottingham, and two other men arrived at the Willson plantation with Henry's body. She screamed frantically, "Oh, Ms. Alice, Ms. Alice....come quickly."

Alice rushed to the door just as the men approached the long front porch. "Why Anne, whatever are ye screaming about?" Alice asked. Then seeing Henry's body, she cried softly, "Oh no, Henry...what has happened?" Not realizing that Henry was dead, she told the men to take his body to the adjoining room and ordered Anne to send for Doc. Holloway.

Ambrose Dixon, gently said, "Ms. Alice, I'm afraid a doctor is no longer needed."

As her mind registered the import of his words, Alice drew away from the men and began repeating, "Nay, Nay, Nay, tis not true...tis not true." She collapsed on a chair near the door and closed her eyes and began mumbling as if in prayer. The men stood awkwardly at the entrance of the house, holding Henry's body...not sure what to do next.

After a few seconds went by, Alice stood and stoically asked the men to lay her husband's body in the Parlour. When this was done, she closed the door and refused to let anyone in the room until she alone prepared his body for burial. At times, soft weeping could be heard from the room but no one interfered while she completed her administrations.

Mary, became quite distraught at the news and when her husband later arrived, he immediately sent his wife to bed with some chamomile tea to help her sleep. He told Anne to make sure Mary remained in bed until he returned, then left with John Trehearne to find Rev. Cotton and make arrangements for the double funerals.

As Pattenden, Trehearne and Rev. Cotton returned to Berriman's house, Rev. Cotton said, "I really don't know what to tell William but ye know his wife cannot be buried in the church grounds. I'm glad ye will be with me to break the news."

"I don't understand; why can't she be buried in the church cemetery?" asked Pattenden.

"Because she took her on life of course, the church does not condone the taking of one's on life so she cannot be buried in the sacred ground of the church."

"Why that's preposterous!" exclaimed Pattenden. "William will be furious. He'll never understand ye reasoning! His wife was a Christian woman that just faced a lot of suffering."

"But in the eyes of God and the Church Sarah has committed a grievous sin. The Church would be condoning her sin if she were buried in the sacred ground of the Church Cemetery."

"I don't know what this will do to William. He feels guilty enough about leaving Sarah here alone so much and now she won't get a Christian burial in the church. Do ye still plan to perform the funeral? "

"Uh, well... I prayed about it....and I feel that since she was a strong Christian before this tragic event that the Church will forgive me if I do conduct the funeral."

"At least, she'll have that. Poor William, he will blame himself for all this!"

"Aye, I'm afraid ye are right. I wish there was something more I could do to ease his pain."

The shallop neared William's dock and Trehearne tied it off while Rev. Cotton and Henry Pattenden trudged up the path to the house. They met Margaret at the door.

"How is Mr. Berriman now Margaret?" asked Pattenden.

"Not taking it well at all, sir, not at all. He has shut himself up in the room with her and won't let anyone in."

"He needs time to adjust, I'm sure. We'll not disturb him for now."

"Perhaps, ye would like to wait in the dining room," said Margaret. "I can make ye some tea and biscuits. I'm sure it's been a while since ye ate anything and maybe Mr. William will join ye there. He hasn't eaten anything since yesterday."

"That sounds fine Margaret."

The two men walked into the sumptuous dining room, filled with the many items William had brought back from England over the years. Some items in crates were still unpacked in a corner of the room. Sarah's portrait hung over the fireplace wall. She was a very beautiful, delicate looking woman with soft, green, sad eyes. Her regal blue dress accentuated her porcelain features and diminutive stature. The men were staring at the picture when Margaret returned with the tea and biscuits.

Noticing their interest in the picture, Margaret said, "Sarah hated that picture. It was painted after she lost her first child and it reminded her of that bad time... Mr. William said that he'd have another one painted to replace it."

"I guess time ran out on me....didna it Margaret?"

They were all startled by William Berriman's discreet entrance into the room.

"Oh, Master Berriman, I didna hear ye come in. Do ye want something to eat?" Margaret asked.

"No, Margaret, just a little tea will be fine. Well, gentlemen, I guess ye have come to make plans for the funeral."

"Aye, Sir," said Rev. Cotton, "And to bring bad news as well, I'm afraid. I hate to provide ye with further suffering but I was not sure ye were aware that Henry Willson died this morning from that Indian skirmish searching for ye wife."

"Henry's dead as well, Oh this is too much!" Berriman replied in an anguished voice. "He was only trying to help me. How is Mum handling Henry's death?"

"As well as can be expected, I suppose," said Rev. Cotton. "She's a strong woman."

"Aye she is at that. Did any other's die due to this tragedy?"

"A few Assateagues and Norton received an arrow in his leg but he should be fine. Henry Willson died trying to carry Norton to safety," said Pattenden

"That's just like Henry, never leaving anyone behind. How did they get in a skirmish with the Assateagues? They were just sent there to search not start a fight."

Rev. Cotton cleared his throat and said, "Well, William, ye

know how hot-headed Scarburgh can be when he's around savages...I guess things just got out of hand."

"All this dying because, Sarah was so alone...I blame myself for that...I should have been here for her. Now we have to plan for two deaths instead of only one and hope the Assateagues don't seek revenge."

Rev. Cotton cleared his throat again. "Uh, William, that brings us to some other bad news, I'm afraid."

"What more could there be?" William asked as he looked quizzically at the minister.

"Uh, well there's the matter of the funeral. Ye know Sarah cannot be buried in the sacred grounds of the Church since she committed the sin of suicide."

"What! Ye mean me strong Christian wife who always supported ye and encouraged ye in the first days here when others attacked. She cannot be buried in the Church grounds! How dare ye say such a thing to me!"

Obviously defeated by Berriman's wrath, Rev. Cotton tried to gain some control and continued, "If it was up to me, William, there would be no problem. I know Sarah was a strong Christian of the Anglican faith but the Church as ye well know since ye are a vestryman does not condone suicide. She just cannot be buried on sacred ground."

All the blood drained from William's face as he realized the significance of Rev. Cotton's words. He collapsed in a chair and shouted, "Get out of my house! Leave now. We don't need ye or the Church."

Rev. Cotton, visibly shaken, stood up and said, "I know ye are distraught now William and not thinking clearly. I do plan to conduct the funeral. It's only that she cannot be buried on Church grounds....I....," Rev. Cotton stammered then looked helplessly at Pattenden and with his eyes tried to solicit his help in defusing the situation.

Margaret walked in with fresh biscuits and set them on the table. William seeing her, said in a plaintive voice, "Margaret did ye hear? They won't let her be buried in the Church grounds. What am I to do?"

"Aye, Mr. William, I heard but I'm wondering if Miss Sarah might rather be buried in the high meadow where we had to bury her wee ones when they died in the winter. Ye know she spent many hours there each day. I think she'd like to be near them now."

William jumped up from the chair, startling everyone. "Ye are right. There is no better place to bury her. She always loved the high meadows. We'd even planned to build a house near there one of these days...but now...." his voice faded away as the realization of her death came over him again.

Sensing William's despondency, Pattenden intervened before Rev. Cotton might say something to upset him again. "Well, it's settled then. Sarah will be buried here at the high meadows near her children. Come Rev. Cotton, we must be on our way. We have many tasks to complete before the funerals."

Hearing the word funerals, William regained some composure and said, "Please give Mum me love and tell her I'll see her as soon as I take care of things here for Sarah."

"Oh, I'm sure she understands but I'll be sure to give her ye message," replied Pattenden.

After taking Rev. Cotton back to Town, Henry Pattenden returned to the Willson's and found Anne with Alice in the hall chamber. They were deep in conversation and he hated to interrupt them. He was worn out from the difficulties of the past few days and just wanted to rest but knew that Alice needed to know about Sarah's death."

Seeing Pattenden standing in the hall, she asked quietly, "How did all this happen? I thought ye and Henry were merely looking for land to patent? How did Henry die?"

Pattenden minced his words as he calmly related the events that had occurred at Berriman's house.

Sarah sat impassively as he spoke but the expression on her face revealed her true feelings. Tears flowed freely down her cheeks but she did not brush them away.

After he finished, Alice asked with little emotion, "How is William taking Sarah's death?"

"Not well, I'm afraid," he replied. "Rev. Cotton told William that Sarah could not be buried in the Church Cemetery because she committed suicide and it upset him greatly."

"Not buried in the Church Cemetery!" she exclaimed. "William must have been furious.....Sarah was one of the most devout Christians in the area. I can't believe Rev. Cotton would say such a thing. Of course, I understand the Church's view of suicide but he could have made an exception....Oh, my poor William. Has he decided on a place for her burial?"

"Aye, thankfully, Margaret remembered Sarah's love for the high meadows where her children are buried and he decided to bury her there."

"Ah....the high meadows, Sarah loved that place and he's right, she would want to be laid to rest beside her wee ones. She spent so much time up there visiting their graves. Ye know I've an idea. I think it is time we have a cemetery here on Plantation Creek. It's so far to the Church Cemetery and we need one closer. I believe I'll insist that Henry be buried at the high meadows too. I know that he would have wanted it that way. He dearly loved Sarah."

"Do ye think Rev. Cotton will allow it?" asked Anne.

"What do I care what he will allow? He's me husband and I can decide where he should be buried." Alice retorted a little too sharply. "Sarah and her wee ones should not be laid to rest alone at the high meadows."

Surprised by Alice's sharp retort, Anne started to reply, "I didn't mean to imply..."

"Oh Anne, don't mind me. I'm not meself today. I shouldn't have been so harsh but it just upsets me that Rev. Cotton caused so much pain for my son, especially at this time. I'm really irritated with Rev. Cotton. Sarah has always been a devout Christian and Rev. Cotton's strongest supporter during his tenure here. Rev. Cotton hasn't always made it so easy to be a supporter. I remember those first few desperate years when he showed no leniency toward those having difficulty in collecting his tithes. Rev. Cotton took anyone late to court where tithes were doubled and only made their strife more difficult. William paid many a tithe for the unfortunate due to Sarah's pleading. Now Rev. Cotton has the audacity to deny her a decent burial in the Church cemetery. I know I should be a better Christian but he just infuriates me sometimes."

"It is a long way to the Church from Plantation Creek," Pattenden said. "Mayhaps we could have the court designate a new cemetery at the high meadows."

"That's a good idea Henry," replied Alice. "We need one on Plantation Creek anyway. Tis virtually impossible at times to reach the Church in inclement weather. That's why Sarah's children were buried at the high meadows when they died shortly after they came into this world. Maybe the court will see fit to grant our wish. Now I know ye must need food and rest. It has been a trying day for ye so let's see what Anne and I can round up for ye to eat..... Anne, let's see what we can find," Alice said as she stood.

After they left, Henry, totally exhausted, collapsed on a nearby chair but looked up when Mary appeared in the doorway.

"Oh Henry, so much needless death, I know it is a strain for ye," said Mary.

"Aye," replied Henry, "But for ye as well. It seems like ye've had nothing but hardship since we left England. I should've left ye with ye're parents until I had things a little more settled here."

"Now, none of that talk. Ye know I'd never want to be in England without ye there. My home is always by ye're side."

He took her in his arms and huskily said, "How did I ever get so lucky....having ye in my life?"

The joint funeral for Sarah and Henry took place on a sunny day. A soft breeze swayed the grasses in the meadow as Rev. Cotton's strong stern voice penetrated the air. The trees adjacent to the meadow stood tall in regal elegance with their colorful leaves reflecting the sunlight belying the solemn occasion taking place before them. Henry Willson's grave was a few feet from Sarah's and three small graves were on the other side of her grave.

Henry clasped Mary's arm tighter as she shivered even in the autumn warmth at the sight of the three small graves.

Am I being foolish coming here with Henry and risking the life of our unborn child? My selfishness may cause us to lose our child just as Sarah lost hers.

Thoughts of home flooded Mary's mind and tears trickled down her cheeks. She glanced around at the people surrounding

109

the graves. One of the ladies present was trying to control four children, three boys and a young girl. All were probably under the age of six and had flaxen hair like their mother's. Her husband stood staunchly at her side. His finely chiseled features and rough hands revealed the hard work he must have known. The mother was not much older than Mary.

Her children have been born here and seem to be doing fine.... I'm sure we'll be fine...after all, I am married to a doctor and Alice will be here as well. I guess I'm just being silly for worrying.

Mary was so deeply engrossed in her thoughts and only became aware that Rev. Cotton had finished when Henry started guiding her away from the graves. She leaned against him and said, "Henry, we've had a rough time so far but I'm sure everything will turn out well, that is.. with God's help, won't it?" she said weakly.

Henry smiled down at her as they walked. "Where's all that overabundance of optimism ye always have? Without it, ye know we're doomed."

"Sometimes it's hard to be optimistic with so much sadness around but I'll try harder," she replied. "I know we can handle anything as long as I have ye with me."

"Now that sounds more like me Mary. I hope the worse is behind us. I wish I could say the same for Alice and William. It will be hard on her without a husband and on William without someone to share his life."

"Ye are right of course" said Mary. "I guess I've been a little selfish thinking we were the only ones with troubles."

"There's not a selfish bone in ye body Mary. This has just been hard on everyone and I'm sure ye are more than a little bit homesick."

Mary grew quiet at the mention of home....afraid that the tears might start again. She bit her lip forcing back the tears and tried to appear brave. Henry felt the tension in her body and pulled her closer to him as they walked toward the waiting shallop.

CHAPTER FIFTEEN

September, 1638, Plantation Creek, Eastern Shore, Virginia

In September, Alice Willson was summoned in the middle of the night to assist Ollive Eaton, a single mother, in the delivery of her child. Not wanting to wake the sleeping house she quietly left in the canoe with the servants of John Roper and headed for his house.

Labor was long for the young mother and while it progressed, Alice Willson urged her to reveal the name of the child's father so the child would be provided with proper care. Finally, after a long night, Ollive admitted that the child's father was William Fisher.

"Aye, I thought as much," Alice said, "but I wasn't sure. We must take him to court and so he will provide for his raising."

"But I wanted to take care of him meself, "cried the young mother.

"Now child," replied Alice. "Ye know that's not possible. Ye are apprenticed to John Roper and he'd never allow ye to keep this young boy. It would take away ye duties to him."

The young mother then began to cry so loudly and hard that Alice was worried about her health. Trying to console her, Alice said, "I can try to see if the court will let ye keep him for a while, at least until he is weanable."

This seemed to calm the young mother a little and she placed the dark-headed boy in his mother's arms while she drifted off to sleep.

Aye, life is so unfair. My poor Sarah could have given a child so much and was unable to have one. Now, here lies this healthy young boy, without a true home and a father who will never really acknowledge him as his own.

After the mother and child were sleeping soundly, Alice left with instructions for their care to the waiting servants and walked to the canoe at the dock. She dreaded the next few days ahead when she would have to attend court and report the events of this night.

The first week in October, Alice was summoned again as midwife. With Dr. Pattenden anxiously by her side, she helped deliver his son, Henry Pattenden, Jr. He was a handsome child with a head full of dark hair like Mary's and big blue eyes. Mary and Henry couldn't have been happier. After both mother and child were settled and resting peacefully. Alice and Henry went downstairs to the Parlour.

"Ye know Alice, I'll never be able to repay ye for all the help ye have given us. I don't know how we would have managed without ye're support."

"The same goes for ye as well, Henry. It would have been very difficult for me after the double tragedy of losing both me husband and Sarah. This house would be mighty sad and lonesome without ye both. Now there's even a new life in here to lift my spirits."

"Once he starts crying all the time, ye'll probably regret saying that," Henry said with a laugh.

"I hope I never get too old to enjoy a child's voice even if it's a wail," replied Alice.

"I doubt that ye ever will Alice. Ye have a big heart and that never changes. I guess this is a good time to tell ye that I've decided to settle here in Accawmacke and even picked out a spot close by in Hungar's so ye will see quite a bit of Henry, Jr. I'm sure, especially, if Mary has anything to say about it."

"That's wonderful news!" exclaimed Alice. I knew ye would love Accawmacke and it will be nice having ye nearby to watch young Henry grow up. I already feel as close to him as I do my own grandchild. It must be because he was born here."

"How many acres will ye patent?"

"I'm due 200 acres for transportation of Mary, me and my two servants, Christopher Bryan and James Hardyn, and I had 200 acres before Mary and I arrived but I plan to try my hand with tobacco planting and I understand I need a good bit more acreage to be successful."

"Four hundred acres will give ye a start but ye do need much more than that. Tobacco wears out the land. My Henry was in the process of buying more from Francis Graves before he died but he never completed the transaction and I'm afraid without it, this plantation cannot continue." Alice looked off in the distance and averted her eyes as she tried to control the anguish in her voice.

"Perhaps I can help ye Alice. I'll be happy to talk to Francis so ye can acquire the land."

"Aye Henry, ye would be of great assistance to me if ye would act as my attorney in the matter. Me husband offered Francis Graves a cow and 100 pounds of tobacco for the land. I'd ask William but he has enough on his hands right now."

"Consider it done, Alice and if ye ever need additional aid with the planting, don't hesitate to ask. We'll never be able to repay ye for ye're kind generosity in allowing us to stay here."

"Aye, the feeling is mutual...ye have been a blessing. I don't know how I'd ever managed without ye when my husband died." She looked away again trying to hide the tears now trickling down her cheeks. After a few moments she continued, "They say God never gives ye more trials than ye can handle but I feel that me cup of tribulations has overflowed....I know God sent ye here to provide the comfort I needed with Henry and Sarah's death and now with the birth of ye're child...God has revealed the joy of a new beginning."

Realizing Alice was close to losing complete control of her emotions, Pattenden tactfully steered her to another subject. "Alice, it looks like I'm in need of a carpenter very soon. I'd like to begin building me own house as soon as possible. Though ye hospitality has been immeasurable, I'm sure Mary would like to have a home of her own again, especially, now that we have Henry, Jr."

"Ye are right of course, Henry. A woman longs for her own home when she has a child." Alice reflected a few moments and she casually brushed away the tears from her cheeks while staring out the window of the Parlour.

After a time she replied, "John Savage is a carpenter, I believe ye're met him but I think it will be sometime before he could start ye house....I believe I know just the carpenter ye need...

Ambrose Dixon. He came over from England a year ago and worked as a ship caulker but he's now a ship builder himself and occasionally he's called on to build a house or two. One thing for sure, ye house will be tight with him starting out as a caulker" she said with a laugh. "He may have some time available to start right away since it's nearing winter....He owns a plantation as well and between building ships and planting, he doesn't have much time left over in the summer...though ye know ye are welcome to stay here as long as ye wish. I love the company....this house will be awful lonesome when ye are gone."

"Ambrose Dixon? Wasn't he in the party that went to the Indian village during the search for William's wife? If I remember correctly, he was quite a character....pretty hot-tempered along with a man named George Cottingham."

"That sounds like Ambrose as well as George. Neither are ones to mince words when it comes to Indians. He and George Cottingham are two of the best Indian fighters in the area. George, is still bound to William Roper for a few more years. He arrived about two years ago but has been on many excursions with Capt. John Smith and Roper looking for gold. I understand that his family is originally from Cottingham, England but the family left there and went to Scotland. They say the family's related some way to Lord Cottingham. George, being a third child didn't receive an inheritance so he came to Virginia to seek his fortune....but there I go chattering again. I really think Ambrose is the carpenter for ye. He may be a bit boisterous at times but he's a good builder and very trustworthy, ye couldn't go wrong by hiring him to build ye house. If ye like, I'll send word for him to drop by as soon as he finds the time."

"Please do, Alice. I'd like to start on a house soon....and with any luck, I should be able to start planting tobacco this spring. It would help to have the house nearby as soon as possible so I could better manage the plantation."

"Well, it's settled then, I'll send word today but we've been chatting away too long. "I imagine Mary's awake by now and I'm sure she's anxious to see ye. Go on up and spend some time with ye wife and son."

"Ye're right. She's probably wondering where I am," he said as he bounded up the stairs two at a time.

After Pattenden left the room, Alice found herself alone in the room where her husband had so meticulously kept the records of their plantation. The strain of Henry, Jr's birth as well as thoughts of her husband consumed her and tears trickled down her cheeks.

Aye dear one, why did ye have to leave me so soon. How will I ever manage without ye? It seems just a few years ago that we were planning our lives like these two young people.

After a time, Alice regained her composure, stood up and walked toward the kitchen to find one of the servants to send a message to Ambrose.

CHAPTER SIXTEEN

Winter, 1638, Plantation Creek, Eastern Shore, Virginia

Henry was sitting on the porch of Alice's house enjoying the pleasant weather as he watched a shallop arrive at her dock. A tall man climbed out and followed the steep path leading to Alice's house while another younger man remained in the shallop. As the man drew near, Henry recognized him as one of the men in the group who had gone to the Indian village to look for Sarah.

The man shouted, "I'm Ambrose Dixon. I understand ye want a house built."

Henry smiled. Alice was true to her word. She must have sent a message to Ambrose shortly after their conversation the day Henry, Jr. was born. Henry studied Ambrose as he approached the house. He was lanky but without an once of fat. He arms revealed strong muscles and appeared to be a few years younger than Henry. He greeted Ambrose, "Aye, we need a house and a shallop built. Have a seat and we can discuss it."

Ambrose sat on the steps and Henry began to describe the large brick house he wanted built, but he was interrupted by Ambrose.

"Sir, when did ye plan to live in this house?"

Startled by the interruption, Henry replied, "Why as soon as possible...I thought maybe it could be completed by spring."

"Well, sir...I'm not building many houses now...me interest has shifted to boats. I've contracted to build a large shallop now and didna have much time to devote to ye house. If ye hope to live in the house this spring, I'd suggest we build a smaller one with plans to add to it later, especially if ye want a shallop built too."

At first, Henry was taken back but the man's abrupt manner but he remembered that Alice highly recommended him. "Aye, tis important to have a place of our own as soon as possible.. then, what size house did ye have in mind?"

"Ye could still have a hall, parlour and two additional

117

chambers next to the parlour and the kitchen and dairy would be detached. Since there's little clay in the area to make bricks and no stone, we'd need to construct the house from pine instead of bricks."

"Build the house of pine?" Henry retorted. "I had hoped for a fine brick house. Well... I guess pine will have to do but, I must insist on a brick or stone fireplace. Can we not find some clay to make bricks for a fireplace?"

"Aye, I'm sure James Ewell, could manage to make enough bricks for a fireplace but I 'd suggest two fireplaces. Tis mighty cold in the winters around here. Being a brickmaker, he's aware of all the clay available on the eastern shore. I'll contact him immediately. Now where did ye plan to build ye house?"

"My land's by William Berriman's on Old Plantation Creek."

"Do ye have time to take me there now? We need to start while we have this good weather. I'm sure another snow is around the corner."

"Aye, tis a fine time now. I'll inform Alice and me wife where I've gone," Henry said as he entered the house.

Ambrose waited on the porch steps and admired the view before him. Alice had a choice location on Plantation Creek. One day he hoped to have a plantation just as big if not bigger.

Henry returned shortly, carrying a large basket and chuckled. "When I informed Alice where we were going, she insisted on sending food for our excursion. I hope ye're hungry ... she sent quite a lot."

Ambrose laughed with Henry. "I'm sure we'll manage to eat it somehow...especially if tis from Miss Alice. Her cook, Anne is the best around."

The two men followed the path toward the waiting shallop and were soon on their way across Old Plantation creek.

Christmas was a subdued affair at the Willson's house December, 1638 with the recent deaths of Sarah and Henry Willson so vivid in everyone's minds. Even the birth of Henry Pattenden, Jr. did little to lift the spirits enough for much of a celebration and the unusually strong winter winds pierced the daub and wattle house the whole month of December creating a miserable environment for the occupants. January was not much better, although the weather improved, there was still a chill in the air forcing Mary to keep Henry, Jr. indoors out of the cold air and she began to get cabin fever.

After the shallop was completed toward the end of January, Henry, with the help of his two servants Christopher Bryan and James Hardyn, worked on clearing his land whenever he found the time so planting could begin as soon as spring approached. Occasionally, members of the community called on him for medical problems and his reputation as a physician quickly became known in the area. He returned home each day thoroughly exhausted, though he never complained. Mary knew he needed a rest and she was particularly delighted when one spring day, Henry agreed to take time off and have a picnic on the beach near the ocean.

The beautiful day was nearing an end too quickly and Mary stared with wistful eyes toward the ocean dreading the thought of returning to their regular routine. Waves crashed on shore then withdrew into the vast ocean. Each one echoed the pattern of Mary's thoughts, reminding her of the great distance that separated her from loved ones in England.

Oh God, please keep them safe from all the turmoil. If only they had come with us....it's so hard not knowing what's happening to them.

Mary, instinctively fingered and twisted the ribbon in her hair as she often did when thoughts of her family raced through her mind. She looked down at the sleeping child lying on the blanket beside his father. Henry, Jr. was nearly seven months old and looked more like his father each day.

Mum and Papa would certainly enjoy seeing ye as well as all ye many aunts and uncles....Oh Papa, we're forging a new path for our family like ye wanted but I wish ye were all here to share it with us...

She quickly, glanced toward the ocean to hide the tears welling in her eyes.

I must get control of myself. Henry was reluctant to stop working long enough for this trip to the shore and he'll not come here again if he thinks it makes me sad...

Mary stood up and dusted the sand off her dress as she

119

regained her composure.

Her movement startled Henry. He looked up and asked, "Are ye ready to return home, Mary?"

"Why Henry Pattenden, we've been here only a few hours and already ye are anxious to go back to work," she said teasingly.

"Ye are right of course," he chuckled. "I just have a hard time leaving work behind, especially on such a beautiful day. I keep thinking of all the things I should be doing."

"I know. But ye shouldn't push so hard...I don't want ye to become ill again."

"No chance of that happening with my dutiful wife taking such good care of me," he said as he pulled her down beside him. Henry held her close and softly caressed her cheek while they both looked lovingly at the sleeping dark-headed child beside them.

"He still seems like a miracle to me," Henry said breaking the complacent silence. "I was so worried before he was born. I don't know how ye endured the trip over as well as all the tragedy that occurred after we arrived here and still managed to produce such a beautiful, healthy son."

"Remember, I told ye that Mum said all the women in our family had an easy time of their lying in, though I do admit, I was a little worried at first."

"Ye worried? I'm surprised to hear ye say that. Not many men much less young ladies would want to go half way around the world, away from family and loved ones to start a new life in a strange country. Ye're one of the bravest women I know and I'm lucky to have ye for me wife."

"I'm not so brave. I just love my husband very much," Mary said, as she snuggled closer to him to reinforce her words.

Henry turned her face toward him and kissed her lips intensely, then slowly and gently kissed her neck and ear. He pressed against hers and she responded to his touch.

Henry, Jr., stirred and began to softly whimper. Alerted by his cry, Henry and Mary broke their embrace. Mary gently stroked Henry, Jr.'s back and after a few minutes he was asleep again, making soft sucking sounds as he slept.

"He is a little miracle, isn't he?" Mary said softly. I know I'm prejudiced but have ye ever seen such a beautiful child. He has his handsome father's good looks."

"Ye are wrong there," Henry laughingly replied. "I'm glad he looks like his Mum."

"He's a ray of sunshine for sure, especially during all that storm of trouble when we first arrived and I think he really helped Alice with her grief."

"I agree. Now there's another strong lady, Henry said as he stroked Mary's cheek. She's done a great job handling her plantation...No man could do better. I've offered to help many times but she never seems to need assistance."

"I guess working alongside her husband all those years prepared her for the day when she'd have to run the plantation alone. I've grown to dearly love her; she's almost like a second Mum to me."

"I wish ye Mum was here with ye now." Then Henry looked deeply into Mary's eyes, "I don't want to alarm ye but I'm concerned about ye're family with all the trouble taking place at home."

"Have ye heard anything new, Henry?" Mary asked with fear in her voice.

"Nothing specific, but I do know that King Charles is building an army to put down the Covenanters. I feel it will be hard on ye're family to continue to avoid conflict. Maybe I can talk them into coming here when I return to England with our shipment."

"Return to England?" Mary exclaimed as she abruptly sat up on the blanket. "Why, Henry when did ye decide to do that? I thought our harvest would just be shipped along with others. I didn't know ye had any intention of going along with the shipment."

"I know, Mary but our house will be completed next week and we need furniture and several more indentured servants as well as additional acreage from buying headrights. Berriman has acquired quite a large holding through headrights and I plan to do the same but to ease my mind about ye and Henry, Jr., I want ye to stay with Alice while I'm gone," he said sternly. "I've already spoken to Alice and she agrees. She assured me that ye both would be welcomed with open arms and I believe ye would be a great comfort to her."

"But Henry, the natives are friendly here and I'm sure I

could manage alone. I'll miss ye desperately and I'll be fine in our new home."

"Ye are probably right, Mary, but I can't help but remember Berriman's wife and how lonely she was. Please agree to stay with Alice," he pleaded. "I will worry a little less about ye and Henry, Jr. if ye stay with her."

"I will Henry if it means so much to ye. But do ye think ye will be able to convince my family to come here......I'm concerned for their safety."

"I'll try me best...I know ye would be more successful in this endeavor. Perhaps, when I tell them about their new grandchild, it could entice them. I know family means a great deal to them."

"Ye're right," Mary replied as she fingered the always present ribbon in her hair. "But both Papa and Mum were so insistent they would never leave England. I guess there's always hope of changing their minds...but Henry, I will miss ye dreadfully while ye're gone. Are ye sure it will be safe to return home? I imagine Laud would still love to get his hands on ye."

"I'm sure Laud is after bigger fish than me, but I promise to be as discreet as possible. I'm more worried about ye and Henry, Jr. Life here is still very primitive compared to home."

"We'll stay with Alice as ye request, Henry. She has been through many more difficulties than we'll ever know. I'm sure she could handle most anything."

"That's what I'm counting on, but I still don't relish the idea of leaving the two of ye here. However, I feel I must take this opportunity to expand our holdings. Tobacco requires a lot of land and labor. Berriman has convinced me of that. Well, it's settled then...when I travel to England with Berriman, ye'll stay with Alice. Chris and James will be able to handle our plantation while I'm gone."

"I understand, Henry.... and we'll be here waiting for ye return but let's not spoil this day by discussing ye departure. Ye've had so little time to spend like this and we must not waste a moment of it on sadness."

"Respectfully noted, Mrs. Pattenden," Henry laughed and he pulled her toward him. She fell into his waiting arms. He gave her a long, passionate kiss and her body began to tingle. She pressed closer to him.

Henry raised his head and looked deeply into Mary's eyes. He gently stroked her cheek and growled huskily, " Ye 're right. We must not waste a moment of this beautiful day."

He hungrily sought her lips and she returned his passion.

Henry, Jr. lying next to them on the blanket, began to cry.

"Well, little man, I guess ye want some attention," Henry laughed as he pulled away from Mary's embrace.

Mary sat up and adjusted her clothes. Henry stood and picked up his child and gently tossed him in the air. Henry, Jr. gasped then began to laugh loudly.

"Little Henry, do ye know that ye have the most beautiful and smartest Mum in the world? Ye're a very lucky young man."

Mary looked at her enthusiastic husband and gleeful son and secretly wished that the day would never end.

CHAPTER SEVENTEEN

June, 1639 Gravesend, England

Henry and William returned to England in June. They experienced only minor difficulties on the trip. The convoy of ships met a few squalls but nothing as severe as the trip to the colonies. As ship surgeon, Henry convinced the Captain to scrub the cabins' floors once a week to avoid ship's fever so very few people became ill. The ship caught very strong trade winds and they arrived in England within a month's time.

As William and Henry disembarked at Gravesend, Henry remarked, "Aye, it's good to see England again....I had forgotten how much I miss me home country, even with all her problems."

"Home country?" replied William. "Ye'll not be thinking that way after a few more years in Accawmacke. Home country to me...is Virginia...there are too many things that I didna agree with here. I love the freedom I have in Virginia and wouldn't give it up for all the amenities England has to offer."

"Ye may be right, but I wish Mary did not have to do without and struggle so much. Mayhaps, when our house is complete and we have more of a town in Accawmacke, life will become a little easier for her. I hope I can talk her parents into returning with us. That would ease her mind considerably."

"Aye, I hope they will listen too," replied William. "I know it would have helped Sarah to have family with her. I feel at fault for not realizing how difficult life was for her. It was a good idea for ye to suggest Mary stay with Alice. Sometimes, we think so much about our own business and forget our wives needs," he replied with an anguished voice.

"I'm sorry, William. I didn't mean to bring ye pain. How thoughtless of me!"

"Not to worry, Henry. I'm afraid I'll feel the pain of Sarah's death for a long time. Now, let's see if we can find what has been happening in merry England, while we were away. I'm famished though now. Let's head for a pub and quench our thirst and appetites"

"I'm with ye there. Ship food leaves a lot to be desired. Some fish and chips and good conversation sounds good to me while we await our shipment to be unloaded."

As the two men walked down the busy quay, Henry and William kept a watchful eye on their surroundings. They remained cautious of the many pickpockets who were always rampant. The dock seemed to be filled with an unusually large number of families awaiting their departure. Crying babes in their mother's arms, children running about and distraught parents sitting on their baggage, keeping a watchful eye on their bairns, crammed the edges of the quay. A short man with a disheveled appearance approached Henry and Berriman as they walked.

"Halloa, are ye returning from America?" the man asked.

"Aye," replied Berriman, and continued walking.

"Could ye tell me a little about the colonies?" the man inquired, as he followed Henry and Berriman. "I hear that a man can grow rich and have freedom to do pretty much as he pleases. Tis it true?"

"Aye," Berriman replied. . "Ye can grow rich, but it takes a lot of hard work....and ye do have more freedom. But don't expect to just have a life of ease..."

"But tis it safe for me family?" the man asked.

Berriman grimaced with this question and didn't respond so Henry replied. "Tis fairly safe...depending on where ye settle."

The man halted his steps, obviously deep in thought, while Henry and Berriman continued down the quay.

"I wish ye success," Henry shouted over his shoulder at the man. Realizing that Berriman had probably recalled the death of his wife and family again, Henry attempted to change the subject.

"Doesn't it seem like a mite large crowd leaving for America, these days, William?" Henry queried as they moved further away from the ship. "I wonder why so many are willing to give up their lives here. Mary and I were trying to get away from Laud but I know all these people can't be that strongly affected by his actions."

"Hope of something better, I imagine," responded Berriman. "Now let's see about that grub before we are accosted again."

"I agree. Let's see if we can find out a little more about what has been happening here as well. I feel like we have been in a void as far as news from England."

The two men found a pub and after seating themselves at an empty table, a serving wrench quickly appeared by their side. "What'll it be for ye, gents?" she inquired.

"The best fish and chips ye have and a pint of ale each," Henry answered.

She nodded then asked, "I seen ye two gents get off the ship from the colonies. What's it like in the colonies?"

"All that a man may desire and more," William retorted. "But, we're in need of some victuals now, so how's about getting some for us? We can talk later if ye like."

She complied and sauntered off to the kitchen to get their food. Henry turned to William and said, "That's the second inquiry in less than ten minutes. Maybe that's just coincidence but people seem to be awfully interested in the Colonies these days."

"I agree," retorted William. "Let's see if we can find out why from those gents over at that table behind ye," he indicated with his eyes. "I noticed them when we came in. They're certainly having a heated discussion about something. Mayhaps, they can reveal this sudden interest in the colonies."

William hollered toward the men behind Henry, "Halloa! We are just back from Virginia and a little short on news around here. Would any of gents care to share a bottle of ale and fill us in on happenings?"

The men disrupted from their conversation, looked in William and Henry's direction uneasily and one of them retorted, "How'd we know ye be from the Colonies?" He was a tall, burly man with a couple of front teeth missing and definitely not someone to become crosswise with.

Henry responded calmly, "We didn't mean to disturb ye? We're just inquisitive. Tis been a while since we've been home and we're curious about any news. I'm Henry Pattenden, the ship's surgeon on the Constant that just returned from the Colonies not more than twenty minutes ago and this be me friend William Berriman. We just wanted to get an update on developments around here. Didna mean to disrupt ye conversation."

A short stout man looked at the burly man and said, "Aw

James, they seem harmless. We shouldn't be so suspicious of everyone."

James, the burly man, gave the others a hard look. "Ye say that, after what happened to Cord. Me think ye are a little too trusting." He looked at Henry and William and demanded, brusquely "Ye say ye've just arrived on the Constant. How long have ye been in the Colonies and why did ye come back here?"

William volunteered cautiously, "I've been there nigh five years but me friend here has only been there around one. We settled on the Eastern Shore of Virginia and only returned to drop off our shipment of tobacco and pick up supplies. We plan to return within the month but we don't mean to cause any problem. If ye don't want to talk, we'll just sit here and mind our own business."

The men seemed to relax a little at William's answer. A short man with a pocked face said, "Aw gentlemen, we be just a little wary of strangers of late with all that's been going on. What do ye want to know?"

"Just a little news, nothing more," replied Henry. "Information in the Colonies is hard to come by, especially where we've settled. We noticed a good many people on the dock set to travel to the Colonies. Why the increase now? Has something happened here, recently?"

"Aye," said the man with the pocked face, "King Charles is forming an army to go against the Scots. He's required a man from every household and many didna agree with his motives and didna want to go against the Covenanters. The Covenanters are a strong lot, having returned from the War in Germany and we are just plain militia. Why give up ye life for a cause ye didna believe in? Many have just decided to flee to the Colonies. Now tis ye turn to share news. What's life like in the Colonies? Is it the paradise we hear?"

"I wouldn't exactly call the Colonies a paradise," Henry replied, "Though me friend here may disagree. If ye are looking for life as it is here, ye will be disappointed because the Colonies are still uncivilized. We depend on supplies from England for our existence and struggle daily making a life for ourselves; but if ye are looking for freedom to do what ye want and willing to work, then I guess ye could call the Colonies a land of opportunity."

Some of the men became interested and a couple joined their table after the serving wrench brought their food. Others crowded round to eavesdrop on the conversation as Henry and William continued to discuss the advantages and disadvantages of living in the Colonies. After their conversation was over, William and Henry had two indentured servants each to take back to Virginia with them.

CHAPTER EIGHTEEN

June 1639, Cranbrook, England

Henry traveled toward Mary's parents' home in Cranbrook two days later. He left Berriman behind to settle some business with his factor. Both William and Henry made a sizable profit from their shipment which enabled them to purchase more indentures, as well as supplies and furniture for their respective homes.

After renting a carriage, Henry decided to take a side trip through Nettlestead where his father had been parson. He trembled as he recalled the horrible days when his father, two brothers and a sister all died within days of each other from 'The Black Death.' He didn't understand the disease then and still knew little about it now. His father became ill after visiting 'the free willers' in Maidstone.

What would life have been like if father had not made that fatal trip? Tis silly to ponder over now.

Henry remembered how passionate his father was about trying to sway the 'free-willers' back to the one true faith of England. Henry's two brothers were working in an outlying field near the family home in Nettlestead, and on their way home, they found their father near the field, feverish and delirious. Henry's sister, Abby, was the only one at the house because his mother was visiting a sister nearby and Henry was staying with Dr. Bastwicke at the time.

Oh, how worried Abby must have been for father and she was alone, trying to take care of him for such a long time.

Of course, a message of her husband's illness was immediately sent to Henry's mother. She left her younger children with her sister and rushed home to take care of her husband. Henry received a message from her ordering him to stay with Dr. Bastwicke. But his mother arrived too late to save her husband. He died within a day of her return.

Then tragedy struck again. Henry's mother didn't have time

to grieve over her husband's death because Abby, and brothers, John and William, came down with the same illness. All died within days of each other. Henry's mother never understood how she avoided the dreaded illness but the deaths of so many members of her family broke her heart and she never was the same after that.

Our family....disintegrated within the span of two weeks and people were so unkind.

Henry remembered how the parishoners of his father's church and the community shunned the remaining members of the family. The words they used still haunted him.

"Ye father was punished because he was not doing the Lord's work."

"He was punished by God for trying to talk to the 'free willers.'"

How ignorant they were!

It all became too much for Henry's mother and she died a couple of years later. After her death, Henry was indentured to Bastwicke and his younger brothers and sisters were raised by his aunt.

"Aye, Mum," Henry said aloud to himself. "I didn't understand how much ye suffered at the time! Now, that I have a wife and a wee one of me own, I can only imagine the pain ye endured. It must have been unbearable because I know it would be unbearable if I lost Mary or Henry, Jr."

Henry drove his carriage up to the Church cemetery where his family was buried. He climbed down from the carriage and walked toward the church. Overwhelmed by memories, from the days he spent here with his brothers and sisters, Henry found himself unable to enter the cemetery but stopped to gaze at the enormous stained glass windows of the church that had been there for ages. St. Mary's of the Virgin stained glass windows were said to have been completed by Reginald de Pympe and his son John. They never ceased to amaze him with their grandeur.

Composing himself again, Henry continued down the path to the graves of his family. So much had changed since they died. His two remaining sisters moved away from the area and he lost track of his youngest brother many years ago. He recalled how much his parents loved children.

How I wish you could meet your wonderful grandson.....and Oh, how I miss them now.

Henry realized that Mary and Henry, Jr. were essentially the only family he had left and they were in the Colonies. Yes, Berriman was right. There was nothing left for him in England now.

A path led down to the Medway River from the church and Henry decided to follow it. He reached the River shortly and gazed off toward the island in the middle of the River. He remembered the times he and his older brothers often rowed a boat to the island. Those days seemed so long ago. After a time, Henry returned up the path and back to the waiting carriage. It was time to leave England behind. His new home would be Virginia.

By mid afternoon, Henry reached Cranbrook. He admired the picturesque scene of the grazing sheep on the gentle hills. He was tired from the trip but it had been good for him. He no longer felt that he was leaving England behind. There was nothing here for him any more and he greatly missed Mary. His life was with her in Virginia. He felt a little guilty though.

She would have been so happy to see her family again. Am I wrong in making her stay home? But it's too late to worry about that now. Somehow, I must convince her family to go to the Colonies. They are not safe here.

Henry contemplated the possible reasons to give them for leaving England but came up short. It would not be an easy decision for them. They had built a life here for many years and would not willingly give that up.

He arrived at their house just as dusk fell over the land. Smoke was coming from the chimney and two young girls were playing in front. They looked cautiously at Henry for a few minutes, then Elizabeth, Mary's younger sister, recognized him and ran toward him with a shout, "Henry, I can't believe ye are here. Where's Mary?"

She gave him a hug while Sarah toddled behind her, looking quizzically at the strange man her sister was so excited to see.

"I'm sorry, Elizabeth, tis just me on this trip," Henry replied to the boisterous youngster. "She's staying in Virginia with ye nephew, Little Henry, Jr."

"My nephew? she exclaimed. "I have a nephew now?"

"Yes, Elizabeth, and he is a beautiful bairn. He looks just like Mary."

Mary's family, hearing all the commotion in front of their house, quickly rushed outside and seeing Henry, began hugging and talking and asking questions all at once.

Henry was overwhelmed by their exuberant response and said, "Whoa, one at a time. I have a lot to tell ye all, but one at a time."

Mary's mother took control and declared, "Okay now, ye all need to settle down. Henry, come inside and we'll see if we can calm down enough to make some sense but first, tell me why Mary's not with ye. She's not sick?"

"She's fine, Margaret," replied Henry, "And ye are now grandparents. We have a fine healthy son. Mary and Henry, Jr. are staying with Alice in Virginia. I didn't want to risk them traveling now due to the extensive pirating that is taking place. She wanted to come with me so much but sent all her love to ye by way of me."

The family became boisterous again at Henry's declaration of the grandchild, Henry, Jr. and peppered questions at him.

Margaret said, "Children, shush, so Henry can tell us about me grandchild. He can't answer us all at the same time. Now Henry, tell us about Henry Jr. What color hair and eyes does he have?"

"He looks like his Mum and has beautiful blue eyes and black hair," he replied. As Henry continued to answer their questions, he realized that Mary's father, Edward and grandfather were not in the exuberant party and asked, "Where's Mary's grandfather and Edward? Are they working somewhere?"

"Aye, ye ask a difficult question," replied Mary's mother, Margaret. "Edward's off in King Charles army. He's part of the militia. The King required one person from every household to go and since Edward is the only one of age, he had to fight in this terrible atrocity against Scotland. As for Grandpa, he died a couple of months back from a fever. The fever came on him quite suddenly but with his age and all, he really couldn't fight it off. I sent Mary a packet about his death but I guess the packet hasn't arrived yet. I'll admit, life hasn't been easy these past few months."

"I'm so sorry to hear this. I know Mary will be devastated by the news of her grandfather's death. I'm glad I asked her to stay with Alice, Henry Willson's wife, so she won't be alone when she receives the packet."

"Aye, ye must tell me about them," Margaret said. "Sit down and have something to eat while we talk. Youngun's, go on with ye chores while Henry eats. We have lots to talk about and don't need all this noise."

Margaret returned her gaze to Henry and asked, "How are Henry and Alice Willson? It's been ages since I've seen them," asked Margaret, as she nudged the children out of the room and then took down the pewter for Henry's meal.

"I'm afraid I have some bad news too. Henry Willson died shortly after we arrived in an incident with the Indians. "

"Henry dead? I can't believe it," Margaret exclaimed. She stopped dipping the stew from the ever present pot on the fire and fell into a chair beside Pattenden with an astonished look. "What happened?"

"He was in a search party looking for a missing woman. The party went to a nearby Indian village to see if she had been captured. They became involved in a fight with the Indians and Henry went back to help a fallen comrade. He was carrying his friend to the boat when an Indian arrow found him. He was killed instantly."

"That sounds like Henry, always thinking of others," Margaret declared. "Poor Alice, being alone like that....I'm glad Mary's with her now."

"Alice took his death hard but is holding up well," Henry replied. "She runs their plantation alone. She's one tough lady and has been a tremendous help to us. She helped deliver Henry, Jr."

"Oh, how wonderful! I'm glad Mary had a woman to help with the birth. I know ye're a doctor and all and she was in good hands but it's always nice to have another woman with ye during delivery. Did they ever find the missing woman?"

"Well, as it turns out, the woman was not really missing. We found her hanging from a rafter in the attic. She committed suicide. I understand that she had been terribly depressed from the death of several children."

"Oh, what a tragedy and I thought life was difficult here in England. Do ye really think Mary will be okay there? Do ye have much trouble with the Indians?"

"Don't worry Margaret, we settled on the Eastern Shore, an area where the Indians are friendly. She will stay with Alice and I feel sure she will be fine but I plan to return as soon as possible. I don't want to be away too long. How have ye been able to manage with Edward being gone?"

"Tis hard but the boys have helped quite a bit, by taking odd jobs and farming the land Edward bought not long ago. That has put food on the table. I recently heard that the army should be back soon. We had word that King Charles worked out some kind of treaty with the Scots. I certainly hope the rumor be true. I'm anxious for Edward to return home. He got the fever before he left and was still weak so naturally, I'm concerned about his health."

"I know ye must be. Ye life here appears to be more and more unsettled and dangerous. Ye know that Mary sent me here to ask ye to return with me....She hoped that ye may have a change of heart since Henry, Jr.'s birth."

"Aye, it has become more dangerous but ye just told me about Henry Willson's death. Sounds like the Colonies may not be such a safe place either. I greatly wish I could see me grandson but ye know Edward would never hear of leaving England. We are just too old to start life anew. Do ye think Mary and Henry, Jr. will ever be able to make the trip back home with ye sometime?"

"I suppose so, if the pirating of ships crossing the Atlantic dissipates some but I think I have given a false impression of Virginia. It's a harsh land that is true but we've settled in a blissful part of the country on the Eastern Shore of Virginia. On the Eastern Shore, we do not have to deal with the legalities of Jamestown. We have fertile land and most of all the Indians are peaceful."

"But I'm confused, ye just said Henry Willson died at the hand of Indians on the Eastern Shore and now ye say they are peaceful. How can that be?"

"The men who were in the search party were led by an intense Indian hater. Actually, the Indians were only defending themselves from the actions led by Edmund Scarburgh. He started killing Indian women and children in retaliation for the supposed capture of Sarah. He just came to the wrong conclusion and Henry's death was the result."

"Oh, that is even worse...so many people dying because of a misunderstanding. Ye said this Sarah committed suicide. I imagine that would be awful hard on her husband."

"Aye, it is. Berriman blamed himself for leaving her alone. He has become a good friend. We met him on the trip to the Colonies, settled near him and now we've returned together with our shipment."

"Berriman, his first name wouldn't happen to be William would it? I remember Alice married a Berriman and had three children by him, William, Joan and Mary. Let's see....if I remember right... Alice's first marriage was to Henry Carsley and they had a son, Henry Jr. before he died. Henry Carsley, Jr. married Elizabeth Traveller. I remember that wedding. Elizabeth's father was a very respectable gentleman....then Alice married Berriman after her first husband died...had the three girls and a son and after his death, married Henry Willson."

"Aye, that is him. I forgot ye would have known him. Alice, told me that she remained in England a few years after she and Henry Willson married, while he lived in the Colonies. She had her children from a former marriage living with her. William Berriman went to the Colonies a few years ago and has done right well for himself lately, though I heard he lost his first plantation before I met him. He started buying headrights and expanded his land holdings. Her daughter-in-law, Elizabeth Carsley with her two girls Agnis and Francis have a plantation next to William but I don't know them well. Mayhaps they are Henry Carsley Jr.'s family. I believe Carsley died a few years ago. They have a large plantation. Berriman helped us tremendously on the trip over and has become a very good friend."

"Aye," Margaret replied. "Alice and I became good friends while Henry was away. William was quite spirited and had a wonderful sense of humor as I recall but he was impetuous. He only had sisters as he grew up and constantly kept Alice appalled at his wild schemes to improve his lot in life. I'm not surprised that he settled in the Colonies. That would have been just like him. I believe her first son by Carsley left home early."

"Now see, that is another good reason for ye to move to the Colonies. There are so many people ye already know settled there," Henry retorted sheepishly.

"Aye, Henry ye never give up," laughed Margaret. "Now, let's see about those victuals. I know ye must be starving after that long trip out here. The bairns will be back soon worrying ye to death about Mary and the baby and I have many more questions as well but we need to feed ye first."

CHAPTER NINETEEN

June, 1639, Plantation Creek, Eastern Shore, Virginia

With Henry's absence, Mary soon grew despondent and worried about him constantly. But thankfully, the routine of life at Alice's home helped relieve her tension a little. There was always something that needed to be done on the large plantation. Mary was glad Henry insisted she stay with Alice. Her company became invaluable as the days drifted by and she seemed to appreciate the visit as well. Before they realized it, a month had come and gone and both were looking forward to Henry's return.

One evening, Mary and Alice sat in the Parlour, sewing and quietly discussing the day's events while Henry Jr. slept blissfully in a cradle beside them. In sharp contrast to the solitude inside, a violent thunderstorm was occurring outdoors. The howling wind and thunder occasionally interrupted their talk and caused Henry Jr. to slightly stir in his sleep so Mary rocked his cradle until he again drifted off in dreamland.

"I love watching Little Henry sleep," Alice said. "He has such sweet expressions. Makes one wonder what he's dreaming."

"Aye, I know," replied Mary. "I feel the same way. I especially, love his sweet smell after I bathe him. I wish I could keep him this age forever. When he awakens in the morning, his bubbly personality and gleeful sounds starts me day off right. I know he misses his Papa, but he doesn't despair over him being gone like I do. I wonder where Henry is right now? I hope the trip back to us will be uneventful."

"I do too, Mary. These days with the rough seas and pirating as well, tis become more dangerous than when I came over with me bairns to the Colonies."

"Aye," Mary replied. I have cried meself to sleep many a night worrying about Henry. He's not completely well and with all the risks of traveling, I wonder if he will safely come back to me."

"Oh Mary, there I go again saying the wrong thing. I didna

mean to make ye worry more. I was just thinking aloud. I'm sure Henry and William will make it back safely. We just have to have faith that God's taking care of them."

Suddenly a loud burst of thunder exploded near the house causing Mary and Alice to jump up and Henry Jr. started crying incessantly.

"Goodness, that was certainly, close!" exclaimed Alice as she looked out the window into the shadows of the night. Off in the distance, Alice saw a flickering light near the tobacco drying barn and shouted in panic, "FIRE!" She dropped her sewing on the floor and rushed to the door shouting, "Stay here with Henry, Jr. I'll summon the help," She disappeared out the front door in the pounding rainstorm before Mary could respond.

Mary picked up Henry, Jr. and tried to control the crying child by rocking and singing to him. The child felt her tension from the events transpiring outside and wouldn't be quieted but continued to howl along with the wind from the storm. Loud shouts, clanging of buckets, and the continual thunder from the storm added to the cacophony of noise outside. Mary glanced out the window and was alarmed at the now blazing fire in the distance.

Oh Alice, where are ye? Please be careful.

Since Mary couldn't help without leaving Henry, Jr. alone, she began to pray for the people fighting the fire. Henry, Jr. continued to wail and did not rest until the noise outside gradually abated. After what seemed like hours, Henry, Jr. fell asleep and Mary placed him gently in his crib. She sat down and tried to wait patiently for Alice to return but could not resist standing up to look out the window and tried to determine if the fire had been brought under control or catch of glimpse of Alice. But all she was able to distinguish in the dark night was the blazing fire and she was astonished to see that it continued to burn during the drenching rain that pelted the house. Finally, the huge blaze appeared only as a flickering light visible from the window but still Mary did not see Alice returning.

Oh Alice, where are ye? Ye should have returned by now.

Glancing back at the sleeping Henry, Jr., Mary decided to at least go out to the porch with the hope that she might have a better view. She stepped outside and saw a group of people heading quickly toward the house and realized that they were carrying someone. As they neared, she was able to recognize the blackened face of her dear friend, Alice and panicked at the sight.

"Oh Alice, what has happened?" she exclaimed but Alice did not respond. Aware that she had to take control of the situation, Mary tried to calm her emotions and ordered the servants to bring Alice into the front downstairs bedroom. Mary immediately checked Alice's pulse after she was placed on the bed and was relieved to find her heart was still beating even though it wasn't strong.

Anne, Alice's cook rushed into the room and cried out "Oh Mary, I came as soon as I heard. How is Ms. Alice?"

"It's not good," Mary quickly replied. "Anne, we need some water to clean this smoke off her to see if there are any injuries." Mary looked around at the worried group of servants standing in the room and said, "Can anyone tell me what happened? Did she get burned?"

"Nay Miss," said Jacob, one of Alice's servants. "We were all fighting the fire and she was right in there with us, lifting those heavy buckets of water, then I guess she fell or something. We were all so busy that no one knew that Miss Alice was not still standing beside us until the fire began to die down. When we saw her on the ground, we picked her up and rushed her back to the house."

"I just wish I knew what happened," Mary replied, trying to keep her voice calm while all she wanted to do was cry. "Is the fire out now?"

"Not completely, Miss. We just felt it was more important to return Ms. Alice to the house."

"Ye did the right thing. I'll take care of Alice. I know she would want the fire completely out. Ye can return to the fire and I'll let ye know how she is doing but Jacob would ye be able to reach Dr. Holloway in this storm?"

"Nay, Miss. Not til the storm dies down some unless I went by land and I couldn't reach him til morning that way."

"Well, I guess we'll just have to wait then and hope the storm ends soon. I know ye are all worried but my husband's a doctor and I helped him some. I believe she will be alright but everyone just pray for her. This will be a rough night."

141

The servants left the room, murmuring quietly and headed for the fire in the distance. Anne returned with water and she helped Mary wash Alice's smoke covered body. Mary told Anne to keep moistening Alice's face with the wet rag while she went to find Henry's medicine bag.

Oh Henry, I need ye now. I know I have helped ye many times but I'm not sure what is wrong. I don't want to make Alice worse. She doesn't appear to be burned and there were no snake bites on her or other injuries. What could have caused her to fall?

Then Mary remembered Henry and his fall on the ship. He said it was his heart.

Mayhaps, it is Alice's heart could not withstand all the excitement and her pulse was not strong. At least it's a possibility. If it tis she may not make it til morning but I don't want to harm her more if it isn't. Oh God, please give me the answer on what to do for Alice. I need ye guidance now.

Suddenly, Mary felt that her reasoning about Alice's heart was right and she went upstairs after Henry's foxglove. She rushed downstairs to the kitchen and prepared the medicine she had made for Henry many times. When it was ready, she returned to the bedroom where Alice still lay limp on the pillow.

"Anne, ye need to help me get this mixture down her. Do ye think ye could hold Alice up while I tried to spoon this in her mouth? I hope she will swallow it."

"Aye Miss Mary," replied Anne and she gently lifted Alice's upper body to an upright position.

Mary carefully spooned a little of the mixture in Alice's mouth because she didn't want to choke her. Alice's reflex took over and she swallowed the medicine. Mary quickly, gave her three more spoonfuls until it was gone. "Now Anne, we'll just have to wait for Doctor Holloway. Will ye sit with her while I check on Henry, Jr.?"

"Why certainly Miss Mary, ye take care of Little Henry and get some rest too. I'll be glad to sit with her all night if ye need me too."

"Thank ye Anne, I think I'll rest a while but only a short while. It will be much easier for me to sit up with Alice while Henry, Jr. is sleeping. We'll both need our rest because tomorrow will be a difficult day. I'll need to give Alice some more medicine

142

tonight anyway. I won't be long."

"Take as long as ye need Miss Mary, I'll be right here. Miss Alice means the world to me and I will watch her carefully."

"Okay, then but be sure to wake me if anything changes and if I'm not back down in four hours, wake me because she will need more medicine."

"Aye, Miss Mary. I'll remember to wake ye."

Mary went into the Parlour and gently picked up Henry, Jr. He was sleeping so soundly that she didn't awaken him as she took him upstairs. Exhausted after the trying ordeal, Mary didn't bother to undress since she would be up again in a few hours.

Henry, how I need ye now. I pray that ye will return home safely soon. I just hope, I gave Alice the proper medicine. Ye have taught me so much but there's so much more I need to know.

Mary knew the days ahead would be trying ones with Alice so ill and she prayed to God for guidance and quickly fell asleep.

CHAPTER TWENTY

June 1639, Plantation Creek, Eastern Shore, Virginia

Mary awoke with a start when Anne touched her shoulder. "Miss Mary, is it time for Miss Alice's medicine?" she quietly asked.

"Aye, Anne, thank ye for waking me. Has there been any change? Is Alice awake?"

"Nay, Miss, she has lain still all this time. I kept a moist rag on her head like ye said, but nothing seemed to rouse her. I'm worried about her Miss Mary."

"Me too, Anne. I'll be glad when Doctor Holloway gets here. Has the storm let up any?"

"Aye, ma'am. It finally let up a little while ago. I 'spect Jacob will be on his way to find Dr. Holloway now."

"I hope so, Anne. I'll feel a lot better when he has a look at her. I certainly miss my husband now. He would have been such a help to Alice and he'll be devastated if anything happens to her while he's gone. She has been through so much this year, the loss of her husband, Sarah's death, the barn burning last night and now this."

"I agree ma'am. She has had her share of problems and she is such a fine lady too. Miss Alice didna deserve all this to happen to her."

"Well, ye get some rest now, I'll stay up with Alice and hopefully the doctor will be here soon."

"Aye ma'am," Anne said. "But ye will let me know if anything changes with Miss Alice."

"Of course, Anne, I'll call ye right away. I know the two of ye have been through a lot together."

"Aye Miss Mary, we have," said Anne. "But I'll help ye with the medicine first." Then she walked quietly out of the room.

Mary stood and washed her face with the water in the pewter bowl on the chest by the door, dried it with a rag sitting beside it and tried to see her face in the looking glass above in the dimly lit room. She pinched her cheeks, trying to add some color and brushed a few straggly hairs back. She glanced back at her sleeping child, and quietly followed Anne's footsteps down the stairs. Mary went to the kitchen to quickly prepare more foxglove medication and took it to Alice in the bedroom.

Anne was waiting in the room and she again lifted Alice off the pillow while Mary spooned the medicine in Alice's mouth. This time, however, they both saw a flicker of Alice's eyelids.

"Did ye see that!" Anne exclaimed.

"I certainly did, Anne. Mayhaps, that is a good sign. Lay her back down gently and I'll watch her while ye rest. I'll need ye help for sure later today."

"Certainly, ma'am. Call me, if ye need me."

"I will, Anne."

Mary sat in the straight chair beside Alice's bed and picked up the rag to moisten her friend's forehead.

Alice, dear friend. Please wake up. I am so worried about ye. I hope I have given ye the right medication and not made ye worse. Ye are so much more than a friend. I miss my family so much and ye has been like a Mum to me. Oh, Mum, I wish ye were here to tell me what to do. With Henry away, I feel so lost. I'm trying to forge a new path in this new world like ye said Papa but I am so frightened. It is so hard without ye. Oh, what I would give for just a moment of time with ye. I took all those moments for granted when I was with ye. Now I may never see any of ye again. Oh God, Please make them listen to Henry and come to stay with us here.

Mary prayed for Alice while she continually moistened her head. The faint rays of dawn began to pierce through the window. She heard some commotion outside so she stood up and started walking toward the front door when she realized that Alice made a moan. Mary returned to the bed and said, "Alice, Alice, do ye hear me?"

Alice flickered her eyes, finally opened them and stared at her friend. "Mary, what happened?" she said weakly.

"Ye didna remember?" Mary asked softly. "Ye fell down in the yard while fighting the fire last night."

"I didna remember falling...just everything becoming blurry and pain in my chest."

"We have been so worried about ye. I believe the Doctor is

here now and I was just on my way to let him in. Will ye be all right while I'm gone for a few minutes?"

"Aye, Mary, I'll be all right," she replied softly. "Let the good Doctor in but I wish ye husband was here."

"Aye, I do too Alice, I do too."

Mary headed for the door and met Anne coming down the stairs. "How is she?" asked Anne quizzically.

"Better, Anne, I was coming to get ye after I let Doctor Holloway in. She awakened just now and started talking."

"Oh that is good news! I'll let the Doctor in, ye go stay with Alice. I know tis hard for ye to leave her side," said Anne.

Mary went back to stay with Alice and shortly afterward Doctor Holloway walked in the bedroom door followed by Anne. He was a short robust man, not nearly as handsome as Henry, Mary thought, but he had an appealing rotund face.

"Why Alice," he said. "What is this I hear about ye falling while fighting a fire? Ye know better than to fight fires at ye age."

"My barn was on fire, Holloway," Alice retorted. "What would ye have me do?....Let it burn."

"I guess there's no stopping ye," he said a little more softly. "Now tell me how ye came to fall."

"All I can remember was one minute, I was standing up and then everything got real blurry-like and my chest hurt. I don't remember anything after that."

"That doesn't sound good, Alice. Have ye had this pain in ye chest before?"

"Oh, it comes and goes....but I'm not as young as I used to be either," she replied.

Doctor Holloway said "Hmmph" and grimaced. He checked Alice's pulse and listened to her heart and after a time said, "Alice, it appears that ye are having heart trouble. That is common at ye age. I'm going to give ye some foxglove and tell Mary how to mix it. I want ye to take it everyday."

"Oh Doctor Holloway, that's what I thought it might be and since my husband has the same problem. I gave her some last night."

"Why it seems, I'm not even needed here. That was good thinking, Mary. It sounds like ye have learned a lot from ye husband. I understand he and Berriman went to England. When do they plan to come back?"

"Any day now, I hope," Mary replied. They didna plan to stay long."

"Well, I'm glad to hear that. Alice, I feel ye' re in good care with Mary here but I don't want ye to get out of bed for at least two weeks and still take the foxglove Mary gives ye after that. Ye probably have a nice bump on ye head from the fall as well. I don't want to hear of ye fighting anymore fires either. Ye have plenty of help and need to let them fight fires. Ye need to rest everyday too."

"Holloway, I can't run a plantation from my bed...ye know that."

"I know Alice, but ye can't run one at all if ye die. Keep working so hard and ye heart will give out....just try to rest a little more at least."

"I won't promise but I'll do my best," Alice said.

"Well at least that's something. Now remember, don't get out of bed for two weeks."

"We'll make her stay there," Mary responded. "I don't want to lose my best friend anytime soon. I can do whatever's needed," she said to Alice. "Just tell me what to do."

Alice nodded but didn't appear to be too happy about the prospect of staying in bed. After Doctor Holloway left, Anne went to the kitchen to prepare breakfast and Mary came back to the room with another dose of the foxglove mixture.

Alice looked worried and asked Mary, "What happened to my drying barn Mary? Was it completely destroyed?"

"Alice, I don't know. I've been here all night but I'll send for Jacob and he'll be able to tell ye."

"I just don't know what I'll do if my barn is destroyed. That was my one shipment for this year and I won't be able to manage this plantation without it. What am I going to do?"

"Ye don't need to be worrying about that now," Mary replied. Just concentrate on getting well. Ye can't run a plantation if ye're sick either."

"Oh Mary, ye are such a comfort to this old lady. I'm so glad ye stayed with me while ye're husband was gone. It has been so lonely here since I lost my Henry and ye little boy has been a joy to have around. I'll be sorry when ye leave."

"I feel the same way about ye Alice. I've been so homesick

for my family and particularly my Mum. Ye have become my second Mum in Virginia."

Mary and Alice talked quietly for a while til Alice drifted off to sleep. Mary stood up and climbed the stairs to check on Henry, Jr.

Three weeks after Alice fell ill, Henry Pattenden and William Berriman arrived home. Mary was upstairs attending to Henry, Jr. when she heard the wagon pull up to Alice's house. She peered out the upstairs window, then rushed over to Henry, Jr., whisked the astonished child from his crib, ran down stairs and reached the door just as Henry was opening the door.

Pattenden was startled by her sudden appearance at the door and leaned back for a moment...then he dropped his valise and grabbed both in a bear hug. The confused Henry, Jr. started to cry at the sudden embrace and Pattenden had to release the two so Mary could comfort him.

"Aye Mary, ye are a sight for sore eyes. I have missed ye so. It seems like we have been away years instead of a few short weeks. I hope I don't have to make a trip again without ye."

"I feel the same way," Mary said. "I don't ever want to be away from ye again. We are so happy ye are home, aren't we Little Henry," she declared.

Henry, Jr. looked up at her quizzically and recognizing his father, held his hands out to him to be held.   Henry took his child from Mary and kissed him on the top of his head.

Mary asked, "Were ye able to see my family, Henry and were ye able to persuade them to come to Virginia?"

"Aye, I saw them, Mary." Trying to hold off the bad news he asked her, "Did ye receive a packet from them, while I was gone? Ye Mum said she sent one."

"Nay, nothing came for me. Why was it important?"

"I'm afraid so Mary. I'm glad ye didn't receive it without me here. It told about ye grandfather's death."

"Grandpapa is dead?" Mary responded without emotion as if she was unable to take in the bad news.

"Aye, Mary, he died a few months ago from a fever. Ye father also had the same fever but he recovered."

"I can't believe it," Mary said as she stared off into emptiness. Then the news of his death finally hit her and all the anguish, fear and frustration she had felt for the past few weeks seemed to be unleashed with the realization. She began to cry and sob uncontrollably and fell in Henry's arms. Henry, Jr. started to cry with his mother and Pattenden tried to hold both of them in his arms.

Henry was thankful to see Anne walk in to check on the wailing noises emanating from the room and she solved his problem by taking Henry, Jr. and tried to comfort him. Henry led Mary to the couch in the parlour and sat her down, held her close and gently stroked her beautiful black hair. She continued to weep for sometime so Anne took Henry, Jr. upstairs because he could not be calmed while his mother was so distraught.

After Mary was finally able to compose herself, she asked Henry the one question she feared the answer to. "Were ye able to talk my family into moving here, Henry?"

Henry took a deep breath and replied with a sigh, "Nay, Mary, ye father was not even there. He had to fight in King Charles War with Scotland." Before she became upset again he quickly added, "However, I understand that a battle was never fought and King Charles worked out a treaty with Scotland so the army should be returning soon. I'm sure he will be fine."

"But how did Mum and the bairns manage with Grandpapa and Papa both gone? How did they live?"

"They had it rough, needless to say but the boys did odd jobs and worked in the fields your family owns. Ye Mum felt they would manage until ye father returned home."

"But are they safe there with all the wars and unrest going on? Wouldn't Mum even consider coming to live here?"

"Nay, Mary. I don't think they will ever leave. We had a long talk and she feels that life will improve eventually for them. She said there are more and more 'non-conformists' everyday and soon they would make their presence known. I do not believe she or ye father will ever leave England so one day we will have to just take a trip back to see them in England.."

"Oh Henry, do ye mean it? Will we return with ye on a trip back home?"

"Aye, Mary. Ye Mum and family want to see Henry, Jr. and once I feel it is safe to travel, we will return home for a visit. We need to wait until pirates aren't so rampant on the waters first. I'm sure the English Navy will crack down on them soon."

Alice had been napping in her bedroom and joined Henry and Mary in the parlour. "Why Henry, ye are back. When did ye arrive? Someone should have awakened me. I am so tired of being tired. I'll be glad when I have my energy back. Oh, here I am chatting away...tell me about ye trip."

"First, tell me about ye illness," Henry replied. "When did this happen?"

"Oh, I just took a fall and they have been all over me about taking medicine and such. I tell ye, it's enough to make a person feel old."

"Now Alice, ye know it wasn't just a fall," Mary retorted and she continued to fill Henry in on all that had transpired in the past three weeks.

Henry's face revealed astonishment as Mary related the events. "I shouldn't have gone to England, ye have been through quite an ordeal."

"Nay, Henry, Alice exclaimed. Ye needed to go and Mary handled everything perfectly. Ye'd have been proud of her."

Henry replied quickly, "Aye, Alice, I'm always extremely proud of Mary," and he gave her a gentle hug. Then he looked seriously at Alice. "Now ye know Alice, I'm a doctor and this heart condition should not be taken lightly. I have a similar condition and ye know I take my medicine daily. Ye need to follow Dr. Holloway's instructions. It sounds like ye've had ye hands full putting out the fire and I feel guilty about leaving . Did ye loose the whole crop?"

"I'm afraid so, Henry. I don't know what I'm going to do. With Henry's death and all, I was only able to produce one crop this year and loosing it just about wiped me out. I don't know how I'll manage to keep this plantation going."

"Well, we'll work on a plan for later. Now the best thing ye can do is get well. We're here to help and I don't want any argument about it. We need the opportunity to repay ye for all your assistance when we first settled here and for taking such good care of my Mary while I was away."

"I guess it's time that I accept ye help, Henry. I don't seem to be moving around as well these days. Now that's enough about talk about my troubles, tell us the news from England. What is King Charles up to these days?"

Henry related the news from England, before they knew it dusk settled over the land and Anne had a nice supper prepared for them.

CHAPTER TWENTY-ONE

February, 1640, Plantation Creek, Eastern Shore, Virginia

Mary Patenden was perplexed. She needed to go outside to attend to her daily chores but she had a problem. There was a strange Indian standing at her front door. After a year and a half, Mary had become use to seeing the Indians around and had, on occasion, even been by her husband's side when he traded with one but she never really stopped fearing them.

Up until today, she managed to avoid personal contact with the Indians by having Marie, Henry and Mary's new cook, give them food whenever they came to their door and the Indians would usually go away afterwards. If that didn't work, then she'd have one of their indentured men tell them to leave. However, today was a problem. Marie had given the Indian food and he had taken it graciously and left for the nearby woods but he returned a few minutes later and was now standing at the locked front door. Mary, Henry, Jr. and Marie were the only ones in the house and she could not depend on any of the men to shoo him away since Henry had gone to assist Alice and all their indentured servants were now in the tobacco fields.

Mary peered out the small front window at the tall, proud Indian. He'd been standing quietly in the same position at their front door for almost a half hour. He appeared to be in his twenties. His face and upper body was painted with red and yellow dye and he had two eagle feathers in his long braided hair. Tattoos with intricate designs covered his arms and small shells, bones and beads dangled from his pierced nose and ears. A large round disk was draped around his neck hanging from a beaded chain. He was scantily dressed with a breech-cloth. Occasionally, he glanced back toward to woods with a worried expression on his face. Mary looked in the same direction but did not see any other Indians in the vicinity but she could never be sure since she had been surprised by their sudden appearance before. The Indian stood at her door for another ten or fifteen minutes, then headed back to the woods and Mary breathed a sigh of relief.

Hopefully, he's left for good this time but I believe I'll wait a while before venturing out.

She looked back at Henry, Jr. playing on the wooden floor with a hickory nut. Most of the houses had sand floors but Henry insisted that Ambrose build them a proper wooden floor. He said it was healthier to have a wooden floor. The walnut rolled under the table where Marie was busily pounding bread dough. He squealed with delight when she tossed it back to him.

Marie, a tall slim woman with graying hair was a godsend to Mary. She appreciated having another woman in the household with her. Henry was so thoughtful to bring Marie back with him as their indentured servant. Marie was a fantastic cook and wonderful help with Henry, Jr. Her husband and both of her children died from typhoid fever in England and Marie said she just had to get away from the bad memories so she indentured herself to Henry's family for seven years in order to obtain passage. Mary looked back out the window and didn't see the Indian anywhere.

I wonder if he's still lurking out there in the woods waiting for someone to come out....he came back before... but I really need to take care of my chores....Oh well just to be safe, I think I'll do a little sewing before I feed the chickens and tend the garden. I'm really such a baby when it comes to dealing with Indians...I'll just catch up on me sewing though for a while and give him a little time to make sure he is gone for good. Now where did I put my sewing basket?

Seeing Mary search for her basket, Marie inquired, "Did ye think he left for good, Mam?"

"I believe so," Mary replied, "but I'm going to wait a while to be sure. I wish I could just accept the Indians around us. Henry tells me over and over again that they are friendly but I guess I've heard too many stories to the contrary before we moved here, and I just can't seem to get over my fear of them."

"They've always seemed nice enough when I give them food, But it could be because of the food," Marie laughed.

"Aye, I agree. I know I will have to face my fears someday but I just hope its not today," Mary declared as she retrieved her basket from a shelf over the table.

"Well, I'm afraid it may be today," Marie said with a frightened look on her face while she stared at the small window in the room.

"NAY! NAY!" Mary screamed when she glanced toward the window and saw an Indian's face peering in the window inquisitively. Startled by her scream, the Indian jumped back and moved away from the house.

"Oh what are we to do, Marie? What can he want? I wish Henry was here."

"I think the only thing we can do is ask him, Mam." Marie replied softly.

"But how am I supposed to do that if I can't speak his language?" Mary retorted a little too sharply. "I'm sorry, Marie, I didn't mean to sound so harsh. I guess I'm just unnerved by the situation."

"Well, anyone would be. Mayhaps, I can give him more food and try some hand signs like the men do. I watched them and believe I know a few."

"Oh, Marie, I can't depend on ye for everything. I must learn how to deal with the Indians too. We'll try to see what we can find out together. Wait and let me put little Henry in his crib whilst we both try."

"Dear God, please help me, I really need ye now," Mary prayed as she lifted Henry, Jr. from the floor.

Mary took a sharp knife from a rack near the fire and carefully, drew back the iron bar across the door. She and Marie stepped out uneasily to face the Indian.

When the two women appeared on the porch, the Indian moved further away and began motioning for them to follow him. His countenance did not seem threatening but neither moved from the doorstep.

"Why can he possibly want us to follow him to the woods?" Mary said anxiously.

"I don't know Mam but I think we'd both best stay right here."

"I agree, Marie. Let's wait and see what he does next. There may be more Indians out in the woods."

The Indian realized the women wouldn't follow him and ran off among the trees again.

Perplexed, the two women waited a few minutes to see if he would return, then they heard a muffled cry and the Indian appeared carrying something in his arms. As he drew nearer, they were shocked to see it was a small newborn baby.

Forgetting her fear, Mary sped toward the Indian and held out her arms. He gave her a concerned look and with some hesitation, relinquished the infant in her waiting arms then to her astonishment sprinted toward the woods. Mary looked at Marie and asked, "I wonder what happened to this baby's Mum?"

"Ye don't have to wait long to find out, Mam. Here he comes again and I believe he has the Mum in his arms."

Mary turned to see the Indian racing toward them carrying a small limp figure in his arms.

"Something must be wrong, Marie. Here take the bairn and I'll have him take the Mum to my bed."

"Oh, Mam, are ye sure that ye want to do that? After all, they are Indians. Do ye want them in the house?"

"Why, of course, Marie. Something is clearly wrong with her or he would not bring her here."

Mary motioned the Indian into the house toward the bed. When he entered, Mary immediately saw the problem. The listless mother was bleeding profusely and obviously in danger of bleeding to death. "Quick, Marie, lay the infant down beside his Mum and give me those cloths by my sewing. We must stop her bleeding at once."

Oh what would Henry do..think..bleeding...Yarrow..that's it!

"Marie, cut some of those yarrow leaves in my garden. We need some large ones and we need to make a tea."

Marie had to move around the tall Indian standing with quiet dignity in the middle of the room as she ran out the front door. Mary used the cloths to try and stop the flow of blood from the young Indian maiden and glanced over at the infant beside her. She realized that the baby was not making much noise so she rushed over and began to clear out the mucus in his mouth and nose with a cloth. In a couple of minutes, the infant began squalling loudly and Mary was startled by the Indian behind her when he clapped his hands and laughed with joy. She couldn't help herself and laughed as well but quickly turned her attention again to the unresponsive mother.

When Marie returned with the yarrow leaves, Mary pressed them between the young mother's legs and told Marie how to prepare the tea. The leaves quickly became soaked with blood and did not seem to be stopping the bleeding. Mary realized that the young mother was no longer making any sounds and she checked her pulse. It was very faint.

Oh Henry, I wish ye were here. Ye would know what to do.

She again checked the pulse of the young woman but this time, she found none. Mary turned and looked at the Indian behind her and with a grim face, shook her head. His face contorted with anguish when the reality of the situation hit him.

He pointed to the infant and gestured toward Mary then grabbed his left index finger and moved it left and right. Mary looked at him inquisitively, trying to understand. Seeing her confusion, he tried again by pointing at the baby, grasping both his arms as if holding a child and then pointing to her.

Mary realized that he wanted her to keep the child and said "Nay, Nay!" shaking her head.

The Indian tried again with the same signs but also extended right hand and swept it toward his face, then placed his hands on the side of his head as if he was combing his hair.

Mary struggled to understand but did not know what he meant. Finally, he gave up trying to communicate and looked lovingly down at the small dark haired woman lying on the bed. He gently picked her up with tears in his eyes and darted out the door.

"Where is he going Marie?" Mary pondered. "He can't leave this bairn with us."

"If I understood him, correctly, I think he meant he was going to bring back another woman," replied Marie.

"I hope so," said Mary. She turned to the small dark haired child lying on the bed who was now crying loudly. "I'm sure the poor thing must be hungry. I guess there is nothing to do but feed him."

"Ye are not going to let him suckle?"

"What else do ye propose I do? I have plenty of milk for this bairn since Henry Jr. is almost weaned now. I don't intend to let this little one starve when I can do something about it."

"But he's an Indian bairn," Marie said.

"Aye, I'm aware of that but that doesn't negate the fact that he's hungry and I intend to take care of him as long as he's here. If ye're correct about the signs; he'll be back soon for him."

"But what if I'm wrong about what he meant? Mayhaps he doesn't come back? What will Mr. Pattenden think of having an Indian bairn in the house?"

"Then he and I will decide what to do then. Right now this wee one needs food and I can provide it. First, let's clean him up. His poor Mum was so beautiful, wasn't she, Marie?" said Mary as she picked up the young infant and laid him on the table to wash. "I wish I could have helped her. If Henry had been here, I'm sure she wouldn't have died."

"I think ye did very well, Mam. I don't think ye husband could have taken care of her any better. She just lost too much blood and was barely alive when that Indian brought her to us."

"I guess ye are right," Mary responded. "This bairn is beautiful too. Look at those dark eyes. Oh what a difficult time ye have ahead of ye little one. I wish I could have saved ye mum. Marie, could ye hand me that small quilt in the stack by the fire? I'll wrap him in it then we'll see about feeding him."

Marie handed the quilt to Mary and she swaddled the screaming infant in the quilt and sat down in a chair by the fire to nurse him while Marie freshen the bed with new straw. In short order the house looked as if nothing out of the ordinary had transpired except for the Indian infant lying in a quilt on the bed.

No longer frightened by the Indian's presence, Mary went outside and completed her daily chores before her husband returned at noon.

The wonderful smells emanating from Marie's cooking drew Henry in the house with a smile on his face and he searched around the pleasant parlour for Mary and Henry, Jr. Mary was knitting while little Henry stacked wooden blocks on the floor and Henry walked over to give Mary a peck on her cheek.

She grows more beautiful everyday. Oh how lucky I am to have such a wonderful woman by my side.

"Aye, Mary, what a wonderful day it has been!" Henry

exclaimed. Willson was right about the climate here. It couldn't be better. I think we'll be able to have three crops this year if the weather continues like it has."

"That's great, Henry! I just wish my family would come and join us and then everything would be perfect."

"Mayhaps, they will in time, Mary. We won't give up hope. Now those breathtaking food smells are driving me crazy. I'm famished. Come join me at the table," he said as he sat down.

"Wait, Henry....first I have something to tell ye....we had some visitors today."

Henry sat with an astonished look on his face as she unfolded the day's events. Then she led him to the bed where the small infant quietly slept.

"Why, Mary, I'm so proud of ye," Henry whispered softly. "Ye have been through quite a trial, especially considering ye're fear I of Indians. What made ye overcome ye're fear?"

"I guess it was the bairn, Henry. I didn't stop to think when I saw the poor wee one carried by his father. I knew he needed help."

"Mary, ye never cease to surprise me. I know life has been hard here but each day ye become stronger. I felt guilty about bringing ye to such a barren land and away from family yet I don't know how I'd manage without ye near."

"I admit...I do miss my family quite a bit but my life is with ye, Henry. We're creating a new path in this great land together...that's what my father told me before we left and I believe it more everyday. I know they are praying for us and I feel their strength....I just wish they would come and join us someday."

"I do too, Mary, I do too," Henry responded as he drew her close to him with a passionate embrace.

Three days later, Mary was spinning and singing to John, Jr. when Marie called, "Miss Mary, you need to come out and see this."

Mary jumped up and ran to the door. A small assemblage of Indians, with one elderly, a young women, a young men and children were heading toward their house. All were carrying something in their arms. Leading the group, she recognized the

Indian father of the infant in the house. He approached Mary and placed his right closed hand across his left wrist, palm side up, as if he was holding a baby.

Mary smiled and went to retrieve the infant. "I knew you would come back," Mary said shyly....as she handed the infant to him. "Ye have a fine son."

Then the Indian said something to his group and they carried beaver pelts, otter pelts, corn and hops to Mary and set them down beside her.

Mary thanked them for their gifts and the Indians departed. As she watched them depart, Mary said, "Marie, I think I'm over my fear of Indians."

"Aye, Miss Mary," Marie exclaimed. "I think ye are at that."

CHAPTER TWENTY-TWO

June 1640, Plantation Creek, Eastern Shore, Virginia

Days went by quickly for Mary. It seemed there was always something requiring her attention. Her daily life soon developed into a never-ending routine of completing the chores necessary for running a plantation. Henry worked in the fields from dawn to dusk and except for the occasional visits from Indians, few people found time for visiting.

After Mary's episode with the infant, Indians became frequent visitors at the plantation to trade or sometimes just to bring gifts and Mary was thankful that her experience with the Indian infant decreased her fear of them. She was now able to carry on trade with ease, thus freeing her husband of the task.

Henry told her that the tribe's name was Accawmacke which meant "from the other side of the water." The Accawmackes had once been close neighbors to Mary and Henry's plantation. They previously resided on the south side of Old Plantation Creek and had always been staunch friends with the settlers who arrived on the Eastern Shore but as more and more settlers arrived, the Accawmackes sold them land on Plantation Creek and moved further north on the eastern shore.

Mary was grateful for the companionship and assistance of their indentured servant, Marie, but today she wanted more than assistance, she needed to talk with a friend and decided to visit her nearest neighbor, Jane. Marie was busy outside dipping candles and Mary had been confined indoors all morning with Henry, Jr. to keep him away from the fire. There was just too much danger for him around the candle-making process. She dropped her son's britches that she had been mending in her lap and spoke to him as he played with his blocks on the floor.

"Henry, Jr., we need to visit Jane this afternoon, don't we?"

Henry, Jr., seeing his mother's cheerfulness, clapped his hands with glee.

Mary stood up and collected items, starting with the most important, her spinning wheel. Then she stepped outdoors to tell Marie of her plans. Marie was standing over two long lines of cooling candles hanging on parallel poles, sweat was dripping from her brow and she wiped it with her apron.

"Marie," Mary called to her. "I don't want to interrupt ye work but Henry, Jr. and I are going for a short visit with Jane this afternoon. We'll be leaving shortly."

"Fine, Mam, that's a good idea. Henry, Jr. will enjoy getting outside on such a fine day. I'll be glad to saddle ye horse. These candles need to cool a bit before I dip them again....and it would be nice to get away from this hot fire."

"Thank ye Marie. I didna want to leave Henry, Jr. while I saddled Rascal. Just bring him to the post after ye finish and I can handle everything from here."

Mary reflected on what Henry said when he brought Rascal home. Henry had been strangely silent for months after Sarah's suicide and shortly after their own house was built. He took a short trip to a neighbor's house and returned leading the big black horse. She recalled his words of explanation; "Mary," Henry said, "I know living here ye' ll have days when ye need womanly companionship and I didna want ye to lack transportation. Ye needn't ever ask.....but whenever ye want to visit another neighbor.... just feel free to do so. I didna want ye to ever feel alone."

Horses were rare on the Eastern Shore and they could scarcely afford the extravagance of owning one solely for her transportation. Mary was still overwhelmed by Henry's generosity.

She moved the items she intended to carry with her to the door then stood and watched Marie lead the big lumbering horse toward the house. She smiled to herself when she recalled how the horse received his name. Since Henry did not have a pen built before he brought the horse home, he simply tied Rascal to a tree. However, an hour later, the horse was found munching happily in Mary's vegetable and herb garden. She immediately dubbed him Rascal.

As Marie drew near, Mary shouted, "I didna know what I would do without ye Marie. Thank ye so much and remember to

162

take a break now and then. We'll be gone all afternoon so ye will have the house to yeself. The meal is prepared for the men. Ye just have to serve it."

"Thank ye Mam, I can handle everything. Ye and Henry, Jr. have a good time visiting."

Mary mounted the horse with Henry, Jr. and they rode off on their short ride to William Berriman's plantation, where Jane Bevis was residing.

Jane Bevis was the daughter of Alice and William Berriman's sister. She was a young widow, having lost her husband in England the previous year. On William's last trip to England, he encouraged Jane to return with him to the colonies since she, their mother and William were recently widowed and his widowed sister-in-law lived near by, William suggested that a new environment might help with her grief and he certainly needed assistance in maintaining his household. He thought that they might be able to provide some comfort and assistance to each other in their joint bereavement. Jane agreed to this arrangement and upon her arrival, William immediately put her in charge of the housekeeping at his large plantation.

A servant greeted Mary at the gate when she arrived and carried the spinning wheel inside for her. Jane was waiting for Mary at the door.

Unlike her mother and brother, Jane was tall and thin with an angular, almost prominent nose. She had soft brown hair and brown eyes and a smile that made everyone welcome but a control that let you know immediately she was in charge. Mary, had even been a little intimidated when she first met Jane but now they had become close friends, particularly since they were close in age.

"Mary, how great to see ye! Jane exclaimed. We were just talking about ye. Ye ears must be burning. Mum came over to visit this morning and now we will all have a nice visit."

"Alice is here?" queried Mary. "I hope we're not intruding on ye time together."

"Nay, nay, Mary," Jane replied. "Ye know ye and Henry, Jr are always welcome."

"Me thinks Henry, Jr. needs a little rest before his visit," laughed Mary. "He kept falling asleep on the way over."

"Aye, then we'll just have to find a place to let him rest.

"Margaret, help Mary take Henry, Jr. to the nursery," Jane directed "I'm sure he'll be more comfortable there,"

"Ye have a nursery?" Mary asked, surprised.

"Aye, William has not made any changes since Sarah's death," Jane replied. "I was waiting for him to make the suggestion but I may have to make the changes anyway. But let's not talk about that...brings back too many bad memories."

"I'm ...I'm sorry," Mary responded. "I didn't mean..."

"Oh Mary, you didn't say anything wrong...I'm just being too sensitive today. Help Mary with Henry. Jr. Margaret. I'll see about some tea and biscuits for our chat and meet ye in the Parlour."

Mary followed Margaret up the stairs and became instantly aware of how nothing had been altered since the fatal day of Sarah's death. All Sarah's beautiful furnishings stilled remained as if she was just away and would return soon. She recalled Henry once saying that William was always very generous to Sarah since he traveled to England so often, William wanted her to lack for nothing while he was gone.

Nice things do not take the place of the one ye love. Nothing replaces them. Oh Sarah, how lonely ye must have been to take ye own life.

Mary realized that Margaret had stopped at a door and was patiently waiting for her to enter with Henry, Jr.

"Aye, Margaret. This will do nicely," Mary said as she lay the now soundly, sleeping Henry, Jr. in a small bed, covered with beautifully embroidered coverlets.

"Don't worry about him waking, Miss Mary," Margaret ensured Mary. "I'm still cleaning upstairs and will be up here for some time. I'll let ye know if he awakens."

"Aye, thank ye Margaret," declared Mary. "I admit it worried me some that he might try to come down those stairs."

"Nay, ye need not worry. I will be up here til he awakens. Have a nice visit with Miss Jane and Miss Alice."

Mary glanced around her again at the beautiful furniture on her way to the parlour.

I'm sure Sarah would have given up all these things if she just had her wee ones and her husband with her. Material things do not mean much when ye cannot share them with loved ones.

Jane was bringing a tea tray into in the Parlour when Mary

joined her. Alice was busily spinning at her spinning wheel.

"Aye, there ye are Mary!" Alice declared. "I heard ye come in. I should have got these lazy bones up to greet ye but I guess I just didna want to move. Tis nice to sit a spell when ye reach me age."

"Tis nice to sit a spell with young bones too, not that I'm intimating ye are old!" Mary exclaimed. "But with Henry, Jr. walking, he keeps me busy chasing after him."

"Walking, ye say. Why seems only yesterday he was born .....how time flies," Alice declared.

"Now Mum, ye need to stop spinning for a bit. This tea won't stay hot for long and the bread is fresh since we had baking day yesterday. We need some refreshment while we have a chance," Jane implored.

"Spect ye're right Jane," Alice responded with a sigh. "We've been at this spinning a while now." She slowed the spinning wheel and tied the thread.

"Mary, what's Henry, Sr. up to lately," queried Alice. "I usually see him once a week but he hasn't been around for at least two weeks."

"Aye, Alice," Mary responded. "I hardly see him meself these days and I have something important to tell him. Henry acquired additional acreage...He and the men are busy clearing it for planting tobacco....ye know how the men are about tobacco planting."

"Aye, tis true. When we first settled here, I use to work alongside Henry in our fields," Alice added. "Henry always called it 'plowing for gold.' I had a time getting him to remember to plant some crops for our food needs....Ah...those were the days," she continued wistfully.

Jane looked curiously at Mary, "Ye said that there was something important ye must tell Henry. No problem with ye're family in England, I hope?"

"Oh, no.....nothing like that," Mary laughed. "I may be speaking too soon but I guess there's no harm in telling ye....just don't tell Henry yet or anyone else for that matter......but...I believe we'll be having another bairn!" she exclaimed with a beaming smile.

"Another wee one! Ah, Mary....how exciting!" Jane clamored.

Alice nearly dropped her cup of tea on hearing the news,

but quickly set it down. She rushed over to Mary and gave her a big hug. "Tis like hearing the news of another grandchild," she said. "How wonderful!"

Jane looked a little dejected on hearing Alice's comment. "I'd give anything to be in ye shoes, Mary....wish Silas and me could have had a grandchild for ye Mum, before he died."

"Oh, Jane, I'm so sorry. I didna meant to upset ye by me comment. I'm always sticking me foot in me mouth," Alice said and put her arms around her daughter consolingly.

"Mum, don't mind me....I'm just too sensitive today,'" she continued. "tomorrow's one year since Silas died and I've just been thinking too much today....when is the wee one due, Mary?"

"Oh Jane, I'm sorry...I guess I've come at a bad time...I didna know." Mary clamored.

"Mary, of course, ye didna," retorted Jane..."and I'm glad ye both came to visit for that very reason. Now, tell us...when's the bairn due?" she continued, a bit too forcefully.

Sensing that Jane wanted to change the subject, Alice joined Jane in her query..."Aye, Mary....tell us...when can we expect my next grandchild?" she said sheepishly, glancing at Jane to check her reaction.

Mary looked at her two good friends and recalling their pain, found it difficult to respond with her good news, but realized the need to change the subject so she forced a smile and replied softly..."As far as I can guess, probably around January."

"January....tis a good way to start another year....with a wee one...we must make a toast to ye and the new bairn," Alice said gaily with a twinkle in her eye and held her teacup in the air.

"Aye," added Jane gleefully and she raised her cup to touch Alice's cup. "To Mary and Henry's new bairn, may he or....should I say, she....arrive in great health and Mary's lying in be an easy time!"

Mary joined in the whimsical mood, raised her cup and said, "I'll definitely drink to that," and clanked her cup against her two friends.

"Jane, we best finish this repast and get back to work soon," said Alice. "Looks like we will have need of more clothes for a wee one."

"Not just yet, Mum. Ye've been working hard all morning

and need a break," Jane lovingly declared. "Speaking of hard work, I guess our Rev. Cotten, won't have to worry about hard work anymore with his recent marriage, fine new house and servants."

"Ye're right about that, Jane," Alice added. "That marriage really surprised me. I just don't know what Anne Graves sees in him....I understand that their new house....Bunbury...I believe has been completed and he recently acquired many servants for it. To my mind, all Rev. Cotten has ever been interested in tis how to acquire money. He's constantly in court, hassling some poor family about the tithes due him...I know he's a man of God and should be supported as such, but that just didna seem right to take from the poor."

"Ye know, my Henry was assigned Anne's guardian after her father died," said Mary. "Anne's such a sweet girl and I know she really missed her father after his death..... mayhaps... since Rev. Cotten is so much older, she feels secure with him."

"Secure, with him....hmmmph....she'll lose all her money, the way he's spending it," retorted Alice.

"Watch what ye say, Mum," Jane said cautiously. "Ye wouldn't want anyone to hear....remember what ye told me about poor Mister Charlton when he called Rev. Cotton "a black rotted rascal and wanted to kick him over the palisades."

"Aye, I remember," Alice said. "Poor Mister Charlton spent three Sabbath's in the stocks asking for Rev. Cotten's forgiveness....Ah what humiliation....the poor man felt....he's never been the same since...no gumption left. But I'd like to see Rev. Cotten put me in the stocks or better yet, dunk me in the pond like they did poor Eve, when she kept talking back to her husband. That was mean of her husband to turn her over to the court. I have a quick mouth too but my sweet husband never complained. God rest his soul...but ye'd never see me asking for forgiveness from the likes of Rev. Cotten. They'd have to drown me first."

"Aye, Mum, please...someone might hear," Jane implored as she glanced toward the door.

"Oh Jane, didna worry....I think Rev. Cotton has more on his mind than the likes of this old lady," Alice retorted. "But I have rattled on too much....I'm guess I'm still mad at him for not allowing Sarah to be buried at the Church. Thank goodness, the court recognized his action for what they were and created a new cemetery where my Henry and Sarah are buried in the high meadow"

"Ye are probably right about having other things on his mind, Alice," Mary added. "Henry was at court recently and said that Rev. Cotten was there making out his will. I understand that he has been feeling poorly...and Henry said he didna look too well when he saw him."

"Ah, well I regret my statements then," said Alice. "Tis not right to talk bad of the ill. I hope it's nothing serious...what with he and Anne having that wee one...no matter how bad a match...a child needs a father....and a wife needs a husband." Then she glanced at Jane. "I've been wondering, Jane. There's quite a few servants cleaning around here today.....do ye have something planned and for that matter... when we William and the men return for dinner? Should we help ye with the meal? I don't want to be in the way...I know what it takes to run this big house."

"Nothing's planned Mum," Jane replied. "This house just needed a good spring cleaning. After Sarah's death, the servants, especially Margaret, took care of the house pretty well but there had not been a real spring cleaning in a while. I asked William and the men to meet in one of the outhouses for dinner today so the servants could give the house a good cleaning. Margaret is taking care of their dinner and William will be back early this evening. He wouldn't miss spending time with ye"

"Aye....Jane, I must say ye are doing a wonderful job but didna neglect yeself. ye needs ye own household," Alice said affectionately. "By the way, I haven't seen that nice John Jackson around lately. I understand that his indenture will be complete this year. Is that right?"

"Oh Mum, ye are so obvious. Aye, John finished his indenture last month and he bought a little acreage. I assume that he's clearing it...not that his business has anything to do with me," Jane added.

"John Jackson," Mary responded, "I think Henry and I know him...Henry introduced a John Jackson to me at church one day...he said they were both traveled on the Abigail when Henry made his first trip to America. I remember John was quite taken with Henry, Jr. and said he'd like to have a son just like Henry, Jr. one day....that makes him a very nice man in my book," Mary continued. "I didna know ye knew him, Jane."

"Well, not too well..." Jane started to respond.

"Hmmph, not too well," Alice interrupted. "Why, I heard the man's made every excuse to come over here whenever he can!"

"Now, Mum....where did ye ever hear such a thing!" retorted Jane emphatically.

"Let's say, I have me sources, Jane," she replied "and leave it at that. Anyway, most important....what do YE think of him, Jane?"

"Mum.....I don't know"....replied Jane bashfully. "Let's talk about something else. My, we need to get back to our spinning...."

As if on cue, Margaret appeared at the door with Henry, Jr. in tow. He was quiet but had a frightened look on his face that quickly diminished once he saw his mother. He released his grip on Margaret's hand and ran to his mother, and attached himself to the side of her dress.

"My Henry Jr., where have ye been? I've missed ye, Mary said as she gave him a big hug."

Alice and Jane requested hugs from Henry, Jr., and he bashfully assented then the ladies returned to their spinning while Henry, Jr. wandered back and forth among the spinning wheels. Jane found some blocks and he began to stack them and laughed when he knocked them over. After a time Henry, Jr. became bored and Alice began humming a tune to distract him.

Mary, said, "I know the words to that song...me Mum use to sing it to me. "Henry, Jr. come sing with me....

    'All around the mulberry bush,
    The monkey chased the weasel..
    The monkey thought twas all in fun..
    (she waited for the spinning wheel to pop then continued)
    POP, goes the weasel.

Henry, Jr. laughed, then started singing with her. Alice and Jane joined in....and another pleasant hour of singing and chatting went by.

Presently, Margaret appeared in the door and said timidly, "Pardon my interruption Miss Jane, but one of ye servants came and I knew ye'd want to know immediately."

"Aye, Margaret, what is it," replied Jane.

"He asked that Miss Mary come home as soon as possible...there's been an accident."

"An accident, what kind of accident...who...", Mary exclaimed.

"I didna know any more than that, Miss Mary," Margaret interrupted. "Just that ye should come home as soon as possible."

"Of course," Mary responded. "Will ye tell someone to saddle me horse....Alice, Jane ...I'm sorry.. but..."

"I've already done that," Miss Alice," Margaret related. "Ye horse will be ready whenever ye are ready,"

"Don't worry, tis probably nothing or he would have given ye more information"....Jane said, trying to reassure Mary.

Alice added. "Just, send someone back with news....we'll pray for ye and that nothing serious has happened."

"Thank ye, both. I'll let ye know as soon as I can. Come on Henry, Jr.," Mary said as she scooped him up in her arms. Margaret followed her carrying Mary's spinning wheel and Mary was soon on her way home.

Oh God, please guide me in whatever I'm about to face...and most of all...if Henry is hurt...keep him safe.

Mary traveled home with their servant as fast as she dared with Henry, Jr. bouncing in the saddle with her.

CHAPTER TWENTY-THREE

June, 1840, Plantation Creek, Eastern Shore, Virginia
All Henry and Mary's servants were clustered around the front of the house when Mary arrived on horseback....no one seemed willing to look her in the eye and Mary's heart was in her throat as she handed Henry, Jr. to the sympathetic hands of Marie.

Oh God, please don't let it be Henry...please God...

Mary rushed into the house and found her husband lying on their table with blood dripping to the floor around him. His eyes were closed but upon hearing her arrival, he opened them and quickly began to reassure her.

"Now Mary, I'm okay, just need a little bandaging and I knew ye'd best know how. I'm sorry I spoiled ye visit love."

"Nonsense, Henry, I should never have left. Now, tell me, what can I do to help."

"Well, it seems my leg is broken and I probably have a few ribs cracked. Do ye remember how to set a leg?"

"Aye, Henry, but what do we do about ye ribs?"

"Not much, I'm afraid....just bind me up....but start with the leg first."

Mary then looked down for the first time at his left leg. She began to tear away at his pants leg and realized that the bone was protruding through the skin....she felt faint for a minute, at the site, but forced herself to regain her composure.

"Henry, I'm not sure I can do this."

"Aye, I know it's bad, Mary but ye can do it....now give me some of that strong whiskey and have Chris help ye."

Marie was at her side in a minute with the whiskey and Henry took a long drink. Chris heard his name mentioned and waited for Mary's direction.

"Chris, ye must hold Henry very still while I try to put the bone back in place," Mary said. "Marie, I'll probably need ye help too. Can ye hold the bottom of his leg still."

Chris and Marie moved in position and Mary said, "Okay, Henry, I'm going to try."

Henry held as still as possible and managed to keep from screaming out as Mary manipulated the bone while Chris and Marie assisted. After the bone was in place, Henry collapsed on the table, apparently in a faint. Mary, quickly, gave orders to the other servants and soon Henry's leg was in splints and tightly wrapped so as to avoid movement.

Then Mary tore open Henry's shirt. There was a huge gash across his chest. Marie was at her fingertips with hot water and Mary deftly cleaned the wound.

What do I use for this wound? I must think....Oh God....help me think....yes...now I know.

Mary rushed over to the cabinet where Henry kept his medicinal supplies and pulled out a jar labeled gum of white popular. With a clean cloth she gently applied the balm to the wound and covered it with a clean cloth.

"Well, that takes care of the wound and leg, I hope, but Henry said we need to bind his ribs. Marie, help me tear this petticoat into strips. Chris and James, do ye think ye can move him to the bed before he awakens. I know he will be more comfortable there."

Chris and James gently lifted Henry off the table and moved him to the bed while Mary and Marie went to work on tearing the strips. Henry, Jr. had been strangely quiet but when he saw his Papa so quiet and being moved to the bed, he began to wail.

"Henry, Jr., Henry, Jr., oh, I'm so sorry....I've been so busy with ye Papa.... come here little one...sit by Mum...everything will be fine."

Henry Jr., toddled over to her side and hid himself in the folds of her petticoats. Mary patted his head occasionally to give him reassurance while she tore the strips.

"How did this happen, Chris?" Mary asked.

"As ye know miss, we were clearing the new acreage today," Chris answered. "We gird the trees so they will die and then we plant below them."

"Aye, Henry told me....but how could he get hurt from girding trees."

"Well, Miss Mary, the reason we gird the trees instead of

172

chopping them down is that most of the trees are four or five feet across....they are too big to chop down....but once in a while we find a smaller tree and Mr. Henry likes to chop them down so the tobacco has more room to grow. "

"Aye, that makes sense. But that still doesn't answer how he got hurt," she said impatiently.

"I'm getting to that," Chris retorted. "Mr. Henry worked hard all day and I guess he be tired. Anyway, he chopped down a small tree but it started to fall before he was ready and he didna get out of the way in time. ...it landed on top of him. We had a time just trying to find him in all them branches and such...it took us about an hour to even reach him."

"Oh Chris, thank God ye did reach him. I didna mean to sound harsh. I'm just upset. I don't know what we'd do without ye."

"I'm sorry Miss Mary. I wish we could've convinced him to stop before he got to tired....Mr. Henry....he's one of the hardest working men I've ever seen. Sometimes, he has a hard time catching his breath but he keeps on working. I know he was just tired or this wouldn't have happened."

"Aye," James added. "We've been worried about him for some time....he sure does work hard.....not that we're complaining...just worried about him....he always treats us right."

"Thank ye gentlemen for telling me this," said Mary. "I know it wasn't easy. Could I ask ye to do one more thing?"

"Anything, Miss Mary."

"I need to bind his ribs tightly with these strips and I'd like to do it before he awakens if possible so we don't cause him so much pain. Could ye lift him while I slide these strips under him? Then I'll tie them in the front."

"Sure, Miss Mary."

Chris and James gently lifted Henry as if he was a child and Mary slid the strips of cloth under him as quickly as she could, then the men lowered Henry to bed. She tied the strips as tightly as she could around his chest.

"If that's all mam, Chris and I we go fetch the tools. We left them in a hurry to get Mr. Henry home," James said.

"Aye, I appreciate ye consideration for me husband. Oh,.....I forgot...could ye send a message to William Berriman's house about what happened to Henry? I promised I'd let them know immediately. Please reassure them that he seems to be okay right now....I wish Dr. Holloway would come to check him though....I would feel much better."

"Aye, Mam. Chris can get Dr. Holloway for ye and stop by Mr. Berriman's too. I can see to the tools...just let us know if ye need anything else."

"Nay, I think that will be enough for now. Thank ye both for ye help. I'm so glad ye were with him today."

Henry, Jr. started to cry again when the men left. Mary picked him up and gave him a special hug.

"Oh Henry Jr., ye be a good boy now. Ye Papa needs his rest."

"Whhaat...s wrong with Henry, Jr.," said Henry, Sr. as he was aroused by the crying.

"Henry, how do ye feel?" inquired Mary as she handed her child to Marie.

"Like something took a whoopin to me," was his reply. He glanced at his leg in the splints, "Ye seems to have patched me up pretty well."

"I don't know, Henry. We'll see how ye heal. I did my best."

He looked at the colorful blue strips surrounding his chest. "What's this? It looks like I'm in a colorful costume."

"Well, Henry, ye said bind ye up around ye ribs...that's all I knew to do."

"Ye did fine, Mary. I'm proud of ye."

Marie interrupted their discourse, "Miss Mary, I thought I'd feed Henry, Jr. I finished the candles and could take him outside til dusk so Mr. Henry can rest. Would ye and Mr. Henry like something to eat?"

"Aye, I could eat something. What about ye Henry?"

"Nay, thanks Marie. I just want to rest."

"I think that's a good idea," said Mary. "Rest will be best for ye."

Mary followed Marie to the table where her husband had lain a few minutes before and she began to wipe it clean. Then tears of relief began to flow down her face.

Marie seeing the tears, gave Mary a hug. "Thee did great Miss Mary," he'll be okay she whispered so Henry Sr. could not hear.

"Oh, Marie, what if he had died out there today. What would

I do?" whispered Mary.

"He didn't die Miss Mary, and ye knew what to do to help him. Think on that....don't waste ye time of what if's. Mr. Henry needs ye to be strong now."

"Ye are right, Marie, forgive me for being weak with these tears."

"Miss Mary, there's not a weak bone in ye body. Don't ever say that...and everybody needs a good cry sometimes. Now sit down and eat something. Thee need ye strength to take care of the new bairn ye are about to have as well as Mr. Henry," Marie whispered.

"How did ye know?" Mary asked softly.

"I've been around ye enough to know something was making ye sick every morning and just put two and two together. When will it be born?"

"Sometime after Christmas but I haven't told Henry yet so let's keep it between ye and me," Mary whispered.

"Of course Miss Mary, I won't tell anyone....but sit down and eat something. Mr. Henry will probably need ye help after a while.

Mary sat down but found she did not have much taste for food. Her mind was focused on 'what if thoughts' as Marie called them. How would she have ever managed to live in this country alone without Henry?

Oh thank ye God for saving his life. Now please if I can ask just one more favor....please help him heal.

CHAPTER TWENTY-FOUR

June 1640, Plantation Creek, Eastern Shore, Virginia

Henry spent a fitful night in a great deal of pain...but Mary gave him aconite from his medicinal chest and it seemed to help. He even felt like eating a little soup the next morning. Dr. Holloway arrived after he finished eating and Mary was anxious to hear the doctor's opinion.

After examining Henry, Dr. Holloway sat with Mary at the table. "I'm sorry if I worried ye by not coming last night but I was with Mrs. Bayly when Chris found me. She was having a very difficult delivery and Chris described what happened and how ye handled the accident. I felt Henry was in good hands. Ye did a great job on his leg...couldn't have done better myself. Those busted ribs will give Henry some pain for quite a while but ye did a good job binding him. The binding may have loosened some during the night so with Chris and James' assistance, I'll tighten them a little more before I go. Check the bindings daily to keep them tight."

"Is there anything else I missed?" Mary asked. "Am I giving him the right medicine.... and what about that gash on his chest?"

"Mary, ye have taken as good care of Henry as I would have. Ye've learned a lot from Henry. The only thing I can think of is if he has a fever, then I would consider bleeding him but I discussed that with Henry and he said nay...I really don't think there is anything else I can do to help him. He needs to stay off that leg until it heals and rest as much as he can, but he knows that....I'm sorry I can't be more help."

"Dr. Holloway, ye've been a great help just coming out here. Ye're right...I learned a lot from him but I still was not sure I did everything right. Ye've made me feel a lot better."

"Mary, I hope Henry realizes what a jewel ye are...now just keep him off that leg...and continue doing what ye've been doing and I'm sure in time those bones will heal. But if anything changes...send one of ye're men for me. Now, if Chris and James will help me, we can bind up his ribs again."

"Aye, Doctor and here let me get ye a piece of pie and some tea while ye are waiting."

Marie interrupted, "Miss Mary, I can find Chris and James, ye stay with the doctor and have some pie and tea yeself. It was a long night and ye had nothing to eat this morning."

"Thank ye Marie," Mary said...then she fainted and fell on the floor.

Someone's slapping me cheeks and what was that awful smell...Stop slapping me...

"Mary, Mary" wake up Mary."

Mary opened her eyes to see Doctor Holloway and Marie's worried eyes staring down at her.

Concern on Marie's face changed to relief....."Miss Mary are ye okay?" Marie asked.

Mary tried to sit up but Dr. Holloway pressed on her shoulders, preventing her from rising.

"Nay, Mary....not just yet. Ye took a bad fall. Are ye hurt anywhere?' he asked gently.

"Nay," Mary responded. "What happened?"

"Ye are probably just overwrought," he replied. "Marie told me that ye're with child."

"Marie, I wanted to keep the bairn a secret....," Mary said as she gave Marie and accusing look.

"I know Miss Mary but the doctor needed to know to help ye. Please forgive me," Marie pleaded.

"Marie was right to tell me Mary. Women with child often faint and if I didna know this...I would've suspected something else was wrong with ye. Now...let's see if ye can sit up, but do so slowly. We didna want ye to faint again," the doctor declared.

"Fainted...tis that what happened?" Mary asked.

"Tis true Mary, and that indicates that ye may have more difficulty in the months ahead. Ye must take better care of yeself." The doctor continued. "Marie said ye haven't eaten much nor slept since Henry was hurt. Sit down now and eat something and then ye must rest. Marie can see to Henry's needs for a few hours. Ye must get some rest or ye'll lose this wee one."

"But, Henry needs me Doctor."

"The bairn ye're carrying needs ye as well. Now do as I say or ye'll be of no help to Henry or this unborn bairn," he said emphatically.

Tears trickled down Mary's face and Doctor Holloway changed his demeanor and began to speak softly to Mary.

"Ah Mary, I didna mean to sound so harsh. Ye've been under a terrible strain.... here let me help ye to ye feet.....now sit here," he indicated the bench by the table. "Marie, I think Mary should try a little soup first."

"I have it ready, Doctor Holloway." Marie set the bowl of soup in front of Mary. "And I have a piece of pie and tea for ye."

"Thank ye, Marie." he replied.

Mary silently followed the doctor's directions and began to eat her soup without further complaint...her thoughts running wild.

Mum said the women in our family had no trouble with child-bearing. What did she say? Oh, I remember....like cats having kittens....why am I having trouble....and why I am having trouble now when Henry needs me to be strong.....Oh God, please help me.

"Doctor, will I faint again?....and most of all," Mary's voice trembled..."will I lose me bairn?"

"I hope not Mary........all women are different ...but ye must eat and rest whenever ye're able. I know it will be difficult with Henry's injuries but that is all I can tell ye to do. When ye need to move Henry, let Marie or better yet Chris or James help. Ye should not lift him."

"Oh, Doctor, how will I manage all this."

Marie patted Mary's shoulder...."Now Miss Mary, ye are not alone...we'll be here to help."

"Ye're right Marie.....thank goodness ye are here," Mary said as she looked up at her....then continued... "And God will help me too."

"Aye, Aye" Doctor Holloway and Marie replied together.

Henry, Jr. had slept through all the commotion, but awakened and began to call for his Mum.

179

Marie said quickly, "Ye stay here, Miss Mary, I'll see to Henry, Jr."

Mary found she didna have the energy to refuse. "Doctor, will Henry be alright?" she asked.

"Honestly, I cannot answer that Mary," he replied. "I wish I could. Henry had a pretty bad break in his leg and I'm not sure about his ribs. I'll know a little more about his ribs once we bind him again. It just depends on how well he heals."

Marie brought Henry, Jr. into the room and placed him on the bench beside his mother. She spooned some gruel in a bowl for him and set the bowl on the table. "Miss Mary, I'll go find Chris and James now if ye didna need me for anything else so Dr. Holloway can bind up Mr. Henry."

"Thanks Marie. I can take care of Henry, Jr. I'm sure Dr. Holloway needs to be on his way."

"That's true, Marie. I wanted to check on Mrs. Bayly again today."

"Oh, I neglected to ask," Mary said. Did she have a boy or girl? I know they were hoping for a boy....."

"Neither, I'm afraid. The wee one was stillborn. He was a boy though but that is why I wanted to check on her. She is taking it kind of hard....wouldn't talk to anyone. I'm hoping she is better today."

"Stillborn, oh I'm so sorry.....I had hoped she would not have difficulty this time,"

"Aye, I had the same hope...but it was out of our hands to change things. That is why I want ye to be especially careful."

"I will, Doctor Holloway. I'll do as ye say," Mary tried to sound more convinced than she felt.

Chris and James arrived with Marie following. The three men went to the bed where Henry, Sr. was sleeping soundly and Dr. Holloway tapped Henry, Sr. on the shoulder. "Henry, I'm afraid we have to cause ye some more pain...but we need to tighten those bindings."

Mary sat at the table a few minutes and fed Henry, Jr. but Henry Sr's agonizing groans as the men moved him overwhelmed her, and Henry, Jr. began to whimper when he heard his father. She stood and said, "Henry, Jr., let's go see if there be any new baby chicks outside," and hurriedly picked her child up and rushed out the door.

Oh God, forgive me for being so weak and please ease Henry's pain. Please give me strength.....

CHAPTER TWENTY-FIVE

August 1640, Plantation Creek, Eastern Shore, Virginia

The next two months flew by quickly. Mary developed a schedule that helped everyone stay on tract. First, she unwrapped her husband's bandages, check and reapplied balm then Chris and James would arrive. They supported Henry, Sr. while Mary wrapped the bindings tightly around his chest. Each day became less and less painful and Mary was thankful. While they were busy tending to Henry, Sr., Marie began preparation for dinner but she also included tea and biscuits for Chris and James. Mary insisted that the two men receive biscuits before leaving for the tobacco fields.

"After all she exclaimed, ye're coming to the house earlier than normal to help me with Henry....it's the least we can do."

Sometimes the men stayed a few minutes to enjoy some tea and update Henry, Sr. about the tobacco fields and the clearing of the new acreage. Eventually, Henry was able to move around the house with the assistance of a walking stick by holding on to walls and furniture. He could sit at the table and talk face to face with his men and Mary knew this time was valuable to him. He was always happier after their talks and less prone to the melancholy moods he often had after spending so much time in bed.

"Miss Mary, ye know ye're spoiling Chris and me," said James one day as he and Chris were leaving. "Don't know how we'll stand not having a hot biscuit and tea each morning when Mr. Henry's well," he laughed.

"Well, we just might continue... We appreciate all ye do in the fields. Henry said we should have a great harvest this year," she said as she stood in the door watching them leave.

"Tis right, Miss Mary. Things look good right now and Mr. Henry seems to be healing. Well, we best get to the fields...see ye at dinner."

Mary watched the men depart for the fields and stopped to

enjoy the moment. Life was better....the harvest was good, Henry's injuries were healing nicely and she had not had another episode of fainting since that first day. Yet she couldn't shake the uneasy feeling that stayed with her since Henry's accident.

I'm just being silly. Mayhaps it's because I'm with child....I've heard sometimes women with child have strange moods. I'll probably feel better soon....Oh, I still need to tell Henry, about the bairn....I didn't want to tell him while he was feeling so bad and worry him but he needs to know.

She looked back in the house at Henry, Sr. sitting and happily chatting with Marie and decided now would be a good time before Henry, Jr. awakened and Mary became busy with her endless chores. She turned and said.

"Henry, I have something important to tell ye."

Marie, sensing that Mary and Henry needed to be alone stated softly, "Miss Mary, I'll feed the chickens now, before Henry, Jr. wakes up," as she grabbed the pail and headed for the door.

"That would be great, Marie," Mary responded with grateful eyes.

"What is it Mary?....sounds serious!" exclaimed Henry.

"Not serious really....just important and I hope more happy news," she replied. She set beside him on the bench and placed her hand over his hand.

"Henry, we will be having another bairn soon."

Henry burst out laughing. Mary did not expect this reaction and immediately put her head down. "Why do ye think it's so funny? Do ye not want another bairn?"

"Oh Mary, I'm sorry.....of course I want another wee one," he said as he put his arm around her. "I'm just laughing because I've known for over a month that we would be having another bairn...I was just wondering when and how ye would tell me...and ye were so serious...I thought there may have been a problem. I'm laughing because I'm so happy."

"Ye knew....but how? Did Marie or Doctor Holloway tell ye? I told them to not to tell ye." she stammered.

"Nay Mary, no one told me. Ye forget, I'm a doctor too. I know the signs and I know ye. As if ye hadn't noticed, ye have grown a little plump around the belly."

"Oh Henry, do I look that bad?"

"Nay, Nay Mary.... ye're beautiful as always....and even more beautiful with our wee one growing inside ye."

"Then ye are not worried."

"Nay, Mary...why should I be? Are ye having any difficulties? Ye didna have trouble the first time and I thought...."

"Oh nay," Mary quickly responded. "I just didna want to burden ye when ye were injured."

"A wee one is never a burden, Mary. Just as long as ye and the bairn are healthy, that's all I want."

Relieved by her husband's response, Mary rested her head on his shoulder and exclaimed, "Henry, I love ye so much!"

"And I love ye, Mary....I love ye," and he encircled her in his arms."

Henry and Mary remained in this position for a few minutes, both enjoying their shared closeness and the quiet silence of contentment.

They jumped apart when the door opened abruptly and Marie rushed in to exclaim, "Miss Mary, Mr. Henry... I just heard"....she stopped talking a minute to take a breath.

"What Marie...what did ye hear?"

"Why Rev. Cotten, he's gone...he's gone..."

"Gone Marie, what do ye mean gone....where did he go?" stammered Henry.

"Why I mean he died....very quickly they said...one minute he was talking and then he just collapsed and died."

"I didna believe it.........he was a stern man but a Godly one," Henry said. "He will certainly be missed."

"What will happen to poor Anne and their bairn?" Mary added. "They had that new home and so many servants....how will she manage everything herself?"

"Aye, she will need help. Ye know I feel somewhat responsible for her since I was her guardian before she wed Rev. Cotten," Henry stated. "I must see what I can do to assist her."

"Henry, how will ye do that? Mary asked quizzically. "Thee can barely make it around room with ye leg and ribs injured."

"Ye're right....it's so frustrating to be so helpless," he said angrily.

"Well, she does have her servants to assist," Marie said stoically. "I'm sure she will be fine."

Realizing they may have misspoke in front of Marie, Mary quickly countered, "If her servants are anything like ye Marie, I'm sure she will not have any trouble. Now, Henry, I hate to say it...but ye do need rest. Ye've been up all morning and Henry, Jr. will be awake any minute. I think we should help ye back to bed."

"Nay, I didna need help today, Mary. "I've been practicing...watch."

Henry using only his walking stick, slowly, hobbled over to the bed.

Mary squealed with delight. "Henry, that's wonderful!" .

"Mayhaps, I'll be able to get out of this house soon," he said. "Not that I haven't enjoyed being around ye ladies and spending so much time with Henry, Jr. while ye were outside, but if I didna get out of here in a few days, I think I'll go mad."

"Soon...Henry, very soon," Mary smiled. "Now be a good patient a little while longer and rest. Henry, Jr. will be wanting to play with his Papa shortly."

"Aye, Mary....I'll rest for now...but tis mighty hard to be a good patient when I see the two of ye working so hard."

Henry, Jr., hearing his name mentioned said, "Play Papa, Play Papa"

And all three adults in the room laughed.

CHAPTER TWENTY-SIX

August 1640, Eastern Shore, Virginia

Rev. Cotton's funeral took place the last week of August. Henry was still unable to walk very far so Henry, Jr. remained home with him while Mary and their servants attended the funeral. As the shallop left the dock headed for Hungar's church, Mary felt very alone. This was the first time she attended a funeral without Henry by her side. Her thoughts dwelled on the fact that the two people she cared most about, her husband and child were not with her. As she always did, when she felt alone, she instinctively reached up to touch the ribbon in her hair. The ribbon always brought her comfort but this time the comfort was waning.

Oh Papa, I miss ye but I miss my new family too. I need them with me now....God please protect them while I'm away.

The small craft floated toward the dock at Hungar's Church. While Chris tied the shallop to the dock, Mary visually searched for her friends....especially her good friend Alice. She saw William Berriman and Jane in the distance, then the Carsley family.

Elizabeth's girls are growing so tall. I should be ashamed of meself....Elizabeth manages her plantation without her husband...and I'm feeling sorry for meself and I still have Henry. God please forgive me.

She caught a glimpse of Ambrose Dixon, the man who built their house and George Cottingham. It appeared that everyone was in attendance for the funeral...but where was Alice Wilson. She certainly should be here...she'd never miss attending Rev. Cotton's funeral even if she was still upset with him at times.

Mayhaps she's in the church...

"Watch, ye step, Miss Mary," Chris said to her and she realized he had been patiently waiting for her to climb out of the shallop. Chris was always so considerate of her. Mary walked up the well-worn path to Hungar's Church and wondered if she would be able to find a seat. Of course, there was a large attendance since

Rev. Cotton had been the rector.

She climbed the steps to enter the women's door of the church and looked for her friend...but she was no where to be found. Seeing a seat by Alice's daughter, Jane, on the ladies and children's side of the aisle, Mary moved toward it.

"I don't see Alice," she whispered to Jane. "Will she be here?"

"Nay, Mary," replied Jane. "We stopped by to take her with us but she was feeling too poorly and unable to come."

"Oh...I hope tis nothing serious." Mary whispered.

"Me too, she's really felt bad for about a week now....I plan to ask Dr. Holloway to visit her."

"That's probably a good idea....." Mary's voice trailed off as the service began.

The funeral service lasted three hours and was very elaborate so Mary did not return home til early evening. She found a thoroughly exhausted Henry, Sr. and a very hungry Henry, Jr. She sent her husband to bed immediately and prepared to feed Henry, Jr.

"Now Henry, Jr., ye shouldn't have worn ye poor Papa out like that," she fussed good-naturedly as she fed him some gruel. "Ye have enough energy for three boys sometimes."

Henry, Jr. clapped his hands...and started shouting "Papa, Papa, play."

"Nay, Henry, Jr. not now," she laughed. Mary's thoughts returned to Alice.

I really must visit her soon. Mayhaps Henry and I could pay her a visit next week. He is doing so much better. A trip to her house would probably do wonders for him.

After Mary finished feeding Henry, Jr. she set him on the floor to play with his blocks and asked Marie to watch him. She went to the bed chamber to change her clothes. Henry, Sr. was lying with his back toward her but turned over slowly when she walked in the room.

"I'm sorry, I didna mean to disturb ye Henry," Mary said

"Ye never disturb me love, tell me about the funeral. I'm

188

starved for news."

"Oh, it was something to behold. It was a very pompous affair.....ye'd have thought it was King Charles' funeral."

"That elaborate, huh."

"Well, almost...considering we're in the colonies....but I guess it would be elaborate since he was the rector. I heard he made all the funeral arrangements himself two years ago."

"How were Anne and the daughter holding up?"

"Anne seemed fine. Their daughter Verlinda is a beautiful child, very well-behaved."

"I don't imagine Rev. Cotton allowed for much misbaviour in his children."

"I looked for Alice but she didna go to the funeral. Jane said that she was feeling too poorly. I need to visit her soon....but I have some good news...Jane and John Jackson are to be married."

"Well, that is good news....I'm sure William will miss her though."

"Do ye believe William will ever marry again, Henry?"

"That's hard to say....I know he's still not over Sarah's death.....particularly, the way she died. He blames himself and guilt can eat a man alive. Until he can come to terms with that....then I don't think he will consider another marriage."

"Tis such a shame...William deserves better. I have some more news.....good news."

"What's that, love,"

"It seems, we won't have to wait long for a new rector. Rev. Cotton's replacement will be arriving next week."

"Aye, that is good news..."

"His name is Rev. John Rozier, and rumor is that he is a non-conformist."

"Non-conformist? I wish I'd been able to attend church when the discussions were being conducted...this bum leg," Henry scowled and hit his leg with his fist...."I'd like to know more about him."

"I know, Henry. But ye should just be thankful ye accident wasn't worse," Mary replied with tears in her eyes.

"Ye are right Mary...I shouldn't complain...tis hard to sit in this house day after day...useless to anyone."

"I've been thinking about that Henry...why don't I ask Chris and James to help ye outside tomorrow.....ye always said that ye wanted to make some new tools and furniture but never had the time before. Since ye kin move around some with that walking stick then mayhaps we could put the bench under a tree by the tool shed. Ye could sit and whittle some at least and rest on the bench....when ye became tired...at least ye'd be outside."

"Mary, that's a great idea....staying indoors....at least, I'll not feel so useless...I was dreading another day indoors and this infernal bed."

"Henry, ye are never useless....just being here...when I think about what might have happened to ye...." Mary stammered. "Ye shouldn't complain."

"Ye're right, Mary,.....but ye're working so hard and all I ever do is rest...I become so frustrated at times."

Henry looked at his beautiful wife. Mary had removed her rochet and begun brushing her long dark hair. She was standing with her back to him but her image was reflected in the old cracked looking-glass they had brought with them years ago and he could see her deep-set gray eyes...misty from the tears she was trying so desperately to control and a desire to be near her came over him.

"Come here, love," Henry said as he patted the bed...."I'm here with ye, ye're safe and I'm feeling better...mayhaps we could find another use for this bed that doesn't involve resting."

Mary turned around and laughed, then fell into his waiting arms....

CHAPTER TWENTY-SEVEN

September, 1640, Plantation Creek, Eastern Shore, Virginia
Henry Pattenden, Sr. was feeling much better by the first week in September. He was still unable to work in his tobacco fields but Chris and James seemed to be managing fine for now. They had even girded the trees on a quarter of the new acreage without his assistance. Now that Henry was able to move around a bit....he was enjoying the days making and repairing tools outdoors and he reflected on his good fortune while he worked.

Chris and James are certainly good men.... I hate to lose them when their indentures are over. 'Spect I could get some more indentures .... it takes time to train new men.... I should have kept one or two from my last trip to England...but then again...we needed the money from selling their indentures to plant this year's crop....and what a bountiful crop it is....it should fetch a fair price.

Henry looked around at his growing plantation and beamed with pride. He now had four additional out buildings plus his house sprawling about the landscape. Henry smiled to himself when he recalled how happy Mary was when the out building for tools was built.

"Finally, the tools will be out of me buttery!" she exclaimed. As if hearing his thoughts about her, Mary appeared at the corner of tool shed.

"Why Henry," Mary said as she looked inside the small waddle and taub cabin at his handiwork. "Thee have been quite busy...I never saw so many tools! But didna ye plan to make some additional furniture, too?"

"Aye Mary.... that was me plan.....but then I thought, ye deserve better furniture than I might build and since we should do well on selling our next crop of tobacco......we will be able to buy furniture in England on our next shipment."

"Oh Henry, how wonderful! Ye're too good to me!" she exclaimed.

191

"Nothing's too good for ye, love," he replied enthusiastically. "But what brings ye out here...it's too early for me to stop working...I feel fine today."

Henry's injuries were healing but he still had not regained his stamina and Mary encouraged him to take a nap each day after dinner.

Mary smiled, "Tis true...ye are better Henry...I just received some good news and thought ye might want to hear. Agnis, Elizabeth Carsley's daughter dropped by for a short visit with me...she's really a beautiful girl.....anyway she said that Jane and John Jackson are to be married this Saturday when we have the welcoming meal for our new Rector."

"Well that is good news....but I thought they planned to wait until John's house was built."

"Aye, Agnis said that they just didn't want to wait any longer and Alice said they could live with her until his house was completed. Alice is still feeling poorly and Agnis felt she really wanted their company so Jane readily agreed. Jane's been worried about her mother. John and Jane decided Saturday would be a good day to wed since most of the neighbors will be at the church anyway."

"That makes sense but I know William will miss Jane. She has done a great job of taking care of his household. I'm looking forward to seeing everyone Saturday."

"Ye plan to attend?" Mary asked. "Are ye feeling that much better?"

"Aye, Mary...it will do me good to see all our friends again...I may limp around a bit...but I'm fine, thanks to ye fine doctoring."

"Oh Henry, that's great news...I was dreading having to attend another meeting without ye."

"And I was not looking forward to another day here without ye around, Mary," he responded. "I may not be able to dance with ye anytime soon," he added, "but at least I can walk again."

"Thee didna have to ever dance with me again," Mary responded affectionately. "But ye must promise to always be with me," she said.

At that, Henry hobbled over to her and took her in his arms... "Mary," he said, "I promise to always be with ye from this day forward." Then he gave her a kiss that erased away all her

192

doubts.

On Saturday, the Pattenden family and their servants, decked out in their finest, were on Henry's shallop meandering among the small islands on Plantation Creek as they headed for Hungar's church. Around them, various shades of red, orange, brown, and yellow sparkled in the forests as if someone had dropped paint over the land. A brisk wind rustled the brown marsh grasses and small animals could be seen scurrying on the ground and in the trees. Whiffs of hickory, walnut, and pine scent from the many trees, mingled with the pungent perfume of wild flowers, tickled the silent passengers' nostrils. Occasionally, Indians were seen on the banks of Plantation Creek, evidently curious about the gala taking place at Hungar's church.

Seeing the Indians, Mary reflected on the Indian bairn she had nursed for three days.

I wonder if I will ever see ye again wee one.

Henry scanned the people on the bank near the church and asked, "Mary, isn't that Alice on the hill by the church?"

"Aye, Henry, I believe it is. I'm happy to see her here." Mary answered gleefully, "I was worried she may not be able to attend since she was feeling so poorly."

As Henry's family disembarked, they heard a loud agitated voice rise from a cluster of men talking near the bank of Plantation Creek.

"Sounds like Scarburgh's voicing his objections to Indians again. Wonder what's got him so riled this time?" Henry declared.

"Aye, he sure hates Indians, sir," Chris commented.

As Henry, Sr. and Mary tread up the well-worn path on the river bank, Edmund Scarburgh's words were easily distinguished as he bellowed.

"We need to kill the whole lot of them! I lost two beeves and a horse last week! They're nothing but thievin savages...and should be driven away from descent society," Scarburgh shouted.

Ambrose Dixon, George Cottingham and Henry Weede were standing in the group of men.

George Cottingham said, "We're gladly help ye retrieve the stock. I've just acquired some acreage and stock of me own...and don't relish the idea of thievin Indians."

The other men nodded in agreement.

Henry, Sr. joined the group and interjected, "Aye, George no one wants to lose stock but Edmund ye might fence the stock in as I have instead of letting them roam free. I believe the Indians think that stock roaming free is theirs for the taking just like the wild animals."

"Why, Henry...good to see ye up and around but maybe the accident affected ye thinking".....Edmund retorted. "I'm not wasting valuable planting time fencing in me stock...besides it takes additional time to feed fenced stock, ye know that. Tis better for stock to roam free and find their own feed. Money's in tobacco, not stock."

"Thee have a point," Ambrose Dixon declared.

"Seems to me tis time wasted hunting stock and fighting Indians," Henry countered.

Sensing her husband's desire to converse with the men, Mary continued along the path toward Alice Wilson with Henry, Jr. in tow.

"Tis great to see ye today, Alice," Mary said when she reached the top of the hill. "I was concerned about ye when ye missed the funeral."

"Aye, Mary, I have been a mite poorly," Alice said as she patted Henry, Jr.'s head and continued, "Dr. Holloway came by last week and told me to get out more...said I was still grieving too much over Henry...seems to have helped because I'm better today. Who wouldn't be better though on their daughter's wedding day? Doesn't she look beautiful? Even if it is her second wedding, she's still beautiful."

Mary grazed in the direction Alice was looking at Jane standing tall and thin as ever, dressed in many petticoats with a dark blue bodice laced tightly around her waist. Her outer petticoat was fashionably drawn up to her waist on either side, and the hem was lined with dark blue ruffles. She wore a matching bonnet on her head.

"She is beautiful Alice. I know ye are happy for her. John Jackson is a lucky man to have her for his wife. I understand that they will be living with ye for a while."

"That's true, Mary. Jane has been worried about me and I admit I wouldn't mind the company on me bad days...but tis just til

194

their house is built."

"Do ye still take the foxglove Henry sent to ye?"

"When I remember to," Alice laughed. "But today's not a day to talk about me....How is Henry? I saw him climb the bank. He seems to be walking pretty well."

"Aye, he's walking better...just tires easily....Stop that Henry, Jr." Mary admonished her son as he tried to pull away from her grasp.

"Well, I have a favor to ask him and didn't want to bother Henry when he was still recovering...but if he has a chance I'd like him to drop by someday and help me with my will."

"What's this talk of a will? I thought ye were feeling better."

"Aye, Mary, I am but ye never know at me age....it's just since Jane was the only daughter not married...I wanted her to have something and I left my house to her while she was a widow. Now that she is married...I want to be fair to all me children and make some changes."

"I understand, Alice but let's not hear any more talk of wills now. Ye will be around for a long time and this is a day of joy. Have ye met Rev. Rozier?"

"He visited me last week, can ye believe that? Rev. Cotton never came calling when I was poorly. But he scared poor Anne to death when this strange, good-looking man shows up at me door," Alice laughed. "He seems to be a very personable man......had me laughing at his jokes. Ye need to meet him...he was here a moment ago. Ah....there he is...yonder on the hill..."

Mary glanced in the direction Alice was pointing. The Rector seemed to be deeply engrossed in conversation with their new neighbor, John Custis and a stranger. "We'll wait till later, Alice. He's busy now but who is that man standing by Rev. Rozier?"

Alice replied, "Aye, that must be Nataniel Eaton....Rev. Rozier said that he had hired a vestry clerk but I never met him. Rev. Rozier said that Mr. Eaton had been the master of Harvard College...I wonder why he left such a prestigious position to come here?"

"That is strange but it sounds like he is very qualified for the office of vestry."

"Aye, and Rev. Rozier tis a far cry from that stern and pompous Rev. Cotton, God rest his soul," Alice added.

"Have ye seen Anne Cotton? I meant to visit her this week and offer my condolences but with Henry's situation....I never seemed to find time."

"She was here early today to welcome Rev. Rozier but left soon after...I'm sure she's still pretty upset over her husband's death."

"Well it certainly seems we will be in for a change with Rev. Rozier," Mary declared.

People began entering the church for the wedding and the two ladies followed with Henry, Jr. leading the way. Mary glanced back at her husband who was still deeply engrossed in conversation. She thought about calling to him but decided against it.

He needs this time after all those days of recovery...even if he misses the wedding.

She turned back toward the church with Edmund Scarburgh's loud voice bellowing across the church yard. "I tell ye now the only good Indian is a dead Indian.....we need to get rid of them all!"

CHAPTER TWENTY-EIGHT

September, 1640 Plantation Creek, Eastern Shore, Virginia

Storm clouds moved in the day after Jane and John Jackson's wedding. Brisk winds, thunder, lighting and hard rain pelted the area for three days making much outdoor work impossible. On the third night of the raging storm, Henry, Sr. sat at the table working on his accounts. A candle on the table flickered whenever a strong gust of wind blew against the house.

Mary was busy spinning by firelight as she usually did every evening. The whrr..., click and pop of the spinning wheel mesmerized Henry, Jr. and he had fallen asleep and was lying on a quilt by the fireplace.

Mary interrupted the silence with a question, "Henry, what do ye think of our new rector Rev Rozier and his new vestry clerk? I saw ye talking with him after the wedding."

Henry looked up at Mary and answered, "Rev. Rozier seem to be a very affable man Mary, and from what I understand tolerant of non-conformists views...which I am happy to see...as for Eaton, I didna find out much about him...there is a hint of some trouble at Harvard before he left, Rev. Rozier hired him to provide some assistance. Eaton still has a wife in Massachusetts and needed funds to send for her. Eaton seems friendly enough according to Dixon and Cottingham. They shared a pint of ale with him last week shortly after he arrived."

"I wonder why Eaton left his wife behind Henry?" Mary asked.

"Seems strange to me as well. I'd like to find out more about him, but I guess that is Rev. Rozier's business. I saw ye talking a good while with Alice. Is she feeling better?"

"She seemed in good spirits but I'm still a little worried about her. Did I mention that she wanted ye to visit her one day soon? She said she needed ye help in changing her will."

"Changes in her will? Why would she be worrying about her

will? Since she was at the wedding, I assumed she was better."

"Aye, I agree...the talk of her will worries me some but mayhaps she would just like a visit from ye. I know she always enjoyed talking over her accounts with ye."

"Well, I'll try to visit her one day next week...I've been looking at our accounts, Mary and if the harvest goes as well as planned, we could add some additions to the house and order more furniture after our next shipment of tobacco....so ye need to think about items ye need."

"Oh Henry, how wonderful...I have lots of wishes."

"I'm sure ye do," he laughed. "We couldn't have done it without Chris and James help. I will certainly miss those two when their indentures are completed. I'm going to purchase a couple more indentures on the next shipment so they will be well trained when Chris and James leave."

"I can't imagine life without Chris and James....and Marie," her indenture will be complete about the same time."

"I know. They seem like our family now but tis not right to think that way....they only signed for seven years and have every intention of starting their own planting. Several good men.....and good friends started here as indentured servants and look how successful they have become, George Cottingham and Ambrose Dixon to name a couple."

"Thee are right. I forgot....still I will miss them," Mary added. "Have ye heard any more about the Covenanters, Henry, or any news from England? I haven't received a packet from Mum and Papa for a while and I'm worried about them?"

"Not much news, the Covenanters raised an army of around 20,000 and were marching toward England but that's all I know."

"Oh, I wish Papa and Mum would come to the Colonies."

"Mary, I had hoped to take ye back for a visit with our shipment in the spring but I hesitate since we will have another wee one before the trip. The journey is much too difficult for a bairn, especially with the piracy still so prevalent. I hope ye understand."

"I understand, Henry. I wouldn't want to endanger either of our bairns. This wee one is becoming quite active now," she laughed. "I don't think he cares much for my spinning."

"Ye do need to rest more, Mary....ye never stop working...and

I've added to ye're burden with me stupid accident," Henry massaged his leg and scowled.

"Nay, Henry, all that's important is ye're alive and here with me now...I didna need anything else," she said lovingly.

"And I enjoy being here with ye," Henry replied. "But if this weather ever breaks...I plan to return to the fields. Chris has given good reports but I need to see for meself how the harvest is coming. We need the rain but I hope this storm hasn't damaged the crop."

"God has been good to us, hasn't He, Henry."

"Aye, He has, Mary, He has indeed."

The morning after the violent storm broke bright and clear. A fresh balmy breeze blew across the fields and the smell of cured tobacco from the barn permeated the air. Henry, Chris and James were gathering their equipment in preparation for their day in the fields when John Trehearne rode quickly toward them on horseback.

"John, what brings ye here so early?" Henry exclaimed.

"Tis Alice," John replied. "William knew that ye would want to know right away."

"Is she ill?"

"Nay, Henry...much worse. She died last night."

"But how......what?"

"She never woke up, Henry. Anne went to check on her this morning....She was not feeling well the night before...and just died in her sleep."

"Tis hard to believe......this will be hard on Mary. She thinks of Alice like her Mum. How's William?"

"He's distraught but handling the news well enough. He went to his sister-in-law Elizabeth's house to inform her. Of course, his sister Mary is in England and Jane's still at Alice's house. Jane's taking her Mum's death hard but her husband is with her."

"I can't believe Alice is really gone." Henry gave a huge sigh. "She appeared to be fine at Jane's wedding. I'd planned to visit her this week." After a few moments reflection, He said, "Tell William we will be there as soon as possible."

"I will, Henry. I need to notify a few other neighbors and of course, Rev. Rozier."

"Aye, Rev. Rozier, I didna imagine he expected another funeral so soon after his arrival." Henry turned toward Chris and James, "Ye men, go on to the fields without me," Henry directed. "I need to talk to Mary." Henry turned and hobbled with his walking stick dejectedly toward his house.

Oh Mary, I hate to bring ye this heartache.

He stopped at the door of his house and sat down on the bench next to the door.

How quickly life changes?...Mary and I were reflecting on our good life here...now this....How can I tell her about Alice? She has been like Mary's second Mum.

He stood slowly and opened the door. Mary was standing at the table pounding dough. Today was bread making day and she planned to make bread while Marie cooked dinner. She gave a surprised look when she saw Henry enter and asked, "Why Henry, what is wrong, ye didna look well?"

"I'm fine, Mary but sit down please. I have something to tell ye," he said gravely.

Marie sensed Henry and Mary needed to be alone, and exited the house on the pretense of obtaining herbs from the garden.

Henry's eyes followed Marie as she left the room, and then quietly sat down on the bench facing Mary. "Love, I have some bad news. Alice passed away."

"Nay, nay, Henry, tis not true...I talked to her just a few days ago. Didna tell me this!" she continued with pleading eyes.

"Mary, tis true, John Trehearne came by to tell us, William wanted us to know as soon as possible." Henry clasped both her hands in his.

Mary pulled her hands away... "Tis not true, tis not true!" she exclaimed but as realization began to sink in she collapsed on the bench across from Henry, whimpering. Her whimpering turned to sobs. Henry stood up, hobbled over to her and pulled her up into his arms. She continued to sob on his chest.

Her cries woke Henry, Jr. Seeing his mother upset, he joined in and cried loudly. Henry, Sr. was thankful when Marie appeared at the door...took a quick appraisal of the situation, picked up Henry, Jr. and took him outside to comfort him.

Gradually, Mary's tears subsided and she asked Henry, "How did she die?"

"She passed away peacefully in her sleep, Mary. I imagine it was her heart."

"Jane must be distraught. I must go to her."

"Nay, Mary, ye must think of the wee one ye are carrying. There is nothing ye can do to help Jane now....she has her husband with her."

"Tis true, Henry, Thanks be to God for that."

"I must do something Henry, What can I do to help them?" she employed.

"Mary, I want ye to rest now...there will be time to help....this has been a shock to ye."

Marie returned with Henry, Jr. and Henry asked, "Marie, would ye make some comfrey tea for Mary? I want her to rest some, now."

"Aye, Mr. Henry. Right away. Chris told me about Miss Alice, sir. I so sorry...she was such a nice lady. We will miss her greatly."

"Tis true, Marie, she will be missed," Henry replied. "Will ye be okay, Mary? I would like to check on the fields this morning but I'll stay if ye need me."

"I'm fine now Henry," Mary replied. "It was just such a surprise. Marie is with me and I'll rest as ye say."

"That's good Mary. I'll return as soon as possible," Henry said as he hobbled to the door.

Marie set the cup of comfrey tea on the table in front of Mary and said, "Tis tragic news, Miss Mary. I really liked Miss Alice."

"Aye, she was like my second Mum, Marie. She helped when Henry, Jr. was born. I don't know how I'll manage this wee one's birth without her."

"I'll be here with ye, Miss Mary. I'm not a mid-wife but I have been around a few births. I will help ye as much as I can and ye husband is a doctor. I'm sure ye will be fine."

"Thank ye Marie. I guess I worry too much. Ye are right. Henry is a doctor and will know what to do."

But he's not me Mum. Oh, Mum...I do miss ye so much.

CHAPTER TWENTY-NINE

September, 1640, Eastern Shore, Virginia

Alice Wilson's funeral took place two days later. She was buried on the highland meadow next to her husband, her daughter-in-law Sarah and the young children of William and Sarah.

Jane was very solemn but remained composed as she stood by her new husband John Jackson. Francis and Agnis were on the Jane's left side. Next was their mother Elizabeth then William Berriman. All appeared to be drained of emotion.

After the simple service, Mary and Henry tread the worn path down the hill to their shallop in silence.

When they reached the quay, Mary finally spoke, "Rev. Rozier said many nice things about Alice even though he knew her such a short time, didna he, Henry?"

"Aye, Mary. It was a fine funeral...befitting of one so loved."

As Henry and Mary boarded the boat, Mary asked, "Henry, have ye heard any more about Mr. Eaton?"

"Aye, Mary, I have and I must say, what I've heard troubles me."

"What do ye mean Henry?"

"Well, it appears that Mr. Eaton was found guilty of irregularities and was censured by the General Court at Boston for flagrant offenses....I believe that he came here to escape their punishment."

"Escape?" she asked incredulously. "How did he manage to escape?"

"It was said that he was bound for Pasctaquack and placed his effects on board but soldiers apprehended him before he left. The Governor allowed him to go aboard the ship with three guards to retrieve his belongings. While two guards stayed on shore to await his return, one guard went on board with him and somehow he managed to overcome the guard, throw him overboard and

203

escape in a small boat. That is how he arrived here."

"Henry, that's quite a story. Do ye believe it is true? If so, why would Rev. Rozier hire him as vestry?"

"I don't believe Rev. Rozier had any idea of his past when he hired him. He only knew that Eaton was penniless and tried to assist him. Eaton is a very learned man and was obviously in need of assistance. All his belongings were sold to satisfy creditors in Boston."

"Do ye think he will dismiss him? There seems to be reason for him to be dismissed?"

"I didna believe Rev. Rozier will dismiss him yet...at least not until Eaton is able to provide for his wife and children to join him here. I understand they are destitute and dependent on the Court in Cambridge for survival. Rev. Rozier said that Eaton has sent for them and they should arrive soon. Actually, some of the men believe that Eaton may have been treated unfairly in Boston. They say he is a very agreeable fellow and often shares a pint of ale with them. Rev. Rozier said Eaton has been very considerate of Anne Cotton, and visited her frequently, trying to comfort her in her bereavement."

"Then mayhaps he was treated unfairly. When will his wife arrive? I will enjoy meeting her."

"She and the children will arrive this week."

"Good, we'll make her welcome. Do ye know how many children they have?"

"Nay, Mary, I didna know."

"I hope there will be some Henry, Jr.'s age. He would enjoy playing with other children."

When Henry, and Mary arrived home, they noticed another shallop tied to their pier.

"Henry, were ye expecting someone to visit us today?" Mary asked.

"Nay, I was not expecting anyone.....but it seems we have a visitor."

Henry, Sr. carried Henry, Jr. and Mary followed him up the

204

path to their house. Marie appeared in the doorway.

"Oh, Mr. Henry and Miss Mary, ye have visitors and ye'll never guess who it is," she said with a smile.

Henry and Mary followed Marie inside their house to the Parlour. Seated in one of the two chairs in the room was a thin young man with jet black hair and blue eyes. He stood when Mary and Henry entered the room.

Mary stared at him a moment the exclaimed "Why, Richard, what are ye doing here?" as she ran to him and gave the man a big hug. Then she looked at her surprised husband and said, "Henry, do ye remember Uncle Richard....Papa's youngest brother? He and his wife came to our wedding."

Henry was pensive for a moment and then said, "Aye, ye have two sons and ye wife, is her name Priscilla?"

"Aye, Henry," Richard responded. "And they are all with me, I left them all at the ordinary by Hungar's church. The boys were tired and I was not sure I would be able to find ye house."

"We are delighted ye're here, but ye still didna answer me question? Are ye here for a visit or have ye come to stay in Virginia?" Mary asked.

"We're here to stay, Mary," replied Richard Wilson. "Ye letters have been so appealing and life in England didna look promising so we decided to start anew as ye have, in the Colonies."

"Oh, what wonderful news," Mary enthusiastically responded. She twirled around to pick up her child and said, "Henry ,Jr. , ye will have two cousins to play with and we'll have such fun. Where will ye live, Richard...will ye live in Accawmacke?"

"Aye, I hope to Mary. I hoped Henry could advise me on some land to patent. We will be able to acquire 200 acres with our headrights."

"I'll be happy to assist ye," Henry, Sr. stated emphatically.

Mary put Henry, Jr. on the floor to play with his blocks and inquired, "Richard, ye must have news about Mum and Papa. We haven't received a packet from them for a long while."

"Aye, Mary...I have news but I hesitated telling ye at once because tis not good news."

"Oh, Richard....please tell me...I must know at once whether bad or good," she pleaded.

"I sorry to tell ye Mary...but ye Papa has passed away."

"Nay, nay...oh, tis too much," Mary cried as she ran to her bedroom, almost tripping over Henry, Jr. as she fled.

Henry gave an appealing look to Richard and said, "Please excuse me Richard...I need to see to Mary."

"Of course, Henry, of course. I'll stay here and become acquainted with little Henry, Jr." Richard stooped down and began stacking blocks for Henry, Jr. while Henry, Sr. followed his wife to the bedroom.

"Mary, love," Henry said as he embraced his wife. "I know there's nothing I can say to ease ye pain but is there anything I can do?"

Mary sobbed softly on his shoulder and shook her head, unable to speak. Henry held her close then moved her face to his and gently kissed the tears rolling down her cheeks. After a few minutes, she began to gain control and said in a trembling voice, "Henry, I need to be alone for a while, will ye tell Richard that I'm sorry, I will have to visit with him later."

"Certainly Mary, I'm sure he will understand. He'll come again when ye feel like talking."

"Please ask him how Papa died, Henry. I forgot to ask."

"I will my love....ye just rest now. I'll check on ye after a while."

Henry returned to his guest and found Henry, Jr. enjoying the attention he was receiving from Richard. "I'm afraid Mary is upset over the news Richard...and needs to rest. She wanted me to tell ye to please excuse her."

"No need, Henry. I knew the news would upset her. George died over three weeks ago but her Mum didna want to send word in a packet. She knew it would be hard on Mary and since I was traveling here, she asked that I tell her instead."

"How did he die, Richard?"

"As ye probably know, Edward had to serve in the King's army. He became quite ill while serving and was allowed to return home but I'm afraid the ordeal was too much for him. He never fully recovered from his illness."

"Mary will be glad to know that he died at home with his family at least. How is her Mum? I'm sure it is difficult without George to provide for them."

"While Edward was in the King's army, Robert and George

acquired some employment to assist the family so they are managing though I cannot say it's easy for them. Nothing in England is easy any more. That's why we're starting anew here."

"I thought things were going well for the Covenanters. Didna the King sign a peace treaty in Berwick?"

"King Charles signed it but he didna concede, he was not successful last spring in forcing Parliament to finance his army but I'm sure he plans to try again and I didna want to be there when he succeeded. I cannot bring meself to fight the Scots. Me brother had to do so to save his family...I didna want the same pressure put on me."

"I certainly understand that and we're happy ye decided to come to the Colonies. Ye'll find Accawmacke is a great place, far away from the troubles in England. I only wish Mary's Mum and family would join us here."

"They will never come....I pleaded with them but her Mum was insistent that they remain in England because it was too hard for the little ones and after our trip over...I can't say as I blame her."

"Ye had a difficult time?" asked Henry.

"Aye, the weather was vicious...I worried many times that we'd made a mistake and should have stayed in England but it is over now and I'm thankful we're here. I'm anxious to patent me land and we need to build a house. I understand the weather will grow cold soon."

"True, but it will take time to build. Do ye have a place to stay til it's built?" Henry asked.

"Nay, not if we build in Accawmacke. We stayed two weeks with John at Elizabeth City and I'm sure we could return. I might send Priscilla and the children back to their house if I can not find a place here while I stay and build our house."

"We could have ye stay with us...it would be a mite crowded but I have another idea. Ye brother's wife, Alice, died recently. If she were still alive, I know she'd want ye to stay with her. She had a large plantation and only her daughter and her husband live there now. I'm sure they'd welcome ye. John and Jane Jackson are building a house and they'll move there soon. Then Alice's house will be empty until sold. Ye could stay there at least until ye house was built."

"That sounds like an answer to prayer!" Richard exclaimed.

"I'll check with Jane tomorrow," Henry replied. Mayhaps ye can move there immediately."

"Well, Henry tis late and I must return to Priscilla before nightfall. Shall I check with ye tomorrow?"

"Aye, and bring Priscilla and ye two sons. Mayhaps they will cheer Mary. I'm afraid the news of her father's death will bear on her mind for a while. Alice was also a very good friend and she only died this week. We have just returned from her funeral."

"Tis hard news for Mary, I'm sure. Only time will help her to bear it."

"Aye, Richard. Only time and God"

Richard walked to the dock, climbed in and slowly maneuvered the small craft through the mashes toward Hungar's church as Henry watched from the door.

The days ahead will be rough on ye Mary but at least ye will have some of ye family near ye now.

Henry continued to stand at the door long after the shallop disappeared from view.

CHAPTER THIRTY

October 1640, Plantation Creek, Eastern Shore, Virginia

Even after Mary drank a cup of comfrey tea, she still had difficulty sleeping with the wee one kicking in her belly and the thoughts of her Papa's death preying on her mind. She was exhausted when the cock crowed the next morning. Henry urged her to stay in bed and asked Marie to watch her as he left to join Chris and James in the fields. After he left, Mary tried to sleep but sleep would not come, she finally decided she should just get up and start on her chores. She dressed quickly. Then she picked up the ribbon her father gave her before she left England. Tears flowed down her cheeks.

Oh Papa. I can't believe ye are gone. Mum I miss ye so. I must stop thinking about ye so much or I'll never stop crying. Mayhaps, me work will keep me from thinking too much.

Marie was feeding Henry, Jr. some gruel when Mary walked in the parlour. "Here Marie, ye can go about ye work. I'll take care of Henry, Jr. There is no hope for me sleeping...this wee one in me belly wants to stay awake."

"Aye, Miss Mary. I understand. Would ye like another cup of comfrey tea?"

"Nay, Marie. I just need to have a normal day and stop thinking so much. There's nothing I can do to change things. I must just accept what God has planned for me day."

"Well, if it's alright, I'll feed the chickens and other stock," said Marie. "But I can stay if ye need me," she added as she walked toward the door.

"We'll be fine, Marie. Won't we Henry, Jr?....now if ye will just eat some of this gruel instead of covering ye face with food, then we'll be fine."

Henry, Jr. squealed and stuck out his tongue and refused to eat anymore so Mary sat him on the floor to play. She sat down on the bench by the table and stared out the small window, deep in thought. Her gray eyes were red and misty from all the tears she shed.

A knock at the door startled her and she looked toward the door as it opened. Jane called out, "Halloa Mary, Marie told me to go on in. I hope I'm not intruding."

"Oh Jane, how nice to see ye," Mary replied, choking back tears that were on the verge of overpowering her again.

"I came over as soon as I heard about ye Papa," Jane said softly. "I am so sorry Mary...I know how difficult the news must have been for ye."

"Aye, Jane. I so hoped that I would be able to see him again and now....I just never thought..." the tears started and it took a couple of minutes for Mary to regain control again. Jane held her hand and gave Mary the time she needed to cry.

"Well, that's enough of that," Mary said. "I don't think I've ever cried so much in my life as I have the past three weeks....first with Alice's death and now with Papa. I shouldn't have any tears left. Tis probably because I'm carrying this wee one."

"If that's the case, then I'll probably be joining ye soon, Mary."

"What do ye mean?"

Jane looked down at Henry, Jr. as he lined his blocks up along the floor. "Mayhaps it is not the time to tell ye...but then the news might cheer ye...I believe a bairn will be in me future too."

"Oh Jane, that's wonderful news and good news I needed to hear, today of all days. Thank ye for coming by to tell me. What do ye wish for? A boy or a girl?"

"Why, I hadn't thought about it...but I imagine John wants a boy....most men do."

"Aye, they do...but girls are nice too. When will the bairn be born?"

"This spring....probably May."

"That's a good time to bring a bairn into the world...there will be no harsh winters to endure."

"That's true. Mum would have loved to know that she would be having another grandchild, wouldn't she Mary?" Jane said wistfully.

"Aye, somehow, I think she will know anyway, Jane."

"Ye are right of course. Oh, I meant to tell ye...if ye can bear some more sad news."

"I don't know, Jane," Mary said hesitantly.

"Tis not about anyone ye know. It's about Rev. Eaton's family. Ye know that he sent for his wife and children. Well, they were to arrive this week on a small boat but there was a mishap and his whole family was lost at sea."

"Oh Jane, how terrible! The poor man seems to attract tragedy."

"Aye, Mary. John said that the poor man has been drinking quite a bit to ease his sorrows."

"I can understand why but he should turn to God instead."

"I agree, Mary. Do ye feel well enough to do some spinning while we talk? I can't afford to get behind on me work with a wee one on the way."

"Aye, Jane, I believe I am up to some work too and I will enjoy the company."

"I'll bring in me spinning wheel and we'll get started. Remember those wonderful days we spent with Mum spinning and talking?"

"I do, Jane...we will miss ye Mum."

"We will at that," Jane replied as she left to retrieve her spinning wheel from her horse.

Oh Jane, Ye are such a blessing! God thank ye for such a gracious friend.

Henry returned to rest that afternoon and found the two friends pleasantly chatting spinning while Henry, Jr. played at their feet.

Ah, Mary... what a brave lass ye are....ye have so much heartbreak and still manage to smile. How lucky I am to have ye as my wife.

211

CHAPTER THIRTY-ONE

November, 1640, Plantation Creek, Eastern Shore, Virginia

Henry was walking much better by November. He no longer needed a walking stick but he still had a limp. Mary, however, found her work more and more difficult as the date of delivery for their 'wee one' neared.

"Henry, I feel like a fat butter ball," she exclaimed one evening after she nearly toppled over leaning down to pick up Henry, Jr.

"Nay, Mary, ye are just more to love," Henry said.

Henry was hunched over the table in the center of the room, studying his accounts as he often did in the evening and was particularly pleased at what he found. The tobacco harvest had been as good as he predicted and the tobacco plants were now safely hanging in the barn to cure. Soon it would be time to strip the leaves from the stalks and bunch them in flat, fan-shaped 'hands' and stack them flat in burdens thirty inches high till the following summer. Then the tobacco would be placed in hogsheads and rolled to the quay by oxen for shipment to England. His thoughts went toward future plans.

Mayhaps we will be able to add additional rooms to their house if we get a good price for the tobacco this spring. It shouldn't be long before we have a plantation the size of William Berriman's or even larger. I should see about more indentures this spring we will soon be in need of more land and workers.

He studied Mary spinning thread on the spinning wheel, quietly humming as the wheel turned. The sound and site of the spinning wheel was comforting.

How lucky I am to have a wife like Mary. She has left her home, family and sacrificed many wants to come with me to the colonies and never complained. I hope one day I can give her everything she deserves.

Henry stood up and stretched. Then he walked over to

213

Mary and rubbed her neck.

"Thee must rest some Mary. Ye are working too hard as always," he said.

"In a while, Henry. I want to finish this hank. I usually spin at least six skeins a day and I am far behind. With this wee one coming soon, we need even more yarn. Winter will be here very soon and we will have need of more clothes."

"I understand, Mary. But the bairn may come earlier than ye expect if ye don't rest."

"I guess ye are right. I have not felt my best today. I promise I'll stop after I finish this hank," she said quietly.

Henry walked to the fireplace to warm himself. A brisk wind was blowing outside from the northwest and chilled the small house. An occasional strong gust caused the candle on the table to flicker and create ghostly shadows on the wall behind Mary.

Henry asked, "Mary, how are our food supplies for the winter? Do ye think we will have enough since we had to share with so many others?"

"We should be fine, Henry," Mary replied. "Though I admit, there may have been some trouble if Big Tom had not brought us that additional corn. We had to share so much of our own corn with the new people from Holland that I was a mite worried how we would manage."

"Big Tom has become a very good friend indeed....thanks to ye Mary. I believe he will be a friend for life since ye took care of his bairn last spring."

"I often wonder if I will ever see the wee one again.....I guess that is silly of me.. but even though it was a few days, I became fond of him."

"Aye, ye love all bairns," Henry laughed, "even Indians. I talked to our new neighbors from Holland today when we were surveying Anne Wilson's estate.....John Custis and his wife Joanne. John Custis patented land beside Alice Willson's plantation. It seems Argoll Yeadley married their daughter and they decided to move here to be near her. They're originally from England where John kept a tavern. He and his brother William first moved to Holland before coming here. They arrived in Virginia on the ship with the Dutch and seem to be nice enough people."

214

"We'll have to invite them over for a visit and welcome them to Accawmacke," Mary said as she tied off her yarn, turned and looked into Henry's eyes. "There, I'm finished for now," she laughed. After a studying him for a moment, she said, "Henry, ye look like ye need to rest as well."

"I admit the days become quite long at times....I'm still not able to accomplish as much as Chris and James but I'm a bit older too."

Mary gave him a worried look but she knew from past experience that Henry would not allow further discussion of his health so she changed the subject. "Henry, when will Richard's and Priscilla's house be complete? I know Priscilla is anxious to move before the first snow comes."

Henry, Chris and James were helping Richard Wilson build a cottage on his land. The cottage was only one large room and was framed with hewn timbers. Riven clapboards covered the outside, a brick fireplace took up one whole outside wall.

"Tis almost done. We completed the thatched roof yesterday and James finished the clapboards today. The fireplace needs to be bricked and the brick must be laid on the sand so they will have a solid floor.   Ambrose came by and helped with the indoor woodwork today. I'll finish the door tomorrow. I hope they will be happy with one room but it's all we've had time to build since winter's nearly here."

"Do they need any furnishings?"

"Richard built a sawbuck table with benches for seating and a frame for a bedstead. He seemed pleased with everything. I know he was thankful for the crops everyone shared since he and Priscilla arrived too late in the year for him to put in a crop."

"I'm so happy they decided to settle here in Accawmacke. Tis nice having some family here."

"I wish we could convince ye Mum into moving here. I know ye would like to have her with us in Accawmacke."

"True, Henry, but I know it will never happen. The last packet she sent indicated more trouble in England and she still will not consider coming here. Now that Papa's gone, she said it would be too difficult and dangerous to travel by ship to Virginia."

"I'm afraid I agree with her Mary. Piracy is still prevalent and the trip would be difficult for a woman alone with her children. Mayhaps one day the voyage will be safer and we can visit them in England."

"I hope so, Henry. I certainly hope so. Henry, have ye heard that a possible marriage might be taking place soon between Rev. Eaton and Anne Cotton?"

"When did ye hear this?"

"Jane mentioned the news when she and Priscilla visited last week. Ye have been so busy with Richard and Priscilla's house and I forgot to tell ye til now. Jane said that Rev. Eaton visited Anne frequently and both had recently lost their mates and I guess their loss gave them a common bond. They plan to wed Christmas day."

"I understand what drew them together, but I hope Anne knows what she is doing. The marriage seems to be too quick after her husband's death and we do not know much about Rev. Eaton. I still worry some about the stories we heard of the incident in Boston."

"The same thought occurred to me, Henry."

"I wonder if I should talk to her about the marriage," Henry continued. "I'm her guardian but she is no longer a child and I didna have much control in her decisions."

"From what Jane said, Anne feels strongly about the marriage. Jane hinted that a wedding so soon after Rev. Cotton's death might not be prudent and Anne became indignant and she dropped the subject. I don't think ye will have much success in dissuading her."

"Ye are probably right but I feel I owe it to her father to at least try. Anne is a wealthy woman and she needs to protect her assets. I will visit her after we finished Richard's house. Mayhaps it will be complete this week."

"Aye, Henry that would be good idea," said Mary. She looked down at Henry, Jr. sweet face, sound asleep at her feet. "Me thinks, it will be a good idea to put this wee one in his bed before he wakes up and thinks it's morning," she laughed. Then she carefully lifted Henry, Jr., placed him over her shoulder and carried him to his bed. She laid him down gently and covered him with a quilt, as she straightened her body, a sharp pain went across the lower part of her back causing her to gasp.

Wee One, tis too early for ye to be born now. Thee must wait.

Mary waited by Henry, Jr's bed a moment to see if another

pain occurred. When nothing happened, she gave a sigh of relief and returned to the Parlour.

Henry blew out the candle on the table and said, "Mary, I believe it would be a good idea if we also retire for the night....tomorrow will be here too soon."

Mary awoke three hours later with a severe contraction.

Oh, wee one....tis too soon....tis too soon. God please stop these pains. It's not time for this wee one to be born.

Another contraction was not forthcoming so she dozed off to sleep again, only to be awakened by another contraction thirty minutes later. Mary remained still, willing the pain to stop, but without success.....another contraction followed around fifteen minutes later. Tears clouded her eyes as she lay silently by Henry's side.

What can I do to stop the pains. Mayhaps some comfrey tea.

Mary eased out of bed slowly so as not to disturb Henry. She managed to make it to the fireplace....then her water broke.

Oh, little one...there is no turning back now....ye has decided to be born tonight....God please keep my bairn safe....tis not time.

Mary lit the candle on the table and waddled back to wake Henry for the worrisome night ahead.

Before dawn, the bairn was born........a beautiful girl with dark, feathery hair. She was very small, no bigger than Henry's palm, perfectly formed but so delicate. They decided to name her Mary Margaret after Mary and her mother.

"She is so small, Henry," Mary whispered as she looked at her tiny daughter lying beside her. She's much smaller than Henry, Jr. when he was when he was born."

"But she will be like ye, Mary...she will be strong."

"I hope so Henry...but..."

"Thee need rest, love....and so does Mary Margaret. I'll put her in the crib."

As Henry took Mary Margaret from Mary's arms, her small hand encircled Henry's finger. He gently placed her in the crib beside their bed.

Be strong Mary Margaret Pattenden. Be strong for ye Mum and Papa.

CHAPTER THIRTY-TWO

November, 1640, Plantation Creek, Eastern Shore, Virginia

Henry, Jr. awoke an hour later and was surprised to find Marie preparing bread and his father sitting at the table. Normally, his mother woke him and his father had already left for work in the fields.

"Why, Henry, Jr.," his father said. "We have a surprise for ye this morning. Ye have a little sister."

"Sister! Sister!" Henry, Jr. shouted.

"Shhhh, Henry, Jr., not so loud.....ye Mum is sleeping," Marie laughed.

"Mum, ..where Mummy?"

"Ye Mum is asleep but if ye be a good boy...I will take ye to see ye Mum and sister when they wake up," his father replied. "Marie, I appreciate ye're help last night. It was a big surprise with the bairn coming so early."

"I was glad to help. Do ye think the wee one will be okay?" she asked hesitantly.

"I hope so Marie. We will have to be very careful with her. I plan to stay at home this week for that reason. I'm a little worried about Mary Margaret's breathing."

"Mary Margaret, that is a very pretty name," said Marie.

There was a knock at the door. Henry was startled briefly then walked to the door. A strong gust of wind blew in the house when it was opened. "It is going to be a cold one today, Mr. Henry. I imagine we'll have snow soon," greeted Chris.

"Why don't ye two come in and warm by the fire a moment before ye head to Richard's house," said Henry. "I'll not be going with ye today...Mary had the bairn last night and...."

"She what?" exclaimed James, as the two men followed Henry to the fire.

"Ye bairn was born last night?" Chris whistled. "That's a mite early, isn't it. I thought Miss Mary said January."

"True, she was a surprise....but Mary Margaret and her Mum are fine," Henry added.

"Mary Margaret, that's a fine name...so the bairn was a girl," James laughed. "Well, congratulations, Mr. Henry! I'm happy for ye."

Henry answered gravely, "They are both fine for now...but I need to stay here to keep an eye on Mary Margaret....tell Richard I'm sorry....I won't be able to help with his house."

"Sure, Mr. Henry. We'll tell him. We've almost finished anyway."

James looked at Henry, Jr. and smiled, "Well, Henry, Jr. what do ye think of ye sister?"

Henry, Jr. shouted, "Sister! See sister!"

"Would ye men like a cup of hot tea before ye head for the fields?" Henry asked.

"Nay, Mr. Henry. We'll be fine...it's probably best that we be on our way....tell Miss Mary we are happy for her," Chris said as he put his hat back on his head and the two men walked toward the door and bowed their head into the wind.

Later that morning, Henry went into the bedroom to check on his wife and Mary Margaret. He found Mary wide awake staring at the ceiling. "How do ye feel, love?" he asked.

"I feel fine, Henry. I was just thinking how I should have listened to ye. Mayhaps I endangered Mary Margaret working too much and not resting more."

"Ah Mary, we never know about why this happens. Don't blame yeself...and Mary Margaret is doing well. Let's not look for trouble."

"Still, Henry....I'm to blame if anything happens to her."

"Nay, Mary, nay. I won't hear ye talk that way. Now I think Mary Margaret might be hungry. Would ye like me to give her to ye to suckle?"

"Oh, of course, Henry....what have I been thinking."

"Henry lifted his small daughter and placed her gingerly in Mary's waiting arms."

Mary guided her mouth to her nipple and Mary Margaret began to suckle at her mother's breast. An intense feeling of emotion overwhelmed Mary as she held her small daughter and tears came to her eyes.

"Oh Henry, there's nothing like holding me own wee one in me arms. Mary Margaret, grow strong for ye Mum and Papa. Grow strong wee one."

Henry smiled at the picture of his beautiful wife with his daughter.

Life is good -----Aye -----Life is good!

A few minutes later the quiet moment was interrupted when Henry, Jr. darted into the room followed closely by Marie. "I'm sorry Miss Mary," said Marie. "But he heard ye voice and would not wait another minute to see ye."

"It's alright Marie. Henry, Jr. what do ye think of ye little sister?" Mary asked her son as he scrambled onto the bed beside her.

"Little sister play."

"I guess ye do have a new playmate son," Henry, Sr. laughed "but ye must wait a while til she can grow a little more."

They were startled by a knock at the front door and Marie went to greet the visitors. Henry, Sr. and Mary heard some women chattering happily and a few minutes later, Jane Jackson and Priscilla Willson followed her into the bedroom.

"Chris told us ye wee one arrived last night and we just couldn't wait another minute to see ye little girl," Jane exclaimed.

Mary Margaret, fully satisfied from her feeding, now lay on the quilt next to her mother. Henry, Jr. was on the other side of Mary.

"Sister, Sister," he said proudly as he tried to reach over his Mum to touch her. Mary managed to block his advances.

"Aye, Henry, Jr., ye have a sister now," Jane responded. "Thee must be gentle with her."

"Gracious she is tiny," Priscilla said softly as she touched Mary Margaret's small finger. "But so perfect."

"What's her name, Mary? I think Chris told us but we left so quickly, I don't remember what he said," asked Jane.

"We named her Mary Margaret.... after me Mum," Mary answered.

Henry was standing on the side of the room, listening as the ladies talk. He said, "Henry, Jr., come with me, we'll let the ladies

221

visit while ye help me feed the chickens and stock."

"Feed chickens, Papa?"

"Aye, son....I think it's time we teach ye how to help ye Mum. With a new sister to take care of, she will have her hands full for a while."

Henry, Jr. crawled off the bed, jumped down and grasped his father's hand. He exclaimed gleefully, "Feed chickens, me feed chickens!" and the two left the house, leaving the women to visit and chat about Mary Margaret.

CHAPTER THIRTY-THREE

December, 1640, Plantation Creek, Eastern Shore, Virginia
Three weeks after Mary Margaret's birth, the first snow storm of the year arrived in Accawmacke. Luckily, Richard Willson's family was safely sheltered in their new home when the storm came. Most of the men in Accawmacke gave up trying to work in their fields but a few die-hards still attempted to girdle trees on newly patented land and two men were found dead in their fields after the storm subsided.

In past years, the annual hog-killing was in early November but the early snow storm delayed the event and everyone scrambled to make up for lost time when warm days returned.

Henry, Sr., Chris and James prepared the gigantic iron kettle the night before by placing it on an enormous tree stump. Then they piled firewood, logs and branches on and around the kettle for the huge fire that would be lit the following day. Next they placed large stones and scrap metal on the edges of the firewood, then, the men built a tripod near the kettle and secured the tackle over the huge pot.

"Well, I guess that's all we can do for tonight men," Henry declared. "It should be a fine day tomorrow for the killing."

"Aye, Mr. Henry. I'm looking forward to the 'cracklin' tomorrow....been thinking about that taste for quite a few days now, especially since we be cooped up in that cabin for four days," Chris exclaimed.

"Me taste buds been a tingling too," James added. "But I'm can't wait to have some of that good fresh sausage."

"Aye, men, we should have plenty....judging by the size of the hogs," Henry replied. "Get some sleep, it is going to be a long day tomorrow."

Henry woke long before first light the next morning. The air was crisp and clear when he met Chris and James at the kettle. The men were hard at work filling the kettle with water.

As Henry approached the men, he exclaimed, "Didna the two of ye get any sleep? I thought I'd be out here before ye'd appear."

"Ah, Mr. Henry...we had trouble sleeping, thinking about them good cracklins," Chris replied.

"And sausage," James said. "Nobody makes better sausage than Miss Mary and Miss Marie."

"Thee are right about that!" Henry exclaimed and he picked up a bucket to help the men.

When the huge kettle was full of water, Henry lit the fire and after a time, the men began throwing the now hot stones and metal lining the fire into the kettle. By sunrise, a tremendous fire was glowing under the kettle that was visible from across the creek and the water in the kettle was boiling.

Henry said, "Well men, I guess it's time and the three men walked toward the pigpen.

Mary and Marie were in the house preparing for the inevitable visitors who attended and assisted in the hog-killing. Mary gathered the seasonings for the sausage while Marie pulled the loaves of fresh baked bread from the oven built into the fireplace wall. The two women had been cooking food for the event for a week.

"Ah, Marie, the bread smells good. I just hope we made enough food for the men."

"Miss Mary, I didna think the men will ever think there is enough, especially on hog-killing day...seems their appetites grow on those days"

"Well, it will just have to do. I'm sure Jane and Priscilla intend to bring food too...it will just have to do," Mary reiterated.

An ear-piercing squeal came from outside, and Henry, Jr. woke with a start and started crying loudly.

"Oh, Henry, Jr., tis okay...I'm here," Mary said as she rushed to his bed and tried to cover his ears.

Not understanding, the child pushed her hands away, crying even louder....then Mary Margaret joined in the chorus of Henry, Jr's crying and the ear-splitting squeals coming from the pig-sty.

Marie covered her ears and tried to shout above the cacophony of sounds all around her, "It will end soon Henry, Jr., it will end soon,"

The squeals from outside stopped just as suddenly as they had started and Henry, Jr's sobs gradually reduced to a whimper. Mary held him to her breast trying to console him and gently patted Mary Margaret's back. After a few minutes, peace was restored to the household. Mary Margaret slept and Henry, Jr. leaned against his mother sucking his thumb while she rocked back and forth on the bed, humming softly. Henry, Jr.'s eyelids became heavy and he nodded off. Mary gently placed him on his bed and he drifted off to sleep.

"Mayhaps, we'll have a few more minutes to prepare before they are up," she whispered to Marie as she returned to the table.

"A few minutes is all we need Miss Mary, I didna think we have enough room to place another thing on the table," Marie retorted with a mischievous smile on her face.

Mary looked at the abundance of fowl, fish, vegetables, fruits and bread placed and piled on every conceivable space of the table top, "I think ye are right, Marie," she laughed. If we add more, we'll have to make Henry build me another table."

After Henry, Chris and James slaughtered four large hogs, they began to drag the carcasses onto a large sled or 'pung' as it was called.

Richard Willson and William Berriman appeared before the first carcass was placed on the pung and Berriman laughed and said, "Are ye trying to have a hog-killing without us? I heard all that racket clear to me house."

"I was wondering when ye would show up....figured ye decided to sleep in so we thought we'd wake ye," Henry responded.

"No chance of oversleeping with all the squealing coming from ye place," Richard laughed.

The men helped pull the pung with the first carcass to the kettle, removed and placed it near the tripod. Then they returned to retrieve the other carcasses.

Ambrose Dixon, George Cottingham and John Custis joined

the group of men. By mid morning, around ten men had arrived to assist Henry in the day's hog-killing event.

Chris and James attached the first hog to the tackle on the tripod then Ambrose, George, Henry, Richard and Berriman elevated the carcass over the boiling kettle, and dipped it into the scalding pot of water. The men talked while the carcass cooked in the boiling water. Then it was hoisted out of the kettle and lowered to a wooden rack nearby.

Chris and James began scraping off the hair with bell-shaped scrapers. The hog was beheaded and halved.

"Chris, ye and James haul that carcass over to Mary, we need some good cracklins to gnaw on with this work," Henry shouted.

"Aye, Mr. Henry but strong as Chris and me look, I didna think we kin lug this carcass by ourselves," he laughed.

"Why, we just came to watch,....but if'en that's the only way we'll get some cracklin's, we'll help, Ambrose whooped. "C'mon men," he continued as he pointed to three men near him. "Let's help these weak pup's"

Sawhorses were placed around Henry's house with planks placed across them as improvised tables for the processing of the meat. Mary, Marie and the wives of the men helping Henry with the hog-killing, chatted while they waited for the meat. Their children were playing near them, darting in and out among the women.

Mary saw the men dragging the carcass toward them and said, "Ah, Marie, guess it's time to get busy. The men will be wanting some cracklin's soon."

"Aye, Miss Mary," she replied.

The men placed the first hog beside Mary and she cut some of the fat away and gave it to Marie, who in turn cut it into smaller strips.

" Marie, I'll cook the meat," Jane offered.

"Thank ye, Mam," Marie replied as she gave the strips to Jane.

Jane took the meat to the house where a large hot kettle of lard hung by the fireplace on a hinge. She put the strips in the lard then swung the hinge so that the kettle was hanging over the fire.

Priscilla entered the house. After a few minutes the fat began to sizzle and pop as the meat cooked.

"I believe they're ready," Jane said.

"Sure smells like it," Priscilla acknowledged.

Jane swung the kettle out and carefully removed the hot cracklin from the pot then placed the meat on a wooden board to cool.

"We'd better not take any out till we have enough for all the men," Jane commented.

"I agree," Priscilla responded.

Later, Henry and five men hoisted another carcass out of the hot kettle. Chris and James waited for the hog to be guided to the rack.

"Them cracklins sure smell good," Chris said to James. "I plan to eat me fill of them today."

"Not, if I get to them first," James retorted.

As if on cue, Priscilla arrived with the first batch of cracklins and the men gathered round.....leaving the second hog on the rack to cool.

Henry was standing near the fire waiting on the third hog to be secured on the tackle, when Priscilla came toward him.

"Priscilla, now ye know I'll never get another moment's work out of these men now," Henry chortled.

"Ah, Henry, a man's gotta eat," George Cottingham retorted, good-naturedly.

"Ye are right....and that includes me.. Guess it is time we take a break."

"Mighty right!" James added.

"Priscilla, ye outdone yeself, cooking these cracklin's!" Henry exclaimed.

"Oh, it wasn't, my cooking, it was Jane's," she replied shyly as she walked away from the men.

"Then John, ye married a right good cook," Henry said.

"The other men nodded in agreement.

"Aye, I have at that," John said. "Say, have ye heard that Rev. Eaton plans to marry Mrs. Cotton Christmas Day?"

"I heard something like that," Ambrose replied. "But I

wonder about the match."

"Why's that, Ambrose?" Henry asked.

"Ye haven't heard?" Ambrose asked. "Why, all Rev. Eaton cares about is the drinking and gambling........he's down at the ordinary every night...don't know where he gets his money....but he sure loses a lot."

Henry frowned. "Is that true, Ambrose? I heard that he drank quite a bit but I figured it was because he's grieving over the loss of his wife and children."

"Tis, true, Henry," Richard added. 'We stayed at the Ordinary when we first arrived and Rev. Eaton was there all the time. From what I hear, he gambles every night."

"I don't know Mrs. Cotton," John Custis said. "I'm new here meself but if she has any money, then she better guard it tightly....I understand that Rev. Eaton has quite a few debts owed to some, including me. I foolishly befriended him and even gave him a loan the first week we arrived. I thought it was secure, with him working for the Reverend but I haven't seen him since. He seems to be avoiding me and several others he is indebted to."

"This news concerns me mightedly," Henry said gravely. "I was guardian for Anne Cotton after her father, Thomas Graves died. Why, he'd turn over in his grave if he knew the money he worked for and left for his Anne was squandered by such a rascal. 'Spect I'd better have a talk with Anne before this marriage takes place and hope she will change her mind."

"Good luck doing that," Ambrose snorted. "I've not seen many men been able to change a woman's mind once tis set on something."

The men chuckled.

"Well, we can't solve the problem of our so-called REVEREND Eaton now...we still have us some hog's to boil.....break's over, men if ye want some sausage this winter," Henry declared.

The men all moved in unison. James and Chris returned to the rack and began scraping the second hog while Henry directed five men to elevate the third hog into the kettle.

When the second hog carcass was brought to the improvised tables at the front of Henry's house, all the women gathered round and helped Mary process the meat.

Mary directed the woman to the task at hand.

"Jane, why don't ye handle the cracklin's and Priscilla could ye chop the back meat for sausage. Francis and I will remove the intestines for stuffing. Marie, will ye handle the seasoning of the sausage, ye know how I want it. Joane could ye cut the ham, shoulders and bacon to put in the brine....the barrel is yonder," Mary pointed toward a barrel near the smoke shed. "Let's see, Sarah, could ye take the head, feet, liver inside for the kettle. Marie will show ye where the vinegar and spices are for head cheese, souse and pudding."

All the women followed Mary's request without question. They knew that time was important in preparing the meat. Twilight fell on the group of people before all the meat was completely processed and they returned to their respective homes leaving Mary and Marie to finish by candlelight. Henry, thanked everyone for their help and gave each neighbor fresh meat to take with them. He took charge of Henry, Jr. and put him to bed since both Mary and Marie were still processing the meat. He was exhausted after the long day and decided to rest a minute and collapsed on their bed. In a few minutes, he was in a sound sleep.

It was late evening when Mary and Marie stuffed the final sausages and their hands were raw from the day's work.

"Marie, ye are as exhausted as I am.....we'll not reddy up the kitchen tonight....we both need to rest."

"Most times I'd disagree with ye Miss Mary but I didna think I can do one more thing tonight."

"Go on to bed, Marie....we'll tackle this mess tomorrow."

"Aye, Mam. Thank ye!" Marie said as she left the room.

Mary hobbled to her bedroom and smiled at her sleeping husband. She took two steps toward her bed, lay down beside him and curled herself against his back. She was asleep in less than a minute.

CHAPTER THIRTY-FOUR

December 25, 1640, Plantation Creek, Eastern Shore, Virginia

December brought vicious storms to Accawmacke. Travel between the plantations became impossible and Henry was unable to visit Anne Cotton. The weather cleared by Christmas day in time for the wedding but it was brutally cold and Mary hesitated taking little Mary Margaret out into the severe weather and Henry agreed so it was decided that Henry would attend the wedding alone.

Mary busied herself by baking bread since she had to remain indoors anyway. Marie attended the wedding with Chris and James. When dusk fell over the plantation and they had not returned, Mary began to worry.

"Henry, Jr., ye Papa needs to come home soon," Mary said to her son.

"Papa play?"

"Aye, Henry, Jr., Papa needs to come home and play with ye."

The wind picked up and howled around the corners of the house. Mary's worries intensified. Everyone had traveled in the shallop to the wedding and she feared there might have been an accident.

As dark fell over the land, Mary heard the front door open and she gave a sigh of relief when she heard Henry and Marie's chatter as they entered. Marie continued to her room leaving Henry in the Parlour.

"Ah, Henry," Mary said with relief in her voice. "I was beginning to worry."

"I'm sorry, love," Henry responded. "They had quite an elaborate wedding....and an enormous feast. I'm sorry ye could not attend. Ye would have enjoyed it, though I imagine it was very costly. It worries me how Rev. Eaton seems to enjoy spending money."

"Our wedding was the only one I cared to attend, Henry," Mary said with a smile. "None other interests me at all."

"Ye are a treasure love," Henry laughed. "I do bring good news, I have a packet from England for ye."

"Oh, Henry. How wonderful! It's been ages since I heard from Mum."

Henry produced the packet and Mary clasped it to her breast a moment before tearing the seal open.

She sat on the bench near the table and read by flickering candlelight.

"What does she say love?"

"Not good news I'm afraid. King Charles called Parliament again and it's still meeting....he continually cajoles them to finance his war with Scotland....so far they've not met his demands....but she fears war is coming...there was a call for an impeachment of Wentworth." Mary looked at Henry. "What are we to do? I am so frightened for me family."

"Mary, there's nothing we can do but continue to implore her to come to the Colonies....but we both know her answer."

"Ah, tis true....tis true..." Mary said, then, unaware that she was doing so, Mary reached up and touched the ever present ribbon in her hair and twisted an end sticking out from under her rochet as she always did when she was troubled.

Henry smiled when she touch her head.

Aye Mary I wish I could bring ye more comfort but I'm glad ye have that ribbon to help.

Henry was compelled to protect and comfort her. He walked over to Mary, clasped her in his arms and softly whispered in her ear, "Oh Mary, love, I wish I could take away all the pain ye feel for ye family. I know I have made life hard on ye bringing ye to Virginia."

"Nonsense," Mary quickly replied as she caressed his cheek. "My life is with ye. Henry, Jr., Mary Margaret and ye are my family now. I would not want to be any other place."

Henry bent down and gave her a languishing kiss. Henry, Jr. started pulling his father's pants leg and crying, "Papa, play, "

Henry bent down and picked his son up and held him out in front of his face, "Henry, Jr., ye must learn to wait ye turn. Thee

Papa needs to play with ye Mum first."

Mary laughed sheepishly, "Oh Henry, don't tell our son such things."

Henry convulsed with laughter at her embarrassment as Mary retreated from the room.

CHAPTER THIRTY-FIVE

February, 1641, Eastern Shore, Virginia

For years the people of Accawmacke complained about the great hardship they encountered in conducting legal business due to the great distance from James City. Finally, the court in Jamestown agreed to give power to the Commander and Commissioners of Accawmacke to determine causes between inhabitants in controversies not exceeding twenty pounds sterling or four hundred pounds tobacco.

Henry had been a respected resident of Accawmacke for a number of years and knew many of the residents so he was often called as a witness in legal proceedings. But attending the legal hearings quickly became a burden and caused him to neglect work on his plantation. Tools often broke and needed mending and this morning Henry decided to send Chris and James to the fields without him while he repaired them. He was hard at work on the task when William Berriman arrived on horseback.

"What brings ye here William? Nothing wrong, I hope." Henry queried.

"Nothing's wrong. I just came by to see what plans ye might have when the tobacco's ready to be shipped. I want to return with the shipment this spring for more indentures," William continued. I don't trust me factor to choose them well. Do ye fancy traveling back to England with me?"

"Not this year William. I didna want to leave Mary alone with little Mary Margaret and Henry, Jr., especially since there's talk of Indian troubles lately."

"Ah, pay that talk no mind, the Indians around Jamestown are the ones to be worried about, not here. Our Indians give us no trouble as long as Scarbrugh leaves them along."

"That's true, but I still plan to stay here this spring. Would ye mind taking care of some things in England for me? I'd like to acquire a few more indentures and order some furniture for Mary....that is if the tobacco prices are still good."

"Aye, I'll be happy too. What kind of furniture would ye like?"

"I'll let Mary instruct ye about that. She knows what she needs. I hope we get a good price since we have restrictions for planting next year."

"Restrictions on planting tobacco? I haven't heard anything about restrictions."

"Remember, last winter when we had that shortage of corn and such?"

"Aye, it was the fault all those people from Holland arriving so late in the year," William retorted harshly. "We'd have had plenty without all those new residents."

"True enough, but it seems the justices are worried about next winter so they issued a proclamation forbidding any planter to set out more than 1,000 tobacco plants, and commission merchants, as well as masters of ships can't accept tobacco except through established warehouses."

"But, that didna seem fair. Some planters have more land than others. I set out more than 1,000 tobacco plants already. I'm not destroying them."

"I didna know what to tell ye, Will. I'm not sure how close they'll check."

"Mayhaps they won't check. I have plenty of land devoted to crops and it didna seem fair to punish me because others planted too little food crops."

"I agree. Ye might talk with Yeardley I saw him at the other day and he told me that he and John Custis planted too many tobacco plants as well."

"That reminds me, when I was at the Ordinary last night and saw Rev. Eaton...that man....I don't know what to think of him," William exclaimed.

"Seems like our concerns about Rev. Eaton were justified. He was seen gambling and drinking most of last week at the Ordinary. From what I understand, he does nothing but drink and gamble. I didna know how Rev. Rozier puts up with him. He's spending Anne's money like there's no tomorrow."

"Ah, that's a shame. I wish ye had a chance to talk some sense into her before she married the scoundrel."

"I do too, William.....I do too, but there's nothing I can do to

236

help her now."

Mary appeared in the doorway of the main house and said, "Why William, tis great to see ye. Come share a meal with us and tell me all the news."

"I didna have much news but I would sure enjoy a meal. I miss Jane since she moved out...can't say much about my new cook. That's one reason I want to go to England with the shipment. I might starve without another cook soon."

"Ye are welcome to a meal here anytime William. I just didna know how good it will be," Mary replied.

"Aye, every meal from ye home is good, Mary. 'Sides, it will give us time to discuss ye new furniture I'm to purchase on me trip to England."

"New furniture, Oh, Henry, is it true?" Mary exclaimed.

"Aye, Mary," said Henry amused at Mary's enthusiasm. "I've asked William to purchase furniture for us on his next trip."

"Then ye are very welcome today William. I have a long list of wishes," Mary declared excitedly as the two men joined her on the porch.

Later that evening, Henry and William relaxed by the warmth of the fire quietly talking, while Mary pounded dough for baking the following day.

"I heard ye were in Court yesterday Henry," William stated. "Any news from Accawmacke or Jamestown?"

"Nothing really new....just a bit of humorous gossip."

Mary heard the exchange and said, "Henry, do tell us the gossip. I'm tired of listening to all this serious talk."

"Well, Mary, ye may have already heard it."

"I doubt that. And I'm sure William might enjoy hearing anyway."

"True, Henry, I enjoy a good tale any day," William added.

"Well, there was a case in court yesterday involving Goody Custis and Widow Taylor...."

"What could the two of them have a court case about?" Mary queried. "Why Goody Cusitis is only newly arrived and surely doesn't know many people that well yet."

"Well...as I understand...it seems poor Goody Custis was milking her cow in Widow Taylor's cowpen. Goody Custis always had trouble with this particular cow and evidently thought if the cow was confined in a pen she would have more success."

"That sounds reasonable," William remarked.

"Sounds reasonable but not to the cow," Henry continued. "The old cow got to kicking and turning and just wouldn't be still."

"Mayhaps the cow was not use to the pen. I know, Goody Custis lets her cows roam," Mary added.

"Right...but that made Goody Custis mad and she said a few words to the cow that didna bear repeating," continued Henry.

"Did anyone hear her? I hope Rev. Rozier wasn't around," Mary inquired.

"Not Rev. Rozier, but Widow Taylor heard her and she didna like what Goody Custis said and told her so," laughed Henry. "Then Widow Taylor started making suggestions on how to milk the cow like Goody Custis was doing it all wrong."

"I bet Goody Custis didna like that," Mary retorted with a laugh. "She doesn't like people telling her how to do things."

"Ye are right. She started calling Widow Taylor names and then Widow Taylor had all she could take and started calling her names right back."

Berriman chuckled aloud and asked. "What happened then?"

"Well, finally Widow Taylor smacked Goody Custis face. Luckily John Custis came along and stopped his wife from hitting Widow Taylor, but Goody Custis decided to take her complaint to court."

"She took Widow Taylor to court?" asked Mary incredulously.

Henry continued, "Aye, and Widow Taylor was ordered by the court to provide John Custis with a pot of milk every day until the end of September."

"Goodness, Henry! I guess Goody Custis didna have to worry about milking her old cow for a while," she exclaimed. Then she looked at Henry and William and they all started laughing so hard no one could speak.

CHAPTER THIRTY-SIX

July, 1641, Plantation Creek, Eastern Shore, Virginia
     William left for England in May and returned in July with many new indentured servants for Henry, and himself. He decided to deliver the them immediately to Henry and Mary. As he tied his shallop to Henry's pier, he noticed some additions to his plantation. Henry greeted him and the two men walked around the house while Henry showed William the improvements.

"Henry, ye have been busy while I was gone."

"Aye, we needed more room for the children and we had such a good tobacco crop last year, I had Ambrose Dixon add two additional rooms."

"I've found the two bed frames ye wanted and other items that Mary requested, though I had me doubts for a while that they'd get here."

"Oh, why is that?" Henry inquired.

"The trip back was almost as bad as that voyage with ye and Mary. I had me doubts at times that I'd ever see Accawmacke again."

"Did ye see any pirates?"

"A few, from afar, but we managed to outrun them. It was the weather that was so bad, one of the worst storms I've ever seen."

"I'm glad ye arrived safely but after hearing about the trip, I'm even more glad that I didna go with ye...What's the news from England?"

"Can ye believe that Parliament is still in session. They didna meet every day but the King won't let them end. He's still demanding more money for his war."

"Is there much fighting taking place?"

"Skirmishes and raids.....lots of unrest, I'm glad I'm in the Colonies, especially Accawmacke. I'll take troubles with our Indians any day over life in England at this time but I do have some good news. Dr. Henry Burton, Dr. John Bastwick, and William Prynne were released by Parliament."

"That is good news. Then Protestants must be in control of Parliament."

"Aye, that's why, King Charles is having so much trouble raising funds for his bloody war."

"But how's ye family? I didna see Mary when I arrived."

"She's over at John Jackson's plantation. Ye sister, Jane had her son while ye were gone and Mary wanted to visit her. Both Henry, Jr. and Mary Margaret are with Mary."

"So, I have a nephew," exclaimed William. "How's Jane?"

"Couldn't be better, she and John are very happy and all three are in good health."

"I'm sorry I missed me nephew's birth but it couldn't be helped and I'm sorry Mary's not here.   I wanted to see what she thought of the furniture."

"I'm sure she'll be delighted. She loved the furniture in your house and told me many times she trusted ye judgment. Did ye receive a fair price for our tobacco?"

"Aye, Henry....a very good price, I'd say. We'll go over the accounts now if ye wish."

"With Mary and the children gone, it's probably a good time," Henry chuckled. "The noise of two youngun's tis a bit loud some days."

The two men walked into the house. Marie was preparing a stew in the fireplace.

"Marie, could we trouble ye for a pint of ale? I'm sure William would like to quench his thirst."

"Certainly, Mr. Henry."

The two men were still sitting at the table talking when Mary returned home.

"Why, William, it's great to see ye back," exclaimed Mary. "When did ye return?"

"Today, Mary. And I came at once to see me favorite people. I understand ye have been visiting Jane and her bairn."

"Aye, and a fine, handsome nephew ye have too."

"Then, he didna look much like his uncle Will, I warrant," retorted William with a laugh. "I'm very happy for John and Jane. I'll stop by to see me nephew as soon as we finish here. What did they name him?"

"His name is Jonas, and I'm sure they will all be happy to see ye back safe and sound. Did ye have a good trip?"

Henry snorted, "Ye might not want to ask him that question Mary."

"Why, was there a problem?"

"I'll say," William exclaimed. "Let's just say I'm glad to be back in Accawmacke. Jonas Jackson, that's a fine name. I know Jane must be happy."

"Extremely happy, I'd say. I'm sorry the trip was so difficult for ye. Will ye be staying for dinner?" .

"Not this time, Mary. I just wanted to deliver the furniture and other items ye requested."

"Oh, Mary squealed. The furniture is here now! Where?"

Henry and Will laughed at her excitement.

Mary realized how childish she sounded and said. "I'm sorry, Will. I guess I'm more excited about new furniture than I thought."

"I'm glad it makes ye so happy," Will replied between chuckles.

"The furniture is in Henry, Jr's room Mary but it's still in crates. Chris and James helped us bring them inside," Henry said after he controlled his laughter. "But let's wait until tomorrow to uncrate........it will take some time and it looks like Henry, Jr. and Mary Margaret are worn out from their visit."

Henry, Jr. was lying in front of the fireplace, almost asleep and Mary Margaret was sleeping soundly on Mary's shoulder. Even Mary's sudden outburst had not awakened her.

"Ye are right, Henry, I need to put these bairns to bed. But do come visit again soon Will."

"Aye," he replied.

Henry walked him to the door and watched William walk down the path to his shallop.

Will needs a good wife like Mary. I imagine it's hard to go home to an empty house all the time ....but I don't imagine he'll find anyone as good as Mary in the Colonies.

241

CHAPTER THIRTY-SEVEN

September, 1641, Plantation Creek, Eastern Shore, Virginia

"I cannot believe that woman. After her husband has given her so much and him sick and mayhaps dying," Henry exclaimed. He had just returned from court and was livid with anger.

"Are ye sure, it was Alice Traveller, William? Adultery is a serious crime to make," Mary asked gently as she tried to cool his temper.

"Aye, I'm sure. George Vaux was the one making the accusation. George Traveller has been a friend of mind for years and I'll not have him treated badly. Why, he is near death right now. Robert Ward is a witness against her. I can't believe Capt. Yeardley fell for her wicked ways!"

"Well, I can't say I'm surprised. After the way she treated that innocent child Elizabeth Bibby, throwing her in the creek, tying her up and beating her......Alice could be guilty of most anything. Why Elizabeth was merely a toddler when she came to live with the Travellers!" Mary responded while filling a bowlful of hot stew for Henry's dinner.

"Aye, Alice Traveller deserves to be punished for many reasons," Henry said as he sat down at the table near the fire, then continued. "I met our new Governor Berkeley today."

"Did ye?" Mary sat down beside him and gathered up her sewing.

"Aye, and I like the fellow though I must say, anyone would be better than old Gov. Harvey. But I'm not sure I like his plans to divide up Accawmacke into more counties. Obedience Robbins wants to change the county name from Accawmacke, to Northhampton."

"Change the county name? I didna think people will like that."

"I agree and told him so but he's insistent and ye know how he likes to get his way...it will be voted on in March. He wants to name it Northampton after the Earl of Northampton, Spencer

Compton."

"Well, he can change the name but Accawmacke will always be Accawmacke to me."

"Ye are probably right. I imagine most people will have trouble with a new name."

"Did ye hear any news about Henry Weede? Jane mentioned that he was not doing well."

"She's right. He sent word that he wanted me to come by and help prepare his will. I don't think he's expected to live much longer. I thought I'd visit him this week."

"Poor Elizabeth...I don't know how she will manage that large plantation without he husband."

"I'm sure it will be difficult but her three sons should be a good deal of help. They are older now."

"Still, it will be hard. Henry has been such a blessing to her after her first husband, John Fisher, died. But the thought of losing her second husband after only three years of marriage. I just can't imagine how she must feel."

"At least Weede will be leaving her well provided for with that large plantation and they have quite a few indentured servants for protection...but that reminds me... I'm still hearing rumors about the Indians being rambunctious around here. There must be something to it because an order was made not to leave home without arms or ammunition."

"I can't believe that Henry. The Accawmackes have always been friendly," Mary responded adamantly.

"It may not be the Accawmackse. The Assategues have been known to come this way. We should be cautious, at least for a while," Henry said vehemently. "I don't want ye to take any chances. We really don't know what any Indian is thinking."

"I will Henry, I wouldn't endanger our children's lives," Mary responded quietly.

"Speaking of bairns....where are they? Tis mighty quiet around here."

"It's late, Henry, they're both asleep. Mary Margaret had a bad cough all day and I put her to bed early."

"A bad cough? I don't like the sound of that. Mayhaps I should check her."

"I think that would be a good idea, Henry. I'm a little

worried about her. She's still so frail," Mary said as she picked up Henry's empty bowl. "Would ye like more Henry?"

"Nay, Mary. I think I'll just check on Mary Margaret now. Does Henry, Jr. have a cough as well?"

"Nay, just Mary Margaret. Henry, Jr. has been his usual mischievous self," laughed Mary. "Nothing ever slows that child down. He was chasing the poor hens all day. He wants to feed them all the time. It's a wonder they're able to walk or lay eggs after eating so much."

Henry laughed and said, "I guess I'm to blame for that. I wanted to teach him to feed the hens to help ye, not fatten them up."

"He's growing up and becoming more help everyday. I just wish Mary Margaret would improve. She never seems to gain much weight."

"She will in time, Mary. She just had a rough start in life. I'll check her now, then I think I'll follow our bairns to bed a little early tonight. It has been a long day and I want to get an early start on the fields tomorrow since I lost the day attending court."

Mary wiped a cloth across the table and looked after him as she replied, "I'm right behind ye when I finish here. Tomorrow is baking day and with Mary Margaret not feeling well, it will probably be a long hard day."

Henry entered the children's bedroom and looked down at his sleeping daughter.

Mary's right.....our little girl is still very frail. I wish I knew how to help her gain weight. What use is it being a doctor when ye can't help the ones ye love the most?

Henry touched Mary Margaret's forehead. It was a little warm, but she was sleeping so peacefully, he decided not to awaken her to examine her further.

I'll just check her again in the morning. She probably needs rest more than anything right now.

Henry returned to the parlour and found Mary working at her spinning wheel. Puzzled to find her still working, he said, "I thought ye said ye would be retiring early tonight Mary. Why are ye spinning?"

"I changed my mind, Henry, I decided that I might stay up awhile and see if Mary Margaret awakens. Is she still asleep?"

"Aye, Mary, but I think she may have a slight fever. I didn't disturb her since she was asleep but I'll check her again before I go to the fields in the morning."

Mary's heart jumped when she heard the word 'fever' and she stopped spinning. "Do ye think I need to bathe her with wet cloths for the fever?"

"Nay, Mary....not now. I'm not even sure she has a fever. She just felt a little warm. Ye might check her again before ye come to bed."

"Aye, Henry, it is so comforting that ye are a physick. I worry less about our bairns health."

Henry grimaced at her comment then quickly turned and moved toward the bedroom so Mary could not see his reaction, "I'm glad it helps, but don't stay up too late, love. Thee need ye rest too."

Oh, Mary...I'm glad ye are comforted, but I wish I had the answer to all sickness... sometimes I feel like being a physick is just a guessing game... with me on the losing side much of the time.

Mary continued to spin for another hour. Then she tied off her thread and went to the check Mary Margaret before retiring. Ringlets of dark wet flaxen curls encircled the sleeping child's head but her cheeks were bright red. Mary Margaret was whimpering a little and Mary touched her forehead and panicked.

Why Mary Margaret...ye are burning with fever!

Mary rushed to the parlour and gathered some cloths and a small pail of water. She returned to her sleeping child, dampened the cloths in the cool water and began to bathe Mary Margaret very gently. When the wet cloth touched her skin, Mary Margaret began to cry and Henry, Jr. wakened by her cry, turned over in his bed and asked, "Mummy, baby crying?"

"Aye, Henry, Jr. She's okay. Go back to sleep little one," Mary said as she continued to bathe Mary Margaret.

Henry, Jr. smiled at his mother and said, "Baby want to play."

Mary stopped bathing Mary Margaret and stood up and tucked Henry, Jr.'s blanket around him. "Go back to sleep, Henry, Jr. Mary Margaret will stop crying soon."

She touched Mary Margaret's head but it still felt warm so Mary took the clothes off her tiny body and continued to bathe her from head to toe. "Hush, little one," Mary softly whispered. "I know this isn't pleasant but it must be done."

Mary Margaret was so thin that her ribs were easily visible under her skin. She began to cough convulsively and her body stiffened with each coughing spell. Tears filled Mary's eyes at her child's suffering but she continued to tenderly bathe her.

Henry, Jr. turned fitfully in his sleep, unable to sleep through Mary Margaret's crying so Mary picked up a quilt near his bed, along with the wet cloth and water and carried them to the Parlour. She spread the quilt in front of the fireplace and returned for Mary Margaret, lovingly laid her on the blanket and continued bathing the wiggling child with the damp cloths.

After a time, Mary Margaret's fever diminished so Mary stopped bathing her and covered her with the corner of the quilt but continued to stroke her child's back and whisper softly to her until Mary Margaret fell asleep.

Mary stood up and debated what to do.

I can't take a chance that ye fever might rise again and I don't want to disturb ye sleep. I'll just stay up with ye tonight. I can rest tomorrow.

Mary quietly picked up her sewing basket and began mending and quietly humming while Mary Margaret slept fitfully on the quilt.

Another hour went by and Mary stood up and stretched then bent over to check Mary Margaret's forehead and discovered that it was extremely hot. Frantically, Mary picked her up and placed Mary Margaret in the pail of water. Mary Margaret gave a loud cry so Mary took her out of the water and cradled her against her breast. Mary Margaret hungrily searched for Mary's nipple.

Oh, sweet one...ye are hungry...That is good.

Mary, slipped her breast out of her dress so Mary Margaret could suckle but each time Mary Margaret began to suck on Mary's breast, the infant cried out in pain.

Oh, Mary Margaret.....Mary Margaret what can I do to help ye.

Mary stroked and hummed softly while she bathed her with a cloth. After a time, the small child fell asleep in Mary's arms. Not wanting to disturb her sleeping child, Mary held her against her breast until dawn.

Marie arrived early to help Mary with the baking and found

Mary sitting in the chair, eyes closed with Mary Margaret cradled in her arms. She softly tapped Mary on the shoulder and whispered, "Miss Mary, have ye been awake all night with Mary Margaret?"

It took Mary a minute to register where she was...then she responded in a whisper, "Aye, Marie. Mary Margaret was burning up with fever last night and it pains her to suckle. I'm very worried about her."

"Well, ye need ye rest too. She seems to be sleeping now. Why don't ye lay her on the quilt? I'll watch her while ye rest some before Henry, Jr. wakes up."

"Oh, I don't know Marie."

"Mr. Henry will be up soon too. He can check on Mary Margaret and I'll fetch ye if there be any need."

"Ye are probably right, Marie. Her fever seems to be down and Henry said he would examine Mary Margaret more thoroughly this morning. I guess I do need to rest a little. She may need me later."

Marie gently lifted Mary Margaret from Mary's arms and placed her on the quilt by the fire. Mary stood up and gently patted her sleeping child before leaving the Parlour She met Henry at the door of their bedroom.

"Have ye been awake all night, Mary?"

"Mary Margaret had a burning fever most of the night Henry. I was worried about her and she won't suckle," Mary said tearfully.

"I'll check her immediately, Mary. Ye should have awakened me, but, ye must rest now," he countered when he realized Mary was upset.

"I will, but make sure Marie awakens me if her fever goes up."

"Aye, Mary Margaret will be fine. See if ye can sleep a little," Henry said as he headed for the Parlour.

CHAPTER THIRTY-EIGHT

September 1641, Plantation Creek, Eastern Shore, Virginia
Mary tried to relax but her mind was filled with worry for Mary Margaret. She tossed and turned a while, then she heard, Henry, Jr.'s voice as he excitedly talked to Marie so Mary decided to arise and help Marie with Henry, Jr.'s breakfast.

She stood up and looked at herself in the new looking glass William purchased in London on his last trip. Her eyes had dark circles under them from lack of sleep but otherwise no one would notice that she'd been awake all night. She pinched her cheeks, brushed her dark hair and splashed cold water on her face and eyes in an attempt to rejuvenate herself for the long day ahead. Then she went to the Parlour.

Henry, Jr. was sitting at the table eating while Marie stood on the opposite side, pounding bread dough. Mary Margaret was asleep on the quilt.

Marie looked up as Mary entered, "Why Miss Mary...ye didna rest any time....ye should have slept longer."

"I couldn't sleep Marie...I'm too worried about Mary Margaret. Did Henry say anything after he looked at her?"

"Aye, he said her fever was down but her throat was very red. That may have been why she wouldn't suckle. We managed to get some willow bark tea down her and she has been sleeping quietly for a little while."

"Good," Mary declared. "Mayhaps she will improve today. I think I'll take her back to her crib so Henry Jr. won't wake her."

"That's a good idea. This bairn is full of talk this morning," said Marie as she winked at Henry, Jr.

Mary gently picked up her small child and Mary Margaret began to whimper. She gently patted her back and whispered soothingly in her ear as she carried her to the crib. Mary Margaret fussed a little when she was placed in her crib but in a few minutes drifted off to sleep, then Mary returned to the Parlour.

"I wish today wasn't baking day, Marie but there is no getting around the task." Mary pulled another loaf of fresh dough from the shelf where it had been placed to rise and started kneading. Then she said, "Henry, Jr., I can really use ye help today feeding the chickens but first ye must finish that gruel so stop playing with ye food and eat it."

Henry, Jr. looked up at his mother and grinned then started eating his gruel very quickly, getting most of it around his mouth in the process. A few moments later he gave a shout, "All finished, Mum! Me feed chickens now?"

Mary laughed and said, "Thee are a sight for sore eyes, Henry, Jr. Come here first and let me wipe ye mouth. The chickens may want to eat ye with all that food on ye mouth."

Henry ran over to his mother and she wiped his mouth with the corner of her apron. He hugged her legs then ran to get the feed pail and was out the door in a flash.

"Stay close to the house, Henry, Jr. and when ye finish come right back inside," Mary shouted after him. Then Mary turned to Marie and said, "We must watch Henry, Jr. and make sure that he doesn't stray too far from the house. Henry said there is still talk about Indian trouble."

Marie nodded, "I heard the same Miss Mary. I hope it's only rumors." Marie put her loaf of bread in a pan to rise again.

"Me too, but we must be careful. Oh Marie, I can't keep my mind off Mary Margaret. Would ye mind finishing this loaf? I feel I must stay close to her today."

"Certainly, Miss Mary. Let me handle the baking today. Thee needs to take care of Mary Margaret."

"Marie, ye are such a dear...I didna know how I'd manage without ye."

"I know what it is like to be worried about a loved one and ye must stay close when they are ill." Marie's eyes were filled with misty tears as she looked at Mary.

"Oh, Marie. I'm sorry. I hope I didn't bring up any unpleasant memories. I forgot about ye losing ye own family."

"Memories...pleasant or unpleasant...they are the same to me Miss Mary. It will always hurt to remember but I could never give up my memories. I cherish each one because they are all I have." Marie's voice broke and she turned away to avoid shedding

250

tears.

"Marie, I'm still sorry for upsetting ye and I thank God everyday for sending ye to us." Mary said and she gave Marie a hug.

"I'm fine Miss Mary. Ye must take care of Mary Margaret. I'll handle the baking."

"Well, if ye are sure," Mary answered, then she walked to the door to check on Henry, Jr. who was running around in circles slinging the feed pail while the chickens chased him.

"Now Henry, Jr., ye must feed the chickens, not tease them. Stop running with that pail right now and feed them, then come right back in this house. I'm sure Marie has other chores for ye to do." Mary turned and gave Marie a wink and went to check on Mary Margaret.

She soon returned to get the water pail and cloth. "Her fever is up again Marie. I will probably be with her most of the day. Send Henry, Jr. to me if he gives ye much trouble."

"Henry, Jr. will be fine, Miss Mary. Ye just take care of little Mary Margaret."

Mary stayed by her child the remainder of the day. She bathed her when her fever went up and sang to her when she fussed. When Mary Margaret slept, Mary pulled out her sewing basket and managed to mend a few items. But try as she might, Mary could not coax Mary Margaret to suckle.

Henry, Jr. was in and out of the room frequently during the day and Marie kept him busy with small tasks he could handle. Each time he completed one, he had to traipse into the room and proudly tell his Mum about his accomplishment.

Henry returned home early that evening and immediately checked on Mary Margaret.

"Her throat is still very red and raw, Mary," said Henry. "But when her fever breaks, she should improve. Let's see if she will take some more willow bark tea. That should help with the fever."

"Isn't there anything else we can do, Henry?" Mary pleaded. "She seems to be weaker this evening and she just can not suckle because it pains her."

"I don't want to bleed her. I just don't feel like that will help her," Henry replied strongly. "All we can do is try willow bark tea, bathe and pray. Everything is in God's hands now."

"Oh, Henry...I didna mean to pressure ye. I'm just so worried. I know ye are doing everything possible. I just feel so helpless."

"I do as well, Mary. I wish I had the cure for her. I should be able to help my own bairn," Henry responded in anguish. "All we can do is pray her fever breaks soon. I'll stay with her. Marie said that ye haven't eaten all day. Thee must keep up ye strength. Mary Margaret will probably want to suckle soon."

"Ye are right, I didna think about that. I've not been interested in eating with her so sick. Call me if she awakens. I'll try to get her to suckle again."

Henry and Mary took turns staying with Mary Margaret the rest of the evening but she remained unchanged. When Henry Jr. went to bed, Mary carried her daughter into the Parlour and laid her on the quilt by the fire. She sang and stroked Mary Margaret's back as she slept fitfully. Henry sat at the table and tried to go over his accounts but his eyes continually wandered to Mary and his daughter by the fireside.

God why did ye give me knowledge to treat the sick but not enough to take care of Mary Margaret? She is so much weaker tonight but I dare not tell Mary. I'm truly worried about our wee one....but what else can I do to help her.

Henry finally gave up trying to work on his accounts and pulled his Bible from a shelf. "Mary, let's read the 23rd Psalm together. I think we both need to hear it tonight."

Mary turned to him with tears misting in her eyes. "Aye, Henry. Please read it to me."

Henry softly read the beloved words:
'The Lord is my shepherd; I shall not want.

He maketh me to lie down in green pastures; he leadeth me beside the still waters.

He retoreth my soul; he leadeth me in the paths of righteousness for his name's sake.

Yea, though I walk through the valley of the shadow of death,

*I will fear no evil; for thou art with me; thy rod and thy staff
they comfort me.*

*Thou preparest a table before me in the presence of mine
enemies; thou anointest my head with oil; my cup runneth
over.*

*Surely goodness and mercy shall follow me all the days of my
life; and I will dwell in the house of the Lord forever. Amen*

"Henry, those words are all so beautiful but can we really
trust that God will lead us through this and heal Mary Margaret?"
Mary asked with pleading eyes.

"We must have faith, Mary." Henry walked over to Mary. She
was sitting on the floor by Mary Margaret. He pulled Mary up and
into his arms. "We must do everything we can to take care of Mary
Margaret, and trust God to heal her."

Henry and Mary stood and held each other close while they
gazed at their daughter sleeping on the quilt and they prayed for
God to make her well.

Mary Margaret's fever was lower by late evening and Mary
urged Henry to rest, insisting that they both did not need to lose
sleep and she would awaken him if Mary Margaret's fever rose
again.

A long piercing scream penetrated the air. Henry awoke
with a start and realized it was dawn. He sat for a moment trying
to determine where it came from. The screaming continued and
Henry realized it was coming from the Parlour.

Tis Mary! Why didn't she wake me?...

Henry quickly rushed to the source of the screams and
discovered Mary sitting on the floor, with Mary Margaret clutched
to her breast.

Mary wailed, "She's gone. Henry! .Mary Margaret's gone!
Will ye ever forgive me?"

"Mary, Mary...there's nothing to forgive...oh love, tis God's
will," Henry encircled Mary and Mary Margaret into his arms.

"But, she died because I fell asleep....I fell asleep while my
bairn was dying," Mary cried. "She needed me Henry. Oh Henry,
God let her die because I fell asleep. It's just as ye said. He let her

253

die because I didna take care of her. I fell asleep."

"Nay, Nay, Mary...ye mustn't blame yeself."

"Then why did she die. Oh, Henry....can ye ever forgive me?....Mary Margaret's gone and it's my fault. I didna take care of Mary Margaret....I fell asleep....I fell asleep."

"Oh, love...tis not ye fault...not ye fault."

Marie, hearing the screams, arrived on the scene in the Parlour and stood puzzled as to how she could help...she heard Henry Jr. crying in his room and rushed to comfort him.

"Mary, oh Mary, how can I make ye understand," Henry continued. "Thee did nothing wrong....I should never have left ye alone....I'm to blame if anyone is...I'm a doctor," Henry said in a tormented voice.

Henry held his wife and dead child for what seemed like an eternity until Mary's cries diminished. "Here, Mary....let me take Mary Margaret. Ye are exhausted."

Mary jerked away from Henry and tightened her grip on her child. "Nay, Mary Margaret needs me."

"Mary Margaret is with God now Mary. She has no need for us any longer. She is with God."

Mary began to cry again then fell into a chair, still clutching Mary Margaret to her breast and moaning softly. "She's gone and it's my fault."

Henry stood with a pained expression on his face as he tried to decide how to help Mary.

Marie returned to the parlour and asked, "Mr. Henry, let me try. I think Henry, Jr. needs ye. He heard his Mum crying and could not be consoled. He wants to see her. Mayhaps he will be content with seeing ye."

Henry turned toward Marie. His face was filled with agony as he said, "Can ye help Mary?"

"I'll try, Mr. Henry....but it is hard to lose a bairn. I don't know if anyone can truly help her."

Mary continued to hold Mary Margaret tightly to her chest as she cried over and over, "I fell asleep....I fell asleep."

Henry looked at Mary again, then turned and walked dejectedly toward his son's room. Henry, Jr. could be heard bellowing, "Me want Mum....Me want Mummy!"

Mary's cry turned to soft whimpers so Marie approached

her.

Mary looked up at Marie and said, "I killed my bairn, Marie. God will never forgive me."

"Nay, Miss Mary....Nay, tis God's will."

"It can't be God's will to take one so innocent. I fell asleep and did not take care of her so God let her die."

"Nay, Miss Mary...that's not true. Thee be a good Mum."

"I can not let her go, Marie."

"I understand, Miss Mary," said Marie soothingly. "But she is with God. Mary Margaret is with God now. We need to prepare her for burial." Marie reached out her hands for Mary Margaret.

"Nay, Marie. Not yet. I can't let her go yet," Mary said as she gently rocked her dead child back and forth.

Marie waited. After a time Mary finally stopped crying so Marie questioned her again. "May I take her now Miss Mary?"

"Aye, Marie, but hold her gently. I need to prepare her."

Marie took the small child from Mary and carried the infant to her parents' bedroom. She wrapped Mary Margaret in a blanket and placed her on the blanket chest at the foot of the bed, then returned to the Parlour. Mary was standing near the table with a pail of water and bar of soap.

"I must cleanse her for God, Marie. I will not disobey God again. Would ye feed Henry, Jr. his breakfast? I heard him crying earlier."

"Aye, Miss Mary."

Mary turned and walked toward her bedroom with the soap and pail of water.

CHAPTER THIRTY-NINE

September, 1641, Eastern Shore, Virginia

Two days later, in a misty rain, Mary and Henry held Henry Jr.'s hands as they walked down the well-trodden path toward their waiting shallop. Marie followed close behind. As they drew near the pier, Mary spied the small wooden box containing Mary Margaret's tiny body at the stern of the boat. She trembled and stumbled briefly, then regained her footing and continued toward the pier.

Chris and James were waiting on the boat. All their indentured servants planned to attend the funeral so William Berriman provided his larger shallop for additional transportation. It was tied up on the opposite side of the pier.

Mary and Henry climbed aboard first then Marie passed Henry, Jr. to Henry's waiting arms and climbed in after them. The short ride to William Berriman's house was completed in silence. Even 'chatty' Henry, Jr. did not feel compelled to talk.

When they arrived at Berriman's quay, Mary and Henry disembarked slowly and deliberately. Henry picked up Henry, Jr. grasped Mary's hand and led the small group up the path to the cemetery on the high meadows where Alice and Henry Wilson and their daughter-in-law, along with Sarah's bairns were buried.

James and Chris trailed behind everyone, carrying the small pine box to the burial site. Mary and Henry stood in solemn silence, side by side. Henry, Jr. was wedged between them and his parents had a firm grasp on his hands.

Soon, other visitors and the remaining Pattenden's servants arrived and gathered in a small cluster around the gravesite. Rev. Rozier began to speak but Mary did not hear his words, She was in a fog and could only hear her thoughts.

God I am so sorry I failed the child you entrusted in my care. Oh, Mary Margaret...oh how my arms will miss ye. Will the pain of ye absence ever go away?

"The Lord Guide ye and Keep Thee Forever, Amen" Rev. Rozier completed his speech and walked over to the Pattendens. He took Mary's hand and said, "God bless ye Mary...If ye have need for anything, just let me know. And the same for ye Henry." He patted Henry, Jr. on the head and said, "Take care of ye Mum, Henry, Jr."

Henry, Jr. looked confused and said, "But she takes care of me."

Rev. Rozier smiled discreetly and said, "Ye are right, How about just being a good boy for ye Mum?"

"Aye, I can do that," Henry, Jr. replied with a grin.

Henry patted his son on his shoulder and Henry, Jr. looked up and smiled at his father. Henry picked his son up and squeezed him affectionately.

Mary stared at the hole in the ground where the small box lay and shuddered. She turned away and began quickly walking down the path to the shallop before anyone could speak to her. Henry started to follow but then he saw Jane Jackson moving toward Mary in attempt to talk so he remained and began talking with Berriman.

When Jane reached Mary, she said, "Mary wait a minute. I wanted to tell ye how sorry I am about Mary Margaret's death."

Mary stopped and turned toward her friend. "Tis not me ye should be sorry for Jane. I'm the reason Mary Margaret is dead. My bairn needed me and I failed her so God took her from me."

"Nay, nay, Mary. She was ill. There was nothing ye could have done."

"I should have stayed awake," Mary sharply retorted. "That mistake cost Mary Margaret her life."

"Ye are wrong Mary. Ye had no control over what happened to Mary Margaret."

"Don't ye understand Jane? I went to sleep while my bairn was dying. I'll never forgive myself for that and I know Henry won't either," she cried. "But for the rest of my life, I will try to make it up to Henry and Henry, Jr."

Henry joined them in time to hear Mary's words and said, "Jane, I'm sorry. Mary is exhausted and overwrought. Mayhaps we should return home now."

Jane nodded but she stated again. "It does ye no good to

feel at fault. Didna blame yeself."

Mary smiled at her friend and said, "Nay, Jane, it is ye who ye didna understand." Mary continued toward the path, climbed into the waiting shallop and reached up to take Henry, Jr. from his father.

Henry looked up the hill and motioned for Chris, James and Marie to come down to the quay. They arrived quickly, climbed aboard and the shallop gently glided across the water.

After the group disembarked, Mary led Henry, Jr. to the house. Earlier, tables made with sawhorses and boards had been set outdoors for the funeral meal so neighbors could come by and pay their respects.

Food from the surrounding community arrived all morning. Mary went inside her house. She remained indoors the whole evening and seldom engaged in talk with others, instead she preferred to sit alone at the table with her thoughts. Henry apologized for her absence and everyone said they understood.

"I'm sure she is grief-stricken and heart-broken. She just needs time to adjust," Berriman said to Henry.

"I hope ye are right but I'm concerned about her," responded Henry. "She keeps blaming herself for Mary Margaret's death."

Toward evening, the crowd started to disperse and return to their respected homes. Henry began helping Marie while Marie cleared away the remaining food on the tables.

After a few minutes, she said, "Mr. Henry, why don't ye go on in with Miss Mary. Chris and James can help me clean this up. Miss Mary didna eat much of anything. Mayhaps ye can talk her into eating."

"I'll try, Marie, but ye know she's been pretty stubborn lately about eating."

Henry went in the house and found Mary sitting on the floor by the fireplace with a forlorn look on her face.

"Marie said ye haven't eaten, love. Everyone has gone. Why don't ye try to eat a little now? Ye must take care of yeself."

"Why does everyone think I need to be taken care of," she barked. "I'm the one who needs to learn how to take care of others. I let me bairn die.....I let her die. I don't deserve any special treatment. I'm to blame for her death."

"Mary that's just not true. The illness took Mary Margaret from us. There was nothing ye could do. I'm going to make ye some comfrey tea and I want ye to rest. Mayhaps things will look better tomorrow if ye rest."

"I don't want to rest. I can't rest. All I think about is Mary Margaret."

"The tea will help Mary and I'm ordering ye to drink it," he said harshly. "Henry, Jr. will need ye tomorrow and ye must rest."

Astonished by Henry's harsh tone, Mary looked up at him with bewilderment. Then she said, "I'll only drink it because ye ordered me to. I don't want to do anything else wrong."

Henry felt guilty for speaking so roughly. He tried to draw Mary into his arms but she pushed him away.

"I'll drink the tea and rest, Henry. That's all. I need no comfort from anyone......I didna deserve comfort from anyone."

Henry prepared the cup of tea and sat it on the table. Mary remained on the floor so Henry picked up the cup and handed it to her.

"Mary, I heard today that Henry Weede is in a bad way so I thought I'd drop by his house tomorrow. He wants me to draw up a will for him. Will ye be okay while I'm gone?"

Mary did not reply but she nodded her head and sipped the tea.

Henry went back outside to help with the tables and Mary stared into the fire as she continued to sip her tea.

The next week, the Pattenden house was filled with visitors almost daily as they came by to pay their respects. Mary usually worked during the whole time of each visit and seldom participated in conversation. Whenever she did converse, she continually repeated that she was responsible for Mary Margaret's death.

As the days passed, Henry worked longer and longer hours in the fields as he tried to deal with his own grief. Thanks to Marie's attention, Henry, Jr.'s life stayed pretty much the same. However, he frequently asked Marie, "Where's Mary Margaret? Me want to play with Mary Margaret," and she could not give an answer to appease him.

Three weeks later, William stopped by to tell them of the death of Henry Weede. Henry was able to visit Weede, before he died, to discuss his will but the will was not completed or signed prior to his death.

"Well, at least I know what he wanted in his will," Henry declared to William. "Mayhaps my word will mean something when it comes time to probate his estate."

On the day of Henry Weede's funeral, a blustery wind began blowing in Accawmacke. Many people, worried about an approaching storm, decided to stay home rather than risk traveling by water to the funeral. The hardy souls who attended arrived on horseback. Henry and Mary chose the later since the cemetery was but a short distance from their plantation. As the horses plodded along the well-worn Indian trail, Henry and Mary rode in silence, both lost in their own thoughts. Mary Margaret's funeral and the pain of her death was still too fresh in their minds to attempt conversation.

Mary was dressed in black as was Henry. Her hair was tucked under her rochet and as usual, tied with the ribbon her family gave her before she left England. When they arrived at the cemetery, Henry dismounted then assisted Mary as she dismounted. He held her close to him for a brief second.

They looked in each other's eyes, then Mary quickly averted her gaze and said, "Is that Scarbrough I hear shouting? The man has nerve to disrupt a funeral with all that angry talk."

Henry followed her gaze as he tied the horse to a nearby tree, and he replied, "If he isn't careful with that talk, we may have trouble with the Indians one day. I really think at times he's looking forward to a confrontation. There's a rumor that he may be a Burgess soon. He may have good qualifications for the position but he needs to become a little more mellow when it comes to dealing with Indians if he's to be a good representative."

"I agree, Henry. We don't need to look for trouble. There's enough that follows us."

They trudged up the footpath to the cemetery on the hill with others attending the funeral.

Jane Jackson noticed Mary's arrival and immediately walked over to give her an affectionate hug. "I'd hoped I'd see ye here, Mary. I've missed our visits."

"I miss ye too but there's so many things to do at home and I didna have much time for visiting and such foolishness."

"Foolishness? I didna think our visiting is foolishness, Mary. We women need to stay close. There are so few of us in the Colonies. We need each other. Remember what happened to William's wife, Sarah."

"We didna know what caused her to take her life, Jane. We will never really know."

"True, but we do know she was lonely. I'm aware of how alone it feels after losing someone ye love and I don't want to feel that way again. I don't want my friends to feel that way either. We need each other to help us through the dark times."

Suddenly, Mary said sharply, "I didna come here to discuss Sarah's death, Jane. Let's talk another time."

Then Mary abruptly walked away in the direction of the gravesite, leaving Jane standing with an open mouth and a confused look at her friend's rude behavior.

Mary joined Henry and tried to hold back the tears filling her eyes.

Why did Jane have to mention Sarah? Oh God, please help me. If the tears start...they won't stop. I have to pull myself together. Oh Mary Margaret I miss ye so.

Mary stood solemnly next to Henry and attempted to listen to Rev. Rozier words but her thoughts raced. She grabbed Henry's hand and he glanced down at her, then gave her hand a gentle squeeze and Mary began to relax.

Suddenly a strong blast of wind swept over the hilltop cemetery. The gust partially pulled Mary's rochet from her head, and freed a few tendrils of hair but she quickly grabbed the cap and managed to hold it tightly with her other hand until the breeze diminished.

After the funeral service was over, Mary whispered to Henry, "I didna think I feel up to conversation now. Could we go home?"

"Aye, Mary. We've had too many funerals of late and we need to stay ahead of this storm. I'm sure Mrs. Weede will understand."

Henry and Mary moved quickly down the path to their

horses. A powerful gust of wind swept across the hill as Henry helped Mary mount Rascal.

"I'm afraid we might be in for quite a storm. I hope we make it home before it cuts loose," Henry said as he mounted his horse. "Hang on tight Mary. I think we need to speed up some to beat this storm."

Henry switched his horse lightly as he galloped toward the path to their home and Mary followed without hesitation. She held tight to Rascal's mane as she followed Henry's horse and plunged headlong toward the dark hollow path, shrouded by angry trees as the wind battered and bent their branches. Eventually, the trees parted in a clearing as they neared their house and the wind gave way to large drops of rain, that changed to a torrent by the time Henry and Mary reached their front porch.

Henry shouted, "I'll settle the horses in the barn. Ye go on in and get dry, Mary."

Mary laughed as she slid quickly from Rascal's back when they reached the front of the house. Marie met her at the door. Mary's hair was flying free, her wet dress clung to her body but she had a smile on her face.

"Miss Mary ye are soaked to the skin."

Mary laughed, "I certainly am Marie. That was quite an adventure."

"Well, it seems to have helped ye spirits some considering ye have been to a funeral," Marie laughed with her. "And I'm glad of that."

"I believe I actually enjoyed the ride a little. I forgot what it was like to ride with such reckless abandon. Has Henry, Jr. given ye trouble?"

"Nay, Miss Mary. He has been good as gold today. He's taking his nap now."

"Well, I'm glad. He can be a hand-ful at times. I 'spect I'd better get out of these wet clothes before I soak the whole Parlour," Mary laughed again as she walked toward her room.

As Mary removed her clothes, she glanced at herself in the looking glass. The face that greeted her was different somehow. The dark circles under her large eyes were still there but now her eyes gleamed with a spirit that had disappeared with her child's death and the little wrinkles that had gathered around her mouth were no longer visible.

It feels good to laugh again maybe I've been too harsh on meself and everyone else since Mary Margaret died.. Mayhaps Jane is right. We need companionship of others to get through the dark times. I think I'll visit her next week and apologize.

Mary grabbed a cloth and began to dry her hair.

I wonder what happened to my rochet. Thank goodness I have another. I would create quite a sensation wearing my hair down on my shoulders at my age. Oh no, no....it can't be.... Where is my ribbon? How can I manage without my ribbon!

Mary frantically felt through her hair to see if it was caught among her thick tresses, then rushed to her clothes in the hope of finding the ribbon there but she knew at the same time it would be in vain. The ribbon was probably on the path she and Henry had ridden down so swiftly moments before. She fell to the floor in despair.

How could I have been so foolish!! I have responsibilities. Hasn't Mary Margaret's death caused me enough pain? Have I learned nothing from her death? My negligence caused her to die and now my reckless spirit has caused me to lose something precious to me. That ribbon was like having a part of my family with me. God has punished me again! I must no longer be so uncontrolled and impulsive but diligent in my duties or I will lose even more that is dear to me.

When Mary returned to the Parlour in dry clothes, Marie was aware that Mary's demeanor had changed but said nothing. A few minutes later, Henry opened the door, tramped in and found Mary sitting in her usual spot by the fire quietly mending one of Henry, Jr.'s shirts.

CHAPTER FORTY

March, 1642, Eastern Shore, Virginia

Spring arrived early in the Eastern Shore and what should have been a joyous time was anything but joyous at the Pattenden plantation.

Mary never made her planned visit to Jane to apologize. Instead she became extra attentive toward her household duties and withdrew even more within herself. She pulled a veil around her emotions that no one, not even Henry could penetrate.

Henry, Jr. was constantly at Mary's side since she refused to let him out of her sight. He was no longer allowed to feed the chickens as he had done in the past. As a result, Henry, Jr. became very clingy toward his mother and cried frequently.

He constantly asked, "Where's Mary Margaret?" to which Mary answered, "She's in heaven, darling," but Henry, Jr. was never satisfied with her answer. He would ask the question again and again, and each query stabbed Mary's wounded heart like a sharp knife, only intensifying her pain.

Since home was so miserable without Mary's laughter, Henry spent longer days in his fields to deal with his grief and returned each evening too exhausted to attempt conversation. He ate his dinner in silence, then after he finished his meal collapsed on his bed but he could not control his thoughts before he slept and they were always of Mary.

How can I reach ye my dear Mary? I will not survive without ye loving optimism. I should never have brought ye to this country away from ye family. God please help her come back to me.

One morning, Henry was leaving his house for a long day in his fields. The sky was cloudy and air hinted of rain. He heard a horse galloping rapidly toward him and realized it was Berriman.

"Halloa, Will, what brings ye here so early and in such haste?"

"Tis John Jackson, Henry. He died last night!" Berriman shouted. "I need Mary's assistance. Could she sit with Jane while I make preparations for burial? I hesitate leaving her alone. We have the servants but I feel she needs a friend and she and Mary....," Berriman's voice trailed off.

"Certainly William, I'm sure she will help. How did he die?"

"He just collapsed from what I understand. He and Jane were talking and without any warning, he grabbed his chest and fell to the floor. He was dead moments later. I haven't notified anyone else....Would ye be kind enough to send word?....I've been trying to console Jane since last night and I need to contact Rev. Rozier now."

"I'll send Chris. Is there anything else I can do to help?"

"Nay, Henry. That will be fine for now. I should be on my way. Tell Mary I appreciate her help." Berriman turned his horse around and galloped quickly toward the path to Hungar's church.

Henry entered his house. Mary was giving orders to Marie about the men's dinner. She turned to Henry and said, "I heard what William said. I'll leave immediately."

Henry nodded. "Send for me if I'm needed. I'll be clearing the new field today."

She nodded and said, "Henry, Jr. and I will be all right but I didna know how long I will be gone. Would ye tell James to saddle Rascal?"

"I'll take care of Rascal," he replied firmly. "Just send word if I'm needed." Then he turned and exited the house in despair. His thoughts were racing again as he walked toward the barn.

Another death! What will this do to Mary? Oh God, please let me have my Mary back. I should never have brought her to this God forsaken land.

A few months after John Jackson's funeral, Berriman left for England and took his sister Jane and her son Jonas with him. He returned in August. His servant Trehearne met him at Hungar's quay to load the many crates of merchandise Berriman acquired in England .

"Any Indian troubles while I was gone, Trehearne?" Berriman inquired as he smoked his pipe on the pier.

"Well, sir," Trehearne replied, "There's talk that some

266

disturbance occurred. I heard three men were killed and four men and an Indian maid were cast in the Bay so Sheriff Taylor had to take a company of men with arms and go to Ginguhcloust to try and appease the Indians. He left a few days ago and I haven't heard anything since he left but we've been ordered to take shot and powder with us everywhere, even Church."

"Even Church? I didna think Rev. Rozier likes that."

"Ye are probably right, Mr. Berriman." Trehearne glanced down the creek and pointed, "Isn't that Mr. Pattenden shallop, sir?"

Henry gazed in the direction Trehearne pointed and replied, "I believe it is, Trehearne. How is Miss Mary doing?"

"I hear she's the same, sir."

"That's too bad. I brought something with me that may cheer her up." Berriman walked to the end of the pier and shouted. "Pattenden, it's good to see ye again. Come drink a pint of ale with me and we'll catch up on the news."

Henry carefully glided his shallop against the quay, climbed on the platform beside William and tied his boat as he replied. "It's good to see ye back William. When did ye arrive?"

"Just now, Trehearne's loading the crates I purchased in England."

"Ye must have received a good price for our tobacco considering the number of crates ye have," Henry laughed. "I didna see Jane. Did she stay in England with her sister?"

"Nay, she's inside with Jonas. Who didna ye think bought all these crates? Don't ever take Mary to England Henry, unless ye want to return near bankrupt, like me," Berriman chortled. "But as far as the price on tobacco....it was a fair price considering the trouble in England."

The two men began walking toward the ordinary but Henry halted and asked, "Troubles in England? What's the news William?"

"Well, King Charles is at odds with Parliament. He even attempted to arrest five men in Parliament for treason....why he raised an army of 400 soldiers and went right into the House of Commons but the men were no where to be found. But our brave King had to flee London in fear of being captured. I'm not sure where he is now. Everyone in England is taking sides. England's not a safe place to be and right now I'm glad we're in Virginia."

Henry looked down then continued his walk toward the ordinary and said, "I hate to give Mary this news. She'll be so worried about her family."

Berriman opened the door and Henry stepped inside the dark room. William followed him and asked. "How's Mary these days, Henry?"

"Much the same, Will. She still blames herself for Mary Margaret's death and try as I might I can't convince her different."

"Mayhaps this will cheer her," Berriman said and produced a packet from inside his jerkin. "Tis a packet from home. It arrived just before I left London."

"I hope it brings good news, Will. I didna think Mary can handle more bad news."

"I hope so too, Henry. Now let's get that pint of ale. I'm parched."

It was almost dusk when Henry maneuvered the shallop around the dense marsh grass near his quay. As he drew close to the pier, he spied Mary and Henry, Jr. sitting on the side of the dock. Henry, Jr. was bobbing a fishing pole up and down in the water.

Once he was within hearing distance, Henry laughed and said, "Henry, Jr. those fish are going to be plumb worn out by the time they finished chasing ye pole. Ye must hold the pole still to catch anything."

"I already caught three Papa....see," Henry Jr. gave his pole to his mother, then pulled a line out of the water with three good sized fish on the end.

"Well, I stand corrected," Henry declared. "Ye may have a new fishing method. Mayhaps I need lessons from ye."

"Now, Henry, Jr., ye must tell the truth," his mother scolded.

"Well, umm....I did have a little help from Mum when I caught the first three. But this one I plan to catch all by meself," Henry, Jr. stated emphatically.

His father laughed out loud then said to Mary, "It's good to see ye out fishing with Henry, Jr. Ye have been working much too hard indoors."

"Marie is making candles and it was so warm today that I

thought it would be nice to see if we could catch a breeze near the water as well as some fish for tomorrow's dinner," Mary explained. "Ye are later than usual coming from Hungar's. Is there news about the Indians in Ginguhcloust?"

"Nay, but I do have news. William Berriman has returned with Jane and Jonas." Henry stepped on the pier beside Mary and continued, "He was loading his shallop with crates from England."

"Jane came back with him? I thought she might stay with her sister in England."

"Nay, she came back with Will." Henry paused and decided not to tell Mary about the problems in England yet. He didn't want to spoil her mood with bad news from home. Then he remembered the packet. "Will brought something to ye and I hope tis good news." Henry retrieved the packet from his jerkin and handed it to Mary.

Mary took the packet and held it in her lap for a moment then carefully broke the seal. "It's from my brother instead of Mum. I recognize his writing." She read for a few minutes then exclaimed. "Oh Henry, Mum is ill. That is why she has not written for so long. She has consumption. Oh, I can't bear it. My whole family will be gone soon and I'll never see any of them again." Mary jumped up and ran toward the house, stumbling and crying as she ran.

Henry was torn between staying with his son or following after Mary and trying to console her but he knew that Mary would never forgive him if anything happened to Henry, Jr. There would be little he could do to ease Mary's mind so he remained on the pier.

"Why is Mummy crying?" Henry, Jr., asked.

"She received some sad news son, but she will be okay soon. Now let's see those three fish ye caught. They look like they are almost as big as ye."

Henry, Jr. beamed at his father's attention and pulled on the line with the three fish attached until the fish were visible.

"Why they are as big as ye!" his father exclaimed as he put his arm around his small son's shoulder and gazed sadly in the direction of his house. "I know Marie would love to see those fish. Let's pull them in and we'll take them to her."

"But I wanted to catch another," Henry, Jr. pleaded.

269

"It's late now son. Mayhaps ye can try again tomorrow. Here let me help ye with those fish."

Henry carried the three fish and the pole while Henry, Jr. slowly followed his father up the path his mother had just taken to the house.

CHAPTER FORTY-ONE

August 1642, Plantation Creek, Eastern Shore, Virginia

The last week in August, nature put on a spectacular show in Accawmacke. A bounteous crop of Indian corn and tobacco whispered in the wind as the soft breeze from the bay swept across cleared land. A delightful scent of wild flowers formed a fragrant, soft carpet in the dense woods tickled one's nose and captivated the eyes.

It was a perfect time for the wedding of Alice Traveller, the recent widow of George Traveller. She had been the subject of many scandals concerning adulterous affairs while married to her first husband George Traveller. Her second husband, William Burdett, was a respected planter, at Hungar's Parish Church in Accawmacke. Since the wedding took place on the Sabbath after the regular Church service, everyone was in attendance. An extravagant feast was held after the ceremony giving an opportunity for parishioners to discuss the news and latest gossip.

Jane Jackson spread a quilt under a huge oak tree so Jonas could nap and Mary, happy to see her old friend back, sat down beside her to exchange pleasantries while Henry went off to join William and several other men. Henry, Jr. was playing chase with two other children.

"Did ye enjoy ye visit to England, Jane?" Mary inquired.

"Not as much as I thought I would. The situation with the King and Parliament was quite unpleasant."

"Henry told me about King Charles attempting to arrest those men in Parliament, but how are the people directly affected. It seems that it's an argument between the King and Parliament."

"It would appear so but everyone is being forced to take sides since both Parliament and the King are raising armies."

"I didna realize that Parliament was trying to raise an army. Are they allowed to do that?"

"Allowed? I didna think they are allowed. They just took it

upon themselves to do so."

"Then, I am worried about me family in Cranbrook. Papa died because he had to serve in one of the King's armies, I hope me brothers are not forced to do so as well. Mum is ill and I didna know what she would do without me brothers at home to help her."

"Oh, Mary. I'm sorry to hear ye Mum is ill. William said that he had a packet for ye. We hoped it would bring good news but obviously it was bad," Jane said in a consoling voice.

"Let's talk no more of them. I'm afraid I will start to cry again. I do that too much already and I also want to apologize for speaking so harshly to ye after Mary Margaret died and I should have helped ye more after ye husband died. I've missed our friendship and I was so afraid ye would stay in England. I didna seem to do anything right lately," Mary stammered.

"Oh Mary, there is nothing to forgive. We will always be friends," Jane said as she leaned over to hug Mary. Recognizing that Mary was near tears, Jane changed the subject. "This wedding is quite exorbitant, isn't it? I knew Alice would marry again soon but I thought she'd marry someone a little younger this time."

"I guess she is marrying for wealth but I didna know why," Mary continued. "George Traveller left her well taken care of in spite of all the rumors about her."

"Days like today remind me of Mum," Jane said with sadness. "She'd have a lot to say about Alice Traveller Burdett. Abusing a bairn is something Mum would never tolerate."

"I miss ye Mum everyday. She was like me second Mum. I didna know how I would have managed when I first came here without her."

"Have ye heard any news about Rev. Eaton and Anne?" Jane asked.

"Henry said that all Anne's inheritance has been assigned to Rev. Eaton and Henry is very worried. Rev. Eaton is constantly gambling, drinking and spending money. They won't have much left at the rate he is spending," Mary replied.

"Poor Anne. She seems to have married the wrong person. I guess all the rumors we heard about him when he was at Harvard must have been true."

A young girl in a yellow dress walked by the two friends as

they chatted and something caught Mary's eye. "Why that can't be!" she stammered. Then she stood up to get a better look as the girl moved farther away. Mary walked toward the girl as she said, "Excuse me Jane, but I must see..." her voice trailed off and she moved more quickly to catch up with the girl.

As she drew close, she touched the girl's arm and declared loudly, "Where did ye get that ribbon?"

The young girl was startled and hesitated for a minute then said, "Tis none of ye business but it was given to me."

Mary said with anger in her voice, "Who gave it to ye?"

"Why...uh...uh Henry Weede, Jr.," replied the girl timidly as she backed away from Mary.

"Well, it was not his to give. Tis mine and I will have it back."

"Nay, Henry gave it to me," she reiterated while her eyes searched the crowd for someone to assist her. She continued to back away.

"I said I mean to have it back and I will," Mary said. Then Mary reached up and snatched the ribbon from the girl's hair. The girl was still backing away and tripped when Mary reached for her hair. She landed in a bush and a ripping sound was heard as her yellow dress was torn by a limb."

Several people saw the commotion and gathered around Mary and the girl. Henry was talking to William and they both glanced at the gathering crowd.

"What could be taking place over there?" William wondered aloud.

Henry examined the scene and was astonished to see Mary standing with something clasped in her hand as she stared at a girl lying in a bush. He rushed over to Mary, and put his arms around her shoulders while another man helped the young girl to her feet.

"The girl began crying hysterically...she's mad. She attacked me. Ye all saw it. She attacked me. Look at me torn dress."

Henry whispered to his wife. "What is the meaning of this Mary? Did ye attack this girl?"

Then Mary fainted and would have fallen to the ground had not Henry caught her in his arms. He carried her to Jane's quilt and gently placed her on it.

The girl continued to scream hysterically in the background.

Henry, Jr. saw his mother lying on the quilt and ran to join them. "Why is Mummy sleeping, Papa?" he asked.

"I don't know son," Henry answered. Jane pulled Henry, Jr. in her lap.

Henry looked at Jane and asked "Do ye know what happened, Jane?"

"Not much," she replied. "Mary got up and followed that girl and jerked a ribbon out of her hair."

"Ribbon....so that's it." He gently, uncurled Mary's fingers from the ribbon she held tightly in a fist. "This ribbon is special to Mary. It was a gift from her family before she left England. It meant everything to her and she always wore it, but it was lost recently. She thought it was gone forever."

Mary began to move her lips and mutter. In a few minutes, she was able to sit up.

"Mary, sip this," Henry said as he offered her some water from a gourd.

Mary complied, then asked, "What happened, Henry?"

"Ye fainted, love. But before ye fainted, ye caused quite a ruckus."

"What do ye mean?" she queried with a puzzled look on her face.

"Didna ye not remember?"

"Nay, Henry...what did I do?"

"Evidently, ye found ye're ribbon. See it's in ye hand. Ye pulled it out of Anne Smyth's hair."

"What? I don't remember anything Henry. Please believe me."

"I understand. Mary. Ye have just been overwrought and worried about ye family in England and I intend to do something about it. We will make plans for a trip to England as soon as ye're able. It's time ye Mum meets her grandson."

"Do ye mean it Henry? I will see Mum again soon. Is it safe for ye? What about Arshbishop Laud?"

"Aye, Mary. Laud is imprisoned in the Tower of London. It will be safe for us to visit. But first we have to calm the girl ye took the ribbon from. She thinks ye are mad."

274

"Oh Henry. I'm so sorry. I didna mean to scare anyone."

"I know ye didna love," Henry looked at Berriman and asked, "Do ye think ye can apologize to the Miss Smyth for us. Right now I think I need to take Mary home."

"Certainly Henry," William replied.

"Thanks Will," Henry said then he turned to Mary and asked, "Do ye feel well enough to walk?"

"Aye, Henry. I can do anything now that I know I will soon see me Mum."

CHAPTER FORTY-TWO

September, 1642, Eastern Shore, Virginia

Mary and Henry were force to delay their trip to England because Anne Smyth's father filed a court complaint against Mary. Henry and Mary were summoned to court in early September to explain her actions against Anne Smyth.

Since there were many witnesses to the incident, the court had no trouble finding someone willing to testify. When Henry and Mary arrived, the small room was full.

Mary was frightened. The court sometimes applied harsh punishments to women. She remembered what happened to poor Joane Butler for talking back and using vile language against her husband. The court ordered Joane to be pulled across King's Creek at the stern of canoe.

Alice told me that Joane nearly lost her mind after the humiliation. How will the court punish me? I don't even remember what happened? How can I even defend what I did?

Mary trembled as she set on the hard bench beside her husband.

Col. Yeardley began the inquiry stating the complaint made by Anne Smyth. "Miss Anne Smyth has stated in her complaint that Mrs. Pattenden attacked her on August 28, struck her, tore a ribbon from her hair and pushed her in a bush. Then she tore her dress. We are here today to determine what took place and assign punishment if punishment is due."

Henry stood and asked, "If the court will allow, I would like to testify on my wife, Mary's behalf."

The court often allowed husband's to speak for their wives so Col. Yeardley stated, "I see no problem with ye're request. Ye will be allowed to speak for Mrs. Pattenden."

Mary gave a sigh of relief. She looked up at her husband with love and gratitude.

Henry is well respected and has been a frequent witness for others in the community. Mayhaps this will help me now.

Thomas Clifton, had been one of the first to arrive at the incident that took place between Mary and Anne so he was the first witness questioned.

Col. Yeardley asked, "Thomas, can ye describe what took place between Mrs. Pattenden and Anne Smyth."

"Why, Mrs. Pattenden followed Anne Smyth, stopped her and fell into words of distaste. She tore a ribbon from Anne Smyth's hair. Then Anne lost her balance and fell in the bush," said Clifton.

Yeardley inquired, "Did Mrs. Pattenden strike Anne Smyth at any time in the incident?"

"Nay, sir. Mrs. Pattenden only took the ribbon from Miss Smyth's hair. She did not strike her."

A few other witnesses were called and they all gave approximately the same testimony.

Since Anne was underage, her father was called next to testify for her.

Col. Yeardley asked, "Can ye describe the incident, Mr. Smyth?"

"Aye, sir, vividly." Smyth replied. "Anne said Mrs. Pattenden came to her like a mad women, she struck her, tore the ribbon from her hair and pushed her in the bush."

"Did ye actually see Mrs. Pattenden strike Anne or are ye describing what Anne told ye?"

"Well, I didna see what happened, sir. But my Anne didna lie," he replied and he glared at Mary as he spoke.

"Did Mrs. Pattenden say why she wanted the ribbon?" Col. Yeadley asked.

"Aye Sir. She said it t'was hers but Henry Weede, Jr. gave that ribbon to Anne. It weren't Mrs. Pattendens. I think he's sweet on Anne."

Anne Smyth blushed as laughter broke out in the room among the visitors.

"Ah, we must hear from Henry Weede, Jr, then,. Is Henry Weede, Jr. here?" Col. Yeardley asked as he looked into the crowd.

"Aye Sir," a young boy shouted from the back of the crowded room.

"Swear him in," Yeardley ordered the sheriff.

Henry Weede, Jr. moved to the front and was quickly sworn in. Then Col. Yeardley asked him, "Son, did ye give the alleged ribbon to Anne Smyth?"

"Aye, sir," Weede replied, "I found the ribbon in the woods near our house, cleaned it and gave it to Anne. I thought it would look pretty in her hair," he continued as he glanced in the direction of Anne and grinned.

Laughter and guffaws rang among the crowd.

"He's sweet on her all right," a man shouted.

Anne Smyth's cheeks turned bright red. She threw her hands up and tried to cover her face.

"That's good son, ye may step down." Col. Yeardley said. " Mr. Pattenden, I think we are ready to hear from ye now."

Henry stood and was sworn in and Col. Yeardley asked, "Can ye describe what took place?"

"I didna actually see what happened between Mary and Anne. I arrived afterward but Mary was holding a ribbon and Anne was being helped out of the bush by Clifton. I didna ask questions because Mary fainted shortly after I arrived. I had to see to her health. But, as ye know, we recently lost our bairn and Mary has been mightly grieved over her death. The ribbon was a special present from her family in England and she valued it highly. She wore it everywhere and it was a devastating blow when she lost it the day of Henry Weede's funeral."

Mary bowed her head and tried to become invisible as her husband talked about her.

Henry continued, "As ye all know, Mary has always been a caring, loving person and I believe she only acted out of overwhelming grief. She would never intentionally hurt anyone and would like to apologize for any pain she has caused Anne Smyth."

Col. Yeardley said, "I believe we have heard enough. Gentlemen we must now make a decision."

Henry sat down next to Mary, took her hand in his and patted it softly.

"Henry, I'm so frightened," Mary whispered.

Henry lovingly squeezed her hand. People in the small room were muttering among themselves.

After a few moments of consultation with his fellow court

members, Col. Yeardley spoke. "We have made a decision. Mary ye are found guilty of attacking Anne Smyth and tearing a ribbon from her hair but since ye didna strike her or otherwise cause harm to her and considering the burden of grief ye carry, the court orders that a penalty rather than punishment is due Anne Smyth. Henry ye are ordered to pay Mr. Smyth, one-hundred pounds of tobacco as penalty for ye wife, Mary's action against the said Anne Smyth. The payment should be made at the end of ye next harvest."

Mary fell against Henry in relief. "Henry, I'm so sorry to cause ye this trouble," she whispered.

"Mary, I would gladly pay this penalty one hundred times for ye," he responded and pressed her hand in his palm. "Now we'll make our plans to travel to England."

"Oh Henry, ye are too good to me," Mary whispered as she looked into his eyes.

They stood and Henry approached Col. Yeardley while Mary waited. Soon they both left the room. Henry's protective arm encircled Mary and he pressed her close to him as they walked through the crowd.

CHAPTER FORTY-THREE

October, 1642, London, England

By early October, Henry, Mary and Henry, Jr. were on their way to England. The weather was fair throughout the trip and they arrived in London by the end of the October, only to find the normally busy streets almost vacant. They easily found a room and Henry inquired, "I notice the streets are empty, has something happened?"

"Aye, sir, have ye not heard that King Charles is advancing on London with his army?"

Henry turned to Mary, "What situation have I brought us to?"

"Mayhaps tis not as bad as it seems, Henry," Mary countered. "The King has not yet arrived and we will be leaving soon for Cranbrook."

Henry asked the innkeeper, "Where may I acquire transportation? We'd like to depart immediately."

"Ye might not want to leave right away, sir. Parliament's army has left to meet the King and we didna know where the two armies are located at present time. But we know they are nearby. It might be safer staying here. Rumor has it that the armies met seven days ago, and engaged in battle between the towns of Keinton and Edgehill. They say that during the battle, the King's standard was taken and his standard-bearer, Edmund Berney, was killed. But two royalists managed to retrieve it later. I heard that King Charles spent the night on the field of battle."

"Do ye know who won?" Henry asked.

"Both armies claim victory," the innkeeper replied.

Henry looked at Mary, "It seems best that we remain here until we know more Mary."

"Aye, Henry, we will wait."

"Good man," Henry inquired, "Will ye keep me informed of any news? We would like to travel to Cranbrook as soon as possible."

"Aye, sir. But ye may find it hard obtaining transportation due to the uncertainties."

"I understand. Just keep us informed."

As Henry and his family climbed the stairs to their rooms, Henry said, "It appears we have arrived in London in the middle of a hornet's nest. I hope the armies stay away from London."

Two days later, the innkeeper stopped Henry as he was leaving the inn.

"Mr. Pattenden, ye wanted me to inform ye of news," the innkeeper said in a nervous voice.

"Aye."

"Lord Essex is returning to London with his army. He is quartered at Northampton."

"What about the King?" Henry asked. "He was in Oxford a few days ago but it is said he is now advancing on London. Rupert is quartered at Maidenhead now."

"Then I guess we have no choice but to remain here longer," said Henry.

Oh Mary, I hope I haven't brought ye and Henry, Jr. to danger. I wish we were at home in Virginia. What are we doing in England? This is what we wanted to get away from.

The next day, Lord Essex arrived in London and received thanks from both Houses of Parliament. Hoping to avert further conflict, Parliament sent word to the King that they might designate a safe place for the King to reside near London until both parties of Parliament could determine a compromise to submit to the King. King Charles responded by marching his army within half a mile Brentford, where part of Essex army resided. He was soon discovered and panic filled the streets of London.

The Earls of Pembroke, Holland and Say and Sele gave speeches at Guildhall. Henry was in attendance at some of the speeches and he was especially inspired by Say and Sele.

"Let every man shut up his shop; let him take his musket; let him offer himself readily and willingly. Let him not think with himself who shall pay me? but rather think this, I will come forth to

save the kingdom, to serve my God, to maintain his true religion, to save the parliament, to save this noble city."

After hearing the words, Henry rushed back to the inn and asked the innkeeper, "Where might I acquire arms? It appears we will soon be in battle with the King's army."

The innkeeper mentioned a shop near Aldersgate street and Henry left to find the shop.

Henry and Mary woke to the sound of distant guns on the 12th of November.

"Henry what shall we do," Mary cried. "Me selfish desire to see Mum has brought us to this danger."

"God will be with us, Mary. Don't worry love." Henry tried to sound more convinced than he felt.

Before noon, the innkeeper reported to Henry, "Prince Rupert charged down the barricaded streets of Brentford and met Hollis's regiment. Mayhaps ye family would like to join us downstairs."

"We would," Henry replied.

The sounds of guns continued till evening, reverberating throughout the inn and shaking the windows. Henry, Jr. and the innkeeper's son and daughter, screamed and cried incessantly. Finally, when night fell and the guns stopped, the exhausted children fell asleep on pallets on the floor near the fireplace. But confusion and alarm remained in the streets. Young men throughout the city of London filled the streets.

The innkeeper stepped outside and asked a couple of the men, "Where are ye bound?"

"To join Parliament's army on Turnham Green," one of the men shouted back. "And ye would do well to join us. We're fighting for God, our wives and our children. God will bless us."

Henry heard the interchange between the innkeeper and the young man. He looked at Mary.

"Didna say it Henry," she pleaded. "We need ye here."

"Mary, ye know I can not remain here in hiding. I must stand up with these men." Henry turned to the innkeeper, "Will ye take care of me family?"

"Aye, I wish I was younger and I'd go with ye. God bless ye. I will protect ye family as me own."

Henry grabbed his musket and ammunition and joined the

men in the street.

By morning over 24,000 men filled Turnham Green. They were provided with provisions of meat, beer, tobacco and wine by the housewives of London and ready for battle with the King. Plans of attack on the King's forces were being made when a rumor began to circulate that the King had retreated. By noon, word from the commanders verified that the King's army was seen marching toward his summer house at Oatlands. Cheers rang out and the men gradually dispersed to their respective homes and shops.

Henry returned to the inn to an anxious Mary who met him at the door. "Oh Henry, I was so worried. We should never have come to England. Let's go to Cranford before there is more trouble."

"We will Mary," Henry replied. "Once we have word that King Charles does not plan to return, I'll find transportation."

The Pattenden's remained in London for two more weeks. By the end of November the King was residing in his winter quarters at Oxford so Henry immediately acquired transportation to Cranbrook.

CHAPTER FORTY-FOUR

December, 1642, England

Mary snuggled closer to Henry in an attempt to stay warm in the cold coach. Henry, Jr. was sleeping soundly with his head in his mother's lap and a quilt tucked securely around him. They were alone in the usually crowded coach since most citizens stayed home, not willing to risk traveling with the hostilities taking place between the King and Parliament. So far, their journey had been uneventful except for the two times the coach was stopped and the family forced to disembark while the cabin was searched.

"Henry, I'll be so glad to see Cranbrook," Mary said softly. "Tis all me fault our family has been placed in such danger."

"There was no way of knowing this confrontation would take place, love. That was quite an adventure in London but I think it made the citizens realize that there must be a compromise soon. I heard Parliament is trying to arrange a place for King Charles to reside safely while they work on a proposition to restore peace."

"I hope they're successful," Mary replied as she stroked Henry, Jr's hair, "Though tis me greatest desire to see Mum, I would feel so much safer in our home in Virginia right now, even with the Indians close by."

"Would ye really, Mary?" Henry asked incredulously. "I never thought ye would feel safer in Virginia than England."

"We have freedom to do as we like in the Colonies, Henry without fear. That is not the case here. I wish Mum would understand that and return with us but I know I'll never convince her to leave England."

"Mayhaps this fight between Parliament and King Charles will change her mind," Henry added.

"If it doesn't, then nothing will. I'm never been as frightened as I was when ye left for Turnham Green. I thought I'd never see ye again."

"I'm sorry, ye were frightened, Mary, but I could not stand

by and watch others die over such a cause."

"I know, Henry. I would not expect ye to do otherwise. Mayhaps ye will not have to make such a decision in Cranbrook. The majority of people there sympathize with Parliament. King Charles dare not attack Cranbook."

As if on cue, the gentle hills of Cranbrook came into view and Mary woke her sleeping son. "Henry, Jr., ye must wake up... there's me home!"

As they drew near the town, Henry smiled as Mary excitedly pointed to houses and objects within view, and related stories from her childhood to Henry, Jr. The town was quiet when they arrived.

"Tis strange," Mary stated with some confusion. "It's December. Cranbrook is usually busy with Christmas activities and where are the decorations?"

Overhearing her comment, as he unloaded their baggage, the coach driver commented, "Have ye not heard about the ban? Parliament ruled last September that there should be no observation of Christmas, no plays, feasts of other events. No singing of carols or gifts should be given since all such things are Popery. Only the fast on Christmas day should be observed."

Mary replied with astonishment, "No Christmas plays? I can't believe it. That seems harsh."

The coach driver looked at Mary critically and Henry realized that her comment might be misconstrued as a Royalist viewpoint so he added, "All those events do take away from the true purpose of Christmas...Christ's birth. I can see the reasoning. A fast does seem more appropriate."

"Aye, that is what Parliament concluded," the coach driver said. Then he pointed, "See that cottage, three doors down. Ye folks can probably acquire a wagon there." Then he climbed up on the coach and shouted, "Good luck to ye!"

Mary looked at Henry as the left, "Did ye mean that, Henry? I can't imagine not celebrating Christmas."

"I agree, Mary. But we do have to watch what we say here. Ye never know who is listening."

"Aye, ye are right. I guess I'm grown accustomed to safely saying what I feel in Virginia."

Henry looked in the direction the stage driver pointed and

said, "I'll see if I can acquire transportation. Ye remain here with Henry, Jr. and our baggage."

The Pattenden's arrived at Mary's mother's house late the same evening and excitement reigned as her family greeted them.

Everyone talked at once until her mother finally said. "Henry and Mary, I know ye are exhausted after ye long trip. Ye young bairns take Henry, Jr. to the loft and help him get settled and I'll help ye two settle down here."

Mary's mother started to lift a bag but sat down in the nearest chair instead, then said between coughs, "I don't think I'll be of much help Mary. Ye know what to do."

"Aye, Mum. We'll be fine. Why don't ye rest now! We'll have plenty of time to talk later."

"It's true, I am tired. If ye're sure," Mary's mother said as she slowly trudged toward her room. "God bless ye for coming. We'll talk tomorrow."

Mary's eyes were misty as she watched her mother walk away. After she was gone, Mary whispered softly, "Henry, Mum is so thin and pale. Thank ye for bringing us here even with all the problems in England. I didna know if I could bear not seeing Mum again...." Her voice trailed off and Henry drew her tenderly into his arms and she quietly cried on his shoulder.

The next morning, Mary woke up before anyone and was preparing breakfast when her mother slowly shuffled into the room. "Why Mary, ye mustn't do that. Ye're visiting. Here, I'll take over...sit down and talk to me."

"Nay, ye sit and rest Mum. Tis time I helped ye some after all the years ye took care of me," Mary replied as she pounded soft dough on the table.

Her mother looked at Mary with red eyes and said. "Tis old I've grown since ye left."

Mary looked at her mother's paper thin skin and fought back tears, "Oh, Mum... so much has happened...I thought I'd never see ye again. There's been so much death, tis hard to bear."

"I wish I could have been with ye when Mary Margaret died, Mary. There is nothing as painful as losing a child, especially one so young."

Mary stiffened, "Aye Mum, and since I was to blame for her death, it's doubly hard".

"But I thought she was ill. How can ye be at fault for illness? I didna blame meself for this illness. Tis just part of God's plan."

"God's plan......God's plan. That's what everyone says and I'm sick of hearing it! God punished me. I neglected Mary Margaret when she needed me most and I am the reason she is dead. I am at fault!" Mary exclaimed.

Mary's mother looked at Mary with astonishment. "Why Mary, where did ye ever get such an idea? And most of all, how can ye place yeself higher than God?"

"What......higher than God? What did ye mean? I'm not placing meself higher than God. I am to blame," Mary stammered.

"Ye said that ye're the cause of Mary Margaret's death. Only God controls life and death. No one can ever completely destroy what God has made. Ye would be higher than God if ye could."

"But, He created Mary Margaret and she is dead."

"Only her body died, Mary. Not her soul. God created and decided the fate of Mary Margaret's soul before she was ever born and he decided to take her back to heaven. Ye said that she was never strong. Mayhaps, God wanted her to have a stronger body and save her suffering so he took her back for now. Mayhaps He will send her soul again in a stronger body. We will never know but tis God's will not ours."

"I never thought....then she's not really dead?"

"Nay Mary, as I said before. Only God can completely destroy what He has made. Even our bodies do not completely die. They only change forms. 'Ashes to ashes' so the Bible says. I could not go on if I didna believe that I will see ye father and me family again. They are all in heaven waiting for me along with Mary Margaret and I will join them soon...whole and without this miserable, sick body. I will rejoice in the day and cling to the words of his son Jesus when he said: *I am the resurrection and the life. He who believes in me will live, even though he dies; and whoever lives and believes in me will never die.*"

"Oh, Mum. I've been dwelling on Mary Margaret's death not

her soul in Heaven. Then I didna cause her death?"

"Nay, Mary. Only God is in control of life and death."

Mary's eyes filled with tears... "Then Mary Margaret is with God in heaven and I didna cause her death."

"Nay, Mary...again remember Jesus words, *"Suffer little children, and forbid them not, to come unto me for of such is the kingdom of heaven."'*

Mary could no longer hold back her tears. "Oh, Mum. I didna cause her death. Mary Margaret is not dead. She is with God. She is with Papa in heaven."

"Aye, Mary," Mary's mother stood and took her daughter in her frail arms. "Ye were never at fault, Mary. Ye are a child of God and one day we will all be together in heaven. One day soon, I will see ye Papa again. I rejoice in the day..."

Henry appeared in the doorway but not wanting to disturb their special moment, started to retreat but Mary caught a glimpse of him before he left and said, "Henry, I have been so selfish. I realize now I didna cause Mary Margaret's death. She is not dead. She is with Papa in heaven."

Henry gave a look of astonishment at the change in Mary, then a huge smile filled his face. "Margaret, I'm so glad we came to visit ye. How I've longed for the day when I would hear those words from Mary. Ye have returned Mary to me."

Margeret laughed and said, "Henry, I thank ye for returning Mary to me as well."

Mary, Henry and Margaret began to all talk at once and made so much commotion that the children awoke and scampered down from the loft to see what was happening. The excitement from the previous evening continued the remainder of the day.

CHAPTER FORTY-FIVE

March 1643, Eastern Shore, Virginia

In Early spring of 1643, the Pattendens returned to Virginia with Mary in much better spirits. They had not encountered bad weather nor much iillness on their trip across the Atlantic and were thankful to be out of the turmoil transpiring in England. Berriman and his sister Jane visited the Pattenden plantation shortly after their arrival. Jane's son Jonas was an active toddler and Henry, Jr. enjoyed showing him how to feed the chickens.

Jane helped Mary prepare dinner while William and Henry watched the two boys chase the chickens in the yard and discussed the news of the Civil War in England.

"Jonas certainly has his father's looks with that jet black hair," Mary said.

"It's like seeing John again, each time I look at him," Jane said sadly. "I miss John, I didna know if I will ever love another as much.....but I must provide Jonas with a father. It's hard enough for a boy to grow up in Virginia, but without a father to guide him, it's almost impossible to provide all he needs. William does what he can but he is very busy with his own plantation."

"I thought ye would live with William after John died," Mary replied. "Why did ye not sell the plantation?"

"I know it's not much of a start, but I wanted to save the plantation for Jonas," Jane replied. "John worked hard to build it and it's the only legacy his father can give him. I just hope that I can maintain it,,...And mayhaps I can if I married again."

"Ah, Jane, is there a prospect of a husband? What happened while I was away?"

Jane responded coyly, "Well, Richard Lemmon asked me to marry him. I haven't accepted yet...but..."

"Richard Lemmon, I've heard his name. Doesn't he live by ye brother Will?"

"Aye. William asked him to handle John's estate and we

spent a good deal of time together going over the inventory. He also handles a good deal of William's business now. William thinks a lot of him and he is very nice but I just didna love him as I did John so I've hesitated giving him an answer."

"How do Jonas and Richard get along?"

"Jonas adores him. Jonas was so small when John died that he doesn't remember him. He's called Richard, 'Papa' several times. I know Richard would be good to Jonas. I didna know why I'm so reluctant."

"It's a hard decision to make, but I'm sure ye will make the right one," Mary encouraged her friend, then sensing Jane wanted to change the subject she asked, "Chris mentioned that Alice Burdett's husband passed away while we were gone."

"It appears Alice is as unlucky as I am in marriage. But she is doing quite well though. Between the death of two of the richest men in Accawmacke as her husbands, she has been very well provided for. The funeral was unbelievable. We didna stay but a little while but I understand the funeral feast lasted for two days with considerable drinking and such. As ye can imagine there was much talk about the event afterwards. Do ye know, William Burdett left me a beautiful ring in his will? I can't think why but I did visit him often when he became ill. Perhaps that's the reason. Anyway, Alice is no longer speaking to me because of the ring."

"Alice manages to be the topic of conversation frequently in Accawmacke," Mary mused. "And her moods are changeable as the wind, I imagine she'll speak to ye again soon. How are things with Rev. Eaton and Anne? Henry is so worried about Anne? He felt he should have done more to stop the wedding but of course he was injured at the time."

"The same if not worse.. At the rate Eaton....I'm sorry it's hard for me to call him Rev....but anyway, at the rate he's spending her money, there is talk that she will soon be destitute. Hopefully, he will find some means other than gambling to earn his living."

"Oh, I hope so too."

Henry, William, Henry, Jr. and Jonas entered the house with Henry, Jr. shouting, "Mum, Jonas found three eggs! May we cook them now?"

"Not now," Mary laughed. "Perhaps we'll have them tomorrow. Jane and I have already prepared dinner today. Now ye and Jonas watch that dirt off ye face and hands and come to dinner."

Henry, Jr. scampered to the wash pail pulling little Jonas by the hand.

"That little Jonas is really growing up to be a fine boy, Jane." Henry said.

"Thank ye Henry. William has helped train him quite a bit," Jane added.

"Aye, that reminds me Henry. I forgot to tell ye," William continued, "Berkeley ordered that we form a trained militia in Accawmacke. Everyone must participate in training. The Indian talk became worse, while ye were away. There's fear of an attack, especially in Jamestown."

"I can understand their fear in Jamestown but I see no point in requiring the same of us. We've never had trouble with Indians."

"I agree. But there is talk of Scarburgh becoming a member of the House of Burgess and in that position he might cause trouble with the Indians. I don't think it will harm us none to be prepared. Berkeley appointed William Roper and Edward Douglas commanders here and all who didna follow their regulations will be set to Jamestown to be sentenced."

"Scarburgh in the House of Burgess? That ought to be interesting," Henry laughed. "His hatred for the Indians will not help keep peace with them."

"Enough of this talk about Indians. England and militia," Mary said. "We worked hard on this meal. Let's all sit down and enjoy fellowship and have pleasant talk for a change."

"I say Aye too that," Henry said.

"A toast to our continued friendship," William declared as he lifted his cup of ale.

"Aye," Henry, Jane and Mary said in unison.

Christmas in Virginia in 1643 was very different from the one Henry and Mary spent in England the year before. Many festivals, feats, events and caroling took place throughout the month. Jane Jackson married Richard Lemmon two days before Christmas.

"Richard seems to be a fine man," Mary remarked to Jane at

the wedding feast.

"Aye, Mary. Jonas adores him and he will be a fine father for him," Jane responded.

"Henry and I wish ye and Richard much happiness. And it's great to hear the carols and see Christmas plays this year. Henry, Jr. is certainly enjoying everything. I'm afraid he missed having a Christmas last year in England."

"I didna understand why Christmas was banned. I understand that shops even remained open on Christmas day in England."

"Ye are right. It was a very strange Christmas indeed. I'm so happy that we are home this year, even with the rumors of an Indian attack."

"I can't imagine the Indians around here attacking. But Richard and William both say that the threat is real. There have already been a few skirmishes in Jamestown. Did ye hear that Alice Burnett and Peter Walker are to be wed?"

"Aye, Henry mentioned it. She has done very well for herself by her marriages. I believe she is one of the wealthiest women in Accawmacke. Henry said that there was quite an argument between the Roundheads and Cavaliers after William Burdett's funeral. It became so intense that a fight almost developed. I hope England's war never reaches us."

"I do too, Mary. We have enough troubles with Indian threats."

Mary nodded in the direction of a group of men in a heated discussion, "It looks like those men are trying to start a war over there from the sound of it."

"With Scarburgh in the middle of it I'm sure it's bound to include something about his favorite topic....Indians," Jane remarked.

"Mayhaps we need to interrupt the conversation before it goes any further. I'd hate to have it said that a fight took place at ye wedding," Mary laughed as she and Jane moved toward the men.

"That would be an awful way to start a marriage," Jane added while she walked with Mary. "I hope it's not a sign of things to come."

CHAPTER FORTY-SIX

April 1644, Plantation Creek, Eastern Shore, Virginia

Governor Berkeley, concerned by the spreading of civil war in England, ordered Good Friday, April 18th, 1644 as a day of fasting and prayer for the King. But on April 17th the fears of an Indian attack were realized in Jamestown. Early that morning, Indians massed an attack on outlying plantations around Jamestown.

A few people managed to escape and word of the onslaught caused panic to sweep throughout Virginia like a dark cloud overshadowing the colony. Every person was on high alert. In Accawmacke, the four militia units were immediately summoned to Hungar's church to prepare for the worst. While the commander's formed a strategy to meet the aggressors, members of the militia milled around in front of the church. Suddenly, a rider on horseback galloped toward the group at break-neck speed.

"Tis Opecancanough, leader of the Pamunky Indians, again....it's a massacre!" shouted the young messenger from his horse. He jumped off his horse and tried to catch his breath.

Scarbrugh shouted, "We should have killed that savage after the last attack!"

"Where are they now?" asked Berriman.

"Still in Jamestown," he replied between gasps. "The savages are in groups and attacking outlying homes. They are scalping and mutilating every man, woman and child they find and burning plantations to the ground."

"We need to protect our own families, not stand around talking here," someone yelled.

"Aye, if they're attacking in groups, we need to protect our own!" another man shouted agreement.

"Okay men, I don't see any more we can do here. Go back to ye individual homes but stand guard, ring the church bell if ye see anything. They still have to come across the bay to reach us.

Sounds like our Indians are not involved right now. Let's hope it stays that way," Col. Yeardley ordered.

The men quickly dispersed to their respective plantations to watch and wait. Henry returned home. The rest of the day and all through the night, he and his servants stood guard in shifts but nothing suspicious occurred.

On the morning of the 18th, Henry heard a shout from Chris. He quickly grabbed his musket and ran out the door.

"Mr. Henry," Chris called out. "Come look!"

Henry looked down Plantation Creek in the direction of the bay where Chris pointed and saw hundreds of shallops, sloops and boats gliding across the water toward the eastern shore. A feeling of dread filled his heart. A couple of the shallops moved toward his quay and once they drew closer, he realized they were manned by whites, probably citizens of Jamestown.

"Get the other men, Chris. We need to help these people," Henry shouted as he headed for the quay. He reached the quay just as the first shallop glided to the pier. The boat was filled almost to overflowing with several solemn-faced, women, crying children and a couple of older men.

Henry greeted them, "Halloa, come aboard. How can I help ye?"

A wizened old man stood up, "We've come for temporary shelter sir. Have ye heard about the savages' massacre yesterday?"

"Aye, we heard and have been on guard all night. Ye are welcome here. We don't have much room in the house but we have barns and outbuildings. We'll find some place to shelter ye," Henry continued. "How bad was the attack? Where is the militia?"

"It was a massacre," the old man growled as he climbed onto the pier. "Bloody savages surprised outlying plantations early yesterday morning. They killed and butchered everyone....even women and wee ones. A few of us managed to escape, and those who did, fled to neighbors to warn others or we'd be dead now. We ran to the woods and hid through the night. Our young men went with the militia....I didna know where they are. The fog this morning enabled us to creep through the forest toward the bay and we boarded this shallop and headed across the bay. We heard the Indians were friendly here. Is it true?"

"Aye, we've had no trouble with the Indians here......Any

news of the militia? Have the raids stopped?" Henry inquired.

"Nay, no news but the savages are still invading. As we traveled across the bay, we saw new plumes of smoke almost continuously from the outlying plantations as they set fire to them."

"Well, ye will be safe here for now," Henry declared as he helped a young women who was holding a crying infant to her breast onto the deck. "I hope the militia in Jamestown halts the savages before the assaults spread. Our Indians are friendly here and I hope they stay that way."

Chris and Henry's other indentured servants arrived on the pier and Henry called out to them, "Ye men, help these people get settled in the barn and James, alert Mary...I'm sure they're hungry and in need of victuals."

As soon as the shallop was empty, a sloop pulled into the quay filled with two young men, a woman and children. The young man guided the craft deftly to the pier. Henry greeted him with a nod.

The young man asked, "Sir, will ye house me family temporarily? They have no place to go. Our plantation was destroyed by the savages yesterday evening. Thanks to, Johnny here," the man said as he patted the head of a young boy around the age of fourteen, "we managed to escape and hid in the woods all night...but Johnny's whole family was massacred. This morning we discovered our plantation was burned to the ground and all our livestock killed. We fled across the bay in our sloop. I needed to see me family safe but I must go back after those murderous animals. We lost everything but our lives and I aim to get even with those savages." The young man looked at his wife with anguish then continued, "But I guess we still have more than most."

"Aye, we'll gladly take care of ye family.... James, lead them to the barn with the others," Henry ordered his servant.

Henry, assisted the solemn young lady and her five children on the deck. The boy named Johnny stayed on the sloop. When the children realized that their father was not coming with them, they began to plead and cry, "Please Papa, come with us, didna leave us here."

"Hush, children, hush. Ye Papa must go for now. He'll be back soon," the young mother said as she stooped and drew the children into her arms to comfort them. Then she stood and waved at her husband as he glided away from the pier, "Be safe Robert," she shouted. She turned and said to Henry, "Sir, we thank ye for ye hospitality."

Henry replied, "Ye are welcome.   I'm sorry ye lost everything. Mayhaps we can find a way to help but let's get these wee one's to safety. I'm sure they're hungry and tired."

Henry saw James returning to the quay and shouted, "We have more to house James. Take them to the barn with the others."

Throughout the day, trickles of sloops, shallops and all manner of watercraft drifted across the bay to Accawmacke. By nightfall, the population of the small community had increased ten-fold and was hard-pressed to meet everyone's needs.

On the 21st Robert and Johnny returned in his sloop to join Robert's family. Henry greeted them at the pier.

"I thank ye for taking my family sir," Robert said as he climbed on the deck.

"It is the least I could do. What news do ye bring?" Henry asked.

"Good news sir, most of the raids by the Indians have been stopped. Some of the militia is still tracking down a few stragglers but we did capture Opecancanough.   I heard he was near a hundred years old and was carried into battle but he'll not be leading any more Indian attacks. Can ye take me to me family and we will be on our way?"

"Aye, I'll take ye to them. But ye said....Opecancanough was captured?"

"Aye, sir. "Fighting was fierce. When Opecancanough was taken prisoner, they said he was so emaciated and worn out he couldn't raise his eyelids.   The militia carried him through Jamestown in triumph and a soldier was appointed to guard him. But I guess the guard, recalled all the people Opecancanough had caused to be butchered and he shot him and killed him right in the street."

"Killed him? Ye mean Opecancanough's dead?"

"Aye sir, I didn't see it but they said Opecancanough ordered one of attendants to open his eyelids after he was shot. Then somehow, Opecancanough found the strength to stand on his feet and he asked Governor Berkeley to be brought to him."

"What did Berkeley do?"

"Why he met with Opecancanough when he heard what happened. And I heard old Opecancanough said, 'Had it been my fortune to take Sir William Berkeley prisoner, I would not have meanly exposed him as a show to my people.' A few minutes later he died."

Robert and Henry drew near the barn and his wife caught a glimpse of her husband with Henry. She broke into a run to greet him. "Oh, Robert. Ye are here. Ye are alive."

Robert took his wife in his arms while his children ran to join their parents, and shouted "Papa, Papa..."

Henry watched the happy reunion scene and contemplated.

I wonder how many more families have been displaced. No matter...we must help them. I need to check with William and others. Accawmacke has a huge task in front of us taking care of them.... at least it's not winter. There will be no shortage of food....only places to house them til they can get back on their feet.

After a time, he walked over to Robert and asked. "Son, What will ye do now? Where will ye go? Ye're wife said ye have nothing left."

"Nothing but our land. We'll have to rebuild."

"Where will ye're family live until ye house is rebuilt?"

"I didna know sir. But we will manage."

"Son, me wife would never forgive me if we sent ye away with ye're wee ones and no shelter for ye family. If ye family didna mind the barn, then they may remain with us until ye can provide a roof over their heads."

"Why, sir. That is most kind. It was a hardship spending one night in the woods with the wee ones. I admit I was a might worried about how we'd manage until I could provide shelter for them again."

"Well, consider it done. They can remain here."

"Do we know how many settlers were killed?"

"I heard it was between three to five hundred, sir. Most of the deaths occurred on the south bank of the James River and the peninsula above Middle Plantation. But it could have been much worse. If we hadn't built that palisade of logs and blockhouses across the peninsula from the York to the James River after the last Indian attack in '23, we wouldn't have been able to stop them. We were able to launch an attack against the Indians behind the palisade."

"Thank goodness for that."

"After Opecancanough was captured, we learned that he intended to wipe out all the settlers to the sea."

"Well, I'm glad ye were able to stop them for now. With the death of their leader, mayhaps the attacks will stop."

"Gov. Berkeley is not depending on that sir. A list was being made of all men of military age to join the militia and march against the Indians. There were still a few isolated attacks and since the treaty was broken by Opecancanough, Gov. Berkeley said we were justified in attacking Indian towns."

"Then I guess we'll see more bloodshed before this ends."

"Ye can count on that sir."

CHAPTER FORTY-SEVEN

May, 1644, Plantation Creek, Eastern Shore, Virginia

Immediately after the massacre, many citizens of Jamestown were frightened or homeless and fled to the eastern shore of Virginia for safety with little but their lives. Residents of Accawmacke took in a number of former Jamestown citizens temporarily until housing could be built.

William Berriman had a large plantation with many outhouses to provide shelter from the elements so he took in a great number of Jamestown citizens. Crowded, living conditions were not the best and soon illness and disease began to plague the former Jamestown residents.

Henry was called to Berriman's plantation when a large number of people complained of headache, fever and stomach pains.

"Have ye noticed any other symptoms Will?" Henry asked.

"Mrs. Jamison has a rash," Berriman replied.

"Where is she? I had her moved to the house because I didn't want the rash to spread."

"Good idea. I see Jane and Richard are here with ye."

"Aye, Richard has been here off and on since the sickness started but Jane insisted on helping so she and Jonas moved in the house with me yesterday."

"If this sickness is what I think it is, ye might want Jane and Jonas to leave. They could stay with us until this sickness abates."

"What do you think it is, Henry?" William inquired as the two men walked to the house.

"Let me look at Mrs. Jamison's rash first. I can't be sure till then."

Jane greeted them as they entered Berriman's house.

"Henry wants to see Mrs. Jamison. Is she any better?" Berriman asked.

"Nay, William. She's worse. I was unable to wake her this

301

morning. I'm glad ye're here Henry."

"Jane, I was just telling William, ye may want to take Jonas and stay at my house. The two of ye may be in danger of catching this illness and I especially fear for Jonas. But first, lead me to Mrs. Jamison. I hope this is not what I suspect."

Jane climbed the stairs to and indicated Mrs. Jamison's room, then asked, "What do ye suspect it is, Henry?

Henry said, "Let me examine her first....But, I don't want ye to be around her."

Jane returned to William who was waiting in the Parlour and asked, "Did Henry tell ye what he suspects?"

"Not yet, but I think he's right. Ye and Jonas should stay with Mary until this sickness ends."

"Of course, if ye think that is best. I hate to go but I will not endanger Jonas."

A few minutes later, Henry joined them with a grim expression on his face. "Jane ye and Jonas should pack at once and come with me. I'm afraid Mrs. Jamison has camp fever and it could be fatal, especially to Jonas. I'm not sure Mrs. Jamison will survive. She has a very bad case.

"Aye, Henry! I never dreamed I would be endangering Jonas by bringing him here. I'll pack at once," she said and left the Parlour hurriedly.

"William, ye must not bring anyone else who becomes ill to the house. We'll have to make the sick comfortable in the barn. Move anyone that is well in the barn to another location. All the sick should be in one location. I'll take Jane to my plantation and return with medicine to assist ye."

When Henry returned a couple of hours later, he found William sleeping in a chair in the Parlour. Alarmed at his friend's inactivity, he touched William's forehead. William was startled and said, "I guess I'm not as young as I use to be....can't believe I nodded off."

"William, oh friend, I'm afraid ye may have developed the illness as well."

"Nay, Henry. I've just been working too hard around here. I just need to rest a spell."

Margaret entered the room. "Mr. Henry, thank goodness ye have returned. I noticed Mr. William was a little fatigued for the past couple of days and I tried to get him to rest but he refuses. Maybe he will get some rest now that ye are here."

"I'm afraid ye have no choice, William. Ye may spread the illness by continuing to work among those who aren't yet ill. I must insist ye retire to ye bed."

"Mr. William is sick?" Margaret asked incredulously.

"Aye, Margaret. And I'm afraid it's camp fever."

"Well, I still think I'm just tired but I'll do what ye say. I could use some rest," William replied then stood up and stumbled a little as he walked to his room.

"Margaret, I'm worried about ye staying in the house. This is camp fever and it spreads rapidly.

"No need to worry, Mr. Henry. I had camp fever in London."

"Then it will be safe for ye to administer to Mr. William's needs. I planned to move Mrs. Jamison to the barn but since Berriman has become ill, there's no need. Who else is staying in the house?"

"Only Mr. Richard, sir. He went to check the planting for Mr. William this morning since Mr. William was not feeling well. I'll take good care of him sir."

"Thank ye, Margaret. I'm sure ye will. I want to examine the rest of the ill in the barn and out buildings. Make Henry some willow bark tea. I think it will help him feel better."

"Aye, Mr. William."

Henry found eight more people ill in the barn and seven more in the out buildings. With the assistance of Henry's servants, he had all the ill moved to the barn, then returned to the house to check on Henry. Richard was in the Parlour with a pale look on his face.

"Margaret informed me. I'm glad ye sent Jane and Jonas to ye house. I told her to stay home but she insisted and I admit, I was still a little worried about another Indian attack so I allowed her to come here with us."

"They will be fine with Mary and me servants, Richard, I felt they should stay away from the illness here...especially, Jonas. But how are ye feeling? Ye look pale."

"Well, now that ye mention it. I have this terrible headache."

Henry checked his temperature and pulse and said, "Ye

must go to bed as well. I'll have Margaret make ye some willow tea."

Henry remained at Berriman's plantation to keep close watch on his patients. He slept only a few hours each night and quickly became exhausted. Mrs. Jamison died a day after his arrival and two young people in the barn died. William and Richard declined a little more each day. Henry tried every remedy he knew but to no avail. Only blood-letting remained as a possible cure. Berriman was now in a deep sleep and Henry sat beside him contemplating what to do next.

Dear friend, I do not want to bleed ye but there may be no other choice. I'll wait one more day but ye must awaken from this sleep soon. Be strong William.

Henry looked across the room at Richard Lemmon who was not faring much better. Though still alert, Richard suffered from a high fever and chills. Margaret sat beside him, bathing his forehead with a wet cloth in an attempt to bring down his temperature. Henry said, "I need to check on the sick in the barn, Margaret. Let me know immediately if there's a change with William or Richard."

"Aye, sir. How is Mr. William?"

"Not good, I'm afraid. He's fallen into the deep sleep and if he doesn't awaken soon then, I'm afraid..." Henry said in a quivering voice, not wanting to complete his sentence.

"I understand sir. I remember how it was when I was sick. But Mr. William is strong. He will get better."

"I hope so, Margaret. I hope ye are right," Henry said as he exited the room.

It is times like these, I feel so useless. God give me the knowledge to help these people.

During the night, three more people in the barn died. Their bodies were lying near the barn entrance wrapped in blankets, ready for removal and burial. One was a small boy and Henry frowned as he walked past them. It was always hard to lose an innocent wee one. The previous day, five new cases of camp fever developed and the people had been moved to the barn. Thankfully, two young men appeared to be recovering. Henry found them sitting up and eating some mush from a bowl.

"It is good to see ye're improvement," said Henry.

"And we are grateful for ye care," replied one of the men. "When can I join me family?"

"In about three more days," Henry replied. Then added.... "That is if ye continue to improve."

Suddenly, Trehearne appeared at the barn door. "Mr. Henry, "Margaret asked ye to return to the house. It's Mr. William..."

Henry rushed after Trehearne and entered the room he left only minutes before. William's breathing was now labored and shallow. Henry bent down and listened to his chest.

"I'm afraid we're losing him Margaret," Henry said.

Minutes later, William's breathing ceased and Richard asked, "Is he gone?"

"Aye, Richard. He's gone. Rest in peace, dear friend. Rest in peace." Henry looked at Trehearne standing in the door and asked, Trehearne, will ye go tell Jane of her brother's passing?" Then he hurriedly left the room.

Richard took a turn for the worse the following day and died within hours. Berriman and Richard were buried in the same day in the high meadow where other members of the Berriman's family were buried. Only a small number of people attended the funeral due to the general fear among Accawmacke citizens of contracting the fever that viciously, raged through Berriman's plantation.

After the joint funerals, Mary walked over to Mary Magaret's grave and laid some flowers on the tiny plot. She looked over the cemetery at the surrounding tombstones and remarked to Henry, "When Sarah was buried on this site beside her wee ones, I never envisioned that so many of those we loved would join her this quickly. It seems that all our friends are leaving us much too soon."

"It's true, Mary. But there's no good time to lose a loved one. At least we can take comfort in knowing that we will see them again in Heaven."

Jane was standing on a plot of ground between her husband's grave and her brother's grave, quietly crying on Margaret's shoulder while her son Jonas wrapped his chubby arms around her dress.

"I didna know how Jane will manage with her husband and brother both gone. She's had too much suffering with the death of so many family members. Life has been unfair to her," Mary, commented as she studied her friend.

"Life was never meant to be fair, Mary. We must find the strength to go on. Jane's a strong woman and with friends to help her....she will manage," said Henry.

"When will ye come back home Henry? I'm worried about ye as well. Ye look so tired."

"There are a few people still pretty sick at Berriman's but at least there have been no new cases in the past two days. I should be able to return home in another week or two."

"I think I'll ask Jane to continue to stay with us for a while. Will that be all right with ye, Henry?"

"Aye Mary, it will do her good to have a friend right now."

Mary walked over to her friend and put her arms around her.

"I can't believe they are all gone Mary," Jane said with anguish as she threw her arms around Mary and cried inconsolably.

CHAPTER FORTY-EIGHT

1644-1645, Eastern Shore, Virginia

In June, Governor Berkeley and his councilors consulted with the General Assembly at Jamestown. After the meeting, Gov. Berkeley declared:

"Because the Indians have shown their true colors by the surprise attack, we will forever abandon all forms of peace and familiarity with the whole Nation and will to the utmost of our power pursue and root out those which have in any way had their hands in the shedding of our blood and Massacring of our People."

Gov. Berkeley appointed William Claibourne, a member of the Council to be the General and Chief Commander of a force of 300 men to attack the main Indian villages of the Pamunkeys and to pillage their cornfields and torch their villages. Gradually this effort quieted the Indians around Jamestown and calm prevailed in Virginia by the winter of 1645.

The population of Accawmacke soared after the Massacre in Jamestown. Settlers sought out land near the friendlier Indians on Accawmacke. The increase in population quickly became a burden to Henry since he was now the only doctor in Accawmacke. Dr. Holloway passed away a year prior to the Indian attack. Henry also assisted Jane in managing Berriman and her husband Richard's plantations as well as his own.

"Henry, ye cannot do everything. Ye must rest and take better care of yeself," Mary exclaimed as she prepared his breakfast before dawn. "Ye had very little sleep last night and seldom have time to eat."

Henry nodded and said, "Mary, there are just so many things that must be done. Once Will's and Richard's estates have been inventoried and sold, there will be time to rest, but for now, I have to maintain them."

"Neglecting ye health will not make that happen sooner," she declared.

"I know. I'll try to return home earlier tonight. But please be patient. These long days won't last forever," he said as he quickly ate the mush she prepared for him. He grabbed a large piece of fresh baked bread and stood. "I must be on me way, if I hope to come home early." Then he retrieved his hat, jammed it on his head and walked out the door.

Mary watched from the window as he walked toward his horse.

He's limping again. Oh, God, please take care of Henry. I know he is not well but he won't talk to me about it.

She recalled her panic last week when she saw him clutch his chest and quickly sit down by the tool shed. Mary had been gathering eggs, and was about to call out to him when Henry bent over in pain and sat down. She rushed over to him but he was unaware that she had seen the incident and did not mention it to her. Instead, he smiled and joked about her doing Henry, Jr.'s job.

I know ye are proud and only trying to keep me from worrying but sometimes ye can be so stubborn!

Henry returned home early as he promised and was exuberant. He took off his hat, placed it on Henry, Jr.'s head and said enthusiastically, "Ye are growing so rapidly Henry, Jr. Soon ye will be able to wear me own clothes."

"Nay, Papa," The big hat covered Henry, Jr.'s eyes and he tried to push it up. "I can't see Papa."

Henry laughed, removed the hat and took his son in his arms.

Mary said, "Henry it is good to see ye such good spirits. Has something happened?

"Aye, Mary. There was news of the war in England and Laud was executed in January. We no longer need fear him. I'm sorry to see him die as I would anyone, but his death feels like a dark cloud has lifted over me. I knew he was imprisoned in the Tower of London but when he wasn't convicted of treason last year, I thought he might be freed."

"But how did he die if he was not convicted, Henry?"

"Parliament passed a Bill of attainder declaring that he was guilty of subverting the laws and attempting to overthrow the

Protestant religion. He was declared an enemy of Parliament and guilty of High Treason and beheaded on Tower Hill in January."

"Then we will be free to return to London without fear?" Mary replied.

"Aye, Mary. We will visit ye Mum again. I believe the war will end soon and the Protestants will control government. Mayhaps, with Laud gone, and not pushing the popery, King Charles will have a change of heart and compromise with Parliament. Then we can travel to England again."

Mary excitedly exclaimed, "I never thought we'd see this day. I must send Mum a packet. I'm really worried about her.

It was a beautiful June day in Accawmacke and Henry decided to take a moment to enjoy it. The planting season had gone well. His crop of tobacco and corn grew tall from the abundant rain they had received in May.

We will have a good harvest this fall. I don't know why I ever questioned coming to the Colonies. Where else can a man's hard work allow him to achieve so much? I have a wonderful wife and son, large plantation and freedom to worship and build me life as I see fit. Thank ye God for giving me this opportunity.

Chris and James were hacking the limbs off a tree, the three men had just chopped down. "Tis a fine crop, Mr. Henry....should fetch a fair price."

"Aye, Chris. Ye and James help has made it so. I will hate to lose ye both next year when you indentures are complete," Henry answered then after a pause, continued, "I promised to give both of ye a start. How would ye like some of that bottom land I recently bought?"

James smiled. "I think that would be fine, Mr. Henry, we'd appreciate it."

"Well, we should finish this field by the end of the week, so we'll have a little free time. Why, don't both of ye spend the extra time clearing ye field. Then it should be ready for ye to plant next year. "

Chris beamed. "That's mighty generous of ye sir."

"It's thanks I have for ye help, Chris. Ye and James helped

make this plantation successful. I guess we'd better get back to work. I promised Mary I'd stop work earlier today." Henry picked up his axe, drew his arm back, gave a loud groan then grabbed his chest and fell face forward into the tree branches.

Chris reacted immediately, "Mr. Henry, Mr. Henry, sir!"

James approached the Pattenden house slowly with deliberate steps and knocked on the door. Mary greeted him with a smile then seeing the grim look on his face, started backing away from the door. Behind him, she saw Chris leading a horse with a man draped across the saddle.

"No, didna tell me," she said. "Didna say it. It's not true unless ye say it."

James reached for her hand and said, "Miss Mary, I'm sorry but..."

Mary jerked her hand away, screamed then collapsed to the floor.

Mary held fast to Henry, Jr's hand as she climbed the stepping stones on the footpath to the cemetery. Chris, James, Ambrose Dixon and Trehearne carried the pine box as they followed behind her.

When they reached the top of the hill, the men slowly lowered the box into the hole beside Mary Margaret's grave. Rev. Rozier greeted Mary with a nod and Jane walked over and stood beside her friend. She encircled one arm around Mary's waist and firmly held her son Jonas' hand with the other.

Mary looked around at the people attending the funeral with misty eyes then looked down and closed her eyes.

I can not look at his grave. Not yet! Tis too soon. It will be real if I see the grave.

Mary trembled and Jane squeezed her waist.

Rev. Rozier began to talk but Mary only heard snatches of phrases..."I am the truth and the light...Trust in the name of the Lord.... Though I walk through the shadow of death."

There's that word. Death didna say it...but what did Mum say about death? No one really dies. Henry's in heaven. But he is dead just like Mary Margaret. Mum said Mary Margaret was not really dead. She was with Papa in heaven. What did Mum say? Be joyful. Mary Margaret was with God and Henry was with God.....But I want him here with me! Why did ye take him now!

Rev. Rozier was no longer speaking. Mary looked up to see him standing in front of her. "If there is anything I can do to help, please let me know," he said.

That's what everyone says. The only thing that will help is for you to bring my husband back to me.

Mary tried to smile and said, "Thank ye Rev. Rozier." Henry, Jr. struggled to release his mother's grip from his hand. Finally, he broke free and started running away from the gravesite.

Ambrose Dixon reached out as Henry, Jr. drew near him and with one strong hand, grabbed the errant child and returned him to Mary.

"Thank ye sir," Mary said. She bent down and said, "Henry, Jr., I need ye to be good today. Papa would want ye to be good."

"But Papa's gone," Henry cried. "Ye said Papa went to Heaven to be with Mary Margaret. Didna he love us anymore? Why did he go away?"

Mary fought back her tears and said. "God wanted Papa for a special job in Heaven. He won't be back but he is not gone forever. We will see him one day. Ye can talk to him now if ye wish. We just cannot hear his voice."

"He can hear me?" Henry, Jr. asked.

"Aye, son, he can hear ye and see ye. Papa wants ye to be a good boy and one day ye will be with him in Heaven."

Henry, Jr. stood still and began whispering, "Papa if ye can hear me. I love ye and I'll be good."

Mary's tears began to flow.

Jane took her friend in her arms and said. "It's just us now Mary. We need to stay close. We need each other."

"Aye, Jane. We will, I promise."

Jane stood by her friend as Mary's neighbors came up to offer their condolences.

Gradually the small group dispersed but Mary remained by Henry's grave holding Henry, Jr.'s hand.

She reached up tentatively as she had so many times before

and touched the end of the ribbon her father had given her. She began to slowly twist the ribbon in her fingers as tears fell down her cheeks. A few seconds went by and Henry, Jr. began to squirm.

Mary brushed aside her tears, stooped and softly whispered to Henry, Jr. while she adjusted his shirt, "We must travel this path without ye Papa now Henry, Jr. but we have our family and God's love to guide us as we forge ahead." Then she stood and followed the worn stepping stones down the hill.

APPENDIX

CHAPTER ONE - *The events in this chapter actually occurred in London, England in June, 1637 and are depicted as they took place. Pyrnne, Burton and Bastwick are the real names of the men and received the punishment described by the STAR CHAMBER. The scene with Bastwick's wife, gathering his ears, actually occurred. Henry Pattenden is a fictional character but there were Pattenden's who resided in the area of Canterbury, England around this time.*

CHAPTER TWO - *There is an assumption in historical records that Henry Pattenden married fictional character Mary Willson. The Pattendens can be found in Virginia around 1638. Henry was not a doctor but was given the occupation of a doctor by the author. The description of the wedding is typical of the time period.*

The name William Berriman appears in court records of the Eastern Shore in Virginia. He lived on Old Plantation Creek but a wife's name is not found in the historical records. The other Berriman family relationships are exactly as delineated in this chapter. William Berriman bought many headrights during this time and became very wealthy after initially nearly losing everything.

Henry Wilson resided on Old Plantation Creek with his wife Alice and was an early settler. He also worked in the salt mines and Mile Pirket improved the salt mines. The description of the Eastern Shore, Virginia is accurate. The Accawmacke Indians were friendly and the Laughing King (actual name) warned the Colonist of the Indian attack and massacre in 1622. He saved many lives due to his warning.

CHAPTER THREE - *Mary Willson's family is fictional but there were many Wilson's/Willson's residing in the area of Cranbrook, England in this time period. Cranbrook was known for it's weaving industry* and its description is fairly accurate. The Wilson house is typical of the time period.

CHAPTER FOUR - *The family history related by Grandfather Willson is accurate for many families who were displaced by the sheep industry. Childbirth linen was passed down to the eldest daughter in a family. The word 'pregnant' was not used. Pregnancy was rarely discussed by 'gentle people' and called a 'lying in'*

CHAPTER FIVE - *This journey to the Colonies illustrates the perilous life and danger traveling across the ocean in small ships.*

CHAPTER SIX - *Many lives were lost at sea due to illness, bad food and storms. Devil's dung was supposed to ward off sickness. Medical information is characteristic of the day. Some doctor's began to question bleeding patients during this time period.*

CHAPTER SEVEN - *Ships to America stopped in these Islands to replenish their supplies. The trip to America took longer than the return trip. Colonists on the Eastern Shore had individual quays for ships to load and unload supplies. Accawmacke was referred to as Ye Kingdom of Accawmacke, even in England.*

CHAPTER EIGHT - *Point Comfort was a port for ships arriving and a tax was required to disembark in 1638 at Jamestown. There was a John Willson who was the first minister at Elizabeth City but literary license was used in the relationships between Mary Willson, Henry Willson and John Willson as well as John Willson's family.*

CHAPTER NINE - *The Kecoughtans were a friendly tribe of Indian. Opecancanough led the Indians in the 1622 massacre of the colonists. Mr. Syms left land for a school to be started in Elizabeth City, Virginia in 1638. Children were often sent back to England for an education in the early days of Virginia.*

CHAPTER TEN - *The Eastern Shore was exempt from the tax imposed on new immigrants to Virginia. The first black slave auction took place in 1638 as stated.*

CHAPTER ELEVEN - *Henry Willson arrived in Virginia in 1619 while Alice remained in England but it is speculation whether this is the same Henry Willson who later resided on Plantation Creek with Alice. Doctor Holloway was a physician on the Eastern shore in 1638 and resided on King's Creek. The family relationships Alice delineates are accurate according to historical records. Alice Willson appears to have been a midwife according to court records.*

CHAPTER TWELVE - *Shallops were commonly used as transportation on the Eastern Shore because they could be sailed or rowed and were easy to maneuver in shallow waters as well as the deeper waters of the Chesapeake. Thomas Savage was the first settler on the Eastern Shore. He lived with the Indians and had a son, John Savage. He owned considerable acreage. John Trehearne arrived on the Eastern Shore as Berriman's indentured servant. Sarah is a fictional character as wife of Berriman. The Assategues were known for their war-like tendencies. Rev. Cotton was the minister of Hungar's parish at this time. Captain Scarburgh resided on the Eastern Shore and was a known Indian hater. Ambrose Dixon and George Cottingham resided on the Eastern Shore.*

CHAPTER THIRTEEN - *Sarah is a fictional character and her death is fictional. Tobias Norton and Richard Bayly lived on the Eastern Shore. The attack on the Assategue Indians is fictional but Henry Willson died around this time.*

CHAPTER FOURTEEN - *People who commited suicide could not be buried inside the Church cemetery. A second cemetery was created on William Berriman's land due to the great distance from the Church cemetery according to court records. It is not known where Henry Willson was buried.*

CHAPTER FIFTEEN – *The illegitimate birth of Ollive Eaton's child is recorded in Eastern Shore court records and Alice Willson was the midwife relating the information about the father.*

Henry Pattenden took care of the land purchse from Francis Graves for Alice Wilson according to court records. Ambrose Dixon was a ship caulker and carpenter on the Eastern Shore. Ambrose and George Cottingham were known as good Indian fighters. The information on George Cottingham is speculation by some ancestors. The Pattendens had a son named Henry, Jr. but there is no evidence that Alice was the midwife at his birth.

CHAPTER SIXTEEN - *The Pattenden house is typical of the period. It was often added on to as the planter grew wealthier. James Ewell was a brickmaker in the area. King Charles built an army to go to war against the Scottish Convenantors.*

CHAPTER SEVENTEEN - *Many people left England to go to the Colonies so they could avoid the problems in England and the battling between the Covenanters and King Charles.*

CHAPTER EIGHTEEN - *Henry's family background is pure speculation by the author gleaned from some facts about the Pattenden family in Nettlestead and events taking place regarding the Plague in England. The area around Cranbrook and Canterbury was known to be populated by nonconformists of the Church of England. Margaret's desciption of Alice Willson's family relationships is accurate.*

CHAPTER NINETEEN - *The events in this chapter are fictional but were created from facts of Eastern Shore life.*

CHAPTER TWENTY - *Dr. Holloway was a doctor in the Eastern Shore at this time.*

CHAPTER TWENTY-ONE - *The colonists often traded and communicated with the friendly Assategue Indians on the Eastern Shore. Yarrow was used to stop bleeding.*

CHAPTER TWENTY-TWO - *Women frequently carried their spinning wheels when visiting neighbor's so they could work while catching up on the gossip. Horses were new to the Eastern Shore. Jane Bevis was William Berriman's widowed sister. Rev. Cotton married Anne Graves a wealthy widow and was constantly mentioned in court records trying to collect his tithes. The incidents* *about Mr. Charlton and Eve is true. John Jackson was an indentured servant in the Eastern Shore. The origin of the Pop Goes the Weasel song is reported to be true.*

CHAPTER TWENTY-THREE – *Gum of white popular was used to treat wounds. Accidents frequently occurred in the Eastern Shore, often resulting in death. Girdling the large trees was the best way to clear land for planting but sometimes smaller trees were cut down.*

CHAPTER TWENTY-FOUR – *Henry Pattenden bought the headrights for Chris and James according to court records.*

CHAPTER TWENTY-FIVE – *Henry and Mary Pattenden are reported to only have had one child, Henry, Jr. according the historical records.*

CHAPTER TWENTY-SIX – *Rev. Cotton died August 1640 and had an extravagant funeral. He had a daughter named Verlinda. Rev. John Rozier was the new minister and was a non-conformist.*

CHAPTER TWENTY-SEVEN – *Servants indentures were usually for seven years. Most people built their own furniture. John Jackson was the 2nd husband of Jane Berriman Bevis. John Custis lived on Old Plantation Creek and his descendants built the first Arlington on Old Plantation Creek, the best and biggest house on the Eastern Shore. One of his descendants was Daniel Parke Custis who married Martha Dandridge. After he died she married George Washington, the first president of the United States. Nathaniel Eaton was the vestry clerk for Rev. Rozier.*

CHAPTER TWENTY-EIGHT - *The Covenanters raised an army of 20,000 to fight King Charles. Alice Willson died around this time according to court records.*

CHAPTER TWENTY-NINE - *The information on Nathaniel Eaton is correct according to court records. A Richard Willson was a resident of the Eastern Shore but the family relationship with Mary was created by the author.*

CHAPTER THIRTY - *Rev. Eaton's family was lost at sea on their way to the Eastern Shore.*

CHAPTER THIRTY-ONE - *New residents from Holland created a shortage of food in the Eastern shore around this time. John Custis and his wife Joane's names are mentioned in the court records around this date. The description of Richard Willson's house is typical of the time. Henry and Mary were recorded as having only one son. The birth of a second child was created by the author.*

CHAPTER THIRTY-TWO - *The birth of children was always dangerous in early colonial days.*

CHAPTER THIRTY-THREE - *This description of a hog-killing was typical of the time. Every part of the hog was used.*

CHAPTER THIRTY-FOUR - *Anne Cotton married Rev. Eaton after her Rev. Cotton died and they had an elaborate wedding according to records. The information about England and King Charles is accurate.*

CHAPTER THIRTY-FIVE - *Accawmacke was allowed to settle disputes between residents as depicted. Henry Pattenden's name was often found in court records as a witness. Restrictions on tobacco planting occurred in 1641. The story about Goody Custis and Widow Taylor is true and is in the Eastern Shore court records.*

CHAPTER THIRTY-SIX - *Pirates were becoming a nuisance on trips to and from England during 1641. Jane and John Jackson were residents of the Eastern Shore and had a son named Jonas.*

CHAPTER THIRTY-SEVEN - *Alice Traveller was a resident and wife of George Traveller and she was accused of adultery with Capt. Yeardley in court records by George Vaux and Robert Ward. Alice was previously bought to court after she abused the young toddler Elizabeth Bibby. Her husband George had been made guardian of Elizabeth after her parents died. After Gov. Harvey left, Accawmacke was divided into two counties as depicted in this chapter.*

CHAPTER THIRTY-EIGHT - *Infants often died when the first few years during colonial days. This is a fictional account of Henry and Mary's child. They are recorded with having only one son, Henry, Jr.*

CHAPTER THIRTY-NINE - *Henry Pattenden was a witness regarding the probate of Henry Weede's estate in court records.*

CHAPTER FORTY - *John Jackson died around this time, leaving Jane a widow with their son Jonas. The events described concerning England and King Charles are accurate according to historical records.*

CHAPTER FORTY-ONE - *In court records of the Eastern Shore, Mary did have an altercation with Anne Smyth over a ribbon but Mary went to Anne's house and pulled it from Anne's hair after stating "words of distaste." Literary license was used by the author to create events and importance of the ribbon. In England, Parliament raised an army to fight King Charles. This was the beginning of the English Civil War.*

CHAPTER FORTY-TWO - *Court records state that Henry Weede, Jr. found the ribbon and gave it to Anne Smyth.*

CHAPTER FORTY-THREE - *The events depicted in England took place. The author created a fictitious story around Henry and Mary visiting during this time.*

CHAPTER FORTY-FOUR - *The area around Cranbrook was known to be controlled by Parliament sympathizers during the English Civil War. Parliament created laws against Christmas celebrations in 1641-42.*

CHAPTER FORTY-FIVE - *Jane Jackson married Richard Lemmon as her third husband. Virginia largely ignored the laws against Christmas celebrations instituted by Parliament. The English Civil War began to reach Virginia as citizen took sides, either King Charles or Parliament.*

CHAPTER FORTY-SIX - *The Indian Massacre in Jamestown in 1644* took place much as depicted but literary license was used by the author to create its effect on the Eastern Shore. Many residents of Jamestown did flee to the Eastern Shore for safety. Opecancanough was old when he was killed by a soldier after capture but there are varying accounts as to exactly when his death took place.

CHAPTER FORTY-SEVEN - *The Eastern Shore was overwhelmed by citizens fleeing from Jamestown in 1644. Richard Lemmon and William Berriman died around this time but literary license was used in how they died. George Cottingham died around this time as well.*

CHAPTER FORTY-EIGHT - *Gov. Berkeley made the declaration and put an end to the Indian uprising. Many people moved to the Eastern Shore where the Indians were friendly. Archbishop Laud was beheaded as depicted. Henry Pattenden died around this time according to court records but literary license was used as to how he died.*

Mary's story continues in the next book of the *Tapestry of Love* series by Donna R. Causey: *Faith and Courage*

Made in the USA
Charleston, SC
05 October 2011